ADVANCE PRAISE FOR CHOJUN...

With *Chojun*, Goran Powell spins the tale of a modern martial arts master, Chojun Miyagi (1888 – 1953), the founder of Goju Ryu karate. Sticking close enough to the facts to assure believability while inventing enough drama to keep readers enthralled could have been a significant challenge for this story, but Powell makes it work fla............. ....et riveting tale that enlightens .... g portrait of the real Mr. Miya.................................. . Very highly recommended!

—Lawrence A. ....martial artist, best-selling
..............of *The Little Black Book of Violence*

Goran P...Miyagi and Kenichi..en them skillfully tog.............................and literary fiction. To the martial artist interested in history, *Chojun*, reveals much about the *way* of karate; the original thinking and philosophy of a martial art that today has been distorted by the intru.......................................fiction, *Choj*.........a very human story of emotional dreams and adult adve..hrough the h.......... .. ...

G...s character ... Ota, has constructed an utterly believable world, drawing the reader in to an identifiable milieu in which many of the events in the story really took place. *Chojun* is an exciting next-step in the evolution of how karate's history is told.

—Michael Clarke, martial artist, best-selling
author of *The Art of Hojo Undo*

CHOJUN

CHOJUN

a novel

by Goran Powell

YMAA Publication Center, Inc.
Wolfeboro NH USA

YMAA Publication Center, Inc.
Main Office
PO Box 480
Wolfeboro, NH 03894
800-669-8892 • www.ymaa.com • info@ymaa.com

Paperback edition	Ebook edition
978-1-59439-253-5	978-1-59439-254-2
1-59439-253-6	1-59439-254-4

Editor: Leslie Takao
Cover Design: Axie Breen

10   9   8   7   6   5   4   3   2   1

Publisher's Cataloging in Publication

Powell, Goran, 1965-

    Chojun : a novel / by Goran Powell. -- Wolfeboro, NH : YMAA Publication Center, c2012.

    p. ; cm.

    ISBN: 978-1-59439-253-5 (pbk.) ; 978-1-59439-254-2 (ebk.)

    Summary: When Kenichi Ota retires he decides to honor his own teacher, Chojun Miyagi, by writing his memoirs. As a young man Ota accompanied Miyagi to China searching for the meaning of karate. Upon their return to Okinawa, they learn the Japanese have just destroyed Pearl Harbor. Ota is conscripted as a runner to the Japanese general staff and finds himself in the epicenter of the Battle of Okinawa. After the war, Ota and Miyagi are forced to adapt to a new world order, to rebuild their island, and preserve Miyagi's brand of karate.--Publisher.

    1. Miyagi, Chojun--Fiction. 2. Karate--History--Fiction. 3. World War, 1939-1945--Campaigns--Japan--Okinawa Island--Fiction. 4. Okinawa Island (Japan)--History--Fiction. 5. Americans--Japan--Okinawa Island--Fiction. 6. Historical fiction. 7. Martial arts fiction. I. Title.

PR6116.O944 C46 2012	2012951859
823/.92--dc23	1212

Printed in Canada.

The truth is near but hard to reach

Chojun Miyagi

Most characters in *Chojun* are fictitious, but in the case of Chojun Miyagi himself, the major events described are true and only the dates have been changed to fit the narrative. The Battle of Okinawa is also accurately portrayed, as are the real-life characters of the officers in charge of the Japanese army: Lieutenant General Ushijima, Major General Cho, and Colonel Yahara. The events described in post-war Okinawa are fictitious, but reflect similar happenings during the American occupation that lasted until 1972.

More details on the thin line between fact and fiction can be found in the historical notes at the back.

THE TYPHOON MAN

I sit now to write my memoirs, not because I am a man of any great importance to the world, but rather because I knew such a man. His life changed the lives of millions and changed mine in ways I could never have imagined when I first met him, all those years ago, as a boy of just nine years.

Today his name is written in karate histories as one of the truly great Okinawan masters. It has even been immortalized in a series of Hollywood movies, but apart from featuring a karate master of the same name, the movies bear little resemblance to the man I knew or the times in which he lived. The Mr. Miyagi I knew was called Chojun Miyagi, and he lived and died in Okinawa. He was born in 1888 in the island's capital, Naha, and rarely ventured far from the warm embrace of his Pacific home. He traveled occasionally to China and the Japanese mainland, and once spent several months touring Hawaii and demonstrating his art, but he never made it as far as America where his karate is so popular now.

Miyagi died relatively young, in 1953, at the age of sixty-five. People say karate training is good for the health and promotes longevity, and I believe this to be true. However, no amount of training can protect against heart disease or temper the soul for the tragedies of the war that descended on Okinawa with such ferocity in 1945.

Chojun Miyagi died a long time ago, but to me, he is still alive. Each day when I practice karate he is with me, beside me, his hard hands guiding my own, his soft deep voice in my ear, urging me to stand firm, to tense here, to relax here, to inhale deeply, to exhale slowly.

When I retired from my job at the harbor, I realized I was the same age as Miyagi was when he died, and ever since that realization, I began to feel his presence more persistently. His ghost visited me not only in my karate, but also in my dreams and even in my waking moments, sitting on my tiny balcony, staring out over the uneven rooftops to the sea. It seemed my long-awaited days of lazing in the sunshine in tranquil retirement were not to be. Miyagi had other ideas and I could feel his disapproving gaze upon me as I sat watching the waves while my wife tidied around me and my neighbors tended their gardens below. It took me several days to realize what my heart, and Miyagi's ghost, was telling me: it was time to stop idling and put down on paper my memories of my master, my teacher, my sensei. It was time to pay tribute to the name of Chojun Miyagi.

I am still on my balcony. I have moved my writing table out here, which means there's even less room than before, but if I go inside I won't be able to see the sea, and who would ever choose to go inside when they could watch the waves, forever changing and re-forming, yet never becoming anything more or less than a single ocean? Who would give up seeing the boats going in and out of the harbor, and the wind at play in the palms? Besides, these things remind me of Miyagi. They inspire me, as he inspires me.

I met Chojun Miyagi by the sea, at the end of the long, hot summer of 1933. It was a day I'll always remember, for many reasons, though it began like any other on our island. The sky was a fathomless blue, as vast as the ocean beneath it, the sun was rising slowly over the tall Ryukyu palms, casting pointed shadows on the white sands below, and the sea was moving in gentle swells, with only the occasional ripple of white foam beyond the rocky headland.

I'd been wandering along the shoreline from my hometown of Itoman to the little village of Nashiro, where the long beach provided rich hunting grounds for sharks' teeth and other treasures left by the sea. I was moving quickly, stopping only to examine any unusual shells or stones that caught my eye, or to prod the dried remains of a sea creature lying in the tidemark. When the sand of the sweeping bay gave way to stony ground, I chased crabs in the shallow rock-pools, following a haphazard trail through the rocks to the rugged cliffs of Cape Kyan, the southernmost point of Okinawa. The sea was rougher here, and ten-foot swells surged below me, sending white foam fingers reaching up the cliff-face for my feet, and then retreated to reveal sharp coral rocks hidden beneath. I continued along the cliff-top path until I came to a rockfall at the beginning of a pristine cove and scrambled down the rocks to the deserted beach below. It was a place all to myself, away from the world.

A shallow reef hugs the Okinawan coastline and I swam out to dive among the coral, searching for oysters that might conceal a pearl. I dreamed of going deeper, all the way to the bottom of the sea like a real pearl diver, but my lungs were too small and I was forced to make do with mussels, clams, and starfish. Beyond the coral shelf, the ocean fell away into an abyss. Whenever I found myself at the reef's edge, I was seized by a lurching sense of vertigo and quickly returned to the shallower water, imagining as I did, some terrible creature emerging from the blackness to drag me to my doom. I held my breath as long as I could, staying down a little longer each time. I must have practiced for several hours, unaware of the time, until I emerged from one particularly long dive and found myself in darkness. I wondered, had I really been diving so long that night had fallen? Bewildered, I spun around in the water, examining the sky. I could still make out the faint outline of the sun behind a sprawl of angry black clouds. Warm, fat raindrops splashed on my arms and my shoulders, and I heard the growl of distant thunder. I looked to shore and saw a narrow shaft of sunlight cast by a gap in the clouds, illuminating a thin strip of the rocks behind my beach like a beacon in the gathering storm. I swam hard for that beacon. Giant waves were already crashing on the shore. I was forced to swim with all my might to avoid being cast into the jagged rocks at the beach's end. At last, a benevolent wave hurled me safely ashore and I lay in the seething sand, exhausted.

I cursed myself for my stupidity. The wetness of the wind and the growing swells of the sea should have been my clues. I was a child of Okinawa, and every Okinawan knew that in the summer months, the Kuroshio current brought more than warm water from the tropics—it brought typhoons.

It wasn't the first time I'd seen a typhoon, they're common in Okinawa at that time of year. But it was the first time I'd been so far from home. Worse still, the way home would take me over cliff-tops and open beaches where I'd be at the mercy of the wind. I feared I'd be picked up like a leaf and dashed on some hillside far inland. Going home would be impossible, but I couldn't stay on the beach. New waves were reaching farther up the beach, eager to drag me back into their embrace. I rose unsteadily to my feet. The wind lashed my back with sharp sand, and a sudden gust hurled me toward the rockfall. I slammed into a boulder, taking the impact on my palms and cursing myself once more.

I had to think. I had to find shelter, but my mind was a blank. The answer came to me through my hands. It was in the rocks that I was holding. I remembered a small cave that I'd noticed at the top of the rockfall. I didn't relish the idea of climbing up the rocks in this wind, but it was my best hope of survival, and I had to do it now, before the full force of the storm hit. I pressed my body close to the rocks, my fingers digging hard into the glistening surfaces, and climbed swiftly and evenly up. The wind snatched at my limbs playfully and slapped me heartily on the back with a warmth that belied its murderous intent. I wasn't fooled. This wind was merely flexing its muscles in preparation for what it was to become. Near the top of the rockfall, I caught sight of the cave exactly where I'd remembered it. There was a huge boulder like an enormous stepping-stone lying at its entrance. I stood on it and at that moment, when I wasn't holding on, the wind made its final play for me. A furious gust sent me tumbling over the side of the boulder. I felt myself falling but the sensation lasted only a moment. To my good fortune, there were three smaller boulders on the other side, their ends close together and forming a rough plateau. It was here that I landed on my knees and my forearms. I was shocked rather than injured and breathed hard to recover my composure before turning to assess my situation. The big boulder was acting as a windbreak. For a moment, I considered staying where I was, but it wasn't safe, not like the cave would be. The wind could change directions. The wind was treacherous. I climbed back up onto the boulder and entered the cave on my belly. Inside it was cramped and dark, but that didn't matter. It would make a safe place to wait out the storm. And I was in for a long wait, that much I knew. The storm could last throughout the day. It might be morning before I'd be able to return home. I resigned myself to a long, cold, and miserable wait in the dank cave. Almost immediately, my belly began to grumble. It had been a long time since I'd eaten, and it would be a long time till I ate again.

Outside, the wind announced its mounting anger ever more loudly. I became curious and peered out from the cave mouth to watch it unleash its full fury on the island. The grey air swarmed with leaves, stones, rocks, and sand. Palm trees were bent at impossible angles, their branches thrashing frantically under the frenzied attack. The ink-black sea was an ugly landscape of torn hills and valleys, so different from before that I wondered if I could possibly have been swimming in it just a short time earlier.

I was about to return to the dimness of the cave when to my astonishment, I saw a man on the cliff-top. At first I imagined that, like me, he'd become stranded on the beach and was trying to get away. I shouted to him, urging him to shelter in the cave with me, but the wind stifled my cries. The man was standing on the highest point of the cliff. I watched in horror, sure he would be seized by the dreadful wind at any moment, but he stood firm, facing out to sea, his arms raised before him, his hands balled into fists, and like one of the palm trees, he appeared rooted in the earth.

I saw him punch slowly into the wind, first one hand and then the other, in a silent battle with the typhoon. Occasionally he would turn his back to the sea, fighting to keep his balance, and then spin to face into the wind once more. Suddenly both hands snaked out together, fingertips slicing the air. Three times he repeated the motion, and then stepping back, his arms wheeled before him and extended, one palm high, the other low.

I watched, barely aware of the storm, as he repeated his curious movements over and over. The man was built like a bull. I couldn't tell how old he was, not as old as my father, but he wasn't a young man either. His face was broad and smooth, his lips thick, his jaw strong. The focus of his gaze was on the far horizon, as if challenging the storm. The black hair was oiled and combed back, as was the style in those days. He was naked save for a pair of khaki pants cut off below the knee. His body was heavily muscled, like a strongman's from the comic books I saw from the mainland. His thick neck sloped down to broad shoulders and his chest was deep and powerful. The muscles of his stomach stood out like a ripple of waves. His forearms bulged, and his thick legs held him firm against the wind. But it wasn't the size of his muscles that I found so fascinating, but rather the way they changed and flowed when he moved. I watched him repeat the same movements for what seemed like hours. All fear of the storm banished by the presence of this man who could dominate a typhoon with his bare hands.

The storm battered the island for the rest of the day and into the night. I must have fallen soundly into sleep because when I woke the sun was shining, and I found myself in the strongman's arms. He was carrying me like a baby to my home in Itoman, the storm little more than a bad dream. For a moment I wondered if it had been real at all, but the debris surrounding us confirmed that it had: tree branches in the middle of flattened crops, fencing and roof tiles littering the road, carts upturned and smashed, dead animals dotting the meadows, paper, straw, wood, leaves, stones, strewn across the earth, and a giant boulder at the edge of my village that I'd never seen before.

"Where do you live?" the typhoon-man asked, carrying me as easily as a straw doll. I pointed dumbly to my house, unable to find the courage to speak. My body felt weak, but my mind was alert. The typhoon-man had me in his arms, arms powerful enough to defeat the dreadful wind. I felt warm and safe and not in the least embarrassed at being carried like a small child.

"Kenichi!"

My mother screamed my name and fell to her knees, crying hysterically and beating the hard ground outside our home. I smiled weakly to let her know I was okay but she didn't seem to notice. I was still wondering how to convince her I wasn't dead when father emerged from the house and took me from the typhoon-man's arms, his jaw set tight. He carried me inside and laid me on the couch and then ran his hands over my limbs. Through my skin, I detected a tremor in his fingertips. Mother appeared beside him, muttering incoherently. She began to examine every inch of my skin for cuts from flying metal or glass, sobbing quietly, and even searched through my hair to check my scalp. I reassured them both that I was fine, but they didn't hear me. Father gathered me in his arms once more and carried me to bed. Mother covered me with a blanket despite the heat of the day and ordered me to sleep. I closed my eyes. I could hear father speaking to the typhoon-man while mother prepared refreshments in the kitchen. I didn't feel tired but I must have dozed off, and when I woke, late in the afternoon, the typhoon-man had gone. Mother brought tea to revive me and fed me bean curd soup like an invalid, ignoring my protests that I was perfectly well. It was evening before I was allowed to get out of bed and rejoin my family for our evening meal.

Father waited till the next day before removing his belt and thrashing me. It was the only time in my life that he did such a thing. He was a very gentle man. The pain of the lashes was distant, dulled by the guilt I felt for causing my father to act in such a way.

Mother barely spoke to me for several days. It was as if I'd died and returned a ghost-child. My brothers ignored me too, and only my little sister Yuka, who was too young to know better, spoke to me, reassuring me that I existed at all.

Over the next week, the whole village worked to repair the storm damage, clearing the roads and fields, fixing roof tiles and thatch, mending fences and burying dead animals, until Itoman looked normal again. Only then did I summon the courage to ask my father about the typhoon-man. He told me I'd been rescued by Chojun Miyagi, the head of a family of Okinawan nobility. My parents were doubly embarrassed that such a renowned figure as Miyagi had been forced to rescue their son. I didn't dare mention that I'd been perfectly safe all along. Instead, I asked what Miyagi had been doing on the cliffs.

"Miyagi is a master of to-te," My father told me. He was referring to karate by its old name of *to-te,* which means China Hand, and this piqued my interest further, since China was the home of the classical martial arts.

"Did he learn in China?" I asked.

"I don't know," he answered curtly. "All I know is he's a very famous to-te master and he has a school in Naha."

Naha was the capital of our island, over two hours' walk from Itoman. "I wish to learn to-te from Master Miyagi," I said.

"You're too young."

"How old must I be?"

"I don't know," he shrugged.

"Then how do you know I'm too young?"

Father glowered at me and I knew it was time to be quiet. I sat beside mother, who was grating dried fish, and offered to help. She didn't refuse and I sat beside her for an hour, grating silently. When we had finished, she told me to put the flaked bonito in a jar and seal it tight. They were the first words she'd spoken to me since the storm.

Life returned to normal. School reopened, and I went about my daily chores as before, but a new idea was forming in my mind and I was determined to carry it through, even at the risk of angering my father once again.

When the weekend came, I completed my chores in double-quick time, and by the afternoon, I was free to go to the capital in search of the typhoon-man. I went to Naha harbor, where my uncle had a ship, hoping he could tell me where to find Miyagi's dojo. My uncle wasn't around, but one of his crew told me Miyagi's training hall was in a nearby school. I followed his directions, and when the school came into view, I saw Miyagi's broad frame striding a little way ahead of me on the street. I fell in step behind him, summoning the courage to address him.

"You're too young," he said without looking round.

"Too young for what?" I asked, hoping the answer wasn't what I knew it was going to be.

"To learn to-te."

"How do you know I want to learn to-te?" I asked, running to keep up. I can't explain how I'd suddenly become so bold—addressing Miyagi in such a familiar manner when before I hadn't dared to utter a single word to him—except to say that since the typhoon, I'd the feeling our lives were linked by an invisible bond. Perhaps Miyagi felt it too, since he didn't seem surprised to see me or too put out by my breathless questioning.

"I know."

We walked side by side in silence. "How did you know I was behind you?" I asked at last.

"I have eyes in the back of my head."

"You do?"

I stopped in astonishment, but Miyagi went on without breaking stride and I had to run to catch up, "How did you know?"

He fixed me with his dark eyes, "I have a sixth sense."

"Really? Truly?"

Miyagi didn't answer.

"Can I get it too?"

"If you sharpen your awareness day and night, you may develop it over time."

"How much time?"

"A very long time."

We reached the gate of the school where Miyagi had his dojo and he swung open the heavy iron grille.

"How old must I be to learn to-te?" I asked.

He looked me up and down. "Fourteen."

I was devastated. Fourteen was almost five years away.

"Come back then," he said, entering the yard.

"But what can I do now?" I asked, desperate to learn right away.

"Do you swim?" he asked.

"I dive for pearls," I told him proudly.

"Have you ever found one?" he asked, his eyebrows raised in interest.

"No," I answered truthfully.

"That's no reason to stop searching," he said, the trace of a smile on his lips. He came out and stood before me, then bent down and placed his palm on my stomach, below the navel. It felt like a block of smooth oak that had been in the sunshine all day, its warmth flowing through my entire body. "When you're diving, don't inhale high in your chest but down here," he said, pressing gently, "in the pit of your stomach. To-te requires a strong stomach. Strong breathing. If you practice like this, your Sanchin will be very strong."

"What is Sanchin?" I asked.

"You'll discover when you're fourteen," he answered.

Then he was gone, and I was left to wander the long road back to Itoman alone. By the time I got home, it was dark but my parents didn't ask where I'd been. I think they knew. That night while lying in my bed, I held my breath for as long as I could, wondering what Sanchin could be. It would be five years before I found out.

THE PEOPLE OF THE SEA

We Okinawans are called *Kaiyo Minzoku*: 'people of the sea.' Ours is the largest island in the Ryukyu chain, but even so, it is only sixty-seven miles long and a few miles wide, so you are never far from the sea. Ryukyu means 'rope.' It is the perfect name for our archipelago since on a map the Ryukyu Islands resemble nothing more than a knotted rope, stretching from the southern tip of Japan to Taiwan off the coast of China, and, like a rope, it has traditionally connected the two powers.

The Ryukyu Islands were not always part of Japan. Before the arrival of the Satsuma clan in 1609, they made up an independent kingdom that traded all over Southeast Asia. Okinawa enjoyed close cultural links with China, and in 1393, the Chinese emperor sent artists, merchants, and craftsmen to help the islanders develop specialized arts and crafts. These immigrants, known as the 'thirty-six families,' settled in Kume near the port of Naha and became known as the *Kumemura*.

My father was a descendant of these immigrants, but his family had moved to Itoman in the south to fish in the clear waters of Itoman Bay. Father didn't speak Chinese at home or keep ties with the Chinese community. He rarely spoke of his Chinese heritage, I suspect, because my mother was a native Okinawan from the former capital, Shuri. Mother's family had been against a marriage to a Chinese descendant, no matter how many generations his family had lived in Okinawa, and she'd married without their blessing. For a woman to go against the wishes of her parents was rare, especially in those days, and it wasn't until the birth of my eldest brother, Yasuhiko, that her parents finally accepted the marriage. She gave birth to three more children: my second brother, Tatsuo, then me, and lastly my little sister, Yuka. Our family name is Ota.

Father was a fisherman, like his father before him, and no one knew the waters off Okinawa better. When I wasn't at school, I would go out with him in his boat. I was the only one of his children who loved the sea as he did. Like most fishermen, he spoke little while at sea, as if making a sound might invite the attentions of a malevolent sea-god who would call forth some catastrophe out of spite. Father would mutter a single word, *net* or *sail*, and we'd haul in the nets or raise the sail. There was no need to say more. We shared countless silent hours in this way.

Father's boat was a *yanbarusen*, a sailing boat common to the island. During the typhoon season we stayed close to shore, but at other times we would sail to the other islands in the Ryukyu chain. Near Kerama, we'd see humpback whales gathering in spring. Around Iejima, we'd follow the yellowfin tuna, mahi, and bonito. And within sight of Miyako, we'd track the giant schools of blue mackerel for hours, or catch a marlin and battle for an hour to get it into the boat.

There were all manner of dangerous creatures in those waters: big sharks, poisonous sea snakes, and jellyfish with venom powerful enough to paralyze you before you could swim to safety, but of all the sea creatures, we hated dolphins the most. They would eat the fish in our nets and could easily ruin a whole day of fishing in minutes. Sometimes we would sail to the Yaeyama islands, the farthest in the Ryukyu chain, where on a clear day, you could see the rugged coast of Formosa—now called Taiwan. In the seas around Yonaguni-jima we saw turtles, giant manta rays, and schools of hammerhead sharks milling in the crystal clear waters. Father's lines and nets were usually full, but he never earned much money when he brought his catch to market. Fish was so plentiful that the price was always low. Despite this, we didn't want for anything, and our family, small by local standards, was quite happy.

We lived at the northern edge of Itoman, within sight of the harbor where father kept his boat. Ours was a typical Okinawan house, squat and sturdy. We didn't have a tiled roof like some of the grander houses on the island, but the dense thatch was firmly secured against the storms and the house was further protected by windbreaks—a row of yellow sea hibiscus planted on one side, and a twisted banyan on the other. A stream bubbled by along the back of our house, so we had no need of a well. The sweet water continued even during the frequent droughts, and there was always enough for our needs.

Inside, the house was separated into three rooms by moveable panels. Unlike Japanese houses, each room had a sliding door to the outside, so any part of the house could be entered from the outside. Like every house in Okinawa, we had a partition set aside with a small shrine for ancestor worship, the main spiritual practice on the island.

In the evenings, father would play the three-stringed samisen, an instrument of Chinese origin, and mother cooked. Our wood-burning stove was covered save for two holes just big enough for two pans—once the pans were in place, the stove was entirely sealed to retain the heat. Mother would cook rice or sweet potato to eat with the fish that father brought home, and every so often she would make miso. Each household in Okinawa made its own, and mother's miso was renowned.

When father brought home a catch of bonito, she would dry it and store it to exchange for pork and eggs with the local farmers. I was often sent to make these exchanges, and spent hours walking through the patchwork fields of sugarcane and sweet potato that hugged the craggy landscape. On the higher ground, I would pass the estates of rich landowners. Their grand houses were surrounded by ornate terraced walls, and the stepped gardens contained trees that had been tied as they grew to create beautiful shapes.

The hard-packed roads were just wide enough for two carts to pass. Sometimes I would be lucky enough to hitch a ride on a cart, but most of the time, like most of the people in Okinawa, I walked. The richer folk on the island would sometimes take a rickshaw to spare themselves the sun-baked climb. I'd watch the rickshaw men go by, marveling at their strength in pulling such enormous loads up the hillsides, their sun-blacked bodies as sinewy as the rope that gave our island its name. Very occasionally, a car or truck would go past and I would stop and stare, wondering what it felt like to travel as fast as the wind.

Once I'd visited the farmer and exchanged the bonito, I'd go home by a different route, exploring off the beaten track, following narrow goatherd's trails to see where they led or climbing a new hill to see what was on top. On the higher ground the trees had also been bent into curious shapes, not by human hands, but by the invisible hands of typhoons, while below, the domed roofs of the traditional Okinawan family tombs resembled giant turtles, moving with infinite slowness toward the sea.

MASTER MIYAGI

Over the years, I have learned a lot about Chojun Miyagi. Most of it, I will tell you at the appropriate time in my story, but some of it I will tell you now, so you can know something of the man and his background before we begin our journey in karate together. He was the head of the Miyagi family, a family of *Shikozu* (Okinawan nobility) that owned an import and export business with two ships and traded goods between China and Japan. Chojun's grandfather had been the head of the family, but Chojun's father, Chosho, was the third son, so he could not become head of the family. This changed when the first son died without leaving an heir. At the age of five, Chojun was chosen to take the position of first-born son and went to live with his newly-widowed aunt, who became his new mother. How this affected him as such a young child I do not know. While I was close to my sensei, we never spoke of such personal family matters. All I know is that in those days, it was more common for families to do such things than it is today.

The young Miyagi took over this position of responsibility in a period of uncertainty, with relations worsening between China and Japan, and Okinawa a tiny island in the middle. His new mother decided he could do with toughening-up by sending him to train with a local to-te instructor called Ryuko Aragaki. Fortunately, the young Miyagi was naturally strong and gifted, and he took to his training eagerly. He was also boisterous and often got into scrapes with other boys. He hated to lose a fight, even against bigger boys, and if he did, he would keep challenging the same boy until he won. Ryuko Aragaki's to-te was powerful but rather simple—he concentrated on punching power and body conditioning—so when he saw the immense potential in Miyagi, he sent him to train with a true master, Kanryo Higaonna. Higaonna had trained in China for many years and was one of the foremost masters on Okinawa. Miyagi thrived under his strict tutelage, and Higaonna succeeded in bringing the boy's wild ways under control, at least most of the time. In later years, when Miyagi reminisced about his own training, he would say that the austerity of Higaonna's methods would be too much for the youth of today to bear and complained that after many hours of moving in the low squatting stance of *shiko dachi*, his training would leave him too weak to even squat over a toilet.

Miyagi grew into an accomplished athlete and gymnast, and excelled in sport. He was restless and looked into all aspects of combat that he could find on the island. He trained in judo, which was very popular at the time, and learned *tegumi* (Okinawan wrestling) from a local champion. He experimented in new ways of training, like sparring with protective armor and using full-power blows, and he introduced new equipment into his program like the *kongoken,* a heavy oval iron ring used to develop wrestling strength that he came across in Hawaii.

Unfortunately, Miyagi's talents as a martial artist did not extend to business. This is understandable when you consider that with most great men there is only room for one passion, one driving obsession, and Miyagi's was karate. He took a job in a bank to gain some business experience but it didn't work out and after a year his family urged him to stop, saying he should devote all his energies to the martial arts instead. This allowed

Miyagi to dedicate his life to karate and plumb the depths of his art without constraint. Again, this was not as strange in those days as it might seem today. The martial arts were held in high regard in Okinawa, and Miyagi's noble dedication to their pursuit brought honor and renown to the family. He became a figurehead for the family, while other, more level heads concerned themselves with the day-to-day running of the business.

Unfettered by financial constraints and limited only by the hours in the day, Miyagi was able to dedicate himself body and soul to the art he loved so dearly. The whole island became his dojo. He visited the north of the island, with its thick forests and clean mountain air, and came south, away from the built-up area of the capital, to climb the hills and train on the rugged cliffs of Cape Kyan.

The next time I saw him, I had stopped at the beach to dive and hold my breath as he had instructed, but the sea had been too rough for swimming, so I had sprinted up a nearby hill instead. While recovering at the top, I noticed a strange sight below: a man was running on the dirt track that led down to the sea. On either side of the track was a stone wall, and the man, running in a zigzag, was hurling himself against one side and then the other. It could only be one person, and sure enough, as he passed directly below me, I recognized Miyagi. I watched him, unseen, as he made his way down to the beach, and there he began to exercise on the shifting pebbles. These were not the slow, deliberate movements I'd seen him perform before—these were fast punches and kicks, blocks and strikes, punctuated every so often by a fierce battle cry that carried above the roar of the surf.

Next, he entered the ocean up to his neck. I knew how hard it was to battle the fierce rips and currents in the water at that time of day. He remained among the waves for twenty minutes, and when he emerged, he seized an enormous stone and raised it countless times over his head, then stood before a boulder and struck it with his bare hands. The heavy slap of flesh on stone rang out, loud enough for me to hear on the hilltop.

I didn't approach him. Instead, I simply watched, as I'd done during the typhoon, to see how the great to-te master trained. I saw the same fierce intensity I'd witnessed on the cliff-tops. Miyagi seemed locked in a struggle against the elements that made up our island. He was fighting a hopeless battle—no man could tame the ocean or the wind, or smash the coral rock of Okinawa—but I sensed something noble in Miyagi's struggle, a desire to engage with the elements, a desire that I myself shared.

Over the following months, I saw him every now and then, pitting himself against the elements in his relentless, hopeless struggle. Sometimes he would heft a huge log onto his shoulders, or cradle it in his arms like a baby, and perform hundreds of squats. Once I watched him lifting heavy rice sacks with his teeth to strengthen his neck. Each time I made a note of his training and added it to my own program the next day. The stones and logs I lifted were small in comparison to Miyagi's, little more than pebbles and sticks, but my stones grew bigger and my logs thicker over the weeks, months, and years that I trained in preparation for my first lesson with Sensei Miyagi.

The Emperor's Portrait

My schoolteacher, Mr. Kojima, was from Kagoshima on the Japanese mainland. He spoke with a strange accent—although he claimed it was we who spoke strangely and never tired of reminding us. I can still hear his high-pitched voice ringing out, his words accompanied by the cracking of his ruler, which he carried under his arm like an army officer's swagger stick.

Mr. Kojima was especially concerned with the education of Kumemura children—children of Chinese descent. We added an extra layer of complexity to the already formidable task of teaching the native Okinawans. There were only two other Kumemura children in my class, both of whom were girls and far too quiet to warrant his attention, so Mr. Kojima ignored them completely and I bore the full force of his displeasure.

On this occasion, I'd failed to bow correctly before the emperor's portrait that hung at the front of our classroom and Mr. Kojima had decided to make an example of me. "Emperor Hirohito is a living god!" he shouted, smacking his ruler on my desk. "The father of all Japanese subjects, and despite what you might think, that includes you, Ota!"

He nodded, as if to say he knew what I was thinking, but he didn't. I was staring at the portrait of the fresh-faced young man in uniform, his chest covered with medals, and wondering why he wore spectacles. If he was a god, surely he didn't need them. And if he was my father, then who was the man at home whom I called father? And how could one man be the father of eighty million people? No, Mr. Kojima didn't know what I was thinking, but I thought it best not to correct him. Instead, I went and knelt before the emperor, holding my forehead on the floor for a long time until I was sure Mr. Kojima would be satisfied.

I hadn't intended to be disrespectful. In fact, Mr. Kojima would have been surprised to know that I wanted nothing more than to be a good Japanese citizen. Our empire was the greatest in the world. We'd beaten the Russians, the Koreans, and the Manchurians, and we were destined to rule all of Asia. I dreamed of one day taking my place in this great ruling class.

When I'd returned to my seat, Mr. Kojima proceeded to tell us about the Japanese soldiers in Manchuria. Three young heroes had hit the news for throwing themselves across barbed wire so their comrades could get to grips with the enemy. They were called "soldier-gods" for their sacrifice and Mr. Kojima ordered us to write a poem in praise of their devotion. "Their sacrifice wasn't in vain," he assured us. "Japanese civilization will soon spread throughout all of China." He looked at me as he said this, though I pretended not to notice and kept my eyes downcast at the paper in front of me. "Soon we will free all Asia from the yoke of Western imperialism," he promised, "and one day, the whole world will thank us for showing it a better way."

During our lunch break, we gathered in the yard and made a ring from old rope to play our favorite game, sumo wrestling. I was skinny for my age and rarely won a bout. After two quick defeats, I spent the rest of the break trying to get the dust off my uniform to avoid another dressing down from Mr. Kojima. The winner, as always, was an older student called Jinan Shinzato who, as well as being very skilful, was a powerful athlete. Occasionally he would perform gymnastics on the bars, swinging and dismounting with a beautiful somersault like a professional circus-man. Shinzato took no notice of me, he didn't even know I existed, but I knew about him. He was from a noble family, like Miyagi, and I knew he also studied to-te with Miyagi. I longed to talk to him about it, but could never summon the courage to approach him—Shinzato was as distant to me as those heroes in Manchuria that we heard about.

In the afternoon, we did English. Mr. Kojima had spent a year in Boston, which, he was at pains to explain, was not in England but in Massachusetts in the United States. I was talented in English, even Mr. Kojima had to acknowledge this, but it wasn't such a good thing. During every lesson, Mr. Kojima lectured us long and hard about the moral destitution of the Anglo-Saxon race. America was a land of untold luxury and wealth, but this had been achieved through unabated greed. American people claimed to worship God, but in truth, they worshipped money. They had no emperor. They didn't honor their parents or their ancestors. They acted like spoiled children, and perhaps most important of all, they were not brave—not like our people. Their soldiers were big in size but small in heart. They lacked the samurai spirit of the Japanese. Mr. Kojima assured us that one Japanese soldier was worth ten Americans. Only one country could compare with Japan, albeit dimly, and that was Germany. Germany's new leader was strong and determined. In just a few years, he had achieved an economic miracle comparable to Japan's own, and created a military machine of impressive power. Our country had struck an alliance with his, and together we were set to lead the world in industry, arms, and technology. Germany would be a valuable ally for the time being, though, as the original Anglo-Saxons, they could never share in Japan's long-term plans. Our nation was born of the gods, with a living god as our ruler. We were destined to rule, first Asia and then the four corners of the world.

I wondered whether Germans spoke English, but dared not ask. It was close to home time, and I didn't want to incur Mr. Kojima's wrath and stay behind after class.

The Striking Post

My fourteenth birthday was a special day. Mother cooked *imokuzu*—potato pancakes—for breakfast, and father presented me with a new penknife like the one he used on his boat. I was thrilled and ran to fetch his sharpening stone. He gave me advice, and though I'd sharpened knives many times before, I listened attentively and did as he instructed. I didn't wish to anger him, especially not today. When it was time to go to school, I stood before him and waited to be invited to speak. My father raised his eyebrows at my sudden formality—we didn't stand on ceremony in our household. I think he could guess what I was about to ask.

"Father, I am fourteen now," I began, then waited a moment to gauge his reaction. He nodded once, as if to say there was no doubting it was true. "Do you remember Master Miyagi, who we met a few years ago?" I continued.

"Miyagi? Miyagi?" he said, his brow furrowing as he tried to recall where he'd heard the name before, "there is a noble family in Naha by that name…"

"The to-te man!" I said, frustrated by his forgetfulness.

"Yes, I do believe Chojun Miyagi is a to-te teacher," he said slowly, as if dredging up some long-forgotten memory from the past.

"The typhoon-man!" I exclaimed, fit to burst with impatience.

"That was Chojun Miyagi?" he asked, wide-eyed.

I stared at him in disbelief until I noticed the twinkle in his eye. "You know it is!" I shouted, all formality forgotten.

"Yes, I know all about Master Miyagi," he said. "Now what about him?"

"He told me I could begin training in to-te when I was fourteen," I said breathlessly, "and I am fourteen now, and there is a to-te class tonight."

"You know where his dojo is?"

"Yes, in the elementary school in Naha."

"Naha is a long way, Kenichi."

"I'll come home at once, as soon as the training is finished," I promised.

"Make sure you do!" he said sternly.

It took a moment for it to sink in. "Thank you, father!" I said loudly.

"One more thing," he said, reaching behind his back. He handed me a small flat parcel wrapped in brown paper. I took it and stared at it dumbly. "Open it," he urged gently.

Inside was a crisp white cloth. I looked at him questioningly. "You can wear it as a headband, if Miyagi permits," he said. "It'll stop the sweat stinging your eyes."

I was touched that my father knew me so well and didn't know what to say. Father filled the silence for me. "When you train, do so with all your body and soul. Don't waste Master Miyagi's time."

"I won't," I promised.

"I know you won't," he smiled.

I rolled the cloth into a band and he tied it around my head. I hurried out of the house. Our exchange had made me late for school, and I'd have to run all the way to avoid a ticking-off by Mr. Kojima.

As it happened, Mr. Kojima ignored my hasty entrance that morning. He even overlooked the headband that I'd forgotten to take off when I bowed to the emperor's portrait. He had a very special announcement to make and nothing was going to distract him from that task.

"Today is a proud day for the school," he began, beaming with delight, "a very proud day! One of our teachers—a former student here himself, Mr. Uchihara—has been afforded the singular honor of fighting for the emperor!" At this point Mr. Kojima was so moved by the depth of his own emotions that he was forced to pause for breath. When he spoke again, he hurried to end his sentence before his passion overwhelmed him. "Mr. Uchihara will be leaving for Manchuria in the morning. There is passing-out parade taking place for him now by the school gate."

We made our way into the yard and Mr. Kojima formed us into two lines that created a path that led to the gate. Some of the other teachers distributed flags and banners bearing good-luck messages and slogans: *Protect the Home Front—National Unity—Do Your Best For Your Country*. The girl beside me was given a banner that was too big for her to hold up alone, so I helped her. Our slogan read, *Reproduce and Multiply!* We held it high, beaming with delight, the irony of our particular message lost on us in our youthful zeal.

Mr. Uchihara appeared, accompanied by the head-teacher, who spoke at length of the honor and privilege of serving the emperor. He called Mr. Uchihara a flower of Japan, a hero. When the speech was over, one of the senior girls presented Mr. Uchihara with a *senninbari*, a traditional belt made up of a thousand stitches—a good-luck talisman given to soldiers by wives and daughters. Finally, Mr. Uchihara walked through the lines of students and banners to the car that was waiting to take him to Naha port.

That evening, I made my way to the elementary school in Naha where Miyagi taught to-te. It was larger than my own school, though similar in layout: three sturdy brick build-ings with roofs of corrugated iron and a dusty yard. A row of trees had been planted around the outer edge as a windbreak, a common sight in Okinawa. As I walked I planned what to say to Sensei Miyagi, changing my mind several times on the way. When I arrived, the school gate was open and I wandered inside. I already knew which building Miyagi used as a dojo. The door was ajar and I peered in. Miyagi wasn't there, but there was a small group of boys chatting and three other boys were practicing punches and blocks. Among them I saw Jinan Shinzato, the talented gymnast from my school. One of the boys ambled over to me. "Are you lost?" he asked.

"No, I've come to learn to-te," I answered.

"You can't just turn up like this. You need to make arrange-ments with Master Miyagi. He's not taking any new students at the moment."

"I have made arrangements with Master Miyagi," I blurted out, praying Miyagi would remember me after such a long time. The boy shrugged and returned to his friends. I stepped a little way farther inside the training hall and stood with my back against the wall. Jinan Shinzato glanced over at me, but if he recognized me from school, he didn't let on. Like the other boys, he was bare-skinned save for a pair of rough cut-off pants and his body was already covered in a sheen of sweat. He was the shortest in the class, but his muscles were broad and well defined and he looked the most powerful of them all. It was clear that Shinzato had trained hard with the iron weights that lay around the edge of the room.

I took a closer look at the equipment. Among the barbells and dumbbells, I saw several curious pieces: a short wooden handle sticking out of a stone, a set of iron rings, a giant oval ring about three feet long, two pairs of iron clogs, and several tall earthenware jars. Suddenly all the boys came to attention and I turned to see Miyagi's broad frame in the doorway. They bowed and he returned their bow. I bowed hastily and opened my mouth to speak, but my carefully prepared speech had deserted me. Miyagi waited expectantly. "Master," I stammered finally, "I've come because I am fourteen."

Miyagi peered at me in the dim light. There was no indication that he recognized me. "It's your birthday today?"

"Yes."

I heard the faintest snigger from the other boys behind me, but didn't turn around, "You said, when I met you before, that I should come when I am fourteen..."

"You have come to celebrate your birthday with us?"

"I have come to learn to-te," I corrected him.

"Ah, well why didn't you say so in the first place," Miyagi said, "because we do not hold birthday parties in here."

The older boys laughed openly now and I felt my cheeks burning with shame. "I can pay," I said quickly.

Miyagi ignored this remark. "Remove your shirt," he said instead.

"Can I wear a headband?" I asked.

"If you think it will help you," he said.

"It will keep the sweat from my eyes," I told him.

"Then wear it," he said, and tiring suddenly of our conversation, he turned and clapped his hands loudly for the class to begin. The boys hurried to form a circle in the hall. There was no space left for me to stand, so I stood apart, in the corner, and aped their actions. Miyagi led the class through a series of warming up exercises that stretched every part of our bodies, starting with our toes and finishing with our heads. By the time we had finished, there was a puddle of sweat on the floor beneath each of us. Next, each student took up a different piece of training equipment and began to work out. I'd no idea what to do and turned to Miyagi with a question on my lips.

"You can train with me," he said before I could ask, "since it is your birthday."

He led me outside, to a small area of rough ground behind the dojo where two wooden planks were sunk into the ground. Each one had a straw pad near the top, positioned at chest height and covered with tightly wound string. Both pads had a dark red-brown stain in the middle that spread out and down, getting lighter at the edges. Miyagi placed his fist against one of the pads and planted his feet firmly on the ground. He waited until I'd done the same on the other, then stepped across and adjusted my fist until only the front two knuckles touched the pad.

"Now punch," he ordered.

I struck the pad. The straw offered little padding and the plank didn't bend.

"Again."

I struck again.

"Harder!"

I struck a third time.

Miyagi shook his head in disappointment. "The first and last weapon of a to-te fighter is his punch," he told me. "*One punch, one kill.* That is our motto. Again!"

I hit the board as hard as I could. A sharp pain shot through my hand.

"Grip your hand tightly when you strike," he told me.

I did.

"Again!"

I struck again.

"That is how you must punch," he told me.

I stopped, eager to leave the painful striking post and move onto the next exercise, but Miyagi didn't move, and it dawned on me that the exercise wasn't over.

"One hundred times, with each hand," he said.

I stared at him dumbly, hoping he was joking. "We'll do it together, since it's your birthday," he said. I realized he wasn't.

Miyagi readied himself before the other striking post, then waited for me to do the same. I placed my trembling fist against the pad. He nodded for me to begin. I drew my hand back and struck. At the same moment, there was an explosion beside me. I jumped away in fear, the pain in my hand forgotten. Miyagi had hit the post. He smashed it again. The plank bent back at an impossible angle, then righted itself, only to be driven back by another tremendous blow. Each time he struck, there was an ear-splitting crash and the groaning of wood as the plank bent back. The pounding went on and on until, after perhaps fifteen strikes, he stopped and glared at me. There was a look in his eyes that can only be described as predatory—he was ready to tear me apart like some savage beast from the jungle. I took an involuntary step back. He held me in his gaze, until I realized he was waiting for me to punch and returned to my position.

We struck up a rhythm together. With the sound and fury of Miyagi's punches, I couldn't concentrate on the dreadful pain in my hand. To my astonishment, Miyagi's punches got harder and harder, until the plank began to split and soon broke in two, leaving only a jagged stump sticking up from the ground. Miyagi turned and went back inside the dojo without a word.

I continued tapping my pad, the blood from my torn knuckles adding fresh color to the old brown stain. When I reached one hundred punches, I checked to see if Miyagi was watching. I couldn't see him, but I didn't dare to cheat—he had a sixth sense, after all. I placed the front two knuckles of my left hand against the pad and punched as hard as I could.

When I'd finished, I took a leaf from a nearby tree and dabbed at my bleeding hands to avoid getting blood on my clothes. Mother would be angry, or worse, she might prevent me from training.

I went back inside the hall and watched the older boys. Their training didn't resemble fighting. Jinan Shinzato was holding a heavy earthenware jar in each hand, fingers splayed around the rim, and was walking in slow deliberate steps. Another tall slim boy was training with the stone-hammer known as the *chiishi*. Squatting low with his arm extended, he turned the chiishi up and down to build strength in his wrist. Another boy was moving the giant oval ring called the kongoken around his body. Beside him, an older boy was practicing with heavy iron rings on his forearms, while the last of them held a barbell across his shoulders and, leaning forward, rolled it down the length of his back, controlling it with his arms.

Miyagi saw me and came over to inspect my knuckles. Without a word, he led me to a tap and ran cold water over my hands until all traces of blood were gone. Taking a clean cloth from a cupboard, he dabbed my hands until they were dry. He reached for a bottle of dark liquid and splashed a little into his palm before rubbing it gently into my shredded skin.

I clenched my teeth to avoid making a sound. Finally, he cut two strips of bandages and wrapped them slowly around my hands, securing them with a neat knot. I could hear his steady breathing as he did so and felt a little ashamed that he was forced to spend so long on my injuries. When he'd finished, he clapped his hands twice and each student took up a new piece of equipment.

"Jiru!" he called out, and Jinan Shinzato stepped forward, "Sanchin."

Jiru was Miyagi's nickname for Shinzato. No one else called him by that name. I watched as Shinzato began to perform the same movements I'd seen Miyagi do in the typhoon. This was Sanchin. Miyagi took up position behind Shinzato and began to probe the muscles around Shinzato's shoulder and back with his fingers, testing their condition, searching for weakness, muttering as he did, "Yes, yes." He continued down Shinzato's spine to his hips and onward, down his legs to his feet. All the while Shinzato continued his performance, punching slowly and with tension. Suddenly Miyagi clapped his palms across Shinzato's shoulders and the slap of skin on sweat-soaked skin rang out around the room. He struck Shinzato's sides and his stomach in the same way, and Shinzato kept these areas tense to withstand Miyagi's blows. When Shinzato had finished, Miyagi nodded, but it seemed he wasn't completely satisfied. "Again," he demanded quietly, and Shinzato began once more.

I went to try my hand at the strength training, eager to develop a physique like Shinzato's. The earthenware jars were sitting unused on the floor and I bent to lift them. To my surprise, I found they had been filled with water and were impossibly heavy. I planted my feet firmly between the jars and tried again. I succeeded in raising them off the ground, but when I took a step forward, I felt the jars slipping from my grasp. The thought of broken jars and water over Miyagi's floor was too frightful. I put them back down. Just then, Miyagi clapped his hands and ordered the equipment to be cleared away.

"Kata!" he said loudly, and each student began to practice a sequence of punches, blocks, kicks, and strikes. Sometimes they struck with open hands, using the palm, fingertips, or edge of the hand. I looked on, bewildered, until Miyagi came and put his hand on my shoulder. "You can go home now," he said. "It is getting dark and your lesson is finished for today."

I wanted to stay and watch the other boys, but I dared not contradict him. Instead, I bowed and thanked him for instructing me. I offered to pay but he shook his head and told me I'd already paid. As I left the training hall and followed the long road home, I wondered what he meant by that. It would be some years before I understood.

The next evening when I returned to the dojo, Miyagi wasn't there and Jinan Shinzato was teaching the class instead. They had begun early, and I was left to wait in the doorway for five minutes until Shinzato beckoned me to join in. He led us through the same warm-up exercises that Miyagi had done, then ordered us to begin our strength training with the weights and jars. I looked to Shinzato for instruction, but he shook his head and led me outside saying simply, "Makiwara."

I didn't know what a makiwara was and expected to find some new training aid waiting for me outside, but Shinzato sauntered over to the striking posts, one smashed and broken in two, the other darkened with my blood from the day before, and waited for me to join him. Each step was a step filled with despair. Shinzato glared at me, daring me to contradict him.

I looked into his hard eyes, wondering if he really didn't know that we went to the same school, then placed my raw knuckles against the red-brown stain and got set to punch.

"No!" he said.

I waited, expecting him to correct some aspect of my stance, but instead he pointed to the broken makiwara. "You need to replace it." I must have looked at him dumbly because he spoke as if talking to an imbecile. "Master Miyagi said that if you came tonight, you should build a new makiwara, since you broke it."

"I didn't break it," I protested. "You must know that."

He shrugged, "Miyagi said it's broken because of you, so you can be the one to fix it. There are tools in the shed over there, and some new planks. When you've finished, come back inside and rejoin the class."

That evening I discovered that despite being a simple piece of apparatus, the makiwara is quite difficult to replace. The plank was sunk deep into the ground and the earth around it trodden down hard. A spade made no impression on the sun-baked ground and I was forced to resort to a pickaxe. An hour later, I was down near the base. It was then that I discovered the plank had two crossbars for stability, so I was forced to dig wide as well. When the jagged stump was finally out, I set about making a new one.

I collected a new plank from the shed. It was already tapered at one end, presumably for just such a purpose. I also found straw, rope, and glue and set about replicating the broken makiwara. I was good with wood, thanks to all the time I'd spent with my father mending his boat and recreated the crossbars on the base quite accurately. Next, I attached the straw padding, wrapped over it with rope, and glued it down in a faithful reproduction of the previous makiwara. It wasn't until I'd sunk my new creation into the hole that I noticed night had fallen. I was still stamping the earth down when Shinzato reappeared. He held the makiwara and shook it to check how solid it was, then stamped on the ground to make it firmer. Finally, he balled his fist and struck the pad. I held my breath, praying it would stand up to his blows.

"It's time to go now," he said, without commenting on the makiwara. "Put the tools back and hurry, so I can lock up."

I returned the tools to the shed and then followed him to the gate. The other boys had already left.

"Where was Master Miyagi tonight, Sempai?" I asked, using the polite form of address for the class senior.

"At a meeting in Shuri," Shinzato said, "But don't worry. He'll be back next time."

I wanted to tell Shinzato I wasn't worried, that I would have been happy to learn to-te from him, but it might have sounded stupid. "Goodnight Sempai," I said as he held the gate open for me. I didn't know what else to say.

Shinzato grunted a reply as he turned the key in the lock and I walked down the road casually until I'd turned the corner, then ran, eager to get home and tell father how I'd built a makiwara for Sensei Miyagi.

On my third training session, Miyagi taught me Sanchin. He showed me how to grip the ground with my feet, rooting myself to the floorboards, just as he had rooted himself to the cliff-tops in the storm. He showed me how to create a fist and punch, how to block, and how to breathe slowly and deeply into my *tanden*, the central point of the body two inches below the navel, in the same way he'd shown me to breathe when I was diving.

Sanchin was just one of the sequences known as "kata." It was simple to learn, but, Miyagi warned me, difficult to master. "Practice Sanchin deeply each day and you will always be strong," he said. The other kata were more complex than Sanchin, yet to Miyagi, Sanchin was the trunk from which all the others branched out and the root that pulled them all together.

No one but Miyagi was allowed to teach kata to a student, since it took too long to unlearn bad habits, and no one else was allowed to do the painful *shime* testing that I'd seen him perform on Shinzato. Miyagi stood behind me and pressed my muscles with his fingers.

"Tense here," he would say, tapping my shoulder, or my side, or my thigh. "Bring your muscle up. Good!" If his fingers felt a lack of response, his iron hard palm would slap until I brought the required tension to that part of my body. I was aware that he was slapping very lightly compared to what he had done to Shinzato, but the impact of his heavy hands was still quite dreadful. After what seemed like an hour, but was more likely ten minutes, he placed his palm on my stomach. Exhausted, I tensed nonetheless, but he tapped my belly gently.

"You have been diving for pearls?" he asked.

"Yes Sensei," I said, delighted that he had remembered our conversation of some years earlier.

"Did you find any?"

"Not yet."

"One day, perhaps."

"If I find one, I will give it to you," I said, "as payment for your teachings."

"And I will be happy to accept it," he smiled. "Now practice for a while," he said lightly, turning his attention to another boy.

I performed Sanchin once again, alone this time.

Sanchin means Three Battles, and the first of my battles had begun. In this never-ending struggle to achieve harmony between mind, body, and spirit, the first battle was the body, the simple struggle to position myself correctly and make myself strong. Later, the second battle would join the first, as I sought to develop the subtlety of technique that makes Sanchin so powerful. And lastly, the final battle would enter the fray, the struggle to understand the effect of such an exercise on a man's innermost soul. This final battle was one that I would wage for many years to come.

CHINESE HAND

By the age of fifteen, I'd grown tall and strong despite my skinny frame. Father decided it was time for us to visit his brother Anko, who lived and worked in Naha. Anko owned a trading ship that he sailed around the Ryukyu Islands and farther, to Fuzhou and Shanghai in China, and Kagoshima in Japan.

Father wanted me to help out on my uncle's ship during the holidays. Though he never said it, I knew he wanted me to be more than a fisherman, and he saw this as a way for me to gain new experience in the world. My uncle was dubious at first, saying I was a little young for such work, but my father wouldn't hear of it. "Kenichi is deceptively strong," he insisted. "He's been training for a year with Miyagi Sensei."

This piqued my uncle's interest. "He's lucky to train with such a man," he said, looking me up and down with a fresh eye. "He can start next weekend."

And so I abandoned my weekends of diving and beach training to work on my uncle's ship. Loading cargo and climbing ropes was backbreaking work, but I didn't mind. I knew it would make me even stronger. At first, the other deckhands ignored me. I heard them muttering that I was too small to be any help on a boat, but when Uncle Anko told them I trained with Miyagi, their mutterings ceased. They began to give me tedious tasks to perform, which I did to the best of my ability. Soon, little by little, I was included in their conversations, and when they finally began to call me by my name, I knew I'd been accepted by these rough men.

On the days when I did work for my uncle, I slept on board. I was much closer to Miyagi's dojo and didn't need to hurry home after class. Instead, I was free to stay behind and enjoy Miyagi's impromptu lectures. Miyagi loved to talk and often continued late into the night, allowing us to stay or go as we pleased. To my surprise, I discovered that my sensei was warm and affable once the serious business of training had finished. He took a personal interest in each of his students, questioning the younger ones on their schoolwork and the older ones on their jobs, giving advice on health and lecturing on morality.

The subject of his lectures wandered from one topic to the next as the mood took him. One night he would tell us the history of the Ryukyu Islands before the Japanese invasion. On another, he would mystify us with the concepts of Yin, Yang, and Tao—and in each case, the topic would relate back to his favorite subject of all: to-te. He always referred to it as Chinese Hand rather than simply Hand (Boxing) as many Okinawans did, and I learned his own sensei had studied in China for many years before returning to Okinawa.

Miyagi told us the mythical origins of Kung Fu, which was introduced to the Shaolin Temple in the fifth century by the Indian monk, Da Mo. The Shaolin monks observed the fighting methods of animals and based their strategies on what they saw. Countless styles now existed all over China. In the southern port of Fuzhou, where Miyagi's teacher had mastered his art, the main ones were Crane, Lion, and Dog Boxing.

I learned that Okinawa had had its own fighting art, which, as well as developing powerful punches on the makiwara, combined throwing and grappling. Miyagi believed to-te was a combination of native Okinawan methods and classical Chinese martial arts, which had been introduced by the

Chinese immigrants. These were the legendary Thirty-six Families that had been sent by the Ming emperor. This filled me with pride, since Chinese immigrants were rarely spoken of in such a positive way on Okinawa.

When my uncle realized I was a good diver, I was sent down to scrape barnacles off the hull and free the rudder from tangled netting. Diving in the oily waters of Naha harbor wasn't the same as diving in the clear waters of Itoman Bay, but I was happy to build up my breath and didn't complain. It took three days, and by the evening of the third day the hull was smooth and the rudder in perfect working order. I sat with the rest of the crew as the sun went down and my uncle appeared with a bottle of *awamori,* the local rice brandy. Someone produced cups and handed me one without a word. Uncle Anko poured a tot for me without comment and I drained it quickly as the others had done. My throat was on fire, my eyes watered uncontrollably, but I was determined not to choke, and I fought hard to pretend nothing was amiss.

"You did well today, nephew!" Anko said loudly, pointing in my direction with his empty cup, "Didn't he?" It seemed he'd had a few tots already and didn't wait for a response. "The boy is a to-te man. He trains with Miyagi!" he nodded knowingly, looking from one deckhand to the next. "They all know Miyagi round here. But tell me Kenichi, have you ever seen your master do to-te?"

"Many times," I answered.

"Ha! What did you see?"

"I saw him battling a typhoon," I offered.

It sounded silly now that I'd said it. "On the cliffs-tops near Itoman, facing into the wind," I continued half-heartedly.

Anko didn't know what to make of this information—it was inconceivable that anyone, let alone a native Okinawan, would stand on a cliff during a typhoon. "I saw him break a maki-wara," I added hopefully. I wondered if anyone knew what a makiwara was.

"Have you ever seen him fight?" Anko demanded.

I shook my head.

"I didn't think so. So how do you know if he can?"

I looked from my uncle to the crew. All eyes were on me expectantly. "I just know," I said defiantly.

Anko looked at the faces of the crew too, then nodded slowly and leaned close to me as if talking confidentially, though when he spoke, it was loud enough for all to hear.

"Well guess what Kenichi, you're right! Because I have seen him fight," he said triumphantly. "And so have these guys," he said, pointing his cup at some of the older crew. "It was a long time ago now, but I can still remember it well. I will never forget. In fact, I know quite a lot about Miyagi. I knew him as a boy. He's the same age as me, you see, although we didn't go to school together. In those days we Chinese immigrants had our own school. We weren't allowed to go to the same school as the Okinawans and the Japanese. Besides, he was the head of the noble Miyagi clan, so we had very little in common, but his reputation was well known among the young men of Naha."

Anko smiled and wagged his finger at me, spilling awamori as he did. "Believe it or not, your teacher was a bit of a tear-away in those days. Always getting into fights and scrapes. He was strong, too. None of the other boys wanted to tangle with him, even before he learned to-te." At this, some of the crew nodded their agreement. "When he left school he joined the family business of import and export. One day when he was about eighteen, he came to the docks to solve a dispute with a group of dockers who were refusing to unload cargo from one of his boats.

"The dockers were saying it was more work than they'd been told, and they demanded more money. Miyagi insisted they'd been correctly informed. He offered to help them unload it himself to make the job easier. There were six of them, so a seventh hand, a strong man like Miyagi, would make a big difference. But this gang was notorious for cheating people and refused his offer. It was an old trick: leaving a perishable cargo in the hold all day in the hot sun, until the owner was forced to agree to their demands or lose his cargo completely.

"Well, Miyagi wouldn't be cheated. The discussion got heated. It turned into an argument. Insults were exchanged and then some pushing and shoving began. The dockers were all strong men, you know how they are, and they were not afraid of Miyagi. They surrounded him and they threatened him. They didn't believe a rich merchant like Miyagi could be a threat to the six of them. They were wrong.

"I saw the whole thing from my boat. It was incredible. Miyagi stepped aside and brushed past one of them, who fell to his knees. Miyagi had hit him so fast that nobody saw it. It must have been in the solar plexus because the docker rolled onto his side and curled his knees to his chest. He never got up again.

"It took the others a moment to realize what had happened and by that time, Miyagi had slipped out of their ring. Suddenly, fists were flying. They leapt at him, eager to be the first to strike him. Miyagi ran around a pile of barrels and they split up and went to each side. He chose one side where only two were coming at him and stepped forward, hitting the first man on his neck with the ridge of his hand. The man went down. In the same instant, Miyagi kicked the second man in the stomach, driving him backward into a pile of rubble.

"The other three had gone around the barrels the other way, and the first of them was about to seize Miyagi from behind. Now this is the truly amazing thing. Without even looking, Miyagi kicked backward like a mule, and the man went down! But the next man reached Miyagi and got him in a bear hug. I thought it was all over then, but Miyagi sunk low and shrugged his head backward, smashing the man in the face. The docker wouldn't let go, so Miyagi bent forward and seized his foot, then pulled it upward. The man was forced to let go and fell over backward, clutching his knee in agony.

"By this time, some of the others had recovered and three of them surrounded Miyagi and smashed at him with their fists. I saw them strike him over and over, but it made no impression on him. They might as well have hit a brick wall. He parried one man's punch and seized his arm, and I swear there was a smile on his face. The man struggled furiously to pull his arm free but Miyagi's grip was iron. Meanwhile the other two tried to reach Miyagi, but Miyagi kept thrusting the man in his grip at them, using him like a shield.

"Then the man in Miyagi's grip produced a knife, but before he could use it Miyagi jerked violently on his arm, pulling him forward onto the point of his elbow, and the man collapsed. Miyagi stripped the man of his knife and spun it expertly in his hand, daring the other men to come forward now. Both ran away instead.

"What happened after that?" I demanded.

"The police came by, looking for witnesses, but no one had seen a thing," Anko smirked. "We were all sick and tired of being cheated by those dockers."

"What happened to Miyagi?"

"Nothing, of course," he laughed. "It would take more than the word of a few good-for-nothing dockers to indict a nobleman like Miyagi." Anko refilled my cup with a half-tot, chuckling as he did. "So you see, your master wasn't as virtuous as he likes to make out."

I sipped the burning liquid, wishing I could have water instead, and wondered idly if I would ever get the chance to see my sensei in action. Miyagi was a man of such quiet dignity now that I couldn't imagine him doing the same today. Then I remembered the primal rage in his eyes when he'd broken the makiwara and wondered how completely such an instinct could ever be contained.

AN INCIDENT AT
ROKO BRIDGE

At school, Mr. Kojima could barely contain his excitement. We hurried through the morning ritual of bowing to the emperor and when we were all seated and silent, he waited an extra moment before making his announcement. There had been an incident at the Roko Bridge near Peking. On the night of 7 July 1937, a Japanese soldier had been held captive illegally by the Chinese forces and there had been a battle. This had escalated and now Japan had declared a *seisen* on China. Seisen was a Holy War, which, Mr. Kojima explained, marked the first step in our destiny to bring the four corners of the world under Japanese rule.

Over the following months, we received daily updates on the progress of our imperial forces across the sea. The port of Shanghai had been captured after a long battle. The Chinese capital Nanking had fallen soon after, and our troops were busy bringing order to the city. Enemy forces were on the retreat all over China.

Mr. Kojima explained it was our divine duty to bring Japanese civilization to the rest of the world. Our English classes were canceled in favor of Japanese history and culture. We sang patriotic songs and recited heroic poems, and all the while, a steady stream of young men left Okinawa to go to war.

My mother and my sister Yuka sewed *senninbari* for the soldiers on the front. These good-luck belts were supposed to be made by the mothers, sisters, or wives of the soldiers, but in practice most were sewn by high-school girls. They also put together ration packs known as comfort-bags filled with tins of food, razors, cigarettes, and sake, and decorated the outsides with messages of encouragement. I wondered whether one day in the future, I too would receive a good-luck belt and a comfort-bag in some faraway corner of Asia.

Yuka joined a local girl's brigade called the Wild Lilies and trained in first aid. They would go to Naha port to cheer the departing troop ships with cries of *Banzai!* (Hurrah!) Sometimes I would go with her to watch the new soldiers who were grinning inanely at their newfound hero status, at least for a day. Mr. Kojima was often there too, his eyes alive with joy at the sight of so many brave young fellows going to war, envious of their chance to serve the emperor. I looked forward to the day that I might be on one of those ships, holding my head high as pretty, young girls waved me off from the quayside, but there seemed little hope of that.

When I left school, I worked full-time on my uncle's boat, and no call-up papers ever arrived at my door. Uncle Anko began to give me a little money at the end of each week. Soon I was accompanying him on trips to the outlying islands. It seemed my life on Okinawa was set, never to change. I wasn't unhappy, but at night I lay awake, rocked by the gentle swell of the ocean in Naha harbor, and wondered whether this was all life held in store.

MRS. MIYAGI

It was a baking hot day when I found myself waiting nervously outside the gate to Miyagi's house. I'd been invited to join the classes in his private dojo, a small building in his garden, and not wanting to be late on my first visit, I'd arrived half an hour early. The gate was shut, but unlocked. I wondered whether to go through to the house or wait by the gate. I peered through the bars, trying to decide. Miyagi lived in a grand house, with a tiled roof and ample gardens surrounded by a high wall. The trees and bushes were neatly trimmed. The flowers were in perfect bloom and a pile of chopped wood had been stacked neatly beside the house. It was clear that Miyagi had no shortage of students to perform chores for him.

A woman in a colorful kimono appeared at the gate. "You're here for to-te?" she asked.

"Master Miyagi invited me," I said, "My name is Kenichi Ota."

"You're eager Kenichi, that's good," she laughed, her voice rich and deep "My husband likes students who're eager, but there's no one here to teach you, not yet. Miyagi is out and about, so why don't you come inside and have something to drink? It's hot today."

I accepted gratefully and Mrs. Miyagi led the way to the house. She wasn't as I'd imagined Miyagi's wife, tall and haughty, she was small, with a round face and warm eyes that danced with mischief. Her hair was piled on top of her head and pinned in the traditional style, and she wore a necklace made of different colored precious stones and coral pieces.

"Come in," she said, stepping into the entrance hall. The lofty room was cool after the heat outside. My eyes were drawn to one wall hung with portraits of what must have been Miyagi's ancestors, fine gentlemen and ladies in old-fashioned dress. Some were photographs, professionally taken and of high quality, but the older ones were paintings, and from the quality of the brushwork they had been done by a master. On the opposite side of the room stood a cabinet filled with fine ornaments: lacquerware boxes with unusual designs that didn't look Okinawan but rather Chinese or Japanese in origin, incense burners of a design that could have been Malayan or Indonesian, and fearsome looking warrior masks that could have been from Borneo or the South Sea islands.

Mrs. Miyagi showed me into the lounge and urged me to sit. I was apprehensive, imagining Miyagi returning home to find me seated on his favorite couch and chatting with his wife on my very first visit, but Mrs. Miyagi insisted I should sit, so I had little choice. She brought sweets and a glass of juice and I munched on the sweets guiltily as she demanded to know about my family, the names of my brothers and sisters, the health of my parents and relatives. By the time I'd finished my juice, she knew all about me. Was I polite to my parents, she demanded. I was about to reassure her on this important matter when I heard a soft footstep behind me and turned to see Miyagi in the doorway. I sprung up and thanked Mrs. Miyagi for her hospitality. Miyagi turned without a word and I followed him out of the house to the dojo, wondering if he were annoyed and whether I should explain that Mrs. Miyagi had insisted. In the end I said nothing.

Only three other students turned up that day. It was mid-summer and the humidity was dreadful. Miyagi's private dojo was tiny compared to the one in the elementary school, and there was no air in the room. Nevertheless, no allowances were made for the heat and we performed the usual warm up and conditioning drills. To my regret, I'd abandoned wearing the headband that my father had given me long ago—Shinzato didn't wear a headband so neither did I. The sweat stung my eyes so badly that I blundered around half blind. I was afraid Miyagi would never ask me back, but instead, he took me aside and taught me a new kata. It was very different to the slow, heavy movements of Sanchin. This kata was called *Saifa*. It was filled with explosive punches and strikes using the back-fist and hammer-fist, kicks and knee-strikes, sweeps and stomps, rips and tears. A guttural shout called a *kiai* was required in two places. Miyagi demonstrated this martial roar and the little room shook with thunder. I sensed a frisson of violence running through the kata and felt the violence running through my veins as I performed it. Later, Miyagi demonstrated the meaning of certain movements. I learned to tear free from a grab on the wrist or lapel, deflect a punch or kick and respond with one of my own, to lock the wrist and elbow and throw a man to the floor.

Miyagi had finally begun to teach me the devastating secrets of his art and I returned to his home for training at every opportunity. My nervousness at being in such a grand household was soon lost as I got to know the rest of his family. He had nine children and there was always a happy atmosphere in the Miyagi household, with much laughter and joking. Mrs. Miyagi was a doting mother and I got the feeling Mr. Miyagi was a doting father, though he remained stern whenever I was there.

He would never accept payment for his instruction, so when I wasn't busy on my uncle's boat I would do chores for him instead. One weekend, he asked me to move a pile of heavy stones from one side of the yard to the other. The next weekend, he asked me to move them back again. I didn't mind. I was delighted to be near my sensei, and Miyagi indulged me good-naturedly with work designed to build my strength and stamina.

One day, two rough-looking men appeared in the garden demanding to see Miyagi. When no one answered the door, they banged louder and repeated their demands to see him. I stopped what I was doing and took a closer look at the men. One was tall and broad with a flat nose and fleshy cheeks, but it was the smaller one who drew my eye. His body was lean and hard, his mouth set tight in a sneer. His pale eyes darted around the yard until they fell on me. I looked away quickly but it was too late.

"Hey, where is Miyagi?" he shouted.

For someone to use such a familiar form of address for an Okinawan nobleman in his own garden could only mean one thing. He was here to challenge Miyagi. I'd heard it happened occasionally—Miyagi was one of the most renowned to-te masters in Okinawa and people wanted to prove themselves against him.

"I don't know," I answered.

"Is he in the house?"

I shrugged.

The men returned to the door and banged it again, shouting for Miyagi. As they did, he appeared behind them. "I'm Miyagi," he said.

The men turned to find him standing one step away. "Is there some emergency?" he asked, his voice showing no emotion whatsoever.

The men were lost for words and exchanged furtive glances. "No emergency," the smaller one answered finally. "We were looking for Miyagi."

"If there's no emergency, then why the urgency?" he demanded, and I noticed he had sunk his weight and was planted like a rock in front of them.

"No urgency," the smaller man said, regaining his composure a little. "We were just looking for you, and now we've found you."

"If there was no urgency, then why hammer on my door and conduct yourself in such a manner?" Miyagi demanded, his voice growing louder now.

"You are Miyagi the to-te man?" asked the bigger of the two, ignoring Miyagi's question.

"You know who I am. Who are you?" he said, never taking his eyes from the smaller man.

"We have come to see your to-te," the bigger man said.

"I do not show it," Miyagi said.

The men took a moment to consider their next move. The smaller of them was about to say something but Miyagi spoke first, "There is only one way to see it, but you wouldn't thank me for showing you."

I'd inched closer in case Miyagi needed my help. He glowered at me but I remained where I was. "The wood is all chopped?" he asked, struggling to control his temper.

"Not all of it," I answered.

"Then go and finish," he ordered.

I moved away and returned to my chores. The two men spoke a while longer with Miyagi, but I was too far away to hear what was said. They left meekly enough without a backward glance and I never saw either of them again.

That evening Miyagi was away at a committee meeting so Shinzato taught in his place. When the class had finished and the other boys had left, I cornered Shinzato and asked a question I'd never dared ask before.

"Do we ever spar?"

"Occasionally," he answered.

"Why not more?" I probed. "Isn't it important to practice realistically?"

"Real to-te isn't a game. It's life or death."

"But everything we do is prearranged. It's not the same as a real fight, where you don't know what'll happen."

Shinzato regarded me for a moment and I held his gaze, wondering whether he knew we went to the same school. I thought he was going to refuse, but instead he said we could spar if I wanted.

"What should I do?" I asked.

He raised his arms to the guard position and I did the same.

"Now what should I do?" I asked.

"I can't tell you," he said with the trace of a smile. "You said yourself, sparring's unpredictable."

I looked into his eyes wondering what he was thinking. His expression was void of clues. Then a black explosion went off in my face. He'd stuck me, his movement so fast that I hadn't reacted at all. I stumbled backward in shock. I could taste blood on the inside of my lip and feel the beginnings of a swelling with my tongue. Shinzato circled me. Our sparring wasn't over. I had the sinking feeling it had only just begun. I became hyper-alert, waiting for the next punch, but when Shinzato stepped forward it was with a kick that caught me in the belly. It knocked the air out of me and I doubled over, gasping in pain and cursing my own stupid curiosity.

Shinzato waited for me to recover, eying me like a hawk eyes a wounded bird. Eventually I stood upright and Shinzato nodded for us to continue. I couldn't stop now, it would be unthinkable, so I lunged forward and threw a punch at his face. I felt his hands tap my wrist, parrying my punch aside. I followed up with a punch from my other hand, but somehow he was at my side, no longer in front of me. When I lifted my foot to turn and face him, he swept it from under me. I stumbled. As my head dipped, I saw a flash of something. His kick connected with my jaw, and I saw black.

I woke to find myself on Mrs. Miyagi's couch. I could hear raised voices in the hallway outside, which stopped when they realized I'd come around. Shinzato entered and stood beside me. "You're awake," he said with a frown.

"Yes," I answered groggily.

"You're okay."

Was it a statement or a question? I couldn't tell. I nodded dumbly.

"Now you know why we don't do more sparring," he said with a grin. 'Someone always gets hurt."

It was the first time I'd ever seen him smile. "Yes," I replied with a grin of my own, eager to show I didn't bear a grudge.

At this, it seemed Shinzato felt his duty had been done and he turned to leave. Mrs. Miyagi entered the room with a tray, ignoring Shinzato very deliberately to make her displeasure very clear. There were tea and sweets on the tray and she insisted I drink a cup of sweet tea.

Shinzato murmured a polite good-bye to Mrs. Miyagi but she didn't reply. I tried to sit up but she would have none of it, and I dared not disobey. Several times I tried to get up and leave, but Mrs. Miyagi continued to make polite conversation and I couldn't get away. I haven't even the slightest recollection of the topics we covered, though I imagine it was about the health and wellbeing of my family. A good hour must have passed before Mrs. Miyagi was finally satisfied that I was ready to make my way home.

EMPTY HAND

Miyagi clapped his hands loudly and waited for silence. For an awful moment, I feared he would admonish Shinzato and me for sparring without his permission and make an example of us in front of the whole class, but he had something far more important to say. The very name of our art was about to change.

He explained that despite being a small island, Okinawa had many styles of to-te (or simply 'te' as it was often known). In Naha there was Naha-te, in Shuri there was Shuri-te, in Tomari (a port just a mile up the coast) there was Tomari-te. Every village had its own style. There were even styles kept within a single family and passed down in secret from father to son. This reinforced the opinion of the premier martial arts federation of Japan that 'te' was a local and somewhat primitive native art of Okinawa compared to the classical martial arts of kendo, jujitsu, aikido, and the newly popular judo.

A group of senior Okinawan masters had formed a committee to set certain standards across all the different styles of Te. Miyagi was the chairman of this committee, and a meeting had taken place the night before, when Shinzato had been giving me my painful introduction to sparring. At this meeting, the name of the art itself had been discussed and a momentous decision had been reached. The written characters for to-te, traditionally written as *China Hand*, would now be written as Kara-te: *Empty Hand*. Miyagi sighed before continuing. The committee had decided a more united image of karate would be useful in making it more acceptable on the Japanese mainland. Also, since many Okinawan instructors had no background in Chinese martial arts, it made little sense to call it 'China Hand'. And understandably, some instructors were keen to lose the association with a country that we were at war with. Others, like Master Funakoshi who was teaching in Tokyo, believed the idea of *Empty Hand* carried a deeper meaning than simply *weaponless*. The concept of emptiness is an important one in Zen, and in Miyamoto Musashi's classic samurai text, *The Book of Five Rings*, the highest form of all is known as 'The Void'.

All this made sense when Miyagi explained it. Nevertheless, I sensed his regret in forsaking his connection with the Chinese martial arts, a connection that his master had worked so hard to bring to Okinawa. A few days later, I asked Miyagi in private what he thought of this change. He simply smiled and told me it would take him some time to get used to writing the new character for 'karate' in his notes and articles. He seemed reluctant to say more on the subject, and for once, I didn't press him.

THE HARD AND SOFT
SCHOOL

Shortly after the renaming of our art, another important name was decided upon. Jinan Shinzato had been in Tokyo, where he had performed a demonstration of our karate to the crown prince of Japan. When he returned, he reported that his demonstration had been well received and had created considerable interest in Miyagi's art, but he'd been asked by the prince which style of karate he was demonstrating and hadn't had an answer. Miyagi's personal brand of karate did not have a name.

A few days later, Miyagi called our class together once more and announced that our school needed a name to be known by. He recited a poem from the *Bubishi*—a book of martial strategy from China that he called 'The Bible of Karate'—which read, 'Inhaling is softness, exhaling is hardness.' He'd decided to take his inspiration from this line, calling his karate the 'Hard Soft School' or Goju Ryu—'Go' meaning hard, 'Ju' meaning soft, and 'Ryu' being school or association.

Over the weekend I made a wooden sign and painted the words 'Hard Soft School' in lettering that I was proud of and presented it to Miyagi on Monday.

"What's this, Kenichi?" he asked in surprise.

"A sign, to hang above our door. It will tell everyone about our school."

"Why would I wish to do that?" he asked.

"To attract new students, Sensei. Lots of schools are doing it now. It's called advertising."

Miyagi held the sign at arm's length and regarded the lettering carefully. "It is a nice looking sign," he said at last. "Thank you very much, Kenichi."

He put the sign aside, by the wall, and later took it home. It never hung outside the dojo. Miyagi never advertised his karate, he never courted students, and to do so now would have been one change too many for him.

THE CEMETERY AT TSUJIBARA

It was the monsoon season and the water was running ankle-deep in the streets. Giant puddles had pooled in Miyagi's yard and I brushed the excess water away and laid planks over the mud, so he and his family could come and go more easily. I'd just finished when Miyagi emerged from the house and asked if I would like to accompany him to the cemetery in Tsujibara. I agreed, happy for any chance to spend time with my sensei, and we set off down the hill together. Miyagi was carrying a bag on his shoulder that I offered to take for him, but he declined. I knew he was going to pay his respects to his former teacher, Kanryo Higaonna, who was buried in Tsujibara, and understood that he didn't want to share that duty with another. I didn't insist, despite feeling awkward walking beside my master empty-handed.

At the cemetery, Miyagi set about cleaning the gravestone methodically. I found a second brush in his bag and began to help. Miyagi didn't object. We removed old offerings of fruit and rice from the grave and replaced them with new ones, and when it was immaculate once more, Miyagi lit incense and prayed while I stood silently by. He held his silent discourse with his former master and I sensed a heavy burden of grief in him.

By the time he'd finished, the rain had abated and the sun shone through the clouds, casting a patchwork of light and shade across the cemetery. Miyagi rose from his prayers and looked up at the sky to determine the time of day. It was still early, and he seemed in no hurry to leave. He sat on a low wall near the grave and I sat beside him.

"Master Higaonna was the type of martial artist who only comes along once every hundred years," he whispered, his heart heavy with sadness. "He was *Kumemura*, like you, did you know?"

"I didn't," I said, filled with joy that Miyagi should mention me in the same sentence as his great master.

"His family was descended of the thirty-six families. As a young man he worked as a sailor. His father was killed in a fight when he was fourteen. Higaonna was consumed with grief and wanted revenge. He'd heard of the powerful martial arts of southern China and got himself a passage on a boat to Fuzhou. There was a large Okinawan community in the city and an Okinawan innkeeper helped him find his feet. He told the owner that he wanted to learn the martial arts, and the owner arranged an introduction to one of the foremost teachers of the day, Ryu Ryu Ko.

"Higaonna worked in Ryu Ryu Ko's workshop by day and learned the martial arts by night. Once Ryu Ryu Ko saw his commitment, he allowed Higaonna to become a live-in student and trained him day and night. After nine years, Higaonna's ability was extraordinary and his fame had spread throughout Fuzhou.

The entrance to the Manju Bridge over the Min River is guarded by two stone lions. To sit on the back of one of the lions was to say you were ready to accept challenges from other martial artists or fighters. Higaonna went there to test himself and sat on the lions of Manju Bridge for several days.

At this I could contain myself no longer, "What happened?" I demanded.

Miyagi smiled a knowing smile. "No challenger ever presented himself. I can imagine young fighters turning up and walking on by without a word after looking into his fierce eyes." He chuckled to himself at the thought of this before continuing. "When Ryu Ryu Ko was old and could teach him no more, he told Higaonna to return to Okinawa. Reluctantly, Higaonna did as his master had ordered. When he set foot on Okinawa again, the angry young man had returned a master, and he found the desire for revenge had left him. He had found the true art. He had mastered his own spirit.

"Despite his ability, he was very humble and, at first, didn't seek to promote his martial arts. Instead, he trained alone and returned to his work as a sailor on the yanbarusen. Nevertheless, his ability soon became known and his fame spread throughout Okinawa. The police would often ask him to help them apprehend dangerous criminals, which he usually did with a lightning-fast kick to stun them while the police moved in and made their arrest.

"Higaonna was an excellent sailor and navigator and had no trouble finding a crew for his boat. He borrowed money to buy a cargo of lacquerware to trade in the outlying islands, but lost his cargo not once, but twice, in two successive typhoons. The second time he was blown miles off course and drifted for a week before finding his way back to Okinawa. By the time they reached Naha, they were so hungry they had eaten the rope from the boat. It was a disaster in one sense, since he had no means of earning a living or repaying his loan, but in another it was a blessing. He was forced to fulfill his real destiny and become a karate teacher.

Miyagi sat silent for a minute, reliving his years of training with his master, then shook his head slowly. "I was twenty-seven when he died. Since then I have been without a sensei."

It was incomprehensible to me that a master of Miyagi's ability should still feel the need for a teacher. Miyagi must have sensed my confusion and put his hand on mine and squeezed it affectionately.

"A sensei is more than a teacher, Kenichi. He is someone who has trodden the same path that you now tread, someone to guide you on every stage of your journey. Karate isn't a short thing. It isn't something you can study for a time and then know completely. The true essence of karate is as deep as an abyss. It can take a lifetime to fully know all its secrets—perhaps even longer."

"What kind of secrets?" I asked, unable to resist.

Miyagi shook his head. "So many questions, Kenichi! Always questions.'

I'd annoyed Miyagi and felt ashamed for my rudeness, but he sighed good-naturedly. "It isn't something that is easy to put into words. It's something that can only be drawn deeply into the center of your being through constant training."

"I see," I said, hoping to please him, but Miyagi continued without hearing me. "When Higaonna was alive, he taught me everything he knew. He filled me with knowledge until I could take no more. But now, after so many years, I have so many new questions for him."

"What type of questions?" I asked.

He looked at my expectant face and smiled. "In recent years I have begun to discover connections that I missed earlier."

"What type of connections?" I asked, hungry for insight into the higher levels of karate.

"What you might call the universal principles of karate," he answered, searching for words to explain the unexplainable. "Ultimate truths that never change. Once a principle is grasped, countless things become clear."

I begged Miyagi for an example. He picked up a rock and held it at arm's length before him. "What happens if I let go?"

"It falls."

"How do you know?"

"Gravity."

"Gravity is a principle. Do you know who first put it into words?"

To my shame, I couldn't remember.

"It was an Englishman named Isaac Newton. Newton summed up all the motions of heaven and earth into three simple laws. Can you believe that Kenichi. Three laws?"

I nodded, recalling dimly a lesson from long ago.

"Karate obeys the laws of the universe, Kenichi. For every thousand days I train, a new one reveals itself like a precious jewel hidden in the rock. A thousand days is a long time to wait before learning something new, don't you think?"

I couldn't imagine a thousand days of training. I hadn't trained half that amount. Miyagi went on: "Several years after Higaonna's death I visited a great master from Shuri called Itosu. He refused to teach me, saying that all I needed was contained in Higaonna's kata. I was furious, until several years later when I began to discover certain connections running through all the kata. I returned to Itosu and he confirmed that my analysis was correct. It was a special moment for me, but Itosu died shortly afterward, and I haven't been able to find another master of his standing to be my mentor."

Miyagi rose with a sigh and we left the cemetery together, walking in silence. The monsoon clouds held back and the sun shone but I felt a somber mood descend on me. When Miyagi had begun to speak I'd felt happy at being taken into his confidence, but now, hearing of his lifelong struggle to grasp the ethereal nature of karate, I felt perplexed. If Miyagi couldn't grasp the deeper meaning of karate, what hope was there for anyone? What hope was there for me?

A VISIT FROM DR. KANO

It was another stifling evening in Naha as we packed into the town hall. The doors and windows had been opened wide, but there wasn't a breath of wind to circulate the air. In the eager press of bodies, the sharp smell of fresh sweat stung my nostrils, but I was too excited to care. I was with the other boys from my karate class and we were in high spirits. The reason for this excitement was a visit from the founder of judo, Dr. Jigoro Kano.

Judo was a new and popular way to develop fitness and fighting ability, and with its exciting competitions, it was already being considered as an Olympic sport. Tonight, Dr. Kano himself would be demonstrating his art. As one of the foremost citizens of Okinawa, Miyagi had a seat on the front row next to the mayor. Beside them, a clutch of journalists and photographers were well-placed to capture the evening's events. I'd managed to get a seat only a few rows back from Miyagi, along with the other boys from the karate club. We chatted eagerly as a group of young judo-men in crisp white suits laid mats down in the center of the hall.

The head of the Naha Judo Club strode into the center and the crowd fell silent. He gave a short speech welcoming Dr. Kano, and when Kano stepped out to join him there was rapturous applause. To my surprise Kano was an old man—far older than I'd imagined—with a thick grey moustache and a down-turned mouth, though his stride was sprightly and he bristled with energy.

He was joined on the mat by his senior assistant, whom he introduced as Mr. Nagaoka. I expected Kano to call his students out to demonstrate, but instead he proceeded to perform a flowing two-man drill using only Mr. Nagaoka as his partner. Despite his scholarly appearance, Kano spoke little during his demonstration, offering no more than the name of the technique he was using, or a simple introduction to a new theme such as *locks* or *chokes*. He demonstrated his throwing techniques in groups based on the direction of the opponent's force: throws for an attacker moving toward you, throws for an attacker pulling backward, throws for an opponent moving sideways. Kano and Nagaoka performed a seamless demonstration of the wonderful throws and submissions of judo. It went on for almost an hour and the power and beauty of their actions spoke louder than any words.

In those days, judo was considerably more brutal than its present form. Kano added many subtle strikes into his techniques. The intensity of their performance was incredible and relentless, and the hall watched spellbound. "Ha, yes!" I heard Miyagi exclaim several times, clapping his hands in delight and whispering animatedly to the mayor. He clearly held Dr. Kano to be a martial artist of the highest order. When Kano had finished his own demonstration, he announced that the members of the local judo club would now demonstrate free sparring, and I noticed he wasn't in the least out of breath. The young students engaged in a series of exciting throwing and grappling matches, and the level of their physical conditioning was obvious.

When their matches had finished, another hour had passed in the blink of an eye. Kano left to wash and change into a fresh judo *gi* before returning to mingle with the crowd. He was quickly introduced to the mayor, who in turn introduced him to Miyagi. I squeezed through the throng, determined to be at my teacher's side when he met the great man and hear what they had to say to one another, but when I got there, the mayor was doing most of the talking.

"Master Miyagi is Okinawa's foremost karate master," the mayor told Kano happily, "He is truly one of the natural wonders of the island!"

"There are many fine masters on Okinawa," Miyagi said quickly, then complimented Kano on the quality of his demonstration.

Kano beamed with delight. "Thank you, Master Miyagi. It is always most gratifying when a fellow martial artist appreciates one's art. I've been keen to visit Okinawa for some time, since I am most interested in karate. I have had the pleasure of meeting with several renowned masters in Tokyo and Osaka, Master Funakoshi and Master Mabuni, and I was fascinated to see their demonstrations. Master Funakoshi is a school teacher like myself, and we share the view that martial arts would be a valuable addition to Japan's school curriculum."

"Martial arts is very good for the health and spirit of young people," Miyagi said, then turned with a smile. "These are some of my own students," he said, ushering us forward.

Dr. Kano regarded us with unconcealed pleasure, "Fine young men too, by the looks of them."

"Splendid!" the mayor said, overjoyed that a man such as Kano should express such sentiment, "Perhaps we can persuade Miyagi and his students to give a small demonstration of their karate?" he said mischievously.

"No, no," Miyagi replied raising his hands quickly, "Tonight is a night for judo, not karate, and besides, the hour is getting late."

"Nonsense!" the mayor said, "the sun has still not set! Show Dr. Kano the beauty of our native art."

"There's no need," Miyagi protested, but the mayor persisted.

"Oh come Miyagi, you are always saying that you want to promote karate to the rest of the world."

"Dr. Kano has seen our art before, demonstrated by two fine masters," Miyagi said evasively.

"Ah, but he has not seem the Naha style of karate, and tonight we are in Naha," the mayor said triumphantly.

"That much is true," Kano said with what seemed like genuine interest, "and I understand there are many different schools of karate. What is the name of your school?"

"Our school is called Goju Ryu," Miyagi answered.

"Hard and soft," Kano said, breaking down the *Go* and *Ju* of our title, "fascinating!"

It was interesting, since judo contained the same character of *Ju* meaning soft or, more exactly, compliant or yielding.

"That is why your demonstration was so enjoyable to watch," Miyagi said. "Your methods of using an opponent's strength against him are truly remarkable."

"It has been my life's work to create a style based on these principles," Kano said proudly. "I believe them to be the highest form of combat."

"I agree," Miyagi smiled. "However, the hard part of a style is quicker to learn, and easier to put into practice."

"Most certainly," Dr Kano nodded with a smile. "Even in judo, power and aggression play a vital role. But tell me more of your karate—does it contain Chinese influence? I have heard that some styles do."

"My teacher studied in Fujian Province for many years. Most of our kata are Chinese in origin, though some elements of Okinawa's native martial arts have been blended in."

"Which elements are those?" Kano probed.

Miyagi smiled. "We Okinawans are a simple people, Dr. Kano. We like to rely on simple methods in our fighting." He raised his hand and clenched it slowly into a fist.

"Ha yes, the famous karate punch!" Kano said. "You use a punching post, I believe?"

"The makiwara is one of our primary training tools," Miyagi said, "though there are others. Physical strength and conditioning are also very important."

"Quite so," Kano said, "but the thing that fascinates me most about karate is the practice of kata without a partner. Tell me, what is the purpose of performing a kata alone?"

"That is quite a question," Miyagi said, "and one which I have pondered myself quite often, since it's obvious that training with a partner is more realistic."

Kano put his head to one side, still awaiting an answer.

"There are many explanations," Miyagi continued, "but my final conclusion is that the deeper meaning of karate is not physical, but rather spiritual. Through the practice of kata, the practitioner aims for perfection of form and movement. This can only be achieved by being in harmony with the elements surrounding us, the earth below, and the heavens above. To perfect one's movement in kata is to be perfectly in tune with nature and the universe."

"Quite an achievement," Kano said quietly.

"An impossible dream," Miyagi said quietly, a trace of bitterness in his voice.

Kano nodded. It seemed he had chased the same dream himself. "You are familiar with Yoga, Mr. Miyagi?" he asked suddenly.

Miyagi answered that he was.

"On a recent voyage to Europe, I made the acquaintance of an Indian Guru aboard an ocean liner. We spent many happy hours in discussion, and I learned a great deal about his country and its remarkable spiritual practices. Did you know, for example, that the meaning of the word 'Yoga' comes from the same root as the word *yoke*, and can be translated as *connectedness?*"

It was Miyagi's turn to be impressed, and as he considered the idea, Kano continued cheerfully, "My ultimate aim in judo is also the development of the individual, the perfection of the self."

"A shared ambition," Miyagi said.

"An impossible dream," Kano beamed, and Miyagi chuckled at having his own words quoted back to him. Kano's smile remained, but his eyes were more serious. "I would be fascinated to see a demonstration of your art, Master Miyagi," he said, and it was clear the request was far more than a simple attempt at politeness.

"Yes, come come, Miyagi," the Mayor urged, "demonstrate your art for Dr. Kano. Demonstrate it for all of us."

Miyagi looked about, seeking an excuse to refuse, but the mayor was determined. "Dr. Kano is sailing in the morning," he added. "We cannot delay, Miyagi. It must be tonight!"

Miyagi's eyes returned to Kano's, which hadn't left his since Kano had made his request. He threw up his hands in defeat. He couldn't refuse.

I left the hall at full speed, running alongside my fellow students, all the way to Miyagi's house. Our job was to bring the equipment he needed for his demonstration. My task was to fetch a bundle of bamboo sticks and a clay pot that sat in his garden. The pot was tall, reaching almost to my waist, and heavy. I put the sticks in the pot and struggled back to the hall. My classmates had brought other items, some quite unusual, and when we were all back we gathered the equipment together by the back wall.

It seemed word had got around fast that Miyagi was about to perform a demonstration and the hall had filled to an even greater capacity. In the past, Miyagi had always had his students demonstrate his karate, but after the elderly Dr Kano's impressive personal demonstration, he could hardly refuse to perform himself.

When Miyagi stepped onto the center of the mats, a hush fell over the crowd. He called us forward and guided us through a brief warm-up before demonstrating our conditioning exercises with traditional equipment. Next, we performed Sanchin and Miyagi commented on its importance to the audience. After this, we sat down, and Miyagi had Jinan Shinzato perform Sanchin alone while he tested him. Shinzato's hard body was covered in a thick sheen of sweat that splashed as Miyagi struck, the crack of his iron palms echoing around the hall. I'd never seem Miyagi test Shinzato with such venom, and could only imagine how hard Shinzato must have fought to conceal the pain from his face.

When the dreadful testing had finally finished, Miyagi prepared to perform Sanchin himself. He was considerably taller and bigger than Shinzato, and when he removed his jacket, his body resembled nothing more than a huge bull that had wandered in from the cane fields. He pressed his palms together in readiness to begin and his eyes went to a distant place, as if preparing for battle. In that instant I knew where he was. He was on the cliffs of Itoman Bay—and I was filled with such happiness that I struggled not to cry out.

His arms crossed before him and he stepped forward, breathing loudly. Despite the slow nature of his movement, the audience fell silent and watched spellbound. Rooting his feet into the ground, his huge body became one of the giant boulders on our rocky shoreline. As his arm went back and pushed forward, his limbs became the branches of the Ryukyu palms. As his stance sunk and rose, he carried the power of the ocean swells in his every movement. The elements of Okinawa had come together in the form of a man.

I glanced at Dr. Kano and saw him watching Miyagi with undisguised wonder. Miyagi dipped and turned to face the back of the hall, then rose and locked into his stance once more. "Ha!" Kano exclaimed, noticing the classic judo footwork at play.

Miyagi turned once more. His body was dripping in sweat now and the sheen made it all the more incredible to behold. His hands came forward together and drew back three times, then he finished with two backward steps and wheeling blocks. There was a long moment as the audience waited, uncertain how to respond—then rapturous applause. Miyagi's performance was just beginning. He called for two volunteers from the audience and handed each of them an oak staff, inviting them to strike his body while he performed Sanchin once more. Their blows had no effect. "Harder," he urged with a smile, and they swung with all their might, though it made no difference.

Next, he demonstrated two beautiful kata that flowed from slow, deliberate movements into explosive punches, kicks, and stomps, punctuated by fearsome kiai that sent tremors through the benches where we sat. If Sanchin had been nature's elements at play on a fine day in Okinawa, these kata were storms that left devastation in their wake, and when Miyagi had finished, the hall was held for a moment, suspended in awe before erupting into thunderous applause.

To end the demonstration, Miyagi had us bring our assortment of props onto the mats. I saw my master perform feats that I would not have thought possible. He smashed a giant stack of tiles with his fist, chopped a thick block of wood in half with a knife-hand strike, and thrust his fingers into a tight bundle of bamboo to snatch a single stick from its center.

Two of my companions brought out a table and Shinzato placed a huge slab of beef on it. Miyagi tore it into small chunks with his bare hands. Then he pointed at me. I hurried out with the tall ceramic jar that I'd brought from his garden. Miyagi lifted it onto the table and turned it around so the audience could see it wasn't broken. He stood before the jar in silence for almost a minute, as if summoning a special strength from somewhere—despite his humble manner, my teacher was a quite a showman when he wanted to be—then suddenly, with a sharp cry, he struck the jar. I'd expected a shower of flying shards to fill the air, so I was shocked to see he'd failed to break the jar, or even move it. The audience was equally surprised. There was an embarrassed silence, until Miyagi spun the jar around to reveal a hole, two inches across, drilled through the clay. It was almost a perfect circle. The audience was too stunned to clap or cheer.

Another student brought out a kerosene can and a basin for Miyagi, and the silence remained in the hall. Miyagi lifted the kerosene can and spun it around so we could see each side, then made to open it. The top was too tight. He tried once more, this time with all his might, but the top wouldn't budge. Knowing the strength of his grip, I found it hard to believe he couldn't open the can. He replaced it on the floor and spread his hands in despair. It seemed his demonstration would end with a whimper. Then to everyone's surprise, he turned and kicked the can in anger. The action seemed so out of place for Miyagi that the audience didn't know how to react. He stooped and picked up the can. Tipping it onto its side, a stream of kerosene poured out from a hole in the side into the basin at his feet. Miyagi had punctured the can with his toe.

THE DANCING MAN

"How did you do it?" I asked in wonder, as we walked on the hard-packed dirt road toward Shuri.

"Do what?" Miyagi asked.

"Kick the hole in the can!"

"With my toe."

My questioning was getting me nowhere, but it was a fine day and a long walk to Shuri, and Miyagi seemed to be enjoying our conversation, so I persisted.

"When will we learn to do that?" I asked.

"You already know how to do it."

I turned in exasperation to Shinzato, who was walking with us. Shinzato ignored me. "Do you know the answer, Sempai?" I demanded.

"Practice."

"Jiru is right," Miyagi said, "Practice is the key to this and all things. Didn't you know that already?"

"I suppose so," I admitted reluctantly.

"Good, because I cannot tell you the answers to everything," he smiled. "You must learn to find them for yourself. Once you know where to look, they are easy enough to find, most of the time."

"Where should I look?" I asked.

Miyagi stared out to sea. The road was getting steep and he took several breaths before answering. "All the secrets of karate are in the kata. Learn the universal principles that make the techniques work and you have learned everything there is to know. Then simply practice, as Jiru says."

What are the secrets?" I demanded, unable to resist.

"Ah, Kenichi," Miyagi said sadly, "I knew you would ask me this. Why can't you be more like Jiru, who never asks any questions? Jiru does the training I set for him with every ounce of his heart and soul. That is why he is so good. That is why he is the sempai."

"I can never be as good as Jiru," I said. It was a cheeky thing to say because Jiru was a nickname used only by Miyagi and by rights, I should have referred to Shinzato as sempai, but fortunately Miyagi chuckled at my remark. Shinzato didn't seem annoyed either. Ever since knocking me out, his attitude to me had softened, from a haughty disdain to a more general indifference. He even called me by my name, on occasion, and whenever he did, I felt an inexplicable joy.

"So tell me," I persisted, "the secrets…"

"There are so many that I can't even begin to count them," Miyagi said evasively.

"Do you know them all?" I asked.

"No I don't," he said, and I got the feeling I'd touched on something that troubled Miyagi. I didn't press him, but after a few more paces up the winding road to Shuri, he began to speak again.

"When my teacher, Master Higaonna, was getting old, we spent many hours together training at my home. Afterward, I would have supper prepared for him and we would often talk long into the night. At the time, I asked him everything I wanted to know, and he always had an answer for me." Miyagi paused. It was a painful memory for him. "That was a long time ago. Today I have many more questions. That is why we're going to Shuri."

"What's in Shuri?"

"There is an old man I want to visit."

"A karate master?" I asked, excited.

"A master of Okinawan dance," Miyagi said.

Shinzato and I walked on in silence, our lack of interest obvious.

"Not this modern stuff that young people do today," Miyagi continued, ignoring our unspoken protest, "but the old dances of Okinawa that were practiced last century, when karate was at its peak."

"Why are we going to see a dancer?" I asked, bemused.

"Before he died, Master Higaonna told me that many techniques of battle had been concealed in Okinawan dance."

"Why were they concealed?" I asked.

"Because in those days, the Okinawans were not only banned from using weapons, they were forbidden from practicing any form of martial arts, so it was done in secret and concealed in dance."

We arrived at the outskirts of Shuri and turned off the main road to follow a back street that wound between rude dwellings in a valley. The walls of the castle and the tall Shureimon Gate soon became visible above us.

"The Japanese had only recently invaded our island," Miyagi continued. "Remember, as I've often told you, Okinawa was an independent kingdom before the arrival of the Satsuma clan."

We came to a little wooden house surrounded by a high hedge on the outskirts of Shuri, and Miyagi knocked on the door while Shinzato and I stood a respectful distance behind. An old man answered and Miyagi introduced himself. The old man eyed him suspiciously at first, but as Miyagi spoke, he appeared to recognize him and we were invited inside. The interior was dark, and the few pieces of furniture were old.

The walls were bare, save for two small prints of colorful birds and an old fan of black and gold that had been opened out and attached to the wall. A small cabinet held a blue tea set and some books and papers, curled at the edges and yellow with age. The dented *tatami* on the floor showed the wear of countless footsteps over the year. Despite it meagerness, the house was spotlessly clean and there was a pleasing sense order to the place.

The old man offered us tea and refreshments. I was surprised because he was of the generation that wouldn't deign to prepare such things himself, and he appeared to be alone in the house. I was still wondering how he would conjure up tea for us when he stepped outside and called to a young boy who was playing in the street nearby. The boy ran off with a message and a few moments later a woman appeared, the old man's daughter, I imagined, to make good on her father's offer.

While she prepared tea on the tiny stove behind a dividing partition, the old man spoke to us about Okinawan dance, as Miyagi had requested. He talked for a long time and Miyagi listened attentively, never once interrupting, but Shinzato and I quickly grew bored. In the end, Shinzato could hide his disdain no longer and when the old man paused for breath, he demanded to know whether the dances contained martial techniques.

The old man assured him that they did. Shinzato asked him to demonstrate, and the old man rose and walked to the center of the room. His dance began slowly with a high forward step, and then he placed his front foot lightly on the floor, one hand rising while the other sank. As he stepped forward, his hands changed, flowing smoothly from the wrist. He turned a circle in tight little steps. It didn't seem very martial to me, but

I noticed Miyagi watching very carefully. The old man continued his strange movements for several minutes until Shinzato stood up and the old man stopped in surprise.

"I fail to see the martial techniques in your dance," Shinzato said boldly.

"That doesn't mean they're not there," the old man said, glaring at Shinzato.

"If they're there, then perhaps you can defend yourself with dance," Shinzato said, the trace of a smile on his lips, and before the old man could respond he swung a punch at the old man's head.

In fairness to Shinzato, the punch was slow and not thrown in anger. Even so, he paid the price for his insolence. The old man circled away from the punch and blocked Shinzato's arm with his wrist, his upturned palm flying over the top of Shinzato's forearm like a heavy whip and stopping the punch in its tracks. Shinzato let out a grunt of pain and slumped forward. I hadn't seen the old man's other hand, which had struck Shinzato in the groin at the same time. Continuing his circular motion, the old man squatted and thrust his arm hard between Shinzato's legs, then rose with Shinzato across his shoulders and, still turning, slammed him down on the hard floor.

The man's daughter appeared in the room, ashen-faced. She looked from Shinzato, still lying prone on the threadbare tatami, to her father, whose eyes were aflame with fury, and finally to Miyagi.

"What on earth is happening?" she demanded quickly, not daring to raise her voice at such an elevated member of society as Miyagi, but anxious for her father's welfare. "Your father was teaching my student the finer points of Okinawan dance,"

Miyagi said, rising swiftly from his seat, "but I'm afraid my student is a very clumsy fellow." He bowed low before the old man. "I apologize and thank you sincerely for your enlightening instruction. We will not trouble you further, sir," he smiled, bowing once more, then strode from the house.

Shinzato and I hurried after him. Shinzato walked with obvious difficulty and stayed several steps behind Miyagi, hanging his head in silent shame. We continued until we were far from the old man's house before Shinzato summoned the courage to speak.

"Master, I apologize," he said loudly.

"Why should you apologize?" Miyagi asked in surprise.

"I brought dishonor on you in front of a master."

Shinzato's voice was quavering, and I sensed he was holding back tears of shame.

"Why do you feel I was dishonored?" Miyagi asked.

"I doubted the word of an old man, who really was a master."

We walked on in silence, the gentle hum of the cicadas was suddenly deafening. When Miyagi spoke it was in a low voice, almost to himself. "I was dishonored, but not by you, Jiru. The truth is, I didn't believe the old man either, but I allowed you to put him to the test. He proved us both wrong, but you were the one who paid the price, so perhaps it's I who should apologize to you."

"No!" Shinzato said quickly—he couldn't contemplate such a thing. "Never," he added more quietly.

I stole a glance at Shinzato, who avoided my eye.

"Did you see martial techniques in his dance, Sensei?" I asked Miyagi.

"Yes," Miyagi answered thoughtfully, "I believe I did, but we will never be sure. His secrets will probably go with him to the grave, leaving us groping in the dark, as we have been for so long."

"I am responsible," Jiru said despondently.

"No, you are not," Miyagi said, his face brightening suddenly. "But let us not waste the day entirely, especially after such a long climb. We can visit Shuri Castle instead, and you can still learn something of your heritage—both of you." Not daring to complain, we followed Miyagi up the hill toward the battlements above.

Shuri Castle was built on a prime vantage point and the views were breathtaking. We saw miles of twisting rocky coastline and white breakers to the south and west, swaying fields of rice, sugarcane, and pampas grass to the north, and the distant Kerama Islands visible on the horizon.

The top of the great Shureimon Gate came into sight through the trees, inscribed with the words *Nation of Peace*. Miyagi told us the history of the castle, which had once been the center of the prosperous trading nation, the Ryukyu Kingdom. Such things were of little interest to me at the time, though I was always happy to listen to Miyagi's lectures, and even Shinzato did his best to appear attentive after his harsh lesson earlier in the day. Miyagi pointed to two stone dragons outside the main hall whose style, he told us, came from neither China nor Japan, but from the far-off palaces of Cambodia and Thailand. We strolled in the castle grounds, through walled gardens filled with flowerbeds, and gleaming temples and shrines, and continued to the artificial Dragon Lake.

We stopped at a huge bell called The Nation-Bridging Bell, and Miyagi read out the inscription. I can still hear his voice, speaking each word is his deliberate style—pausing between phrases so the meaning might sink in, and the memory fills me with joy and sadness in equal measure.

> *In the southern seas lie the islands of the Ryukyu Kingdom. The Kingdom embraces the wisdom of Korea and the cultures of China and Japan. Located between these nations, it is the ideal land where peace and long life prevail. The Ryukyu Kingdom bridges the nations with its ships and the land overflows with exotic goods and priceless treasures.*

A PASSAGE TO FUZHOU

The grey freighter seemed hugely out of place beside the little wooden boats in Naha harbor. When it arrived from Kagoshima on the Japanese mainland, we were forced to move Uncle Anko's ship to the far side of the quay to make room for it.

Sailors and local dockers had been working throughout the morning to carry a never-ending stream of cargo. Giant artillery guns were lifted off by crane, while crate after crate of small arms and ammunition were stacked on the quayside. A convoy of army trucks arrived to collect the supplies and soldiers began loading the trucks. When the last of the trucks was emptied, new trucks arrived and the unloading continued. The giant ship began to disgorge the main contents of its belly onto the island. It turned out to be building materials.

The work went on all day. At one point my uncle came and stood beside me. I thought he might complain that I'd not done much work that day, since I'd been mainly gawking at the ship, but instead he put his hand on my shoulder affectionately. "They are turning our island into a giant airbase, Kenichi."

"Is that what the building materials are for?" I asked.

"So I've heard."

"But we already have two runways. Why do we need more?"

"Air power is the key to modern warfare. Okinawa is an important strategic position in the Pacific. We're the last big island before the mainland and a vital part of Japan's defenses."

"Do you think there'll be a war with America?" I asked.

He shrugged, "Who can say?"

"Master Miyagi believes there will be, and if there is, it won't be like the war with China. He says America's a very powerful nation."

"Maybe so, but the Americans don't have the Japanese fighting spirit," my uncle assured me. He sighed, "Even so, it would be good to end the war in China first before we engage such a formidable foe."

My uncle sat beside me and we watched the unloading for a while longer.

"We shouldn't be at war with China anyway. It's bad for business. We Okinawans are traders. We ship household goods, clothing and tea—things people need to live, not to kill each other with, but in wartime, the main trade is in arms."

"Is business really bad?" I asked. It hadn't crossed my mind that the war might have affected us that way.

"It has been bad, but I picked up a new assignment to collect some supplies which should improve things."

"From Kagoshima?" I asked, since Kagoshima was our most frequent port of call.

"No, from Fuzhou."

I was surprised to hear this because trade with China had ceased since the start of the war, and all entry to the ports was strictly controlled by the Japanese Navy.

"We're going to pick up tea for the army," he explained. "I have entry papers from the authorities." He looked at me with a frown, "You've never been to China, have you Kenichi?"

"No," I answered.

"It's the home of your ancestors."

"I know. I've often dreamed of seeing it."

He nodded slowly. "Maybe you can. One of my crew is in jail, and I don't think he'll be out in time to sail with us. You can take his place, if you like."

"I would love to," I said, grinning foolishly.

"Good, then it's settled," he said. "It will be good to see China again. You'll like it Kenichi. I know you will."

Later in the day, a thought struck me. I turned it over in my mind throughout the afternoon and when work finished in the evening, I made my way up the hill to Miyagi's house. There was no training that evening, but I often stopped by to do chores for him, so he wasn't surprised to see me. He was stacking wood in neat piles by the side of the house. I bent down to help him and when we had finished, I told him I had an idea. He looked at me dubiously. "We should go to China," I said eagerly.

"That is your idea?" he asked with a frown.

"Yes. We can go in search of a master, perhaps someone taught by the same teacher as Master Higaonna."

Miyagi grinned and there was a light in his eyes. I saw he liked the idea. "It's a good plan Kenichi, but a little impractical. We can't simply board a ship and sail to China any more. We're at war, in case you didn't know."

"My uncle's ship is sailing to Fuzhou in five days time," I told him.

"My own ships sail to Fuzhou, Kenichi, but all personnel have to stay inside the port. No one's allowed to go beyond."

"But my uncle has a permit to leave the port," I explained. "He's bringing a large consignment of tea for the army. The general is very particular about the quality of his tea, so he's given my uncle a permit to inspect the plantation where it's grown."

Miyagi didn't answer; I could see he was unconvinced.

"My uncle speaks Chinese. He has contacts in the Okinawan community in Fuzhou. He might be able to find someone who trained with Higaonna, someone who's still alive today."

"Your uncle's done well to remember the language of his ancestors," Miyagi said.

"Yes," I agreed, suddenly proud of my heritage.

"Do you speak Chinese yourself?"

"Only a few words," I said, embarrassed by my lack of knowledge or interest in my own heritage. "Let me speak to my uncle, please," I continued quickly. "Let me ask if you can accompany us. I know he'd be honored to have you aboard."

Miyagi stared at me for a long time and I felt suddenly ashamed of myself, to have presumed to suggest such a thing to my teacher.

"You are going yourself?" he asked finally.

"Yes, it will be my first trip to China."

"I've been once before to Fuzhou, when Master Higaonna was still alive. It was most interesting to see the martial arts there."

"That was a long time ago," I reminded him. We both knew Miyagi had many new unanswered questions.

"Yes it was," he agreed.

"One of my own ships is sailing to Fuzhou next week to collect a small shipment of Chinese medicine," he mused. "I could divert it somewhere else if your uncle can fit a few cases of medicines aboard?"

"I'm sure that would be possible," I said confidently, "I'll speak to my uncle."

"Do so," Miyagi said, "and if he agrees, we will go."

Five days later, I was standing beside Uncle Anko on the prow of his ship. We had already cleared the calm waters of Naha harbor and the wind had picked up, blowing a stiff northerly breeze that had us making good time through the grey swells. The sky was overcast and there was a hint of rain in the air, but it was late autumn, and not the time for typhoons. I was filled with excitement and ignored the warm spray on my face and the soft grey brine swirling around my feet. I could hardly wait to see China and help my sensei to discover the deepest secrets of karate.

"Where is Miyagi?" my uncle shouted over the buffeting wind.

"Below deck," I answered.

"He has no sea-legs," Anko laughed.

"Apparently not." I stifled a grin of my own.

"Now you're stronger than Miyagi!" he chuckled.

My uncle was irrepressible, quite unlike my father, who was always so serious. "There's something you should know about China, Kenichi," he went on mischievously, as if giving away a precious secret. "The women are something special."

I must have blushed because he roared with laughter. "Seriously, they are very beautiful, and so refined, not like the country girls of Okinawa—these are city girls, all dressed up in silk and finery, carried by eunuchs on golden sedan chairs." I couldn't tell if my uncle was being serious. "We can get you one, if you want," he continued amiably.

"I don't need that sort of lady," I said stiffly.

"You have a sweetheart in Okinawa?"

"No," I admitted sullenly.

"Whyever not, a good-looking young man like you?" he asked, his face serious, though I knew he was still teasing. I thought of the awkward kisses and fumbled gropes I'd managed with one or two of my classmates and wished Anko would change the subject. "I haven't met the right person," I said glumly.

He looked at me as if I were mad. "Forget the right person, Kenichi! At your age, any person will do, as long as it's a girl. You need practice. That's how you get to be a man. But listen, don't worry, I'll find you a girl in Fuzhou."

"No!" I shouted, but my uncle ignored my protest, "A beautiful Chinese girl, just for you, Kenichi."

"I'll find my own girl," I said desperately.

"Don't worry, she'll be a real lady," he promised, "or at least a real lady of the night." He ruffled my hair.

"I'm going below to check on Master Miyagi," I said to get away.

"Yes, go and check on Miyagi," he said happily, "go and empty the great man's bucket."

The sleeping quarters were cramped and stifling, and no one ever stayed down there unless there was a storm. I found Miyagi looking pale and drawn. The bucket beside his bunk was half-filled with vomit. I emptied it and replaced it for him, then offered him tea to settle his stomach. He refused with a grunt. I knew he wished to be alone and left him to his misery.

We stopped at Kume in the Yaeyama Islands to sell lacquerware and pick up firewood before sailing on to Formosa. By the time we put into the harbor at Keelung, Miyagi was feeling well enough to join us on deck. My uncle was delighted to have the famous karate master on board and even more delighted by his helplessness at sea. "Ha, Miyagi-san, he laughed, "you might be the strongest on land, but I'm the strongest at sea!"

Miyagi shrugged good-naturedly at my uncle's jibes. On Okinawa few would have dared to speak so freely to a nobleman like Miyagi, but we were at sea, and my uncle was the captain of the ship, and on a ship, the captain is also the king.

A light drizzle greeted us as the grey shores of China came into view. The air was warm, despite the weather. The low-lying coastline was soft and fertile, with lush bamboo groves supplied by the ample waters of the Min River delta. Far behind, pointed mountains rose, reminding us of the hinterland beyond, a land so vast that we small-islanders could barely conceive it. We sailed up the Min to the international quay at Mamui. The riverbank became an unending row of ramshackle wooden buildings, their timbers rotten and black, planks missing from gangways and roofs—many seemed deserted. The war had stifled trade, the lifeblood of any river. Several rusty steamers belched black smoke into the already grey air. Smaller sampans and ancient junks crossed the river around us as we pulled into the quay. We waited for several hours in the offices of the Japanese port authority while my uncle smoothed the way for entry into Fuzhou. Eventually our papers were stamped and we were allowed to pass through.

Fuzhou turned out to be an elegant city of white houses with tiled roofs and a tall pagoda that rose high above the rest of the town. When the ship was moored in the port, my uncle hired a smaller boat to take us upriver to the Manju Bridge where a large Okinawan community was living in Fuzhou.

We took rooms at a hostel called the Inn of Heavenly Peace run by an ancient Okinawan called Kanpu Tanmei—a nickname that means *Grandfather with a Topknot*, and an ironic one at that, since the old man was completely bald. My uncle knew Kanpu Tanmei from previous visits and introduced us. When the old innkeeper heard that Miyagi was a former student of Higaonna's, his eyes lit up and he spoke in glowing terms of

Higaonna, who had stayed in the same hostel when he had arrived in Fuzhou.

Kanpu Tanmei also knew of Higaonna's teacher, the renowned Ryu Ryu Ko, but when Miyagi told him of his hopes of finding other students of the Ryu Ryu Ko's, he was skeptical. Ryu Ryu Ko had died many years ago, he explained, and since Fuzhou had fallen under Japanese control, martial arts had been banned. Most masters had disappeared into the interior and Kanpu Tanmei didn't hold out much hope, but he promised to make inquiries on our behalf.

An enormous black car had pulled up outside the inn. I went out to investigate. The giant metal grill was open like a lion's roar, and the bodywork curved back from it, coiled like a panther waiting to spring. The black paintwork gleamed in the morning sunlight like the sheen of sweat on a great beast. I knelt beside the bumper, not daring to touch the car. I could see my face in the polished chrome. The driver ignored me deliberately. He must have been used to boys gawking at his car. I rose and walked around it, wondering what it would be like to sit inside, or better still, to ride in such a vehicle.

My uncle emerged from the hostel and, to my astonishment, opened the passenger door. Miyagi followed a moment later, and my uncle held the door open while he got inside. My uncle waited, while I stood dumbly, uncomprehending. "Well come on Kenichi," he said finally. "Get in. Or would you rather sit on the pavement all day and play with the crickets?"

"Where are we going?" I asked, hurrying inside.

"We're going to do business," he answered, following me into the car and pulling the door shut behind him. I took a seat facing the rear, while Miyagi and my uncle sat opposite.

The car moved off suddenly and I gripped the armrest, I'd not even noticed the engine running. It was like no car I'd ever been in and I felt my senses overload with excitement. Miyagi and Anko discussed the forthcoming business of the day as the car nosed its way slowly through the busy streets of Fuzhou. My eyes flitted restlessly from around the insides of the car to the bustling scenes outside and back to the car's interior once again, not knowing where to settle. My ears were filled with the sounds of the street coming through the open window— the singsong voices of the Chinese, the ringing of a thousand bicycle bells, the roar of diesel truck engines, the continuous blare of a hundred impatient horns. The smell of leather, wax, and stale cigarette smoke mixed with the driver's cologne in my nostrils, making my head spin.

Fuzhou seemed endless, far bigger than any city on Okinawa, one street leading relentlessly to the next, but eventually the buildings began to recede and we climbed a winding road into forested hills. It was well over an hour later that the car pulled onto a road running through row upon row of tea bushes that stretched away up the hillside. We continued for several miles before turning into a wooden gateway and, after another mile, coming to a group of buildings beneath a small copse of bamboo.

There were people working outside, but all work stopped when they saw our car approaching. Someone must have alerted the plantation owner because he was standing beside the car by the time the engine stopped. He greeted Uncle Anko and Miyagi formally in Chinese, but when he realized Miyagi didn't understand, he switched into Japanese, which he spoke well, though with a strong accent.

We were invited inside and tea was quickly served. It was different to the tea we drank in Okinawa, lighter and more fragrant, paler in color and, I learned, served warm rather than hot to avoid scalding the delicate white leaves. The conversation revolved around simple matters, the tea itself, my uncle's health, the health of his family, the health of Miyagi and his family, until finally the tea was finished and we set off on a long tour of the plantation. The owner was at pains to make our visit interesting, but despite his best efforts my attention began to wane, so I was glad when we finally returned to the main house and negotiations could begin in earnest.

Uncle Anko and Miyagi retired to another room with the owner and his assistant. I waited outside for an interminable time, certainly more than two hours, until they emerged. The owner was as polite as ever, though I noticed tight lines in his lips that hadn't been there before. I waited until the car was speeding down the hills before inquiring how the negotiations had gone. "They went well," my uncle said with a sigh and a smile. "Very well, I think."

"Your uncle is a shrewd businessman," Miyagi told me.

"Mr. Miyagi is no slouch himself," my uncle chuckled. "The Chinese are very difficult to negotiate with—it's impossible to know what they're really thinking—but you learn how to deal with them over the years."

"Our suspicions were correct," Miyagi added.

"What suspicions?" I asked.

"With the war on, and the country in chaos, we suspected demand must be at rock bottom. A large plantation like this one would have huge surpluses. They would be desperate for orders, even if it means doing business with their occupiers."

"Not quite their occupiers," my uncle corrected, "That is the beauty of being from Okinawa. We are not exactly Japanese."

"Yes, I believe that makes a difference too," Miyagi said.

"We are middlemen," I said, pleased to be learning a bit about the mysterious world of business.

"As we have been for centuries," Miyagi nodded. "Okinawa is the supply chain that takes tea from China to Japan, and money from Japan to China."

"And along the way, a little tea always falls over the side of the boat," my uncle said with a grin.

"And a little money, too," Miyagi laughed.

I joined in the laughter. Sitting in that grand old car, speeding through the lush countryside of Fujian province in the evening sunshine, sharing the happy atmosphere with my uncle and my sensei, I could think of nothing better in the world and no place I would rather be. It was the beginning of a new chapter in my life—I'd left tiny Okinawa and discovered the whole world lay on our doorstep. China was just the first step, just one of many possibilities. Who knew where my journey would take me next?

The sun was setting when we entered Fuzhou and the car slowed to a crawl. The streets were even more crowded than before, if that was possible. Busy night markets had sprung up on the streets. The driver rested his hand on the horn in protest, but it made no difference. The car inched forward through the whirling throng, pushing people out of the way with its huge chrome bumper.

When we were close to the inn, Miyagi suggested we should get out and walk the rest of the way. My uncle was unsure, but Miyagi dismissed his worries with a wave of his hand. "The markets look fascinating. There's nothing to worry about."

"Well, you are the great *Bushi Magusuku*," my uncle joked, using an Okinawan name for Miyagi meaning Great Warrior, "so we will be perfectly safe."

The tension in the air was palpable as soon as we stepped out of the car. The local people were forced to bow to any occupying Japanese who passed by, and the resentment was clear in their eyes. The Japanese were both hated and feared in the port of Fuzhou. Miyagi ignored the resentful stares and moved from shop to shop and stall to stall, examining the local handicrafts and clothing and choosing souvenirs for his wife and family. My uncle made a point of speaking to the stall owners in Chinese and encouraged me to do the same. It seemed that as Okinawans, we were able to move around the city in relative safety. Nevertheless, I was glad when we finally arrived at the inn.

Kanpu Tanmei greeted us with good news. He had made contact with a woman whose grandfather had trained with the famous Ryu Ryu Ko many years ago and had arranged a meeting with this woman the next evening. Miyagi was intrigued, and thanked him profusely for his efforts.

"Don't thank me too soon," Kanpu Tanmei warned, "I can't vouch for the authenticity of this woman or her grandfather, or for the quality of his martial arts. There are very few genuine masters in Fuzhou nowadays. I hope this one is true."

The next day we visited a pharmacy in the affluent district of Fuzhou where Miyagi bought his medical supplies. The owner was delighted to meet Miyagi in person. They had done business through intermediaries for many years but never met face to face. Miyagi spent several hours inspecting the medicines before placing his order. The negotiations were long and protracted, but Miyagi was a strong negotiator and the price eventually came down to a figure he was prepared to pay. Once the distasteful matter of money had been resolved, the pharmacist invited us to a banquet at a nearby restaurant where we enjoyed fine food and wine until late in the evening. I guessed the merchant wanted to maintain friendly relations with an important client like Miyagi, especially in uncertain times.

By the time we had climbed back into the car and were returning to the Okinawan quarter, we were all in a merry mood. I'd never tasted so many unusual and delicious dishes as were served at the banquet, but Anko and Miyagi assured me that the food had been very limited compared to before the war. They were describing delicacies of such a strange and intricate nature that I was convinced they were pulling my leg, when all of a sudden the car halted at a roadblock. The driver rolled down the window and a policeman informed him there was a disturbance up ahead. From the noise that we could hear, it sounded like a full-scale riot.

The driver turned the car around and tried to approach Manju Bridge from other routes, but they were all blocked off. In the end, he parked the car several blocks from the inn and we made our way on foot through deserted streets, the noise of the rioting still audible in the distance. At one street corner, we found a rickshaw and the driver agreed to take us to the hostel. A rickshaw was safer than walking, so the three of us jumped in while our car-driver returned to his vehicle, promising to return the next day when things had calmed down.

The rickshaw got no further than the end of the street when a gang of men rounded the corner and forced him to stop. There were perhaps nine or ten of them, several carrying sticks and iron bars. They appeared more like looters than dissidents or freedom fighters. Several were carrying bundles of silk and bottles of wine under their arms. They demanded that we get out of the rickshaw. My uncle refused, saying we were late for an appointment and were in a hurry.

"You are Okinawans!" one of the gang said, recognizing my uncle's accent.

"Yes, and we are staying in the Okinawan quarter, so let us pass and we'll be on our way," my uncle said jovially.

"Okinawans, Japanese, same thing," another said, "You're on business?"

"No, we're visiting relatives," my uncle answered. "We're of Chinese descent ourselves."

"Step out of the rickshaw," the looter demanded. It was clear he intended to rob us.

"We don't have time to stop," my uncle began, but Miyagi put his hand on his arm and muttered that we should hand over any money in our pockets. My uncle reassured Miyagi that he would handle it and turned to the leader once more.

"Come, let us pass, we don't want any trouble tonight."

A chain flashed out from the looter's hand and caught my uncle on the temple. He lurched forward, stunned. The looter dragged him from the rickshaw and down onto the cobbles. I leapt out to protect him, but Miyagi was ahead of me and even as he jumped, his left foot lashed out, catching one of the looters flush on the jaw. The man fell with a sharp slap on the hard cobbles and didn't stir.

The leader launched his chain at Miyagi but I threw myself at him, blocking his arm and taking him to the floor. For a moment, I was on top and smashed my fist into his face, but he was like quicksilver beneath me and I failed to hold him. Another looter kicked me hard in the ribs and I couldn't catch my breath, then the leader's chain struck me on the back of my skull and I fell. As I lay on the hard road, my head swimming, my body unable to move, I could see two of them, kneeling beside my uncle and going through his pockets. Through my blur there was an explosion of bodies, split only by a fragment of a second—Miyagi had floored them both with lighting fast kicks to the head.

I watched, still groggy, as the gang leader fell beside me, unconscious. Miyagi must have knocked him out too, though I hadn't seen how. The rest of the gang, realizing their robbery was not going as planned, threw down their loot and three of them smashed at Miyagi with sticks. Miyagi held his arms high to protect his head and their blows had no effect on his iron-hard limbs. He waded through them like water and seized one assailant's stick, his other hand closing on the man's wrist. I saw the robber's face contort in agony as Miyagi's steel fingers crushed his bones. Miyagi turned him in a half circle to use him as a barrier between himself and the other attackers, then pulled the looter close, kneeing him in the groin and twisting the stick from his grasp in one smooth action. The man fell at his feet.

There were still five men against Miyagi. I had to help him. I stood, ignoring the pounding in my skull, the swimming vision, the urgent need to vomit. All eyes were on Miyagi who, armed with a stick, now posed a serious threat. The looter nearest to me inched forward toward Miyagi, unaware of me. I punched him on the back of the neck, a knockout point that Miyagi had taught me, and to my surprise, the man collapsed in a heap at my feet. I took his stick, though I had no idea what to do with it. I shouted to the looters to distract them from Miyagi and drew my stick back like a baseball bat, ready to strike.

Unlike me, Miyagi knew exactly what to do with his stick. Using my shout as the diversion he needed, he knocked away the nearest looter's stick and thrust the point of his own stick into the looter's throat. The man beside him made to strike, but Miyagi spun away, the tip of his stick smashing the man's hand in an upward arc as he did. The looter's stick fell from his grasp. A third man struck Miyagi hard across the neck and I saw him stumble. I thrashed at the man blindly, knowing I had to stop him. He turned and our sticks clashed with sickening force. Mine jumped from my grasp. I lurched forward to close with him before he could strike me and we wrestled for control of his stick. Meanwhile Miyagi fought with two assailants. The man whose hand he had broken was trying to trap Miyagi's arms behind his back so his friend could get a clean swing with his club.

I fought furiously, lashing out with my hands and knees to overpower my opponent but though he was smaller than I was, he was broad and very strong. He smiled as his strength began to tell and mine began to fail. I couldn't hold him and he freed the stick from my grasp. I saw a flash beside his head and he fell—it was the chain, but this time my uncle was wielding it and from his eyes, I could see his head had cleared, and what was more, he was furious.

He strode forward grimly and whipped at Miyagi's assailants with the heavy chain. The man with the club turned to defend himself, leaving Miyagi free to deal with the one behind him. I saw Miyagi's head fly back in a reverse head-butt, then his hips twisted suddenly and his leg was behind his attacker's. The looter was forced over Miyagi's knee and fell to the ground. Miyagi stood over him and the man pleaded for mercy.

I ran forward to stand beside my uncle, a new stick in my hand. The final looter, seeing the odds had turned badly against him, dropped his stick and ran. Miyagi ordered the downed man to run too. He complied urgently, and suddenly the three of us were alone on the streets, except for the bodies of fallen looters strewn across the cobbles.

Back at the Inn of Heavenly Peace, Kanpu Tanmei eyed us in disbelief. My uncle's left eye was purple and closed over. Miyagi was bruised and disheveled, though unhurt. My nose was broken and blood caked my shirt. He hurried to fill a basin with water, shouting for his boy to fetch a doctor, but my uncle and Miyagi assured him that there was no need. The boy waited, unsure what to do, until finally Kanpu Tanmei succumbed and ordered the boy to fetch towels and bandages instead.

Half an hour later, we were clean and our wounds bandaged. Miyagi and my uncle went upstairs, but I stopped to examine my face in the mirror. I barely recognized the young man looking back at me. My eyes were puffy and half-closed. My nose had swollen to twice its normal size, too tender to touch. Miyagi had reset it with one agonizing wrench and I was pleased that at least now, it was back in the center of my face. I thanked Kanpu Tanmei for his help and had begun to climb the stairs slowly, when he called me back. "Wait, I almost forgot! There is someone here to see you," he called up to me.

"Me?" I asked in surprise. "Who wants to see me?"

"To see all of you," he said, still flustered from what had happened.

I came back down the stairs, wondered who it could be at this late hour. "It's Wa Cheun Liu," he informed me, "the granddaughter of Sifu Liu, the Kung Fu master who I told you about yesterday. Come, let me introduce you."

Kanpu Tanmei led the way into the reception area, speaking in Chinese as he did. I couldn't understand the words, but their meaning was obvious. He was apologizing profusely to the woman for keeping her waiting so long. The woman was seated, and Kanpu Tanmei was standing before her so I couldn't see her expression, though from the tone of her voice it was clear her patience was at an end. I wondered what Kanpu Tanmei had done, or promised, to arrange a meeting with such a highly ranked Kung Fu master and felt guilty for causing the old innkeeper such loss of face. I was about to ask him to add my apologies to his own, but when he stepped aside to introduce us, the words shriveled and died in my throat. There before me, rising from the low seat with the grace of a cat, was the most beautiful young woman I'd ever seen, and all I could do was mumble a greeting with a foolish grin on my face.

SINGING CRANE

Wa Cheun knew of the disturbances in the city and understood our lateness once Kanpu Tanmei explained what had happened. Her smooth forehead furrowed and she spat an angry stream of Chinese that I couldn't follow. Then she looked me up and down, her pretty lips curled down in dismay. I didn't know what to do or say. Fortunately, Miyagi and my uncle appeared just then to meet her. I noticed they had cleaned themselves up and looked far more presentable than I did.

Kanpu Tanmei introduced Miyagi first and Wa Cheun assessed him with a fleeting glance before bowing. Miyagi returned the bow and greeted her formally in Chinese. Next, the old innkeeper introduced Uncle Anko, who spoke to Wa Cheun in fluent Chinese. To my delight, I found I could understand him a little, perhaps because his accent made the language more familiar. He apologized for our dreadful appearance, especially before such a beautiful young lady. I groaned inwardly but Wa Cheun inclined her head at the compliment. I was mesmerized by the loveliness of her neck and was staring dumbly at her when my uncle introduced me once again. I said that we'd already been introduced and Wa Cheun did little more than glance at me—I was insignificant compared to Anko and Miyagi. She spoke briefly with Kanpu Tanmei and my uncle and promised to try and arrange a meeting between her grandfather and Miyagi as soon as possible. She couldn't say when that might be.

When she'd gone and Kanpu Tanmei had retired, my uncle clapped me on the shoulder. "What do you think of Chinese women now, eh, Kenichi?"

I shrugged.

"I told you they were beautiful, didn't I? Now tell me if I'm wrong." He turned to Miyagi. "I'm not wrong, am I Miyagi?"

"The girl is very beautiful," Miyagi agreed.

"I didn't notice," I said stubbornly.

"How could you not notice?" my uncle roared, squeezing my shoulder with his hard fingers, "Your eyes were popping out of your head!"

I brushed my uncle's arm off my shoulder angrily.

"Kenichi, wait, don't be angry. This is good news. You know what it means?"

"What?"

"I don't need to find you a lady. You've found one for yourself!"

I stormed from the room without another word, my cheeks flushed and burning.

"It will save me a bit of money," he called after me. "Bravo, Kenichi! You are a good man. Just make sure you gallop her before we leave. A fine mare like that shouldn't be left in the stable!"

I heard Miyagi stifle a laugh as I went up the stairs, but I was too tired to be angry. All I wanted to do was put my head down on a pillow and sleep.

Two days later, we received a message saying Wa Cheun would come for us the following morning. Kanpu Tanmei rose early the next day to prepare breakfast for us himself, but his housekeeper heard him and ushered him out of the way. Kanpu

Tanmei joined us at the breakfast table and we drank tea while we waited for the porridge to arrive.

"You must be happy today, Kenichi," my uncle said.

"Why?" I asked, still bleary eyed.

"Your girlfriend is coming."

"She's not my girlfriend!" I said, too quickly.

"But you'd like her to be."

It was early and I was still half asleep. I couldn't cope with my uncle and looked away in exasperation, but he wouldn't let it go. "It's about time you got yourself a girlfriend. Make some use of that thing between your legs—it's not a toy, you know."

I stood up angrily.

"Wait, Kenichi, wait!" my uncle pleaded, holding my hand. "Don't be angry. Seriously now, you like her, yes?"

I didn't answer.

"She is pretty, yes? At least admit that!"

"Yes, she is," I sighed.

"She's beautiful," my uncle said. "If I were twenty years younger myself I would... well, no matter, she likes you instead."

"She doesn't like me."

"How do you know, Kenichi?"

"She didn't even look at me," I said.

"Exactly! It's a sure sign, trust me."

I looked at Miyagi in exasperation. Miyagi shrugged, "Don't ask me, I know nothing about women—ask Mrs. Miyagi if you don't believe me."

"Oh, don't be too hard on yourself Miyagi," Anko chuckled. "You love karate. That's why you're an expert. I love women, and that's why I'm an expert. It's also why I don't have a wife!" He patted my hand good-naturedly. "But listen, Kenichi, she likes you. Take my word for it. Who wouldn't, a strong young karate-man like you? Come, sit down and eat your porridge while it's hot."

I sat back down and ate in silence, wondering if there was even a grain of truth in what my uncle was saying. Did Wa Cheun like me? I had to admit, I was filled with an uneasy thrill at the prospect of seeing her again.

I heard voices in the adjoining room, footsteps approaching. The housekeeper had let her in and now Wa Cheun was standing in the doorway. Her hair was tied back and she wore no make-up, and I couldn't help staring at her. Her face was like a doll's, her skin smooth and perfect, her eyes round and shimmering, dazzling me. She was wearing a baggy blue cotton suit that hid her figure entirely. I tried to imagine what she looked like without it.

"Good morning," she said in Japanese, and spoken from her lips, they were the loveliest words I'd ever heard.

Uncle Anko engaged her in conversation while I did my best not to stare, sneaking only furtive glances that I hoped went unnoticed. He explained that he had business in Fuzhou and wouldn't be accompanying us to visit her grandfather. He expressed his regret that he wouldn't be spending time with such a beautiful young woman, a Flower of Fuzhou, he called her. He begged her to pass on his sincere regards to her grandfather. He was laying it on a bit thick, I thought, but Wa Cheun didn't seem put out and agreed to his request.

Outside in the morning sunshine, Fuzhou seemed fresh and new, with no hint of the malevolence of three nights ago. People rode on bicycles, carts clattered down the busy streets, coolies carried their passengers in sedan chairs and rickshaws. Wa Cheun led the way while I followed behind with Miyagi, but when we turned a corner onto a wide avenue, Wa Cheun stopped to wait for us and I found myself beside her. We walked ahead together as Miyagi stopped to admire some building or other.

"I didn't know you spoke Japanese," I said, unable to think of anything better to say.

"Everyone speaks Japanese now," she replied.

I felt an edge of resentment in her voice. It wasn't a good start.

"But you speak it very well," I persisted, wishing I hadn't as soon as the words were out.

"You are too kind," she said frostily.

"Do you practice martial arts with your grandfather?" I asked, seeking a more agreeable topic of conversation.

"Yes, since I was a child," she said.

"Your style is White Crane?"

"Singing Crane. It's derived from White Crane."

"It originates from Shaolin?"

"Yes."

"Where's your dojo?" I asked.

"Dojo?"

"Yes, it means a training hall."

"I know what it means. We don't have such a thing any more. Our training takes place in secret now. Didn't you know martial arts have been outlawed in Fuzhou? Only Japanese martial arts are allowed to be practiced, and only then by Japanese living in China."

"I'm sorry," I said.

"For what?"

"Martial arts should not be banned," I said lamely.

We walked on in silence. The road climbed up a hill, past a factory building that looked closed and a drab warehouse locked behind a rusty gate. The gate had extra bars where barbed wire had once been strung, but the wire was gone. I wondered where it had been taken.

"Do you practice in your home?" I asked, aware of the growing silence.

"We use the social club next door to my grandfather's house. We know the owner and he lets us have a key."

"It's good of your grandfather to see us," I said.

"Grandfather only agreed because your master was a student of Higaonna's," she added pointedly, and for once in my life I was glad that I wasn't Japanese.

I wanted to ask about her father and find out if he too trained in the martial arts, but something told me to keep silent. We turned into a narrow street at the top of the hill and she stopped outside one of the tiny houses and told me to wait. Miyagi appeared at my shoulder just as she re-emerged.

"Grandfather is already in the social club."

She led us across a patch of rough ground to a squat one-story building with a flat roof and a small unkempt garden at the front. The old wooden door was unlocked and we followed her into the cramped entrance hall. The place was dark and smelled of stale tobacco and old wine. Chairs were stacked haphazardly against peeling walls. There was a small kitchen to one side with crockery on a counter. The cups and plates were old and chipped, but someone had taken care to clean them and pile them neatly in a corner.

Wa Cheun opened a set of double doors to the main hall, which was lit by two barred windows on one side. The sunlight streamed through, highlighting the dust and cigarette smoke swirling in the air. A young man was performing a kata in the center of the hall, and an old man watched, seated on a stage at the back, smoking. Both wore loose-fitting grey cotton suits that had once, long ago, been black.

The young man's kata was unlike any I'd seen before, yet faintly familiar nonetheless. We waited by the door until he had finished, then Wa Cheun led us to her grandfather to introduce us, but the old man stubbed out his cigarette and, ignoring us, climbed down from the stage slowly to correct his student. He was tall and thin, with pointed features and a narrow grey moustache. His grey eyes were set wide apart and watery, almost dreamy, but there was a firmness to his jaw line and a purpose in his stride that told of a lifetime of martial arts. He corrected his student at length, going over one part of the sequence with him again and again before moving onto another and then another. The old man demonstrated the movements, his steps light and flowing, then waited for his student to repeat them correctly until he was satisfied.

Finally, he turned to Wa Cheun and beamed with delight, as if noticing her for the first time. She stepped forward, a little uncertain, and spoke breathlessly in Chinese, reminding him, or so I gathered, of the Okinawan visitors he'd agreed to meet. The light of recollection went on in his old eyes and as Wa Cheun made the formal introductions, I saw him take in Miyagi and me with undisguised interest. Wa Cheun introduced him as Sifu Liu and his young student as Yong Li. When the formalities were over and the ritual courtesies had been observed, Sifu Liu invited us to sit and spoke a few words in a broad dialect that neither Miyagi nor I could follow. Wa Cheun nodded and asked, somewhat flatly I thought, whether we required tea and refreshments. Miyagi declined politely, not wishing to impose on their hospitality.

"It's no bother, really," she insisted.

"Thank you, but we do not eat or drink at this hour," Miyagi said politely, knowing, or at least hoping, that we might do some training shortly. "Perhaps Sifu Liu could tell us a little about training with Master Ryu Ryu Ko, and my own master, Higaonna?"

Wa Cheun spoke at length with her grandfather, translating as she did that Sifu Liu had trained alongside Higaonna under Master Ryu Ryu Ko. Shortly after Higaonna had returned to Okinawa, Ryu Ryu Ko had died and Sifu Liu had trained with another master in a style called Dog Boxing. Later still, he had also learned another Crane style called Singing Crane from a third master. This was the style he now taught, though he maintained elements from both his previous styles in his art. All his teachers had died long ago.

When he'd finished speaking, Wa Cheun continued with her own explanations. Her grandfather was the only high-ranking Crane master remaining in Fuzhou. The Japanese overlooked his activities because he was so old, and he had only a handful of students. I felt deflated. I'd brought Miyagi all the way to Fuzhou and there was so little martial arts left to see.

Sifu Liu spoke again and Wa Cheun translated. "My grandfather says Kanryo Higaonna was a great martial artist. He is happy to meet his students and very interested to see Okinawan karate. He says the proof of a style isn't in its teachers, but in its students. He asks that you demonstrate your art," she said, looking at me.

I hadn't prepared for this and looked at Miyagi in dismay. He simply smiled and nodded, "You can begin with Sanchin," he said. Three pairs of eyes watched me expectantly. I could hardly refuse and made my way to the center of the hall, where I turned and bowed to the stage, preparing to begin.

"Wait!" Miyagi called out, "Remove your shirt."

I did as instructed, folding it neatly and placing it by my side on the floor, before beginning. By the time I'd finished there was a sheen of sweat on my body and a puddle on the floor at my feet. Miyagi descended the stage and stood behind me. "Once more," he ordered.

I stepped one pace to the right to avoid the puddle of sweat. I needed to grip the ground with my feet and create tension in my legs. Miyagi was about to demonstrate his painful *shime* testing on me. I bowed once more and placed my hands, left over right, in the ready position. Stepping forward, I brought my arms into the guard position, breathing out strong and steady.

An explosion detonated on my shoulders and the world went black. I had no concept of where I was. I opened my eyes and discovered myself standing in the middle of an unknown hall, watched by an old man, a young man, and a beautiful woman. The shock of Miyagi's strike so close to the back of my neck had knocked me out momentarily, and only my strongly rooted stance had kept me upright.

I struggled to recover my senses as I drew back my left arm and punched. His iron-hard palm slammed into my side just below the shoulder. The pain was excruciating. I tried not to grimace. Fresh sweat erupted on my forehead and ran into my eyes, blinding me. Stepping forward and blinking furiously, I punched again and took another sickening blow on my right side. On my third step, Miyagi slammed both hands on my shoulders and then my back in a swift, down-and-up clapping action, and I felt as if a pan of scalding water had been thrown over my back.

There were twelve movements in Sanchin and I'd completed only three. I couldn't imagine how I might reach the end. My legs felt weak beneath me. A howl of protest rose inside me, but I swallowed it back down into my belly. With all my being, I wanted to step away from my tormentor, to turn on him angrily and tell him to go straight to hell, but I could hardly shame him in front of the old Chinese master. I was stuck with the unhappy task of exhibiting the power of my teacher's karate.

Miyagi's iron fingers began working their way down my legs, checking the tone of my thighs and calves, threatening new pain to come. I pushed out my fourth punch, slow and steady, using my breathing to control my muscular contractions. Miyagi placed his palm on my stomach, signaling his next target. The force of his blow knocked me backward half a step and I fought to recover my posture. I gritted my teeth to prevent a choking cough erupting from my mouth and rued the day I ever suggested Miyagi should visit China.

Next, he stood before me and pressed my fist with his hand. I fought to extend my arm but couldn't shift his palm a single inch. I might as well have been pushing against a giant oak. Finally, Miyagi allowed my arm to extend, but when I attempted a short block to return to my guard position, he pressed again and I was powerless to move until he allowed it. My hands snaked forward, fingertips outstretched, then closed into fists, and I pulled them back. He hooked the base of my thumb and made me work hard to retrieve my hands. Twice more my hands snaked out together and pulled back, fighting every inch against Miyagi's shocking strength.

A wave of exhaustion rolled over me. I'd never worked so hard, nor been so tired. There were only two movements remaining, two backward steps with a wheeling block and a two-handed push known as *tiger mouth*. As I stepped, Miyagi moved behind me and smashed my right thigh with his shin, buckling my leg. I gasped in pain, but I couldn't stop now, I'd almost finished. I stepped back into the final position and took the final kick on my left thigh, a savage blow that thudded through to my bone so hard that I worried it might have snapped.

When I bowed, my only thought was of Jinan Shinzato. I'd seen him undergoing Miyagi's testing many times in the dojo. Only now did I know what he had endured.

Miyagi moved ten paces in front and turned to face me, "Saifa," he ordered. It was the only other kata I knew, but my mind was a blank. My mystification must have been obvious because Miyagi turned his body to conceal his action from the others and put his hand on his fist to remind me of the opening movement.

Quickly I stepped forward at an angle, deep and low, but my battered legs gave way and I struggled to remain upright. I continued on trembling legs, my arms refusing to move correctly, my stomach painful with every breath. As I completed the kata, I felt ashamed that Miyagi had such a poor student to reflect his karate.

Fortunately, Sifu Liu seemed oblivious to my ineptitude and asked me to repeat the kata. As I did, he spoke to Wa Cheun, his hands moving in patterns in the air. Wa Cheun listened with a frown until he had finished.

"My grandfather says that the first kata you performed, Sanchin, is a very important kata in the south of China. There are many versions of it existing nowadays, and yours is quite different to the way it is performed in China, but recognizable nonetheless. He has asked Yong Li to demonstrate how we perform it here."

Yong Li jumped down easily from the stage and walked to the center of the hall, where he performed a kata that was remarkably close to Sanchin in style. His movements were a little lighter and faster, his hands open, his steps a little quicker, but it was clearly the same kata. When he had finished, the old man said something to Yong Li, who laughed and shook his head as he returned to his seat on the stage.

"What did Sifu say?" I asked Wa Cheun.

"He asked if Yong Li would like to experience Master Miyagi's testing, but Yong Li declined."

"Very wise," I said bitterly.

"I think so too," she laughed. It was the first time I'd seen anything but a stern expression on her face and I was captivated all over again.

"Saifa is also familiar," she continued. "It contains many techniques of escaping, ripping, and tearing."

Sifu Liu then asked Wa Cheun to demonstrate another kata and she slipped lightly from the stage. The form was long and flowing, unlike any I'd seen before. Her arms wheeled like silk banners in the breeze, her lithe body dipping low to the ground, then rising, skipping, and turning, her feet dancing as lightly as an insect on water. Her kicks were so high they were almost vertical and the concentration in her face captivated me completely.

When she'd finished, she wasn't in the least bit out of breath and there was only the faintest glow on her cheeks. "Exquisite," Miyagi said, though I guessed he was referring to her technique rather than Wa Cheun herself, "Please, show us more," Miyagi asked, his eyes alight with excitement.

Sifu Liu nodded to Wa Cheun and she continued, performing two more kata from the Singing Crane style. When she had finished, Sifu Liu asked Miyagi to demonstrate a little more of his karate.

Miyagi rose and performed five kata, most of which I'd never seen before. He announced the name of each one, which Wa Cheun translated for her grandfather, who related some of the kata to the forms she had performed earlier.

I watched in awe. Miyagi's broad frame and rugged features couldn't have been more unlike Wa Cheun's, yet at times his movements contained the same intricate grace. However, there were other times—like when a kiai erupted in the hall, or his foot smashed the ground, or a savage punch or kick cut the air—that the brutality of his art was ugly beyond words.

When he finished, Sifu Liu beckoned Miyagi to sit beside him and Wa Cheun translated once more: "Grandfather says he is very happy that you came. It has been a long time since he has seen such powerful martial arts. It makes him glad to see it once more before he dies. He says he can see Ryu Ryu Ko's methods in yours. Your master, Higaonna, was a fine teacher, and your student's karate shows that you are a great teacher too."

I could scarcely hide my pleasure for Miyagi on hearing this, but Wa Cheun continued quickly, "Since you've shared your art with him, grandfather will share his with you. He'll perform the most advanced form of the Singing Crane style."

Sifu Liu shuffled to the center of the room with small steps and began his performance with no formality. His old body was suddenly transformed into the body of a young man, his movements smooth and flowing, graceful like his granddaughter's. Then suddenly the flow was punctuated by whip-like actions of strikes or short chopping kicks at knee height, his footwork supremely delicate, pattering on the floor like so many intricate dance steps, and I was reminded of the old dancing man we had seen in Shuri a few months earlier.

When he'd finished, Miyagi clapped in delight and requested a private meeting with Sifu Liu. The old master agreed and the rest of us went outside. Yong Li announced that he had to go, leaving Wa Cheun and me sitting on the low wall outside the social club.

"Do you mind if I ask you a question?" I said. She eyed me suspiciously but I continued regardless, "The rest of your family, do they practice martial arts?"

"My father and my elder brother were martial artists," she answered, "They died in the war."

I realized they must have died fighting the Japanese. "I'm sorry," I said, regretting the question.

"I have two more brothers," she went on, "they are fighting with Chiang Kai Shek." I sensed a note of defiance in her voice—Chiang Kai Shek was leading the Chinese resistance against the Japanese.

I didn't know how to respond. "And Yong Li? He is your boyfriend?" I asked before I could stop myself.

"No, he is my cousin!" Why do you ask?"

"No reason," I answered, too quickly, staring at my feet awkwardly. She stared at me and I avoided her gaze, though I could feel it, heating the side of my neck.

"Your master is very powerful," she said suddenly.

"He is," I agreed.

"His testing looked very painful. Did it hurt?"

I turned to see if she was mocking me, but she seemed serious. Yes," I said grimly. It would have been futile to pretend otherwise, "a lot."

She looked at me for a long moment, then laughed. I couldn't be sure if she was laughing at my remark or at me, but I found myself laughing with her.

"How could you bear it?" she asked between giggles.

I was about to answer that I hadn't borne it very well, but the door opened and her grandfather summoned her inside to translate. When she was gone, I walked around to the side of the building and peered in through the barred windows. I could see her grandfather and Miyagi speaking seriously, with Wa Cheun translating occasionally. I moved away, not wishing to be caught spying on them.

Almost an hour passed before the three of them emerged. Miyagi and I said a formal goodbye to Sifu Liu and walked with Wa Cheun back to the Inn of Heavenly Peace. We spoke little on the way. It was as if Miyagi and Wa Cheun shared a confidence that neither wished to break. When we reached Manju Bridge, Miyagi thanked her warmly for her help. "I have one final request to make," he said. "I wish to give your grandfather a gift for his thoughtfulness and consideration."

"There's really no need Master Miyagi," she said quickly, "seeing your karate was a great pleasure for my grandfather, really."

"Nevertheless, there is an item on our ship that I would like him to have," Miyagi insisted. "I'm going to the port this afternoon on business, so I will collect it then. Perhaps you would meet me here in the evening and take it to him?"

"As you wish," she said with a bow.

"Good, then it's settled," he beamed.

"Until tonight," she said with a sweet smile, then turn rather formally to me, "Goodbye, Kenichi."

The sound of my name on her lips stunned me for a second. "Goodbye Wa Cheun," I croaked finally, watching her back and the gentle sway of her hips as she walked back up the hill.

I went with Miyagi to the port. He was silent on the way, lost in thought, replaying his session with the old master, I imagined. I left him to his musings and when we reached the ship, I waited on deck while he went below to choose a suitable gift for Sifu Liu. When he emerged he held a black lacquer box which he handed me. It was a very expensive piece, decorated with a picture of a *shiisa*, the traditional Okinawan lion-dog that stands guard outside temples and tombs, and inlaid with silver and mother of pearl.

"What do you think?" he asked.

"It's beautiful," I said truthfully. "I'm sure Sifu Liu will be delighted."

"I hope so," Miyagi said seriously.

"He will," I assured him. I examined the design more closely. It was intricately carved and immaculately finished, and I had never seen a piece like it. "I've noticed the guardian-lions here in China, but our shiisa are a little different," I smiled. "Different in what way?" Miyagi probed.

"A little cruder," I ventured carefully, not wishing to offend Miyagi, "but also a little friendlier, perhaps?"

"Well said!" Miyagi laughed.

"It's the perfect choice of gift," I continued.

"Why do you say that?" Miyagi asked.

"The shiisa keeps watch. He's always vigilant, always seeking."

"Quite," Miyagi said happily. "Now look inside."

I opened the box carefully and saw a single pearl nested within. I looked at Miyagi, remembering our long-forgotten conversation when I'd been a boy.

"You came in search of knowledge, and you found it!" I said triumphantly.

Miyagi shook his head with a sad smile, "No."

"You didn't?" I asked, deflated that our trip to Fuzhou had been in vain.

"Not yet, but I believe I've found where to look."

"Where?" I asked eagerly.

"A place I've been avoiding, until now," he smiled. I wanted to probe further, but I knew Miyagi would only evade if I did. "I've you to thank for that," he continued, "which is why I'm going to give you a gift, too."

"No! Please, no," I said hurriedly, afraid that Miyagi would give me a gift of such value that I could never repay it, a gift that was completely unnecessary. Simply being with him was worth more to me than all the gold and jewels on Okinawa.

"You will deliver my gift to Sifu Liu," he said before I could protest further.

It took a moment for me to realize what this meant. I would be the one who met with Wa Cheun that evening. I had to admit Miyagi's gift was a good one, despite feeling embarrassed that my attraction to Wa Cheun was so obvious.

"We're leaving in three days, remember, so make the most of your time here," Miyagi grinned.

"I'll try," I promised, my cheeks flushed now.

"Go," he urged. "I may not be an expert like your uncle, but even I know it's not good to keep a lady waiting."

I left the port with a spring in my stride and a flutter in my belly, clutching Miyagi's gift tightly as I went. With the clammy evening air and the anticipation of meeting Wa Cheun, my palms were damp and I didn't want the precious gift to slip from my grasp. I tried to think of what to say to Wa Cheun when I saw her, but no clever turns of phrase came to mind. All my ideas seemed hopelessly contrived and by the time I arrived at the bridge, half an hour early, I'd given up completely and simply sat in the failing light, watching each approaching silhouette anxiously.

A steady stream of figures came and went, but none was Wa Cheun. I noticed an elegant lady in a dress approaching, the wife of a local official perhaps, or a high-class concubine from the red light district. Her kimono hugged her figure tightly and for a moment I forgot all about Wa Cheun, who seemed like a mere girl in comparison. When she came into the lamplight, I cast my eyes down to avoid being caught staring, and waited for her to pass so I could watch her backside swishing down the street. A pair of high shoes stopped before me. I looked up furtively. The lady was staring at me.

"Where's Master Miyagi?" she asked.

I was about to inform her that Miyagi could be contacted at the Inn of Heavenly Peace when I realized the woman was Wa Cheun. Wearing make-up and high shoes had made her look ten years older, a woman of experience, and not for the first time the words caught in my throat and died.

MANJU BRIDGE

"It's exquisite," Wa Cheun said, examining the lacquer box in the lamplight, "but Master Miyagi is far too generous. My grandfather will never accept it. He'll be embarrassed to receive such a gift."

"He shouldn't be," I said, having recovered from my earlier surprise enough to speak now. "Master Miyagi is from Okinawan nobility. His family trades in fine lacquerware like this. He wants your grandfather to have it."

She looked into my eyes to see if I was telling the truth. I held her gaze, sure of what I was saying. She looked at the box once again. "The design is some sort of dragon?" she asked.

"It's a shiisa," I explained, "a guardian found on Okinawa—half lion, half dog."

"How wonderful," she smiled.

"Look inside," I urged her.

She saw the pearl inside and gasped, closing the box quickly. "We should go. It's best not to stay out on the streets so long with such a valuable piece. And besides, grandfather retires early. We need to hurry if we're to catch him."

"Did you like the pearl?" I asked as we walked.

"Of course," she said, "but your master is far too generous."

"He is renowned for his generosity," I said. "When Master Higaonna was old, he was very poor, and Miyagi brought him to his home every day. He brought him meals on a tray, in the style of an Okinawan nobleman, and cared for all his needs.

This devotion became known as The Tray of Chojun Miyagi, and when his Master Higaonna died, Miyagi built a beautiful grave for him."

"Your master is an impressive man," she said, "but..." She stopped, unwilling to say more. I turned and stole a glimpse of her profile, her skin glowing gold in the dim light of the street lamps. "But what," I prompted.

"There's something disturbing about him. His movements are so beautiful, yet filled with such violence. When he performed, I saw him maiming and killing people in his mind."

"Like swimming with sharks," I murmured.

"Sharks?"

I realized I needed to explain. "There's a reef running along the coast of our island where I used to dive as a boy. Sometimes there would be sharks, mostly reef sharks, harmless. But sometimes bigger sharks swam there too, dangerous sharks. They left me alone—fish were plentiful and I guess they weren't hungry—but I knew how easily they could kill me if they chose. Sometimes, when I'm training with Master Miyagi, I feel the same fear. One day he may forget himself and strike out without restraint."

"He would never do that," she said quickly.

"I know."

"But I know what you mean," she added. "I don't know why he wanted to come here. I doubt if there's anyone more powerful that he is in the whole of Fujian, maybe even in the whole of China."

"He's seeking a deeper meaning to karate. That's all I know," I said. I wanted to ask what Miyagi and her grandfather had discussed, but it would have been inappropriate to ask her to relay a private conversation. We walked in silence for a while, and then she answered the question I'd left unasked.

"Grandfather demonstrated some techniques that your master hadn't considered before, and he seemed delighted with them. Then he spoke of *ki* for some time, but it seemed to me that your master already understood it perfectly well. In the end, my grandfather said there was only one person who could show Miyagi the very deepest meaning of the martial arts. He didn't say who, and Master Miyagi didn't ask."

"Do you know who?" I asked.

"I've no idea," she answered, "I've never heard of anyone so powerful."

The lights of Manju Bridge had disappeared behind us as we climbed the hill to Sifu Liu's house. The streets had become darker, with only the dim glow of lamplight coming from some of the houses to light our way. There were fewer people in the streets. Those that passed us did so quickly, in a hurry to get to where they were going.

"Maybe it's not a person," I said without thinking.

"What then?"

"When I was young I used to dive for pearls. Miyagi knew what I was doing—I don't know how because I never told him—but he has a sixth sense about these things. Anyway, he told me he was seeking pearls too, but I never saw him swimming or diving. I didn't know what he meant, until now."

"I think I understand," she said. Quickly her mood changed and her voice was excited like a little girl's, eager to learn a secret, "Did you ever find a pearl?"

"No," I said, sorry to disappoint her, "the water was too shallow, and I was just a boy."

"Still, how wonderful, to dive for pearls on a Pacific island."

"Come and try it," I offered, "I'll show you how."

She waited a moment before answering and I heard a faint sigh pass her lips. "I can't swim."

I was surprised. I'd heard that there were people who couldn't swim, but had always imagined it was those who lived far inland on some dusty plain or high mountains.

"Don't worry, I'll teach you."

She stopped and we faced one another. A sad smile played on her lips. "Do you think you could?"

"Of course, it'll be easy if you really want to learn."

She nodded. "I do. I would like that very much."

I searched her face, wondering what she was thinking. I wanted to tell her how beautiful she was, but I imagined a hundred young men had already done so. "There's something I wanted to tell you," I began.

She looked at me expectantly.

"The kata you performed earlier today, they were very beautiful."

"I'm glad you think so," she said, suddenly serious again, "the Singing Crane style is known for its grace."

"Grace, yes, very graceful—and elegant too."

"Elegant, yes," she nodded.

We were still standing face to face but I sensed she was about to turn and walk on. "You're very beautiful," I said before I could change my mind or say anything else. She examined my face without replying.

"I'm sure you must know, because lots of men must have told you already, but when I saw you tonight, at Manju Bridge, you looked so…" I stopped. My hands didn't know what to do,

I wanted to reach out and draw her into my arms, but I'd no idea if she would let me.

"You can kiss me if you like, Kenichi," she said quietly, and for a moment, with all the thoughts roaring around inside my head at once, I was unsure if I'd heard her correctly. I didn't wait to find out. I reached for her and pressed my lips to hers. A moment later, I felt the soft warmth of her mouth responding, the sweetness of her breath, the subtle aroma of her hair oil and the gentle press of her breast. I felt my head spin. My hands explored her slender arms, and then moved to her lower back, my fingertips brushing over the silk of her gown. With my left hand I reached to the back of her neck and clasped it in my palm. I felt her hands on my back, drawing me in tight. She was touching me in the same place where Miyagi had slapped me with his iron palms earlier, but the pain only added to the pleasure coursing through my veins. My legs felt watery. A heat was gathering in my thighs. I pushed my groin into her.

She broke away. For a moment I thought I'd gone too far.

"Not here," she said breathlessly, taking my hand. "Come, let's give the gift to grandfather," she said quickly and began to walk before I could argue. When we reached her grandfather's house, I waited outside while she went in.

She emerged a short time later. "It's as I thought. Grandfather is asleep," she whispered.

"We can come back in the morning," I said.

"There's no need. I'll give him the box when he wakes tomorrow."

I didn't want to leave her. Not now. The garden at the front of the house was in deep shadow. No one could see us. I reached for her again.

"No," she said quickly, and for a moment I feared our first kiss would be our last. "Come."

She had the key to the social club. I followed her across the rough ground, surprised by her boldness. She unlocked the door and a moment later, a dim light illuminated the entrance. I slipped inside and shut the door quickly behind me. She went into the little windowless kitchen and a dim bulb threw a soft light across her face.

"I don't normally do this," she said.

"I didn't think you did," I assured her. I waited, a few steps from her, not wishing to appear to take her for granted.

"It is only because you're going back to Okinawa," she said defiantly. "There'll be no ties, no expectations, no false promises."

"I don't make false promises," I said.

She glared at me for a moment then sighed. "I didn't think you did," she said. "But you're leaving soon, and so am I. It's simpler that way."

"You're leaving?" I asked in surprise. "Where are you going?"

"Better you don't know."

I guessed she was going to fight with Chiang Kai Shek to fight against the Japanese. She was right—it was better I didn't know, but the news stopped me in my tracks. I'd no idea what to say or do next. She watched my face for some time, and then stepped closer.

"Also because you're a handsome karate-man," she said, the seriousness gone from her face, replaced with a twinkle of mischief in her eyes. I smiled and stepped forward to grab her, but she was too quick and slipped through my grasp like a butterfly. She went into the kitchen and waited for me to join her. Once inside, she shut the door so no light could escape and alert her neighbors to our presence.

I gathered her in my arms and we kissed again. "And because you dive for pearls," she added breathlessly.

She unfastened her gown. I drank in the pale perfection of her flesh, her tiny brown nipples standing alert on her small breasts, the soft ripple of muscle running down her flat stomach to her pubis. I removed my own clothes, never taking my eyes off her body. I knelt to remove the thin strip of cloth around her hips and lifted her onto the kitchen counter. Standing between her parted thighs, I kissed her breasts until she moaned softly. I felt her small hand reach between my legs, stroking me with her fingertips, until I could wait no longer.

"You mustn't finish inside me," she said huskily. In my aroused state, it took me a moment to realize what she meant.

"I won't," I promised, entering her slowly, all the more inflamed by the risk. She wrapped her legs around me and I felt her heels dig into the back of my thighs.

"Where can I finish?" I asked, turned on by the question.

"On my stomach," she offered, blushing and avoiding my eye.

It was all too much. I withdrew just in time and watched in amazement as my seed spray her body. She leaned back, her eyes closed, waiting for me to compose myself.

"Wait there," I said, reaching for a cloth to clean her. She allowed me to wash her body without comment, then climbed off the counter and put on her gown.

"Are you leaving now?" I asked.

"Are you?"

"We can stay here all night," I said.

She looked at me with an even stare, "Where will we sleep?"

"I'll fetch some of the chairs. We can make a bed."

She considered the idea for some time. "Alright," she said at last.

Our makeshift bed offered little comfort, but it allowed us to lie together through the night and make love twice more. In between, we kissed endlessly and talked of our arts, our teachers, our homes, our families, our friends, our likes and dislikes, our childhood memories—all the things new lovers talk of when first discovering one another. There was only one subject that was avoided, and that was the future. No mention was made of our dreams or ambitions, since to mention the future was to separate from one another.

With so little time together, I didn't want to be parted from Wa Cheun even in my thoughts. I was so intoxicated with her I prayed the night would never end, but the heavens made no exception for me. The earth continued to spin. The moon maintained its orbit. The sun insinuated itself through the barred windows of the social club and forced its unwelcome fingers beneath the old front door, until even in the windowless kitchen where we lay, I was able to make out Wa Cheun's beautiful profile beside me.

"We have to go," she said firmly, turning to face me.

I couldn't argue. We tidied the place up quickly, wordlessly. I kissed her once more and we murmured a swift goodbye before slipping from the club, first one and then the other, faces turned down to avoid the sun's accusing glare.

I called for Wa Cheun in the afternoon on the pretext of paying my respects to her grandfather, but she wasn't in. I called back in the evening and left messages for her, but received no response.

With one day to go before our departure, I begged Kanpu Tanmei to arrange a meeting for us. He promised to try his best, but as the night drew in, I realized I wouldn't be seeing Wa Cheun again. Miyagi and my uncle were subdued at dinner and left me alone to pack for the journey home. Shortly before midnight, the old innkeeper knocked on my door and relayed a message. Wa Cheun had left the city. No one knew where she'd gone. He handed me an envelope with sad a look on his face.

I knew what it would say even before I began to read it. I kept Wa Cheun's note with me for several years, until it was finally lost in the fires of war that descended on Okinawa. When it was gone, I didn't mourn its loss. By that time I knew every word by heart:

> *Kenichi, I am so sorry to say goodbye this way. It would have been so easy to see you again, but so much harder to say goodbye afterward. You know where I must go and what I must do. I was afraid that one more night with you and I would never leave. Instead I would stow away on your uncle's ship and dive for pearls with you in Okinawa. I can think of nothing I would rather do. But duty doesn't listen to wishes.*

> *Please give my regards to Master Miyagi and tell him my grandfather was overjoyed with his gift and deeply touched by his generosity. I hope he finds what he is seeking.*

> *Farewell, my Okinawan boy. I will be thinking of you when I am on the road tomorrow, and missing you.*

Years later, I received another short letter from her cousin Yong Li, which had been included in a longer letter to Miyagi. The note informed me, with regret, that Wa Cheun had died in the final days of Chiang Kai Shek's battle against the Communists. Her body was buried in an unmarked grave in Chengdu, Sichuan province, the site of the Nationalists' last stand, before they fled to the island of Taiwan.

THE HOLY WAR

The return voyage to Okinawa took place without incident. Miyagi overcame his seasickness quickly this time and joined me on deck, looking out over the ever-changing greens and grays of the South China Sea. He kept a small distance from me, leaving me to my own tormented thoughts, and even my uncle Anko didn't tease me but left me alone to my misery, perhaps remembering some lost love of his own from his youth. Meanwhile I contrived endless ways to return to China, to search for Wa Cheun and bring her to Okinawa. The prospect was hopeless, I knew, but I wouldn't be put off. I had to kiss her lips, smell her smell, and feel her body against mine once more.

When we arrived in Naha there was a crowd in the harbor, a celebration was taking place. We hurried onto the quay to discover the cause of all the excitement. I stopped a sailor who I knew from one of the other boats and held him by the arm. "Hey, what's all the commotion?"

He looked at me as if I was crazy. "You don't know?"

"We just got back from China," I explained, "What's going on?"

"We have just attacked Pearl Harbor. The American fleet has been destroyed." He clapped me on the shoulder with a fierce grin, then pulled away and joined the rest of the crowd, shouting, "Long live the emperor! Banzai! Banzai! Banzai!" A radio broadcast we heard later confirmed it. The crackling voice announcing that we'd declared war on British and American forces in the Pacific, and that it was the beginning of the end of Western dominance in Asia.

Throughout the spring of 1942, the same voice announced stunning victories in the Pacific and Southeast Asia. Pride swept the island as we freed our Asian neighbors from the yoke of Western imperialism: Burma, Malaya, Singapore, Philippines, Borneo, Java, Sumatra. The decaying armies of the colonial powers, soft with years of easy living at the expense of their impoverished subjects, crumbled before the might of our armed forces. Japanese soldiers were the best in the world and regularly defeated far larger forces thanks to their unique samurai spirit. I shared in this sense of pride, believing it was our divine duty to bring Asia, and later the world, under Japanese dominance. Japan's was a superior culture, and it was only right and proper for it to extend its power and influence over lesser powers, to show them a better way—the Japanese way.

Despite the momentous events happening all around it, Okinawa itself was barely touched by the war. Work continued on the airstrips in the center of the island, but otherwise life went on as normal. I continued to work on my uncle's boat during the day and train with Miyagi in the evening. My father continued to fish, though he complained that the increased shipping had made the fish disappear. My eldest brother Yasuhiko, who worked on a sugar plantation near Gushikawa, got married and we attended his wedding. My second brother, Tatsuo, got a job on the same plantation and moved out to live nearer to his work. Meanwhile my sister Yuka entered the final year of school. She and her friends got together to sew good-luck belts and comfort-bags for the soldiers on the front.

At Miyagi's school, we learned two new kata. Each of Miyagi's kata had its own name—Sanchin meant Three Battles,

Saifa meant Tear and Smash, Seiunchin meant Trapping Battle. Some were named after significant numbers: Thirteen, Eighteen, Thirty-six, One-hundred-and-eight. The new kata were called *Gekisai Dai Ichi* and *Gekisai Dai Ni,* meaning Attack and Smash One and Two. The two kata were similar, the second slightly more sophisticated than the first, but both were filled with simple, brutal strikes and kicks. Miyagi felt it would help us to develop a strong attacking mindset and indomitable spirit. Unlike the other kata, the final movement included a step forward rather than backward. This might seem like a small difference, but the significance was considerable. Miyagi had always emphasized the saying: *There is no first attack in karate.* The final step backward in the other kata signified that once the karate-man had finished defending himself, he was to step away. *Do not strike. Do not be struck*, he repeated, like a mantra. This final step forward was, he told us, symbolic of the need to develop fighting spirit in a time of war, when, regrettably, no mercy could be shown to the enemy, nor expected in return.

The new kata and their new mindset filled me with foreboding. Miyagi had always preached morality and chivalry. He looked down on anyone who lost his temper or engaged in violence of any kind. If Miyagi felt the need to instill such an attitude in his students, what troubles did he envisage ahead?

One hot night in early June, Miyagi had a visit from his friend Gokenki, who had come to play the strategy game of *Go.* They took advantage of a break in the rains to sit on the porch, and I stayed with them, serving tea so they wouldn't have to get up from their game, enjoying the warm atmosphere and sound of my master's friendly chatter, the click of the *Go* pieces on the polished checkerboard and the patriotic songs crackling on the radio. At midnight a news bulletin came on from Tokyo and we all stopped to listen. The newscaster's voice was as enthusiastic as always, so it took a moment for his words to sink in. He announced a strategic withdrawal from the island of Midway in the central Pacific. When the broadcast finished, we sat in silence for some time.

"It has begun," Miyagi said solemnly.

"What has begun?" I asked, unable to comprehend the significance of what we'd just heard.

"The tide of war has turned against us."

I looked to Gokenki for confirmation and he nodded in agreement. "The American navy is far larger and better equipped than our own."

"But we destroyed it in Pearl Harbor!" I protested.

"That was only one part of their fleet," Gokenki explained. "America's industrial might is ten times that of Japan. The attack only served to wake a slumbering giant."

"And enrage him," Miyagi added ominously.

They sat in silence for a long time, staring at the little round pieces of their forgotten board game, neither daring to say aloud what the news could mean for Japan, and more particularly, for Okinawa.

America's recovery had been swift. A large portion of its Pacific fleet had been damaged in Pearl Harbor, but by no means all of it. Many of the sunken vessels had been due for decommissioning, and those that had been fit for operations had been quickly salvaged and refitted. Moreover, the navy had many more ships in other oceans around the world, including an enormous Atlantic fleet. The unprovoked attack had outraged the American public, and with the wholehearted support of the public, the American war machine had gone into overdrive. Production of new ships, planes, tanks, and weapons had soared.

The attack on Pearl Harbor had also enraged the country's fighting men, who were hungry to get to grips with the nation that had dealt them such a dirty blow. These men hadn't turned out to be the weak-willed fighters our military leaders had promised—quite the opposite. In fact, they had fought with unbridled ferocity and determination. Once they had won the pivotal battle of Midway, the Americans pressed on in a series of hard-fought victories across the Pacific, hopping from one island to the next in a line that led inexorably to the Japanese mainland.

The news bulletins from Tokyo followed a similar pattern, announcing a series of what were called 'strategic withdrawals' from Guadalcanal, Saipan, and the Philippines. With the fall of Saipan and the Marianas, America's giant B29 bombers had a launching pad from which to reach the Japanese mainland. A relentless bombing campaign began over Tokyo and the industrial heartland of Yokohama and Osaka. The US Air Force used firebombs over these cities, cities built extensively of wood, causing firestorms of death and destruction on a scale never before seen. Meanwhile at sea, American submarines blockaded our fuel supplies, hampering industrial production to devastating effect, and sent packed troop ships to the bottom of the ocean. As the American invasion force drew closer, our soldiers fought with ever-greater determination. In steaming island jungles and on deserted atolls they battled to the last man, but they could not hold out against the might of the Americans. By the autumn of 1944, only one obstacle stood between the invaders and their hated objective—the home islands of Japan—and that obstacle was Okinawa.

THE TYPHOON OF STEEL

The dawn sea was tranquil in Naha harbor. I liked the water this way, green and flat as a looking glass before the chopping blue of later in the day. I took advantage of the calm to bring a small rowing boat alongside my uncle's ship and do repairs to the hull. I'd just begun applying tar to the battered wood-work when I heard a motorboat in the distance. The tone was unfamiliar and I wondered what sort of engine it was. When I heard a second engine, I realized the sound wasn't coming from the water but from the air. I looked up to watch the planes fly over, curious to see which type they were. I counted nine black specks flying in a perfect V formation. They were not a shape I recognized. A sudden excitement gripped me—the Japanese Air Force had a new plane! Our engineering was superb—it was a well-known fact. Japanese Zeros had wreaked havoc on the enemy early in the war, and now a new squadron of super-planes was coming to Okinawa to defend us.

The lead plane passed high above me. It was huge, far bigger than any I'd seen before. The rest followed seconds later. To my surprise, I saw black objects falling from the undercar-riage of one of the planes. I guessed they were supplies that had come loose in the cargo hold and fallen out. How careless, I thought—they could fall on someone and kill them! A cluster of what looked like gas cylinders fell toward the harbor. Heavy gas cylinders. Dangerous gas cylinders. It wasn't until I heard the whistling of their deadly approach that the crushing reality hit me. The bombs hit a moment later.

The first of them landed in the water a hundred yards from me, sending a huge funnel of spray into the air. The rest hit the port like giant footsteps trudging across the cluster of ramshackle buildings, each one stunning, deafening, each new explosion robbing me further of my senses. My uncle's warehouse erupted in a shower of wood, glass, and smoke. The café where we ate disappeared into a fireball. A boat at the far side of the quay was smashed into matchwood and sank in seconds. All around I could hear the screams and cries of stricken men. Through a gap in the rising smoke clouds, I saw the planes unleash their deadly cargo over the center of Naha. The distant explosions registered in my chest.

A ringing filled my ears that would last for several days. I didn't hear or see the next wave of planes and only became aware of them when the ship beside my uncle's exploded from a direct hit. The force of the blast flipped my rowing boat over and I found myself underwater. Jagged shards of wood and iron pierced the water beside me. The surface above me churned in a maelstrom of fire and debris. The front of my uncle's boat was already engulfed in flames.

I swam deeper, away from the surface, away from the burning shore, but I hadn't taken in much air. I searched frantically for clear water above me. There was a ragged line of daylight beyond the flames. I made for it. My head cleared the water inches from the flames, but the wind was blowing the fires away from me, toward the quay. I'd survived, at least for the moment.

More planes passed above me and more explosions registered dimly, showering the water around me with more debris. I searched the shoreline for a place to get out. There was a spit of rocks on the southern end of the harbor that wasn't in flames. I swam steadily, forcing my breathing to remain calm, knowing it was an easy swim if I didn't panic. My thoughts turned to my family. Would the Americans bomb Itoman? I wondered. I feared for my parents and my sister, but it was my uncle I feared for most. He'd been in the port when the bombs had hit. I tried not to think about it—it was impossible to contemplate. My thoughts tumbled on, turning to Miyagi. He was in Naha, where smoke plumes rose like pillars to support the blackened sky.

I concentrated on my strokes, casting all other thoughts from my mind. It was only then that I noticed the redness in the water around me. My arms and shoulders had been cut by shards of metal and glass. I'd always feared getting cut on the coral and attracting sharks. Now I was bleeding badly in the water, yet the fear of sharks seemed laughable. No fish would be in the harbor right now.

My brothers were working inland, in Gushikawa, far from the bombing, but the nearby airstrip in Kadena would be a prime target. I forced myself to continue with my steady strokes, I was almost at the rocks, and I needed to save myself before I could worry about my family.

Dragging myself wearily from the water, I examined my arms, my body, my legs. I was covered in glass splinters. I'd no idea how they got there. There had been no glass nearby or anywhere on my uncle's boat. One long triangular shard was embedded in my shoulder. I pulled it out carefully and held my hand over the wound to staunch the bleeding. With my other hand I felt my face, fingertips trembling. There were splinters on my cheeks and in my forehead—I was lucky I could see through both eyes.

Access to the harbor was cut off by flames. I was forced to wait on the rocks until the inferno died down, and from the size of it, I knew it would be a long wait. For three hours, I sat helplessly, watching the destruction of Naha harbor. Begun by the Americans, it seemed to take on a will of its own, propelling itself to its own doom. Boats burned and sank, spewing petrol to feed new surface fires. Buildings cracked and groaned, gaping like stricken monsters breathing smoke and flames before collapsing and writhing in their final death throes. On the far side of the harbor, a factory was ablaze and I watched in horror as running fireballs exited the inferno, unrecognizable as humans, their dreadful screams smothered by the din of the destruction and the ringing in my ears, but piercing my mind, nonetheless, until I was forced to look away.

A dead body bumped up against the rocks. I thought of dragging it out, but I was too terrified to touch a corpse. I moved away and sat on other rocks but the current moved the body and it followed me. A new squadron of bombers passed overhead. They didn't waste their bombs on the harbor. That was already destroyed. They saved them instead to unload over new, still pristine areas of Naha.

When a passage finally opened up through the flames, I re-entered the harbor. Three firemen with a single fire truck were doing their best to contain the flames of a warehouse as other buildings collapsed all around them. Some dockworkers had formed a line and were passing water buckets as we'd been trained to do in last year's fire drills. It seemed so pointless, laughable almost, if it hadn't been for the tragedy of it—like spitting on a volcano.

Others worked frantically to free people trapped in rubble, ignoring their own burned and bleeding limbs. I ran to search for my uncle. The row of huts where he worked was engulfed in flames, and there was no way in. I searched all around, frantically, but there was no sign of him. I joined the work gangs in shifting the rubble, barely able to hear the plaintive cries of those trapped beneath, searching instead for bloodied limbs beckoning through the debris. Wooden wreckage was the most dangerous since it could catch fire at any time. We tried to search it first. Every so often, I looked in the direction of my uncle's office, but that area was still burning intensely. My only hope was that he'd not been inside at the time. The row of wooden cabins collapsed and then there was nothing left but smoldering beams and ash billowing up into the charcoal sky.

More bombers flew over us. New pillars of smoke rose over the city.

Fire crews and ambulances began to arrive from other parts of the island. I felt someone's hand on my arm, pulling me away from the rubble. Furious, I was about to roar in his face that there were still people trapped, but when I turned I found myself face to face with a young nurse. She was speaking, but I could barely make out her words. "I can't hear you!" I said, gesturing to my ears.

"Sit down, just for a moment," she yelled, "I need to attend to your cuts."

"We're still finding people alive," I told her.

"You've lost a lot of blood," she said, pointing at my arms.

I looked down and noticed I was soaked in blood, some of it already dried and dark, some fresh from the broken bodies I'd been hauling free. I felt my head spin suddenly and sat down heavily on a low wall.

She worked efficiently, cleaning my cuts and bandaging my wounds. There was something familiar about her, but I couldn't tell what it was.

"You should go to Itoman and check on your family," she said as she worked.

"Do you know if Itoman was hit?" I asked, painfully aware that I'd forgotten my family in my desire to help those trapped in the harbor.

"I didn't hear of any bombings except in Naha," she said.

Suddenly I knew who she was. "You're Fumiko!" I said, probably a lot louder than I'd intended.

She nodded. She was my sister's friend from school. The nurse's uniform had made her appear much older. It came as a surprise to me that the woman who was taking care of me so ably was younger than I was. She raised my chin in her hand and told me to be still. Then taking a pair of tweezers, she set about removing the shards of glass from my face. I could feel several being removed from beside my eyes. "You're lucky your eyes are alright," she said loudly, so I could hear.

I didn't know what to say. I couldn't even nod as she worked close to my eyelid. Instead, I looked into her eyes and she gave me a faint smile. I examined her face. Her eyes were round and set wide apart, giving her a look of sweet surprise. Her teeth were unbelievably white inside her dark skin. Her lips were thick, a deep natural red. Even with the dead and dying all around, I couldn't help noticing a pretty face. Her uniform was spotless, the only unblemished thing in the harbor. I wanted to stay with her and keep my eyes only on her, and ignore the nightmare around me. I closed my eyes and fought back the tears that threatened to engulf me.

She cleaned up my face and dried it carefully before applying plasters to my face. "You will need stitches in some of these wounds," she told me, "but it is safe to go home now."

"Thank you," I said, touched by her kindness.

"Say hello to Yuka and your parents when you see them," she said.

"I will," I promised, watching her as she turned to the next patient, waiting in a long line beside the ambulance that stretched the entire length of the wall.

I picked my way through the devastation of Naha. Half the buildings were in ruin or aflame. Grief-stricken families sat by the rubble that had once been their homes. Parents carried the limp bodies of their children in their arms. An old woman wandered the streets, bewildered. I didn't stop to help her. I needed to see my family now, to feel each of them in my arms, alive and well. I needed to tell them the terrible news that I hadn't been able to find Uncle Anko. I prayed they might have news to counter my fears.

I left Naha smoking behind me and struck out along the road to Itoman. A bone-deep tiredness overcame me. I stumbled toward my home, determined not to stop, though each step became more painful. I searched the darkening skies ahead for the dreadful columns that would signify bombers had flown over Itoman, but the orange sunset was mercifully clear. Then I saw a figure on the road before me. As we came closer I saw it was Yuka. She ran to me and threw herself into my arms. I felt her hot tears on my neck. "Kenichi, you're alive!"

"I am alive," I confirmed. "How is mother? Father? Have you heard anything about Yasuhiko and Tatsuo?"

"Mother and father are both safe," she sobbed, "but father has gone to Naha to look for you."

"I couldn't find Uncle Anko," I told her. She looked into my eyes, fearing the same thing I feared.

"What about Yasuhiko and Tatsuo?" I asked.

"They should be safe," she said firmly. "The Americans bombed the airstrips at Kadena and Yomitan, but Gushikawa wasn't damaged."

She insisted on putting my arm over her skinny shoulder and helping me to the house. Mother rushed out and fell to her knees with relief, then rose and examined my blood stained bandages urgently.

"I'm alright, mother!" I told her, but she wouldn't be calmed. She insisted on taking my other arm over her shoulder and bringing me into the house, ignoring my protests. I said I had to go back to Naha to find my father, search for Uncle Anko and go to Gushikawa to check on my brothers. Mother begged me to sit down and eat some rice and soup first.

"Water," I urged her, suddenly aware of the thirst raging in me. I hadn't eaten all day, but felt no hunger and ate simply for energy, the energy I would need to go back to Naha.

Yuka brought fresh bandages and began to replace the blood-soaked cloth that Fumiko had applied.

"I saw your friend Fumiko," I told her.

"You did? Where?"

"She was in Naha. She dressed my wounds."

"She did a good job," she smiled.

"The port is completely destroyed," I said, the memories unfolding like the unwelcome scenes from a nightmare, "so is the center of Naha."

"We heard the explosions from here. We thought you were dead."

"I was lucky."

My voice was cracking. I pressed my lips tight together to suppress the tears that threatened to spill out. I felt my hand tremble and clenched my fist to stop it.

Yuka worked with the same gentle neatness as Fumiko, but unlike Fumiko, she hadn't seen the horror that the American bombers could inflict. She would see it soon enough, and I dreaded to think how it would affect her. I thought of all the young girls in the Wild Lilies Nurses Brigade, the little children who played in village streets, the old people who could no longer run or fight and wondered how any of them would survive now that war had finally descended on our island.

There were footsteps in the doorway. I turned to see my brother Tatsuo. He rushed in to embrace me, and then stopped, not wishing to hurt me if I was injured. He was frantic with questions. I reassured him I had no serious injuries. My father and Yasuhiko arrived a few moments later. Their faces told me they hadn't found Uncle Anko even before they spoke. My brothers had met my father by chance at the port while searching for my uncle and me.

That night we all stayed together in our tiny house, as we had done when we were a young family. Despite my exhaustion, I couldn't sleep. When sleep finally came in the early hours of the morning, it was a sleep so deep that no dreams penetrated it, the sleep of a patient on the surgeon's table, and I woke groggy, late in the morning, my limbs so stiff that I could barely rise from my bed.

The ringing in my ears had lessened. I heard the thud of new explosions in the distance. American bombers circled Naha like black crows and new smoke plumes rose into the blue. The attacks continued all day, and the next, and by the end of the third day the capital was razed to the ground.

Each day we searched for my uncle. We visited the makeshift hospitals, we read the hastily erected notice boards, and we spoke to anyone who might have known him. We found nothing, saw nothing, heard nothing. The row of offices where he had worked had disappeared. Naha port, where he had lived all his life, had been wiped from the face of the earth. My uncle's body was never found, and with his ship sunk, and his office burned to ash, there was no trace he ever existed.

I went in search of Miyagi. Hurrying up the hill through his neighborhood, I saw there was no consistency as to which house had survived. In one street, a single house stood in a line of rubble. In another, only one house had been destroyed, while those around it were perfectly intact. I rounded a corner and saw to my relief that Miyagi's house was still standing. The gate was shut, but unlocked. I went inside, calling his name. The place seemed deserted. I went to the front door and knocked but there was no answer. I went around the back and called out, but there was no reply. I tried the door but it was locked. I guessed the family had evacuated when the bombing began.

I was about to leave when something made me try the dojo in Miyagi's garden and I discovered Miyagi inside, kneeling beside a crate, a single candle burning beside him.

"Master! Are you alright? Your family?"

"I am fine, we're all fine," he said without looking around.

"Where is Mrs. Miyagi? Where are your children?"

He seemed distant and disorientated. "They have all left, gone north," he answered slowly.

Northern Okinawa was less populated than the center and south, and most refugees from Naha were heading there. Miyagi collected himself and turned to me, "How are you, Kenichi? I thought of you, working at the port. I prayed for you." I saw the concern in his eyes by the flickering candlelight.

"I'm okay," I assured him, "but Uncle Anko can't be found."

145

His face fell. He opened his mouth and then shook his head, unable to find the right words. "I am terribly sorry to hear that," he said at last. "He was a good man." "Yes," I murmured. He seemed strangely calm, his voice soft, his eyes distant, as if he couldn't fully take in what had happened. He returned to what he was doing. I saw he was wrapping his earthenware jars in cardboard. When the cardboard was securely fastened, he put the jars in the crate with the other equipment already inside: four stone hammers, a set of iron rings, various dumbbells, a pair of iron clogs, and a stack of papers and folders, which, I guessed, were his notes on karate.

"What are you doing, Master?" I asked gently.

"These things can't stay here," he answered. "These notes have been compiled over many years. They are vital to the art of Goju Ryu and to all karate. They must not be lost."

"Where will you put them?" I asked.

"In our family tomb. They will be safe there. Not even the Americans' bombs can destroy our tomb."

"I'll help you take them."

He nodded, and when the packing was complete, we lifted the crate between us. It was impossibly heavy and the tomb was over a mile away. Despite his strength, Miyagi would never have been able to carry it alone. Even with my help, it would be a hard struggle. We stood with the crate raised between us and I saw him thinking the same thing.

"Your notes are the most important thing," I told him. "Everything else can be replaced."

He looked at me for a long moment. As my words reached him, he nodded and we put the crate back on the ground. We unloaded the items of iron and stone and lifted it once more. It was still heavy, but manageable now.

Two hours later, we arrived at the family tomb, dripping in sweat. My fingers were numb and bleeding. I flexed them to try to recover some feeling as Miyagi rolled aside the stone that covered the entrance. Inside the tomb was vast, as befitting a noble family like Miyagi's. Shelves were lined with jars containing the ashes of Miyagi's ancestors, and boxes contained the bones that had been cleaned and stored in the Okinawan tradition. The stench of damp and decay hit me as we brought the crate inside and placed it in a nook by the back wall.

Miyagi must have sensed my revulsion at the smell and ordered me to follow him outside. The evening air had never smelled so sweet. He took my hand in his and clasped it firmly. "Thank you, Kenichi, I won't forget your dedication. Now go, look after yourself and your family. I will stay a while longer with my ancestors. It has been some time since I visited them."

I didn't know what to say. I was worried about him.

"Go," he ordered with a smile. "I will pray for your protection."

"What will you do after that?" I asked.

"I will follow my family north."

"Take care, Sensei," I said. "I will pray for you too."

I turned back only once and watched his broad back disappear into the mouth of the tomb. With an ache in my chest that took my breath away, I wondered if it would be the last time I would ever see my beloved teacher.

SEA OF BLACKNESS

With Naha destroyed, the Americans flew only sporadic raids designed to harass us and destroy our morale. They bombed workshops and factories and strafed innocent farmers at work in the fields, but if the Americans were trying to break our spirit, they were going about it the wrong way—they were only making us more determined to fight.

Normal life in Naha had all but ceased, but life in Itoman remained surprisingly ordinary. Apart from the occasional American spotter plane overhead, the only sign of the war was the steady stream of refugees coming to stay with relatives or passing through the village on their way south to Mabuni or Kyan.

A fortnight after the bombing, I received a letter instructing me to muster at my old school in Itoman. A new militia had been formed for young Okinawan men called The Blood and Iron Brigade. I joined a long line that snaked around the schoolyard and inched forward to the desk where a Japanese officer sat.

"Sailor or farmer?" he asked when I stood before him, his eyes never leaving the paper on his desk. I stifled my annoyance that he should assume we did nothing else on Okinawa.

"Sailor."

I was appointed to a coastal patrol under a Japanese lieutenant called Oshiro, who ordered us to report for duty the next morning in Nakagusuku port on the east of the island. Here we learned what our role in the war would be. Timber was needed to build the fortifications planned for the south of the island, and the north of Okinawa was heavily forested. Good timber was in abundance, but transport was a problem. American submarines had blockaded our fuel supply so effectively that a fleet of trucks stood idle in the port with no gas to run them. Our job was simple. We would sail to the north of the island and bring the timber by sea.

We sailed in a hastily assembled fleet of small craft called *sabenis*, just two sailors and me, following the eastern shoreline to Kunigami in the north. The timber had been collected into small piles and hidden where the rainforest met the beach to avoid detection from the air. We dragged our boat onto the sand and loaded as much timber as we could before returning south with our precious cargo.

We made four successful trips before the Americans noticed us. It was a perfect day. The sea was calm and a gentle breeze was carrying us south. We were only a few hours out of Nakagusuku, our cargo lashed down securely in the bottom of the boat. We'd been ordered not to sail too close to other boats to make ourselves less obvious to the American spotter planes, and from my position on the prow, I could only see one boat ahead of us on the horizon, and one other, far behind.

An angry black spot appeared suddenly in the perfect blue, descending on the boat ahead like a mosquito. My heart was in my mouth. I couldn't swallow. The drone of the engine grew louder and more urgent, working itself into a frenzy. The dreadful chatter of machine gun fire erupted. I could hear the shouts of the distant crew, and thought I could make out the churning water approaching the boat, telling of the awful destruction heading its way. The mosquito was flying along the line of our convoy and we were its next source of blood. I didn't wait to see what happened to the boat ahead.

"Get under the timber!" I shouted to my crewmates. They stared at me, still unable to believe what was happening. "Now!"

We scrambled down among the logs in the bottom of the boat. I pressed myself into the wood as the whine of the engine grew louder. When the shooting began, it was much louder this time. I closed my eyes and waited for the bullets. The boat shook violently, each hit sending new shocks through the hull like an electric charge. The log beside me erupted in a noisy procession of splinters as the plane roared past, moving on to its next target.

I wriggled out from under the timber. "I'm alright," I shouted, "Is anyone hit?"

My comrades were unharmed. We examined the boat quickly. Bullets had chewed up the timber inches away from where we had lain and punctured holes in the boat. Water was coming in. I ripped off my shirt and did what I could to plug the gaps. My crewmates did the same. We were two hundred yards from the beach.

"Head to shore!" I ordered. My crewmates took up the oars and began rowing with all their might. I held the plugs in place with my feet and hands. The sea was still coming in, but more slowly now. We would make it. The boat and timber could be saved.

Then I heard the dreadful whine of the mosquito returning. We had turned toward the shore, which meant the plane now flew across our path. Its bullets missed us completely. I watched it continue onward, praying it wouldn't come around again, but it banked and prepared to pass over us once again.

"Row!" I shouted. "It's coming round again!"

The engine slowed. The pilot was giving himself plenty of time to take aim this time, and we were still a long way from shore. I watched the approaching plane, flying low and steady toward us, and knew we were doomed.

"Jump!" I yelled.

"We can make it!" one of the others shouted, just as the plane opened fire. I stood up on the prow. A line of bullets was heading straight for the back of our boat. It would cleave our little craft in two.

"No, we can't. Jump!" I roared.

I dived as the first bullet hit the boat. Even underwater, I could hear the roar of the engine, the staccato laughter of the machine gun, the bullets beating out their short, frenzied rhythm on our boat.

I surfaced and shouted to my companions. Neither answered. The plane banked to the left and continued down the coastline, its job done.

I swam to the boat, dreading what I might find inside. Both my crewmates had remained on board. One was dead, a neat round hole drilled in the center of his chest. His expression was peaceful. He'd died instantly. The other had been hit in the groin and blood was pooling quickly in his lap. He was pale with shock. I hauled myself in and searched frantically for something to staunch his wound. The hull had been punctured many more times and the boat was already half full of water. I found a knife and began to cut away the shirt of our dead comrade to use as a bandage, but it was no use. By the time I'd created a strip, the boat was sinking. I cut the logs loose. They would make useful floats. My comrade's wound was under water, coloring the sea in wisps of pale red. There was nothing I could do for him. I held his hand. He mouthed incoherently, his eyes already distant. Then the boat disappeared from beneath us.

I tried to lift him onto a floating log, but he slipped from my grasp and then he was gone. I dived down, but couldn't bring him back. All I saw was his body disappearing into the blackness.

I thrashed in the water to reach one of the logs floating nearby and clung on grimly to recover my breath before kicking for shore.

Fifteen sailors died that day. The enemy pilots had found a new sport to occupy their time while they waited for their invasion fleet to reach Okinawa. Ten more sailors died the next day and after that, all operations were suspended. But my relief was short-lived. Two days later, Lieutenant Oshiro announced that operations would continue at night. He reassured us that the Japanese Navy was expert at night maneuvers. He explained that beacon lights had been placed in strategic positions all along the coast to guide us. It was insanity, and we all knew it. We didn't have the radar and sonar of the Japanese Navy, but we were people of the sea, and we knew the dangers of night-sailing well enough. One of our number began pointing out the dangers, but he'd hardly begun when Lieutenant Oshiro punched him in the face. The man fell to the ground and Oshiro struck him twice more.

"Anyone else wish to question an order?" Oshiro roared.

No one did.

I was teamed up with a single new crewmate, a young man called Yoshi. The next night we set out on choppy seas with only faint moonlight and the stars for company. To my great relief and good fortune, Yoshi turned out to be an experienced sailor and a likeable character. We soon became firm friends and spent the time telling jokes and stories of our childhood, lighting endless cigarettes—anything to fill the blackness that threatened to engulf us. The journey north passed without incident and by dawn we were far up the coast. We pulled into shore, hiding in a mangrove swamp and dozing until nightfall when we could continue.

By dawn the next day we had reached the wild shoreline of Kunigami and made our way to the rendezvous beach. We loaded the timber in the morning and lashed our boat in the shallows beneath a clump of palms, then helped out in the timber yard for the rest of the day.

At the yard, I met a young man who'd trained with Miyagi for a short while, and he informed me that Miyagi and his family were in Henoki village, just ten miles to the west. I slipped out of the timber yard and hitched a ride westward to the village, where I quickly found Miyagi and his family, who were staying in a large house with old family friends. Miyagi was happy to see me and told me how they'd come north, staying with relatives and friends in Urasoe, Ginowan, Chatan, and Kadena, moving northward all the time, and onward through Onna, Ogimi, and Kunigami, before arriving in Henoki in the far north, which, he felt, was the safest place for his family.

We sat on the porch, his younger children playing happily and Mrs. Miyagi helping in the kitchen to prepare food for all those in the house.

I told Miyagi of the boat trips we'd done and what had happened to my first crew, and he said I had acted correctly.

"I served as a soldier once," he said. "Before I left for the mainland, Sensei Higaonna helped me to prepare. We didn't have any guns, so he taught me to use a bayonet with wooden sticks. I will show you what he taught me, although thankfully, I didn't have to use it."

He went into the back yard and came out with two Jo—training sticks about four feet long. He showed me how to parry the enemy's thrust with a movement resembling an inside-block before driving my own point into the enemy's guts. Once I had understood the technique, Miyagi came at me again and again, insisting I minimize the time spent on the block until it was little more than a flick of the wrist, allowing the enemy less chance to respond and giving me more opportunity to make the kill.

When he was finally satisfied with my technique, he walked with me to the roadside and waited with me until I succeeded in hitching a lift back to the timber yard.

"Be careful, Kenichi," was all he could say as I clambered into the truck.

"I will," I promised.

"Have you been practicing Sanchin?" he asked.

"No."

I didn't dare lie to him, knowing that he would know if I did. "I've been very busy recently."

"Practice it, Kenichi."

I nodded.

"And come back and see us again next time you're here."

I promised I would, and sadly took leave of him. He watched me go, and I could see him in the side mirror, watching the truck drive away down the old dirt road, the worry still visible on his face even as his form disappeared into the distance.

By evening a stiff breeze blew up and by dark the wind was blowing hard. A growing dread knotted in the pit of my stomach and when it was time to leave, I approached the officer in charge at the timber yard.

"Sir, I regret we cannot go out in these conditions," I said.

He looked me up and down with a frown. "What conditions are they?"

"A storm is coming," I said.

"Hardly a storm," he scoffed, "just a stiff breeze. The timber must be delivered."

"It's too dangerous," I persisted.

His face hardened and he stepped close to me. "Do you know the penalty for insubordination?"

Having seen what Lieutenant Oshiro had done two days earlier, I could well imagine what would happen. "My only concern is the safe delivery of the timber," I told him evenly.

"Then go and deliver it safely," he roared.

I returned to the boat where Yoshi was waiting anxiously. My expression told him we were going out and he untied the boat without a word. We rowed toward the flickering lamp at the end of the harbor. Even in the sheltered bay, the waves were rough. I didn't want to think how they would be in the open sea. The cold wind blew in long drawn-out gusts that set white tips on the waves. The night sky was covered in clouds. It was winter, not the season for typhoons, but I'd seen this weather before and knew it could grow into a serious storm very quickly.

Once we rounded the headland at the harbor's end, the next light on the coast was only a winking in the distance. We rowed farther from the coast, fearing the reefs, and sailed into the blackness. A hard rain began to fall, obliterating the coastal lights. The sky offered no stars to guide us. I had a tiny compass, a gift from my father, which I checked by torchlight to keep us on the right bearing. The wind picked up and the boat began to shudder and smashed against the heavy swells. Yoshi and I clung grimly to the ropes that fastened the timber. Water came over the side of the boat and gathered at our feet. I baled as Yoshi steered. The boat was filling faster than I could empty it with a single bucket. I worked frantically, fearing the extra weight would put us dangerously low in the water.

The rain fell more heavily, soaking our light clothing. Water streamed from my hair into my eyes. I felt I was crying tears of frustration, but I couldn't be sure.

"We're too heavy!" Yoshi yelled.

"What are you saying?" I asked, though I knew what he was driving at.

"The timber—we should get rid of it."

The timber was the reason we were risking our lives. It seemed pointless to do so without it. I ignored him and baled as fast as I could. The wind drove us where it willed. The battery in my torch died. I tried in vain to light our damp matches and cigarettes and soon all our matches were gone. We were at the mercy of the wind, the waves, and the night.

For six straight hours, the storm pitched us through the blackness. We took turns baling, our movements slow from exhaustion, while the other held the rudder steady so it wouldn't break. Finally, an hour before dawn, the wind fell away and we were left on a sea as flat as a millpond. The first rays of dawn set the water aglow and we welcomed the dawn in silent wonder.

There was no land in sight. No familiar rock or distant island, not even a single sail on the far horizon. We had been blown far off course, into the open ocean. I took my best guess at a bearing for Okinawa and we steered toward what we hoped was home.

We saw no land that day and spent another night adrift in the blackness. The weather was fine, but by this time we had finished our small water supply and our throats were parched.

The next day we continued on the same northwesterly bearing that, I prayed, would take us within sight of at least one island of the Ryukyu chain, but by late afternoon there was still nothing on the horizon. Yoshi and I had stopped speaking, our throats were too dry, and there seemed nothing more to say. I watched him sit back against the side of the boat and close his eyes. The fight was going out of him. I wanted to shout at him, to rouse his spirits, but I didn't have the energy myself. His oblivion seemed like a good place to be. Yoshi opened his eyes and looked into mine. He knew what I was thinking. Then he squinted and covered his eyes, staring into the sky behind me. I turned to see a black spot far to west, circling like an angry mosquito, and then it was gone. We guessed it was a hated spotter-plane and headed in that direction. Soon the familiar bulge of the Shuri heights came into view, rising majestically from the ocean. Our island had never looked more beautiful.

The Americans had led us home.

THE STONE DOOR OF HEAVEN

Ours was the only boat to return from the storm. Lieutenant Oshiro allowed us a day off to recover from our ordeal and we slept for thirty hours straight in one of the trucks in Nakagusuku port.

A corporal woke us in the morning and ordered us to form up on the quayside with the rest of our brigade. Lieutenant Oshiro demanded volunteers who knew the countryside in the south of the island. I hesitated, wondering what volunteering might involve, then stepped forward a moment later along with a dozen others—anything would be better than returning to the sea at night. Oshiro scanned our faces, trying to ascertain how much we really knew, but the truth was he had no way of knowing. He ordered us to run up the hill to Shuri Castle and report for duty to a colonel named Yahara.

We left at a sprint, but the road to Shuri was several miles of relentless climb and we were soon out of breath. Most began to walk as soon as we were out of sight of the lieutenant, but I continued to run, feeling that somehow the faster I ran, the farther I would get from the terror of the night sailing. After a mile I was far ahead of the rest, keeping a steady pace. Soon I could see only Yoshi's flagging form trailing behind me in the distance. By the time the walls of Shuri Castle came into view, he had dropped from sight and I was on my own.

A high-ranking officer was waiting by the Shureimon Gate and I guessed it was Colonel Yahara. He was of medium height, a little smaller than I was. His swept-back hair, slim figure, and handsome face gave him the look of a movie star. I stopped a few paces from him and wiped the sweat from my forehead, feeling suddenly scruffy before this immaculate officer.

"Private Ota, Sir," I said, bowing as smartly as I knew how, "I have been ordered to report to Colonel Yahara."

"Where are the others?" he asked quietly.

"They are coming, sir."

He looked over my shoulder but there was no one else in sight. "You're the fittest," he said, looking me up and down. "Are you an athlete?"

"No sir. I'm a karate-man," I answered proudly.

"Karate? I've heard of it, but never seen it in practice. I understand it is a native martial art form?"

"It is, sir."

"Personally, I practice kendo," he said, "but I believe all martial arts are good for body and spirit. I'm Yahara, by the way," he added, almost as an afterthought. "I need runners who know the area well. You've already proved you can run, but how well do you know this part of the island?"

"I'm from Itoman," I told him. "I know it very well."

"How well?" he asked, his languid eyes suddenly locked onto mine, deadly serious.

"I know the whole of the coast from Naha southward, inland to Shuri, and east to Nakagusuku."

"I need someone who knows every beach, every cave, every hill and valley, every stream and spring, every farm and hamlet—do you understand?"

I found myself drawn to this officer. I wanted to serve him. I didn't want to spend one more night at sea. "No one knows it better," I told him firmly, returning his gaze. It was no more than the truth.

"Good, then come with me," he said, ignoring Yoshi, who had just appeared, breathless, beside me. I turned to Yoshi with an apologetic smile, and then followed Yahara toward the daunting walls of Shuri Castle.

The grounds were still beautiful despite the army of trucks parked haphazardly, and the piles of supplies and soldiers crossing like busy ants. We came to a concrete bunker with a steel door that hadn't been there on my last visit with Miyagi and Shinzato. Yahara led the way inside and we descended a vertical shaft. The ladder seemed endless, but eventually we stepped into a wide, well-lit tunnel that stretched away in both directions. Yahara must have seen the amazement on my face.

"Welcome to the Stone Door of Heaven," he smiled, "Headquarters of the 32nd Army. From here we will be perfectly placed to orchestrate the defeat of the foreign devils. As my personal aide, you'll need to get to know your way around quickly. Follow me."

He guided me around the command center himself. It was far larger than I'd imagined, even after seeing the size of the main tunnel. Soon I would come to know the complex so well that I could find my way about in the darkness, but at the time, I wandered through it in barely-concealed wonder. There were over thirty chambers including a kitchen and storeroom, a clinic, a generator room, a telegraph and telephone switchboard, a weather room, separate officers' quarters, and an intelligence-gathering area. The complex was ventilated by giant fans circulating air through vents, keeping the atmosphere tolerable. There were six entry and exit points, and the command center was joined to other strategic locations across the island by a series of interconnecting tunnels.

Yahara took me to a tiny room with two bunks. This would be my quarters. Someone was already occupying one of the bunks. There was a kit bag and papers spread haphazardly over it, but no sign of my new roommate. Yahara told me to return to Nakagusuku to get my kit, then left me to find my own way out.

That evening I returned to the command center with my possessions on my back. As the fans blew the heavy air through the tunnel, I could smell barbecue and spices in the air that reminded me of Naha on a warm evening, before the Americans had come. I stopped by the kitchen and peered inside. A chef was busy preparing what looked like a banquet. I guessed it was for the officers. Then I came across something even more unexpected. I heard the soft chatter of women coming from around the corner. I imagined they must be nurses serving in the clinic, but when I rounded the corner, I realized these women served an entirely different purpose. Both were dressed in tight dresses and wore immaculate make-up. They stopped for a moment, looked me up and down to assess the newcomer, and then continued in their private joke as if they hadn't seen me. I was just a local boy and of no concern to these high-class comfort women.

When I reached my quarters, my roommate was there. I introduced myself.

"Ikkei," he replied with a smile, but without rising from his bunk. He was Japanese, I could tell from his manner. "Colonel Yahara told me to make sure you settle in quickly, so you'd better tell me what you need to know."

I set my kit bag on my bunk and thought of how much I wanted to impress Yahara. "Everything," I answered seriously.

Ikkei stared at me for a moment, then rose slowly, rubbing his eyes, "Okay, we'd better start at the beginning."

He took me to the dining room where the officers had gathered. I peered inside and saw twelve officers, including Yahara, seated around a table. They were all looking at one of their number, a short, powerful man standing with his back to me, his feet spread wide. He was talking loudly and waving a small cup of sake as he spoke. From his actions, it was clear he was describing a battle and droplets of sake were spilling each time he recounted a new turn of events.

"That's Major General Cho," Ikkei explained, "Second in Command on Okinawa. Cho fought the Soviets on the Mongolian border. He's one hell of a soldier. They say ice runs in his veins, and never more so than in battle. One time he fell asleep during a visit to a forward position. While awaiting a division-strength attack by the Soviets he just put his boots up on a crate of ammunition and nodded off. They say he didn't wake up until artillery started landing all around them."

I could feel the force of nature that emanated from Cho. He had an aura that made him seem bigger than his small stature. I could imagine him leading a brigade of battle-hardened troops as naturally as he drank the warm sake.

"That officer over there is Lieutenant General Ushijima," Ikkei continued, "He's in charge of operations on Okinawa." There were other senior officers in the room but I knew instantly whom Ikkei meant. Ushijima was tall and distinguished, with the poise of an elder statesman. He smiled benevolently as Cho continued his furious re-enactment of the engagement. "The general leaves day to day affairs to

Yahara and Cho," Ikkei explained. "Yahara is in charge of strategy and intelligence, a very clever man, but he lacks the warrior spirit of Cho. If you ask me, it will be Cho who leads us to victory."

Ikkei told me the names of the other officers present, each one in charge of a different division deployed around the island, and then took me to the communications room to introduce me to operators who manned the radios and telephone switchboards day and night.

The next morning Yahara summoned me early. We were going to Yomitan, he explained, to check on the progress of several new runways being built in the area. Yahara could have sent a more junior officer, but he preferred to oversee things himself. He had a car and a driver, whom I'd intended to sit by on the journey, but to my surprise Yahara ordered me to sit in the back beside him. I was even more surprised when he engaged me in conversation, shouting to be heard above the rushing wind as we sped down to the coastal plain.

"So you are a karate-man, you say Ota?"

"Yes sir," I answered.

"Then you know something of strategy, I take it?"

"I hope so," I shouted, wondering what he was driving at.

"In battle, strategy is everything," he said seriously. "Man against man, or army against army, it doesn't matter. Strategy is the key."

I nodded, not knowing what Yahara expected of me. It was highly unusual for a high-ranking officer to engage a subordinate in conversation, let alone an Okinawan from the civilian defense force.

"You agree?" he demanded.

I guessed he was testing me. "What about spirit?" I asked, hoping to please him, knowing the importance of Japanese fighting spirit.

Yahara shook his head in annoyance. "Too much reliance is placed on spirit and look where it has gotten us." He looked away. I'd angered him, and didn't know what to do next. Yahara was staring at the back of the driver's head intently.

"Driver, pull over here," he ordered loudly, but the driver couldn't hear him above the roar of the wind and drove on.

Yahara turned back to me. "The Americans haven't turned out to be the spineless imperialists that we thought they would be."

I realized he'd been testing to see if the driver could hear him—what he was saying could be deemed treasonous. He leaned a little closer before continuing, "They've already defeated us at Midway and Guadalcanal. Their marines are fierce fighters, and the attack on Pearl Harbor has made them mad as hell."

"No foreign devil can compare to soldiers of the Japanese army," I said.

"They already have!" Yahara said in frustration, and from his expression I feared I'd soon be back in a little boat on the black sea.

"So tell me," he continued a moment later, "when two karate-men fight, and both are equal in spirit, who will win?"

"The stronger," I answered gloomily, knowing that the Americans were superior to us in military might.

"True," he said, "if both fight the same way. But what if one fighter is smarter than the other, what then?"

"He can win."

"Yes he can," Yahara said, punching his fist into his palm, his eyes suddenly alight with the same zeal I'd seen in General

Cho's eyes the previous night. "We must fight smarter. We must make use of the strategic advantages offered by this island—which are many—and which you will show me."

All of a sudden I was overcome with joy to be sitting beside the colonel, flying down that winding road from the Shuri heights, looking down over my beautiful island. For the first time, I believed we might reverse the misfortune that had overtaken our armed forces. We might take the foreign devils who'd murdered my uncle and destroyed our capital and grind their gloating faces into the dirt.

The next day Yahara announced he'd reassigned his driver, saying I would be his driver instead. There was only one problem with this arrangement. I didn't know how to drive. I didn't tell Yahara, but instead begged one of the regular drivers to teach me, and when he refused, bribed him with cigarettes and food from my rations. He relented, and we drove a staff car to a quiet stretch of road where he showed me how to operate the controls. It was simple enough, and soon I was thrilled at the sensation of speeding across my island with such power beneath the soles of my feet.

I drove Yahara all over Okinawa in haphazard fashion, but he didn't seem to mind. We began in the flat central plain, where he planned to build airstrips from which to unleash the fury of our air force on the enemy. Yahara diverted as much resources and manpower as possible to the task and at one time, eighteen airstrips were under construction on the island. Next, we drove around the south, and Yahara was eager to check the areas marked on his map. We visited remote beaches, craggy hilltops, and escarpments where he sat for hours, planning his lines of fire. It would be his greatest triumph, to watch the Americans smash themselves on the rock of Okinawa.

We talked as we drove. Yahara seemed willing to express ideas to me that he wouldn't share with anyone else. It was a way of testing his arguments without fear of condemnation from his fellow officers, and once I realized I was permitted to question his ideas without fear, I did my best to act as a foil for his razor-sharp mind.

Yahara was working to hone his arguments for his critics, the most powerful of which was General Cho. Cho disagreed with Yahara's reliance on air power, preferring to meet the enemy in the traditional way, face-to-face on the beaches, relying on Japan's ferocious fighting spirit to overwhelm the Americans in one decisive battle. It was the textbook approach, but in recent engagements, it hadn't succeeded against the superior numbers and firepower of the Americans. Yahara's role for the army on Okinawa was simply to defend the airfields and enable the air force to wreak havoc on the American fleet.

In Itoman we stopped by my house and my mother and father came out to see me. From their faces, I could see how proud they were that their son should be accompanying such an important-looking officer. I introduced Yahara to them and he spoke to them for a long time, reassuring them that the defenses on Okinawa were the strongest ever created on an island. When my mother asked how long it would be before the war was over, he told her that the fate of Okinawa would be decided at the time of the cherry blossom next year. That was six months away, in the spring of 1945. His prediction proved eerily correct, but by that time, everything had changed, and Yahara had been forced to change his strategy too.

HENOKI

Once Yahara had scouted out all the areas in the center and south of the island that he wished to visit, we drove north, through the Motobu Peninsula and onto Kunigami, where Miyagi and his family were staying. Yahara stopped to meet with the colonel in charge of the northern defenses, and I asked permission to take the car for an hour. I drove to the little village of Henoki, where I found Miyagi in the same house as before. He got into the car and his children clambered aboard, hanging off the side of the vehicle. We drove for several miles, stopping finally at a scenic viewpoint overlooking the sea. The children remained by the car, sitting in the driver's seat and honking the horn, while Miyagi and I walked among the pines. I told him about Yahara, of his strategies, of the headquarters at Shuri, and of the fortifications around Naha and the south of the island.

I sensed a deep unease in Miyagi as I spoke, and finally he stopped and fixed me with his dark eyes. "I have something important to ask you, Kenichi. I want to join you. I can't stay here any longer."

"Why not?" I asked, surprised. His family was here, and he'd become an informal leader of the local community.

"I can't stay up here while soldiers are preparing to fight the enemy. I need to fight too. You must ask Colonel Yahara to find a post for me."

Miyagi was well over the age of conscription, but he was certainly strong and fit enough to fight. I imagined if I asked

Yahara, he would probably be able to oblige, but the thought of Miyagi carrying a rifle was strangely repugnant to me.

"But your family, Sensei, they are here. They need your protection."

"They will be even safer if I'm able to fight the Americans, rather than hide away from them like a coward."

"You are a civilian and a leader," I said. "They need you here, not just your family, but the local people."

"Speak to Yahara!" Miyagi ordered, his eyes cold and hard.

I stared into them. They were the same eyes I'd seen when he'd broken the makiwara during my first class with him, but I was not the same frightened boy any more.

"I'll see what he says," I answered evenly, knowing I would say nothing to Yahara. I believe Miyagi knew this too, since he had a sixth sense and always knew what I was thinking.

"Thank you, Kenichi," he said grimly, and we turned and walked back toward the car together.

On the way back to the south of the island, I drove the car through Nakagusuku harbor, where a long line of men stood waiting on the quayside to board a troop ship. They looked like local men, newly conscripted, and still uncomfortable in their ill-fitting uniforms. Driving past their lines, I wondered where they were headed: a Pacific island, a jungle in Asia, a mountain fastness in China?

There were no cheering crowds to see them off, no school-children waving flags. No pretty, young girls shouting good-luck slogans or handing out thousand-stitch belts. The faces in the line were somber. As I nudged the car forward, one in particular caught my eye. For a moment I couldn't place the strange-looking soldier. Then I realized it was my former schoolteacher, Mr. Kojima. He was gazing up in trepidation as the enormous grey ship swallowed men and cargo into its yawning hold. His frantic joy at seeing young men leaving for war was gone, but I was surprised to find I couldn't despise him for this, as I once would have so easily.

"May I stop just for a moment, Colonel?" I asked Yahara.

"You wish to say good-bye to a friend?"

"Someone from school," I told him.

"Of course, take your time, Ota," Yahara said benevolently.

It took Mr. Kojima a moment to place me. "Ota! I didn't recognize you."

"Hello Mr. Kojima," I said, with a bow. He returned my bow and glanced at Yahara in the waiting car.

"I am Colonel Yahara's personal assistant," I explained with pride.

"Quite an honor," Mr. Kojima said graciously.

"I wanted to wish you luck in your new posting, Mr. Kojima," I told him. "I know you will defend our country with honor."

"We all will," he said, a little of his former zeal returning to his eyes.

"You are going to Formosa?" I asked.

"No one will say, but there is a rumor it may be Iwo Jima."

"Iwo Jima is a fortress," I assured him. "I have heard Colonel Yahara say it is impregnable."

"Yes!" Mr. Kojima said nodding vigorously, "I have heard that too."

"Long live the emperor," I said, bowing long and low.

"Long live the emperor," Mr. Kojima said briskly, returning my bow with equal enthusiasm.

That evening we received word that Japanese ships would be putting into Nakagusuku harbor. There was a new excitement in the command center. The navy was preparing for a major sea offensive against the Americans. It would be a chance to achieve a decisive victory and reverse our ill fortune. Yahara ordered me to drive to a hill near Yonabaru, from which he could see the fleet for himself. The next morning we found twenty warships in the dark waters of the bay but they were strangely subdued. There was no activity on deck. They looked somehow forlorn below the low-hanging clouds. Yahara examined them with his binoculars, then handed them to me, and returned to the car without a word. As I drove him back toward the command center, we passed Rear Admiral Shinba from the naval base heading in the other direction. His grim expression confirmed our worst fears. The ships had already fought a battle, and lost.

This was confirmed a few days later. The navy had lost a major battle in Saipan, one of the Marianas chain and a vital part of the Tojo line, which had been considered impregnable, until now.

More bad news rocked the command center shortly afterward. A troop ship, the Toyama Maru, had been sunk by an American submarine. Five thousand men from the elite 44th Independent Brigade, earmarked for Okinawa's defense, were lost. The news went from bad to worse. With the American fleet bearing down on the Philippines, Tokyo High Command withdrew the 9th Division from Okinawa—a total of twenty-five thousand men—and sent them to the Philippines.

It left us without the troop strength to defend the entire island, and that evening Yahara met with generals Ushijima and Cho to propose a new strategy. They talked long into the night.

I could hear Cho's voice angrily denouncing Yahara's plan, and Ushijima's occasional comment, little more than a grunt, followed by Yahara's even, reasoned tone, relentlessly stating his logic, pitting his cold assessment against Cho's fiery passion. By morning, a new plan had been agreed. Yahara looked tired and drawn, but I could see the relief in his face. He'd got his way, at least for the moment.

Yahara's new strategy relied on concentrating our troop strength. Okinawa's long coastline, flat central plains, and sparsely populated north were too much to defend effectively. The heavily populated south was the key. With its mass of sharp hills, craggy ridges, lofty escarpments, it offered superb defensive positions, while the honeycombs of caves sunk deep in the hard coral rock meant our soldiers would be immune to even the heaviest artillery bombardment. The airbases at Yomitan and Kadena were abandoned and the gun placements on the beaches were withdrawn and taken south.

For the next three months Yahara concentrated his efforts on creating a network of trenches and tunnels to join the defensive positions that stretched from coast to coast with the commanding heights of Shuri at its center.

Most of this work was carried out by soldiers with picks and shovels. General Cho continued to request rock-cutting equipment from Tokyo but nothing ever came. There were only two bulldozers on the entire island. No dynamite. Not even any concrete. Unbelievably, the timber needed to support the trenches and tunnels was still being delivered from the north in boats, though ever more erratically, and when supplies were low, beams were taken from local houses.

Despite the fearsome defensive positions he had created, Yahara was subdued and I sensed a feeling of resignation descend on him. His dreams of a glorious victory had vanished with the departure of the 9th and the loss of the 44th Independent Brigade. All that remained now, though he would never admit it, was a grim determination to cede every inch of the island in blood.

D-DAY OKINAWA

We had been expecting the invasion fleet and knew of its size. Nevertheless, it was a sobering sight to see it arrive in our waters, a fleet so vast that it stretched for several miles across the ocean, and its rearguard fell away beyond the horizon. I drove Yahara to a vantage point where he could examine it through his binoculars. The exact figures were later confirmed: 40 aircraft carriers, 18 battleships, 32 cruisers, and over 200 destroyers. The total number of ships was 1,600—the largest Pacific fleet ever assembled, and second only to the Normandy landings.

After a feint attack on the southeastern coast, the Americans landed on the west coast near Kadena, exactly as Yahara had predicted. The landing had been preceded by six days of artillery barrages and bombing raids, each one more powerful than the last. American firepower was both awesome and terrible to behold. Giant arcs of fire stretched from the behemoths at sea to the coast. The enemy had the power to light up the sky with thunder and lightning, bending nature itself to its will. On the night before their planned troop landing, they unleashed a sustained three hours of fury that was more terrifying than anything previously. When the maelstrom of shells and bombs finally abated, an eight-mile strip of sandy beach and leafy forest had been annihilated—but nothing else. Our coastal defenses had been withdrawn long ago and the entire show had been a gigantic waste of ammunition.

As soon as the sun peeked over the horizon, streams of enemy landing craft and amphibious tanks began racing for the beach. When they hit the shore, the troops scurried like angry ants, crawling through the sand and digging frantically to create a safe beachhead.

We watched it all from ten miles away on the ramparts of Shuri Castle. Cho bristled with anticipation of the battle, and smirked as he passed his binoculars to Yahara, "The Americans are pissing in their pants on an empty beach." His bravado was infectious and the other officers laughed. Even Yahara couldn't resist a grin of his own, and the corners of General Ushijima's moustache twitched as he watched through his own binoculars. The other officers joined in with jokes of their own, offering cigarettes around and enjoying the spectacle of the American landing.

I noticed Yahara shift the binoculars from the beach to the sky. He was hoping to see the air-attack he'd requested from Tokyo High Command. With so many troops in the open, it was the perfect time to deal the enemy a devastating blow, but there was no sign of the air force. He handed the binoculars back to Cho without comment, but from his expression I could see he shared some of the buoyant mood despite Tokyo's lack of support. This was his chance to put his tactical genius to the test, to lock horns with a truly formidable foe. I knew he relished the prospect of the hated Americans coming up against his iron-clad defenses. The Battle of Okinawa had finally begun.

Over the next three days, the Americans had most of the island to themselves. They took control of the airfields at Kadena and Yomitan with little opposition and crossed to the east coast almost unopposed. They encountered stiffer opposition in the north, but by the end of the first week, they controlled all of central and northern Okinawa. It was only then that the long-promised air support finally arrived.

Seven hundred aircraft flew in from Kyushu and Formosa, including the fearsome Tokkotai squadron of suicide planes. It was the largest kamikaze attack ever launched and inflicted severe damage to the American fleet. The American seamen came to fear the kamikaze above all else, and with good reason. They were responsible for the highest number of US naval casualties in the war. In the next weeks more air raids came from the mainland, but none could match the scale of the first.

I stood beside Yahara on the ramparts of Shuri and we shared the binoculars, watching another furious battle, a maelstrom of smoke, fire, metal, and seething water that didn't belong to the Okinawa I knew.

"Each time there are fewer planes," I said, voicing what we both saw.

"The submarines have blockaded our industry so effectively that we can't produce enough planes to compete with the Americans."

A kamikaze came in from the north, diving from the heavens, its engine noise rising to a fever pitch. A hail of gunfire erupted all around it but the pilot maneuvered expertly, spinning to evade the flak. More American guns trained on the plane as it neared a battleship and they realized it hadn't been stopped. The pilot veered left then right, weaving through the gunfire before settling on a direct course for the battleship. The plane took no more evasive action—I imagined the controls had been too badly damaged to function anyway—but it was traveling on a collision course for the battleship and nothing could stop it. It struck near the front and burst into flames. Soon the entire front of the ship was ablaze.

"So brave," Yahara said, his voice thick with emotion.

I didn't know how to reply. The kamikaze were called Thunder Gods, Flowers of Japan, our proudest fighters. I couldn't imagine what it would take to aim a plane full of explosives at a battleship and fly with such determination.

"Mathematics," Yahara said, almost to himself.

"Sir?"

"Simple mathematics is at the heart of the problem."

"I don't follow, sir," I said.

"Think about it," he said, the frustration clear in his voice. He had hardly slept since the enemy landing. "The more experienced the kamikaze pilot is, the more likely he is to succeed in his mission—and never return. A new pilot must then be trained for the next mission, each less experienced than the last, and a new plane must be built. Now look at the Americans. Their pilots grow more experienced with each mission, and their Hellcats are superb. They'll soon be flying rings around us."

All day we watched the stricken battleship fight the flames. It didn't sink. Instead, blackened and bowed, it limped away from the fleet to effect repairs, to where we didn't know. The air raid had inflicted damage on the American fleet, but not nearly enough to force a withdrawal. The enemy was here to stay.

THE NORTH OF THE
ISLAND

At this point in the battle for Okinawa, I lost touch with Miyagi, and what I recount here is pieced together from what I learned later. However, I will tell it to you now, so you can know what happened to my master when it was happening, and see how his story fits with my own.

The Americans surged eastward and northward from their landing site in Kadena, smashing through the thin resistance in the center and north of the island. As they came closer, village by village, Miyagi took his family away from the house in Henoki to a secluded cave on the northern shore of the island. There was nowhere farther to go. The cave already contained a large group of civilians, mostly old people, women, and children.

It took the Americans almost a week to locate the cave, and by this time the water supplies had all but run out and everyone was sick with hunger and thirst. They lay, half awake, half in delirium, until an unknown voice boomed a message to them from outside. The voice on the loudspeaker was speaking Japanese, but in a strange accent, one that they had never heard before. It ordered them to come out of the cave peacefully and promised that they would not be harmed.

Panic erupted in the cave. Women screamed and several tried to kill themselves by striking rocks against their own heads. Two attempted to strangle one another simultaneously, all without success. The children in the cave wailed pitifully, terrified by the dreadful antics of the adults around them. An old man produced a grenade and ordered his grandchildren to gather around. The children obeyed, fearful, but fearing the voice outside even more, and the old man examined the grenade. It had been given to him by a Japanese soldier, and it was clear he had no idea how to trigger it. Miyagi stepped forward and took the grenade from him, then ordered silence in the cave in the commanding voice he normally reserved for the dojo. It took several minutes for the inhabitants to hear what he had to say. He would go out first and see what would happen. Mrs. Miyagi begged him not to go, but he calmed her fears, assuring her that his assessment of the situation was correct and that the Americans wouldn't harm him, or a group of unarmed civilians.

Stepping out cautiously, blinking in the bright sunlight, his arms high in the air, he approached the enemy soldiers. Eight rifles were trained on him, waiting for him to make a wrong move. One of the soldiers was holding a loudspeaker and appeared to be half-Japanese. Miyagi walked toward him. The soldier demanded to know if he was armed.

"I have a grenade in my pocket," Miyagi told him.

"Put it on the ground slowly."

Miyagi placed it carefully on the dirt.

"Who's in the cave?" the Japanese-American demanded.

"Just civilians. I took the grenade off a crazy old man. There are no soldiers inside, only old people, women, and children."

"How many?"

"About twenty, all starving and terrified."

"They have nothing to fear. Tell them to come out. We have food for them."

"They believe it's poisoned," Miyagi answered.

"It's not poisoned!" the interpreter said angrily. They looked at the cave mouth together and saw that a group of civilians had gathered to see what would happen to Miyagi. At the front were Miyagi's own children. The interpreter took a candy bar from his pack and held it up to Miyagi. "Do you need me to eat it?"

Miyagi saw no guile in the soldier's eyes. He stepped forward, ripped off the wrapper and took a large bite. He had to chew slowly, the texture was so rich and the flavor so alien that he could hardly swallow. He held out the remaining candy to the people gathered in the cave entrance. One small boy ran forward, too hungry to be afraid, and took a bite from it. Slowly, the others followed. The Americans gave them water and candy before herding them into trucks and driving them to Hentona, where an old school building was now serving as a prisoner-of-war camp.

The Battle of Okinawa

In the space of a week, the mood of the American soldiers had changed considerably. They had been expecting a ferocious battle, and while the navy was fighting one against the kamikaze, it seemed the land battle had been won without a fight. From our vantage point on Shuri, we could see the Americans laughing and joking with one another, walking in the open without their helmets, and listening to music on their radios and gramophones. The center and the north of the island were under their control and all that remained was for them to seize control of the south. However, if they thought the Battle of Okinawa was already won, they couldn't have been more wrong.

A mechanized US reconnaissance platoon passed through the village of Chatan before dawn and entered the hilly territory known as Cactus Ridge. They were the eyes and ears of the 96th Division. Their role was to travel an hour ahead of the main force and report enemy activity back to their commanders.

Our gunners waited patiently for the convoy of four jeeps, two half-tracks, and one armored vehicle to penetrate deep into the gully before opening up, and taking out the front and rear vehicles to block the rest. Over a hundred men were trapped under withering fire from all sides. All the months of preparation in the area meant our guns were sighted to perfection. Our gunners could hit any object on the landscape almost at will. The recon platoon took heavy losses and radioed frantically for assistance under a hail of fire.

Reinforcements arrived in the form of three Sherman tanks, which rolled into the valley to rescue the stranded platoon. All three were hit by anti-tank guns in short order, and flaming bodies dived out and sprawled to the sides, only to be gunned down by a savage blast of machine gun fire. The Americans had reached the first line of Yahara's defenses. Their honeymoon in Okinawa was over.

They answered with their most fearsome weapon, overwhelming artillery fire. The effect, as before, was very impressive, but made little difference to their situation. Our men simply retreated into caves of solid rock up to thirty feet thick and waited. When the bombardment ended and the infantry began to advance, they simply re-emerged and opened fire once more. It took the Americans two days and enormous casualties to gain control of Cactus Ridge, a relatively minor position. Then our artillery pounded them from nearby hills where, again, our guns had been sighted to perfection on their position.

Cactus Ridge was just the beginning. Behind it lay the much larger and more formidable Kakazu Ridge. Kakazu stretched for over a thousand yards and was joined to hills in the east and west by a series of trenches and tunnels, forming a defensive line that stretched from coast to coast across the island.

The Americans learned the lessons of Cactus Ridge quickly. Instead of announcing their infantry attacks with artillery bombardment, they climbed silently up Kakazu Ridge in the darkness before dawn and used their bayonets on the handful of unsuspecting troops at the top. They captured the ridge by stealth, but their success was short lived. Our troops had built strong firing positions into the reverse of the slope. As the Americans headed down the other side, they were caught in another hail of mortars and bullets. When they were utterly confused, our troops charged out and regained the ridge. The Americans were forced to retreat under a smokescreen, to lick their wounds.

I learned of these engagements from my roommate Ikkei, who had been delivering messages from the front. Since the battle had started in earnest, I'd only delivered messages behind our own lines. It seemed Yahara was shielding me from danger, but I wondered if he was merely saving me for a later date. Ikkei's boyish smile had gone, giving way to a red-eyed stare and sickly pallor. He spoke in grunts and single syllables, unwilling to say more about what he had seen at Kakazu Ridge. He stayed awake all night, fearing his own dreams, and I lay awake beside him, wondering what horror lay in store for me.

The noise of war continued night and day. The screams of rockets and mortars, the rat-a-tat of machine gun fire, the shriek of flares, the pop of small-arms fire, the dull thud of distant artillery, and the ear-splitting crash of bombs exploding directly above—the unearthly symphony never stopped, conducted by a madman hell-bent on driving his orchestra to death.

The American assault on Kakazu continued for four days. Each time they made progress, our men counterattacked with fanatical bravery, coming within yards of the American dugouts to toss in grenades and satchel-charges. When the Americans won the high ground after a day of fierce fighting and heavy losses, they were forced to spend the night on their hard-won ridge. Our soldiers were well-trained night fighters, expert at infiltrating enemy positions and deadly at close-quarters with knife or bayonet. The Americans were forced to stay awake all night, listening for the gentle sound of an infiltrator coming toward their foxhole.

Kakazu Ridge was a bloody stalemate, and just when it seemed things could get no worse for the Americans, it began to rain. This wasn't the rain of Boston, Massachusetts, or Chicago, Illinois. This was the Pacific monsoon, and they had never seen anything like it. They lay waist deep in water in their foxholes, shivering beneath useless canvas shelters as our artillery pounded them from the distant heights of Shuri.

At the end of the four days, American casualties numbered almost 3,000 and they had advanced only a hundred yards. The push toward Japan that had begun at Midway and continued through Guadalcanal, Saipan, and Iwo Jima had finally ground to a halt on the rock of Okinawa.

"Roosevelt is dead," General Ushijima announced, crumpling the paper that contained the message in his fist. The room broke into spontaneous cheers and applause.

"The timing couldn't be better," Cho shouted above the din.

"It is good news," Yahara agreed guardedly.

Cho continued, his eyes gleaming, "The foreign devils have been bloodied at Cactus Ridge and stopped cold at Kakazu. The kamikaze are wreaking havoc on their fleet. They don't know how to fight us in this terrain, and now their Commander-in-Chief is dead."

"Yes, it is a good day for Japan," Ushijima smiled, "a good day indeed!"

"Don't you see," Cho said eagerly. "Now is the perfect time to launch a counter-offensive, when their morale is at an all-time low."

"A counter-offensive would mean giving up our advantage," Yahara cut in quickly "Our positions have been established and fortified months in advance. The Americans are being forced to attack them. That's why they are suffering such terrible losses."

"Yours is a clever strategy I grant you," Cho said loudly, "but it isn't a plan for victory. It's a battle of attrition that can only end badly for us in the long run. We can't hope to compete with the enemy's supplies of ammunition and manpower. If we continue as we are, they'll grind us slowly into the dirt. What we need is a plan for victory. That's what I am proposing now!"

Yahara's mouth set firm. "We will be attacking American positions instead of vice versa. It will be ruinous," he said evenly, fighting to control his temper.

"Our troops are expert fighters in this terrain!" Cho cut back, searching the faces of the other officers present to see who agreed with him. Suddenly, the atmosphere in the room was stifling. Cho turned to Ushijima and looked him straight in the eye. It was so quiet that I could hear the water trickling down the rough walls. The light flickered on and off several times, as if joining in the struggle.

"What do you propose, General Cho?" Ushijima asked evenly, eager to restore calm and careful consideration to the meeting.

"A decisive action to win back the island," Cho answered swiftly.

"It will only waste good men, General," Yahara said urgently, but Ushijima held up his hand to silence him and allow Cho to continue.

"We send six battalions out under cover of night," Cho went on, "their mission to infiltrate enemy positions. At the same time, we send amphibious units up the coast to land behind enemy lines. These units will cause havoc at the enemy's rear and cut off supply lines. Then, when the enemy is confused, our front-line troops will surge out and attack to achieve a decisive victory."

"Under other circumstances it would be a good plan," Yahara began, "but we are outnumbered and need to concentrate our troop strength. That's why we've been successful so far. It is also why Japanese forces have failed on other islands—such an attack spreads our strength too thinly..."

Ushijima silenced Yahara once more and asked Ikkei and me to leave the room. The steel door closed behind us and the officers in charge of Okinawa's defenses remained to debate the merits of Cho's plan for another hour. When the door reopened, a flurry of radio messages went out and soon the command center was filled with personnel. Urgent preparations began and continued throughout the day. At dusk, a massive bombardment from our own artillery announced that Cho's strategy had been chosen over Yahara's. We would be taking the battle to the Americans.

SUGAR LOAF HILL

Cho's counteroffensive was a disaster. After some initial success, the Americans rallied strongly. Our infiltration units were too small and too scattered. They were quickly surrounded and destroyed. The amphibious landings up the coast were discovered and wiped out. Four battalions were lost, numbers we could ill afford, and the mood in the command center was somber for days afterward.

Despite this setback, our defenses on Kakazu and the surrounding heights were still formidable. The line held for another three weeks of bitter fighting, during which American progress was as slow as it was bloody. Finally, their commanders amassed three divisions and prepared to take Kakazu Ridge in a massive assault.

Yahara urged General Ushijima to withdraw from Kakazu and reinforce our already impressive defenses along the Shuri line, and Ushijima agreed. The maneuver was perfectly timed. Our troops moved out silently during the night and when the Americans stormed the ridge, they found nothing. We watched the enemy from the battlements of Shuri Castle. Yahara's binoculars were powerful enough to reveal the bemusement and annoyance on their faces as they searched the windswept ridge. They found no dead, no wounded, no shell casings, no bullet cartridges, not even food wrappers, or empty mess tins. All trace of our defenses had vanished, and the Americans must have thought they'd been fighting ghosts.

Their commanders were in no hurry to push south to our next line of defense, and with good reason. The Shuri Line was even more formidable than Kakazu. It crossed the island from coast to coast—five miles of commanding positions joined by tunnels, peppered with pillboxes and caves concealing mortars, anti-tank guns, rocket-launchers, and machine-gun nests—and all invisible to the naked eye.

Even before the Americans could reach Shuri itself, there were barriers in their way. The Maeda Escarpment was a craggy, high ground that the Americans called Hacksaw Ridge, which was connected to Conical Hill, Kochi Ridge, and Needle Rock by a maze of tunnels that amounted to an underground fortress.

I found Yahara sitting on his bunk, his elbow on his knees, staring into space. When he spoke, there was a note of resignation in his voice that I'd never heard before. It chilled me to the bone.

"Now that he has taken away all our strength, General Ushijima has finally given me complete control over all strategic operations."

"What can we do now?" I asked, praying Yahara might have a new masterstroke to play.

His bitter smile revealed he had none. "The Americans will take Maeda soon. We should withdraw to our next line of defense at Amekudai, keep our strength close to us. That is the correct strategy."

"Yes," I nodded, struggling to hide my despair. Yahara was getting set to continue his bitter battle of attrition to its logical conclusion. It was an ending I didn't want to contemplate.

Amekudai was a beautiful part of the island. Yahara and I had often driven through the soft, cultivated landscape on our trips around the island. He had even gone horseback riding there with General Ushijima before the invasion. The country was punctuated by a triangle of low hills that blocked the American advance to Shuri. They called these hills Sugar Loaf, Horseshoe, and Half Moon—innocuous sounding names that would go down in history as some of the bloodiest battles of the Pacific.

As before, the Americans began by underestimating the sophistication of Yahara's defenses. Each of the three hills was in sight of the other and joined by underground tunnels. When the Americans stormed to the top of one, our defenders simply disappeared and bombarded them from the tops of the other two hills, forcing them to retreat. When the Americans finally realized that all three hills were joined, they ordered a simultaneous offensive of all three.

The defenders on Sugar Loaf Hill, or Hill 52, as we called it, were commanded by Colonel Mita. When their radio and telephone communications ended, we feared they had been wiped out, but gunfire and shelling could still be heard coming from the hill. It seemed a fierce battle was still in progress. Ikkei had been sent the previous day, but hadn't returned, and I feared the worst.

Yahara entered the communications room, where I sat alone with the radio operator. "I need a runner to go to Hill 52 and report back," he said.

"I'll go," I said.

Yahara waited a moment, as if searching for an alternative. "What happened to yesterday's runner?"

"There has been no word from him, Colonel."

So far, Yahara had been reluctant to send me out. I was never sure whether it was because a certain bond had developed between us over the months, or whether it was simply because he wished to employ my expertise later, in the far south of the island, an area I knew better than anyone else. Perhaps it was a little of both. Nevertheless, he had little choice now. "Go and find Colonel Mita," He nodded curtly. "Check on his position and report back."

I bowed sharply. There was no need for Yahara to tell me what he wanted to know. By this time, I knew his mind well enough. He would want every detail: troop numbers, positions, ammunition and supplies, enemy strengths and positions, and the morale of the men, which, his calculating mind assessed, was vitally important. I turned to leave.

"Ota!" he said suddenly. I turned back. The lamplight cast a beam onto the side of his face, and I noticed a vein pulsating in his temple. He pinched the bridge of his nose and closed his eyes as he spoke, "If the position is hopeless, tell the colonel I order a retreat. His troops can reinforce us here in Shuri."

"Yes Colonel," I said seriously, knowing the responsibility Yahara had just given me. He was leaving the decision to me, based on what I saw. If Hill 52 were taken, there was little standing between the enemy and Naha.

I left under cover of darkness. The Americans lit up the skies with a never-ending stream of flares that allowed me to find my way through the craggy rocks and gullies to Sugar Loaf Hill. The rain that had begun days earlier hadn't stopped. The ground was an ocean of mud. I was forced to keep to the low ground to avoid the skyline, wading knee-deep, often waist-deep, through black water and mud that sucked at my boots with every step. Both armies had abandoned vehicles in the mire. I saw lorries, jeeps, a small Japanese tank, an American Half-track, even a giant Sherman that had got stuck in a ditch and been destroyed by a rocket. I waded past the first of many corpses, four badly burned bodies beside the tank. The smell of death was mercifully dulled by the rain. When a new flare lit up the sky, I noticed a sea of white maggots moving around the bodies and struggled to suppress the noise of my retching.

I listened out for telltale sounds of the enemy, careless talk, the squish of boots in the mud, the click of a grenade pin, the flare of a cigarette. Twice more I stopped when I heard a sound and waited for several minutes before continuing. I carried only a pistol and a knife. A rifle would have made it difficult to move quietly, especially at night, and besides, I was a lousy shot. We'd had very little target practice, and my results had always been poor. I convinced myself I would be better off without it.

I'd scaled a small slope and was descending the other side when I heard a distinct click up ahead. All at once, the darkness exploded in gunfire, pierced by cries of *Banzai!* from a handful of Japanese soldiers, and the furious yells of Americans, the crack of bullets, the screams of stricken men. I scrambled back up the slope, praying the commotion would hide my presence.

Breathless, I peered slowly above the slope. The exchange had ended. Japanese soldiers had tried to infiltrate an American position and drop grenades into their foxholes, but their charge had failed. I knew why. Japanese grenades had a fatal design flaw—their outdated firing pin had no spring and they could be triggered only with a hard knock. Our soldiers had to bang the pin against a rock before hurling the grenade, and if there were no rocks, they would knock it against their own helmets instead. The Americans soon came to know the sound of a triggered grenade, and would open fire instantly in the direction of the noise.

They sent up a flare and checked the area for infiltrators. When a new flare lit up the sky, I saw five dead Japanese still twenty yards from the American foxholes. I made a wide sweep of the area. On my way, I came across the body of a single soldier, with a neat bullet wound in his chest. Even before I saw his face, I knew it was Ikkei. I sat beside him for a minute. His face looked peaceful, now that he had become part of his dreams of death. I hoped his spirit felt the same peace.

My slow journey took most of the night and by morning I'd reached Sugar Loaf Hill. I waited in a concealed cave until I saw two Japanese soldiers carrying a box of ammunition up a slope. I called out to them and explained that I was looking for Colonel Mita, and they took me to him.

I'd seen the colonel many times at the command center. He'd been a robust officer, happy and good-natured, his face round and boyish. Now he looked pale and haggard, his skin pulled taut over his skull. His eyes, bulging manically, bored into me.

"I have been sent by Colonel Yahara," I explained quickly to cover my shock at his appearance.

He nodded slowly, and I wondered how long it had been since he had slept. "Tell Yahara our telephone got smashed by a mortar. The radio is out too. Everything's out."

"The battle is lost?" I asked.

"No, it's not lost!" he shouted, "Those bastards are not getting past. We are going to attack at dawn and drive them back once and for all."

"The colonel has asked me to report on your troop numbers and positions," I said, suddenly unable to remember any of the other details that Yahara would want, as they seemed unimportant now.

"I will know better when we come out of these damned caves and have a look around," Mita said grimly.

Mita's cave was primitive compared to the command center, little more than a waterlogged dugout covered with concrete. There were about a hundred men inside, and many more in nearby caves joined by tunnels. Ours was the only cave with a medic. I was even more surprised when I saw he had only one assistant, a young student nurse. There was something familiar about her, and it took a moment to come to me. It wasn't her face, but the insignia on her shoulder, *Wild Lilies Nurses Brigade*—the same corps my sister and Fumiko had joined. I was horrified to think they might be in a similarly dangerous forward position. I was also ashamed that I'd never considered the possibility before.

The wounded and dying were everywhere, some lying still and silent, some moaning quietly, while others cried out, begging for help loudly, raving and praying for deliverance from their pain. The medic was hopelessly ill equipped. He could do little for the dying men other than promise to send their bones to their families, along with a letter of reassurance that they had served the emperor bravely.

The colonel gathered his officers for a briefing. I listened as he explained his tactics for retaking a small ridge and wondered what they must be feeling, going out once again into a storm of steel and death. I had specific orders from Yahara not to engage in any fighting. He warned me that he needed an aide who knew the country, an aide he could trust, but when they gathered outside and I saw the pitiful size of Mita's force, I couldn't stand idly by. I picked up a rifle from one of the dead and followed the colonel into the battle.

We took up positions on a ridge overlooking a small valley. All was quiet for almost two hours, until word passed down the line of enemy approaching and Mita raised his hand for absolute silence. I lay beside him and we watched as the Americans made their way up the valley. They moved cautiously, checking and clearing each cave before advancing to the next. A massive Sherman lumbered into view, crushing stones beneath its tracks as it went. An unusual gun had been mounted on top, one I'd never seen before. It stopped in the mouth of a cave and a stream of fire erupted from its gun. Three soldiers clambered up the rocks and stood over the cave mouth, their legs splayed for balance, guns at the ready.

"We call it their horse-riding method," Mita said grimly, and from their stances, I could see why.

"They shoot whoever runs out," he continued. "If they don't have a flamethrower, they toss in explosives or smoke grenades. Sometimes they just blast the entrance, sealing our men inside forever." The bitterness in his voice showed how deeply Mita hated the Americans. "Their bodies will never be recovered. No relatives will ever clean their bones and pray for them. No descendants will ever worship them."

No one emerged from the cave. I wondered if they were dead. Mita must have read my mind. "There was no one in that cave," he said. The Americans moved on up the valley, coming ever closer. They were well within firing range now, but Mita's troops waited for his signal. Despite their exhaustion, they were superbly disciplined. Only when the entire platoon was visible did Mita give the signal to open fire.

The Americans dashed for cover as machine gun bullets tore up the mud and rock around them. The Sherman backed away quickly. As it passed close to a jutting rock, two concealed

Japanese sprang out with satchel charges. They didn't shout *Banzai!* Their faces showed none of the wild emotion of a suicide charge. They ran quietly to avoid drawing attention to themselves, and because of this, the American infantry took an extra second to notice them streaking toward the tank. They opened fire. One Japanese went down instantly, but the other continued running at the tank. The tank turret turned, as if looking at the approaching soldier, but by then it was too late. The soldier placed the satchel on the side of the tank and turned his back, his arms raised, a look of ecstasy on his face. Bullets ripped into his body, but he felt no pain. The satchel charge exploded and he departed for the Yasukuni Shrine, where the heroes of Japan gather to bask in glory for all eternity.

When the smoke cleared, the Sherman's tracks were twisted beyond recognition. It wouldn't move again. The soldiers inside hurried to get out before the tank was over-run and a grenade thrown down the hatch. Our gunners waited patiently for them to emerge before opening fire. Two figures scrambled away from the carnage. I fired, aiming for the body of the first. I saw him fall, but couldn't be sure if it was due to my bullet or another's. The second American fell too and the rest retreated back inside the tank. Moments later an anti-tank rocket hissed out from somewhere above me and the Sherman was a burning wreck.

The Americans retreated down the valley, covering each other in the orderly fashion they had perfected after weeks of fighting in this terrain. We waited until nightfall in case they returned, but they didn't.

Despite having not moved from the ridge all day, I felt as weary and parched as I had after being lost at sea for three days and nights, and wondered how any soldier could fight this way, day after day, without end.

After taking water and a simple meal of tinned rations, I found Mita in the cave and asked to speak with him privately. I'd rehearsed what I wanted to say, but now with Mita's wild eyes glaring into mine, I couldn't think how to begin.

"I know what Yahara is thinking," Mita said without waiting. "He believes we should withdraw to Shuri and concentrate our strength there."

"That is his plan," I said.

Mita blinked hard, shaking his head as he spoke. "Which part of the island are you from?" he demanded.

"Itoman," I answered.

"In the south?"

"Yes, Colonel."

"Then your home is still untouched by war."

"So far," I conceded, wondering what he was getting at—I considered the whole island my home.

"Mine too," he said, "I am from Hokkaido. The Americans are still far from my home, but one day they will be there too if we don't stop them. If we allow them to pass us here, there will be nothing stopping them from taking Naha. Then Shuri. Then what will be left to defend on this island, and what will stop them from reaching the next?"

I was overcome with admiration for this man from the far north of Japan who was ready to give his life to defend my southern home. "I will inform Colonel Yahara that Hill 52 is being defended with matchless valor," I said.

Mita smiled. "Convey my compliments to the colonel. He is a good man."

I retreated quickly into the blackness of the cave. My emotions were in tatters and I didn't want the colonel to witness my shameful tears. The American guns continued to pound our position, but I barely noticed. After so many days the incessant shelling had dimmed until it was little more than the hum of cicadas, lulling me to sleep.

The forbidding battlements of Shuri Castle were already visible against the night sky when I saw the enemy soldier, half-concealed in a ditch, his rifle aimed at my chest.

I'd slept for two hours and risen at midnight to return to the command center under the cover of night. A steady rain had given me added protection, reducing visibility and muffling the slap of my footsteps on the mud-soaked ground. I'd felt none of the fear that I'd felt on the way out to Colonel Mita's position. The earlier fighting had drained me of all anxiety, and besides, I'd told myself, no enemy would be out in this weather. If they were out in the open at all, they would be sheltering miserably beneath a sopping canvas in a waterlogged foxhole.

The enemy soldier was close—five more paces and I'd have stumbled over him. I froze, too surprised to try and run or hide and waited for the bullet to hit, chiding myself bitterly for my lack of awareness. He hesitated to pull the trigger. I guessed he was a spy who'd been scouting out the command center and was reluctant to alert the sentries to his position. In the end, he must have decided that since I'd seen him he had no choice, and squeezed the trigger.

"Fuck!" he muttered.

Nothing.

He squeezed again.

"Fuck!"

It was impossible to keep any weapon clean in the morass of mud created by the monsoon. His had jammed. I started from my frozen surrender and hurled myself toward him, my hand seeking my pistol as I did. There was a bayonet on the end of his rifle, but he saw me going for my pistol, and fearing being shot from a distance, threw his rifle aside to draw his own sidearm.

As it was, I was upon him before either of us could bring our pistols to bear. He was still struggling to free his from its holster and his eyes were down, looking at his hip. It was a mistake. I kicked his head, which, since he was standing in a ditch, was at waist-height. He moved at the last moment, but my boot clipped his temple and he fell. I jumped into the ditch after him to finish him off. He was half submerged in the rainwater that had gathered in the bottom. I raised my fist to strike at his head but his helmet was in the way. In the next instant, his feet lashed out at my shins, kicking my legs from under me. I slipped and landed on top of him. Up close, his face wasn't the typical American I'd imagined. He was dark-skinned, with black hair and features that seemed almost Asiatic. I seized the rim of his helmet and pushed his head under the water. He thrashed beneath me but I held him firm, keeping my arms locked and my weight over him to prevent him from rising. I thought he couldn't struggle much longer, but his hands found my wrists and tore them from his helmet. His mouth cleared the surface, gasping for air. I rose up and struck down at him, but he twisted beneath me and scrambled away. I punched him hard on the spine. He grunted in pain and turned to face me, an animal fury in his eyes, the dreadful fury of a man fighting for his life. I hesitated for a moment, shocked by the sickening brutality of our situation, and in that moment, he struck. His fingers clawed at my eyes. I swept them aside before he could gouge me, but his knee struck me low in the abdomen, close to the groin, and I folded in agony. I felt his fists strike at my ears and my neck, exposed beneath my helmet. I knew I had to stand up or die now, in this muddy ditch, within sight of Shuri Castle where I'd once walked happily with Miyagi and Jinan Shinzato.

I drove a tiger-claw strike into the American's groin and stood up. It didn't slow him for more than a fraction, he was so pumped with adrenaline. He swung a huge punch at my chin. I took the impact on my forearm and directed a lightning fast counter at his face. His punch had been savage, but it had traveled in a great arc, covering too much distance. Mine had traveled down the center-line between us—the shortest distance to the target. It knocked him back, but he surged forward again, kicking at my groin. I shifted to the left and shot my right hand across my body, creating a wedge that guided the kick harmlessly away. My fingers hooked around the back of his boot and I pulled up. He overbalanced. I seized his sleeve with my left hand to hold him up. In that moment, his arms flailing to avoid falling, his right cheek angled toward me, he presented the perfect target.

Over the years, the makiwara had been a hard taskmaster. After that first day when I'd bloodied my knuckles at Miyagi's dojo, my progress had been slow and steady. The skin of my knuckles had developed a protective callus so it no longer split, but calluses are not the purpose of the makiwara, merely a useful result of its use. Repeated striking of the makiwara hardens the bones and strengthens the muscles, making them more capable of supporting the skeletal structure of the hand while delivering shocking force. The process cannot be rushed—too fast, and injuries will occur that set you back months, too slow, and you will never push through new barriers to achieve Miyagi's stark motto: *one punch, one kill.*

I smashed my right fist into the soldier's jaw.

Did that single punch kill him? I will never know. All I know is that I drove the full force of it through my front two knuckles—the traditional striking knuckles of karate—into his unprotected jaw and I felt his bones collapse beneath my fist. His head whipped around with shocking force and he fell like a sack of cement against the side of the ditch. His head flew back as he landed, exposing his neck. His mouth was open and his irises had disappeared into the back of his head, leaving only white slits staring sightlessly at me.

From the angle of his body and the ragged splay of his limbs, I knew he wouldn't recover any time soon. I fingered my pistol, wondering whether to make sure with a shot through the brain, but in the end I left it in the holster, fearing the noise might cause the sentries at Shuri to open fire without checking first. Instead, I withdrew my knife from its sheath. It began to shake in my hands. I looked at the American's dark complexion and wondered where he was from? Like most Americans, he was an immigrant, from Russia, or the Middle East, Latin America, perhaps. He may even have been an American Indian—I had no way of knowing. All I knew was I could not plunge the cruel blade into his skin. I walked away, fighting down the nausea that came over me in a wave, and struggling to return the knife to its sheath with hands that would no longer obey me.

A PILLOW FOR THE
MASTER'S HEAD

Miyagi sat hunched on the bunk made of roughly hewn planks and held his head in his hands, fighting to keep the despair from his heart. His wife Makato stepped inside the straw tent that was their new home, holding back tears of her own to see her husband so reduced. His broad frame looked doubly out of place on such a tiny bunk, and his face was even more drawn now that his hair had been shaved off so he could be treated for lice. Her own hair had been shaved off too, as had the hair of all the civilians in the camp, but the loss of her husband's hair hurt her far more than her own.

"You should be happy, my husband," she said with a smile, kneeling beside him and taking his hand in hers. He looked into her eyes absently—there was nothing to be happy about.

"You have led your family to safety, our children are here, alive, and the other people in the cave are all here, alive, all because of you."

"What sort of life is this?" he said grimly.

"A temporary life," she smiled.

They had arrived that morning from the POW camp in Hentona to their new accommodation in Haneji, a sea of straw-tent housing, set around a tiny burnt-out village that was filled with civilians from all over the island.

"It can't stay like this forever," she went on, "One day we'll rebuild what we had, you'll see."

He smiled despite himself.

"What is a little hardship for you, Chojun? You have always sought hardship when you never needed to. Now you have as much as you could ever want. You should be happy."

"I am happy with you, and with our children," he said, his voice thick with emotion. "I only hope that Tsuneko and Shigeko are safe—they must be in Tokyo by now, but it will be a long time before we get any word—and that Jun is safe—he's in the thick of the battle right now."

"I worry for them too," she said, knowing what was happening in Okinawa, and knowing that Tokyo was undergoing a terrible bombing campaign that had created firestorms of unimaginable proportions.

There was a tapping on the wooden frame of the tent, and a head appeared inside. It was the unknown face of a middle-aged man, the left side of his face badly scarred with what looked like burns, but he smiled a dazzling smile that revealed a set of pure white teeth.

"Miyagi San?" he asked.

Miyagi regarded him warily, not wishing to confirm his identity before finding out what the man wanted, but the man didn't wait to find out, "My name is Professor Shimoji. Please come with me. You too, Mrs. Miyagi, and bring your children, of course, and all of your possessions."

"What is it about?" Miyagi demanded, but the man simply waited by the door with a fixed smile until they took up their things and came outside to follow him.

He led them to a small house. The walls had been scarred by bullets and mortar, but the roof was intact and for this reason alone, it stood out among the other houses in the village. "Please, this is your accommodation," Shimoji said with a bow.

They looked inside and saw two clean rooms containing two sturdy beds with thin straw mattresses and blankets, and a small stove. To a family of refugees it was unimaginable luxury, and Miyagi wondered what had prompted the man to bring them here. Professor Shimoji spoke before he could ask.

"I was an English teacher in Hentona before the Americans turned our school into a camp. When they discovered I spoke English, they employed me to help with the administration. I saw your name on a list of new arrivals and made some enquiries. When I discovered Master Miyagi was among us, I decided he could not stay in a straw tent. It would be unfitting. This is not much, but I hope you like your new accommodation."

"It is excellent, Professor Shimoji," Miyagi said, so moved by the man's thoughtfulness that he was unable to say more.

Shimoji beamed.

Later, when Miyagi and his family had finished arranging their few possessions in the little house, there was a knock at the door and a young boy appeared with a pillow under his arm. Mrs. Miyagi invited him inside and discovered that he'd been sent by their new neighbors, who, upon learning that Chojun Miyagi would be living beside them, had sent a pillow for the master's head.

THE FALL OF SHURI

I had expected Yahara to be furious when I reported on Colonel Mita's refusal to retreat, but he took the news calmly. A strategist of his ability knew the value of tenacity in his men, it was an asset as real as any well-entrenched position or secure supply line, and he could hardly complain when it manifested itself in such selfless courage.

Myself, I tried to avoid dwelling on Colonel Mita's fate or the savagery of my fight with the dark American, but images of the American haunted my dreams for weeks: his mouth gasping for breath in the trench water and the animal fury in his eyes when he'd been fighting for his life. Each morning I awoke with his sightless eyes staring at me accusingly and felt them following me in my waking hours.

We got news that all of Amekudai, including Hill 52, had been overrun. The next day thirty enemy tanks rolled into Naha. Elements of the Independent Mixed Brigade held out at the teacher training college. Troops defending the naval base at Okoru fought to the last man. Messages flooded in from positions all around us and I felt my heart would break as I saw them:

> *We fight on to the last, joyful to defend our homeland.*
>
> *Ammunition low, casualties mounting, we make a final charge with a joyful heart.*
>
> *Enemy advancing on all sides. Cut off from main body of troops. Gladly we dash forward with the emperor's name on our lips.*

The USS Mississippi sailed close to shore and trained its sixteen-inch guns on Shuri Castle. The explosions rocked the command center one hundred feet below. It was just the first of countless more that descended like giant raindrops from hell. The storm lasted three days and by its end, our 400-year-old national treasure was reduced to rubble.

Morale plummeted to a new low and just when I thought nothing could bring hope or relief, something happened to brighten my day. Yoshi, my crewmate during the night storm, appeared in the command center. The rest of our Blood and Iron unit had been wiped out in fighting at Yonabaru, and Yoshi hadn't known where else to go. I embraced him like a long lost friend and offered him Ikkei's empty bunk next to mine. Though we had barely spent three days together in that little boat, it was as if we had known one another all our lives, and somehow his appearance gave me renewed hope. We spoke long into the night, despite our exhaustion, neither wishing to close his eyes and risk the fatal dreams of sleep.

It was time to move our headquarters to the southern tip of the island and make our last stand. Yahara presented his plan to generals Cho and Ushijima and they couldn't refuse him. The order was given to withdraw to Mabuni on Cape Kyan.

Yahara told me to get rid of the maids and comfort women who remained in the command center. I gathered them together and advised them to go to the Chinen peninsula—the last unoccupied part of the island apart from Kyan.

"You're abandoning us to the Americans!" they protested.

"No," I reassured them, "There are other civilians in Chinen. Join them and wait until we've won the battle. Then we'll all be rid of the Americans."

It must have been plain from my face that I didn't believe it, but I needed to give them some hope, however thin. "Tokyo will send reinforcements..." I continued.

One of the women stepped forward and held me in her gaze. She was Cho's mistress, the oldest among them and the most beautiful. She smiled reassuringly, "We would rather die fighting with you than fall into enemy hands," she said.

"The troops can't fight bravely if they're worried about women," I told her.

"We can help you. We'll fight too."

"I know you will, but Colonel Yahara has ordered it," I said lamely.

"We are not afraid to die, Kenichi," she said gently.

I was surprised that she knew my name. She continued before I could think of a suitable reply. "We're afraid of being captured. It's as shameful for a woman to be taken prisoner as it is for a man, perhaps even more so. I'm sure you can imagine why."

I began to protest again when one of the maids spoke up, her voice shrill compared to Cho's mistress's. "Do you know what they do to female prisoners? They rape them over and over before torturing them to death. They tear little children limb from limb. They kill babies by smashing their heads against a stones. They..." she choked on her words, and one of her friends held her to comfort her.

I'd seen the leaflets issued by the army and heard the shocking stories told by the Japanese soldiers. I didn't know what to tell them, but I could see that panic threatened to overwhelm them.

"Listen, all of you. Listen!"

When they were quiet, I lowered my voice: "The command center is being evacuated tonight and moved to Mabuni on

Cape Kyan. No women except those serving as nurses will be allowed to accompany us. You have been officially advised to go to the Chinen peninsula, but in the end, where you go now is up to you. That is all I can say."

"Thank you, Kenichi," Cho's mistress said with a smile and a slight incline of her elegant head, "we understand perfectly what you are saying."

I nodded and turned to go, overcome by a feeling of help-lessness, and suddenly sick with worry for my family. Once we were in Mabuni, the Americans would pass through Itoman on their way through the peninsula. The battle would be close and fierce. For weeks, I'd been pushing all worries for my family from my mind, unwilling to consider what fate they might be suffering, but now the same dreadful fears resurfaced. Would we ever sit down together as a family to eat mother's miso? Would we ever listen to father play the samisen again? Would we ever gather, as we did each year, to visit the tomb of our ancestors?

With the final chapter of the battle unfolding, I was forced to accept the very real prospect that I might never see my family again.

THE SINKING OF THE
KONANMARU

Miyagi stood still as a statue, his mind circling, seeking a way out, knowing there was none. The other people in the camp moved around him, some crying and wailing, others shouting and shaking their fists impotently at the American guards. News had just hit the camp of the sinking of the Konanmaru, a passenger ship that had sailed from Okinawa for Tokyo two months earlier. It had been hit by an American torpedo, and there had been no survivors. Two of Miyagi's daughters had been aboard, Tsuneko and Shigeko.

The milling crowd, the noise, the lamenting, the fury—all happened in slow motion around him, distant, the bodies of the people little more than flies buzzing in the humid air, their noise drowned out by the deafening rush of blood in his ears. He became aware that he'd not taken a breath for some time. He willed himself to inhale, but his stomach was frozen. His heart thudded inside his ribcage, beating out its rage against his chest, and then his heart stopped too and he stood, a standing death, knowing he was departing the life he had known. He was not afraid. He welcomed the peace it would bring. But then his final thoughts turned to his wife Makato who had not yet heard the news, and he knew he could not leave her alone in her grief, nor add to it with his own departure.

Reaching into his body with his mind, he drew his diaphragm downward into his lower abdomen as he had so many times before during the practice of Sanchin. New breath entered his lungs. The vital energy of ki slowly coursed through his body once more. His heart began to beat again. Finally, his feet made their reluctant journey to the house to tell Makato the news, and his arms prepared to hold her for however long she needed them, for his whole life, if necessary.

THE JOURNEY TO CAPE KYAN

The remains of the Japanese army traveled south in a convoy from Shuri on one of the few covered roads. Much of the surface had been destroyed by artillery and the rains had made the route all but impassable. Our truck stopped every few miles, sometimes for over an hour at a time. The night sky was lit by a never-ending stream of flares. The surreal orange light afforded me my first glimpse of how the war had affected civilians, and what I saw filled me with despair.

The roadside was packed with refugees who had been moving around the island in ever decreasing circles, trying in vain to avoid the fighting. Soon there would be nowhere left for them to run except into the arms of the enemy, or into the sea. I scanned their faces, both hopeful and fearful of seeing someone who might know the whereabouts of my family. Twice I saw someone I knew and jumped down from the truck to quiz them, but their mumbled replies were incoherent. The trauma they had suffered must have been far beyond anything I could have imagined.

The road was littered with corpses. The sight of the dead was nothing new to me now, but these were not soldiers killed in battle, they were women, children, old people—unarmed, simply caught in the storm of bullets and bombs unleashed when two giants had collided on their tiny island. I struggled to put concerns for my family aside one final time. I would do my duty to the end in the faint hope that we might defeat the invaders before searching for my family in the ruins our island.

Morning came. By the light of the flares at night, the road had seemed an unearthly place, the scene from a nightmare, but by dawn's grim light it could no longer be dismissed as the twisted conjurings of a dream. The once-beautiful countryside around Itoman was a morass of mud. Black wooden spikes jutted from the earth where trees had once stood, a ghoulish cemetery covering the land as far as the eye could see. The bodies of soldiers and civilians lay tangled together, some peaceful, as if taking a nap by the roadside, others burned and broken beyond all recognition. The body of a single young boy was the most pitiful of all. He was sitting with his back to a cart wheel, a pool of blood in his lap. His face looking out, still watchful. He had died alone.

We stopped at a supply depot in Tsukazan where there was still food and supplies. I put on new socks and boots. Our men collected fresh weapons and tins of pineapples. There were crates of sake and beer. As we loaded the trucks, the Americans began shelling our position. The bombardment went on all day and by nightfall, the little village of Tsukazan didn't exist.

We set off again under cover of darkness for our new headquarters in Mabuni, but our truck broke down near the turning for Itoman, and I got out to wait by the roadside. The stench of corpses was unbearable. I thought of heading down the side-road to my home, just fifteen minutes from where I stood, and wondered what I would find of my home, but just then the engine coughed back into life and we moved on. I scarcely recognized the nearby village of Komesu. The local primary school had been completely demolished save for the front gate, which remained standing with a padlock still fixed around it.

Around a bend in the road, we came to a pine grove that was untouched by the shelling. It made the surrounding areas all the more dreadful. We stopped to dig up sweet potatoes from the nearby fields and even found sugarcane, which we brought back in bundles for a feast.

An hour later, we had reached the caves beneath Mabuni Hill that would be our new headquarters. There were three entrances: one to the landward side, one directly above with access via a long shaft, and one that opened onto cliffs above the sea. Our engineers had installed electricity, but there was little in the way of comfort. These caves were a far cry from the command center at Shuri. In an uncharacteristic outburst, Yahara berated the engineers for the lack of facilities. The engineers said the shelling had been too intense to carry out all of his wishes, at which Yahara turned on his heel and left without another word.

The main cave was cramped and dark, with water dripping from the ceiling. The dank air was stale and heavy, and with no fans to circulate it and a new crush of bodies, it quickly became stifling. Nevertheless, compared to our new sleeping quarters, it was luxury. Our room, if you could call it that, was a hole four feet high and just wide enough for two bodies. Stalactites hung down from the ceiling and water dripped from them in a relentless stream. I hung a cover across to divert the water, but it quickly became waterlogged and useless. Lying under the dripping stalactites, I felt I was in the jaws of death itself. I hurried out, and left the caves altogether for the dangerous freedom of the outside air, my heart beating madly in my chest.

The drone of a plane came from overhead, but I didn't bother to look up. I didn't care. Instead I looked out to sea, thinking of the days I'd spent on the waves with my father.

Something caught my eye, descending in the sky. Too slow to be a bomb, it was a parachute drop. I knew it was American—Japanese supply drops had ceased long ago. The wind must have carried it far to the south because it landed a short distance from where I stood. I went to examine it and to my astonishment, found it contained Camel cigarettes. I dragged the crate into the cave and was greeted as a hero. The cigarettes tasted wonderful, strong and smooth. We rationed them out carefully over the next ten days as we waited for the final battle of Okinawa to begin.

Yahara's swift and orderly withdrawal from Shuri took the Americans by surprise and allowed us a period of respite while they prepared to follow us south. We placed rugs and chairs on the cliffs outside the cave and enjoyed the sunshine, ignoring the reconnaissance flights overhead. We laughed and joked and played cards, as if the war were over and would never trouble us again. Our chef cooked outside using water from a natural spring at the bottom of the cliffs. It was our only source of drinking water, apart from the drips that we could collect inside the cave, but it was fresh and sweet.

Yahara wanted to check our new lines of defense so I drove him to our gun placements on Kunishi Ridge, a two-thousand-yard outcrop that was smooth and steep, with an exposed area beneath it that the enemy would have to cross before engaging us. It might have been purpose-built for our needs. Ahead of Kunishi were two tall hills, Yaezu and Yoza. We couldn't establish positions on the peaks due to lack of water, but our formations lower down offered excellent lines of fire on all approaches. Yahara was satisfied our final defensive line was as formidable as it had been at Kakazu, Sugar Loaf Hill, and Shuri.

We returned to find everyone gathered in the sunshine outside the cave. The chef served tinned pineapple and boiled sweet potatoes that he'd obtained from a nearby field at great personal risk. His devotion to duty was appreciated by all. Our native potatoes had never tasted so sweet. The relaxed atmosphere must have dulled our senses because we were slow to react when an American patrol boat rounded the bluff to the north of the cliff. All of a sudden the stones around us rang out with the sharp chimes of machine gun bullets. A lieutenant called Hirai roared in pain. His thumb had been blown off by a bullet. He scrambled inside the cave with the rest of us, cursing the Americans roundly. Yoshi didn't follow us. I rushed back outside to rouse him, thinking he'd drifted off to sleep, but there was a neat hole in his forehead. The war had caught up with us once more.

Yoshi's death affected me greatly. I was the only remaining runner with the general staff, the only remaining member of the Blood and Iron Brigade at the new headquarters. That night I dreamed I was back in the little boat on the black ocean, Yoshi with me, telling filthy jokes one after another and smoking endless cigarettes. Whenever he drew on the cigarette, the tiny flare illuminated a neat black hole in his forehead. He didn't seem aware of it, and I didn't mention it, not wanting to spoil his high spirits or somehow lose his companionship on that unlit ocean.

From that day on, the American patrol boats kept a constant vigil off shore. They issued daily loudspeaker broadcasts urging us to surrender, assuring both civilians and soldiers that they would be treated fairly. "Come to the beach. Swim out to our boats and you won't be harmed," they promised. They dropped propaganda leaflets from the sky with similar lies.

No one believed them. Our soldiers handed out grenades and cyanide to the civilians to spare them the gruesome fate that awaited them if they fell into enemy hands.

The patrol boats guessed the spring was our main source of water because they began to target it. Our soldiers were forced to go there despite the bullets and soon the corpses begin to pile up. The water-powered generator was near the spring. When its cables were severed by gunfire, it was too dangerous to repair and we were forced to use candles. The tiny cave where I slept leaked water so constantly that in desperation I pitched a tent inside it, but the tent was never dry and soon rotted away around me, leaving me below the dripping stalactites once more. I found every excuse to stay in the main caves, running errands for Yahara, carrying supplies in and out, or helping the chef to prepare his meals for the officers.

General Ushijima busied himself with writing letters of commendation for his men. Since we had arrived in Mabuni, his lofty grandeur had evaporated and he had become friendly and talkative. When he saw me grating dried fish for the chef, he enquired what I was doing with what seemed like genuine interest.

"I am grating bonito, General," I answered. He sat beside me, watching with apparent fascination.

"My mother used to do it," I explained. "She used to say that grating bonito is very relaxing."

"And was she right?"

"I think she was."

"May I try?"

"Of course, General," I said, hiding my astonishment and handing him the fish and grater.

"I don't wish to take your only grater," he said.

"There's another one in the kitchen," I said, pressing it upon him. "I'll get it. Please take this one."

We grated together in silence for some minutes, until Ushijima laughed to himself. "Your mother was right. It is very relaxing."

"Chef always has plenty of bonito that needs grating," I said happily.

"Then it seems we have our work cut out for us," he smiled.

After that, we spent many hours grating bonito, sometimes when the heaviest bombardments were taking place above us, and the caves shuddered all around us. The general asked about my family and told me a little of his own, but for the most part we simply sat, in silence, and grated.

General Cho had changed too. His war-like demeanor had gone, replaced by a gallows humor that made those dark days a little more bearable.

"Hey Yahara!" he called out one evening as we were relaxing in the main cave after dinner, "I have a question for our master strategist: would now be a good time to commit *seppuku*, or would it be tactically advantageous to wait until a later date?"

"That isn't a question of strategy, General Cho," Yahara answered warily.

"I'm joking, Hiromichi!" Cho said, using Yahara's first name and laughing heartily, "but seriously though, strategically, when would be the right time?"

Ushijima was grating bonito with me. He didn't look up from his work but I knew he was listening carefully to the exchange. Yahara sighed. He knew there was no way to dissuade the generals from taking their own lives—they were honor-bound by the samurai code to do so—but he tried his best. "The battle isn't yet over, General Cho. The men under our command need leadership. Therefore there can be no correct time for a general to commit seppuku."

"Then I have another question for you," Cho said, his face deadly serious now. Yahara steeled himself visibly.

"Have you got lice?"

"I beg you pardon?" Yahara said, blinking in the dim candlelight.

"Lice… in your hair… do you have any, Hiromichi?"

Yahara's hand rose slowly and he ran his fingers through his lank hair. "Yes, as a matter of fact, I do," he said slowly.

"How many?" Cho asked.

"What do you mean?" Yahara replied, uncomprehending.

"How many have you found, so far, in your hair," Cho persisted patiently.

"Three."

"Hah! I found five." Cho chortled, "I win."

We laughed, and even Yahara joined in the merriment, though in truth lice were no laughing matter. They kept us awake all night with terrible itching and Cho said they caused him more misery than the American artillery. In those final nights in the Mabuni caves, it wasn't far from the truth.

The enemy tanks were a different matter. The Americans had so many in the battle now that they could move around at will. We had only a handful of big guns and scant ammunition. By day, the tanks pounded our positions, but when they withdrew at night, we rebuilt our defenses in readiness for the morning. It was a hopeless task. The tanks broke through our defenses at Yonabaru and messages of defeat began to come in from the surrounding fortifications. Our troops fought heroically to the last man, but they couldn't withstand the relentless onslaught of the Americans. Yaezu Hill was captured. The enemy smashed through Kunishi Ridge. Finally, having taken Yoza Hill, they radioed a message to General Ushijima. The radio operator handed it to me and I ran to deliver it personally.

"What is it, Kenichi?" Ushijima asked, looking up from the letter he was writing with a frown.

"A message from General Buckner," I said nervously.

Ushijima looked over the rim of his glasses with a frown, "General Buko Noh? I know of no such officer."

Ushijima was well aware of General Buckner, I knew, but I played along nonetheless. "Buckner is the hated foreign devil in charge of enemy forces on Okinawa, General," I said earnestly.

"Ah," Ushijima said, nodding slowly. He returned to his letter and continued with his writing. I waited a long time, until I began to think he would take no action, but eventually he spoke again. "What does General Buko Noh have to say? Please tell me."

I read the message aloud:

> *To Lieutenant General Ushijima, commander of Japanese Forces on Okinawa.*
>
> *General, the forces under your command have fought bravely and well. Your infantry tactics have merited the respect of your opponents in the battle for Okinawa. Like me, you are a general who is experienced in infantry warfare. The inadequacy of your defense forces must be obvious to you, and it is clear no reinforcements can reach you. The destruction of all Japanese resistance is only days away. I urge you to surrender, with honor, and spare the lives of your remaining officers and men. You will be treated as prisoners of war according to the Geneva Convention.*

The general didn't look up from his work, but he had stopped writing.

"What do you think our answer should be, Kenichi?" he asked.

"You must do as you see fit, General," I said.

"As I see fit?" he nodded thoughtfully, savoring the words, "Yes, you are right. I must do as I see fit, and there is only one way forward, as I see it, Kenichi. I have sworn to defend this island and the empire until my dying breath, and that is what I must do." He looked into my eyes and smiled such a warm smile, I will never forget it, "You, however, have made no such promise. When the time comes, you must escape, find your family, sit with your mother and grate bonito again."

"I swore loyalty to the emperor when I joined the Blood and Iron Brigade," I corrected him.

"You did, but in reality, we gave you little choice in the matter."

"I didn't need a choice," I said seriously, but Ushijima held up his hand to stop me.

"Please fetch General Cho and Colonel Yahara," he said. "I wish to inform them of Buckner's message and discuss our final plans." He was still smiling, and behind the kindly old eyes I saw the steel that had once made him such a formidable soldier—one whom I would have followed to the ends of the earth without a moment's hesitation.

"Yes, General," I said, the words thick in my throat, and with a swift bow, I hurried from the cave to find Yahara and Cho.

THE SUICIDE CLIFFS

As the American guns drew closer and the bombardment became more constant, conditions in the cave became unbearable. The shortages of food and water caused our men to run the gauntlet for supplies and soon corpses littered the path to the spring and the nearby field of sweet potatoes.

By the time we gathered for Ushijima's final orders, only sixteen remained in the cave. Each of the staff officers was given a mission. Most were ordered to disperse and carry out guerrilla warfare on the island, but Yahara was told to return to Tokyo and report the situation to Imperial Headquarters. I was released from military service with orders to assist with rebuilding the island by any means possible. I tried to protest, but Yahara wouldn't hear my arguments. I sensed he himself was poised on a knife-edge of indecision. Ushijima and Cho would commit ritual suicide as was the custom, and Yahara's fellow officers would carry out a hopeless campaign of sabotage on an island swarming with enemy troops. He, on the other hand, had been given a ticket out of Okinawa. His rational mind told him to take it, while honor demanded he should remain and fight to the death.

That evening we ate a makeshift banquet by candlelight, a final meal together of fish, pineapple, sake, and rice brandy. The conversation was cheerful but muted, each officer doing his best to maintain morale while wrestling with his own fears. Finally, Cho clapped his hands to signal the end of the banquet, and we retired for a few hours of sleep before our final day in the cave.

By this time, I'd moved my bedding to a larger, more comfortable cave, one vacated by an officer who had been killed at Kunishi. The water dripped down the walls instead of on my head, but the same stalactites hovered above me. I closed my eyes and tried to think of Itoman Bay, just a few miles away, picturing the limitless blue sky above me as I strolled along the cliff-tops and ran across the white sand to the cooling ocean. Somehow, I must have fallen asleep because when I woke, there was frantic activity in the cave. Enemy tanks had swarmed into nearby Mabuni. The officers hurried to leave the cave and carry out their missions, but by midday American infantry had gathered on a hilltop overlooking the main entrance and several had been killed trying to exit the cave. An hour later, the Americans sealed the entrance with a huge explosion that rocked the hillside. Our men continued to leave from the overhead shaft on the other side of the hill, but by evening the Americans had located this too and dropped grenades down, killing two more.

By the time the enemy retired at nightfall, only the cliff-side entrance remained open to us. Officers and men disguised themselves as civilians and slipped away during the night, until only the two generals, Yahara, and I were left. We sat in the main cave, waiting for someone to speak first. In the end, it was Cho, who rose and bowed formally to Yahara.

"Colonel Yahara, do you remember the film we watched together in Saigon?"

"Of course," Yahara answered without hesitation, "it was a European film, *Waves of the Danube*."

"It was!" Cho beamed. "Those were good times, were they not?"

"The best of times," Yahara smiled. "And afterward, we went to a sukiyaki restaurant on the riverbank and drank ourselves into oblivion."

"We did!" Cho bellowed, his eyes glistening with emotion. He waited a moment, holding the emotion in check lest it overwhelm him, then, breathing out slowly, he continued, "Yahara, you have been a good companion and, more recently, a worthy adversary, both for me and for the Americans. For that I salute you!"

"It has been an honor to serve with you, General Cho," Yahara replied, the sincerity obvious in his voice.

"Then you must do me one final honor," Cho said quickly.

"Anything," Yahara said, knowing what Cho was about to ask.

"Please assist me in my death."

Yahara rose and bowed, "It will be my deepest honor, General."

"Thank you," Cho said with a warm smile and then continued briskly, "once you have completed this task, your orders are explicit and must be obeyed. General Ushijima and I have discussed the matter at length. You must escape to the mainland and bring details of our valiant defense to the High Command in Tokyo. They must know of the valor of our men, and no one is better qualified than you to tell them this, together with the lessons they can learn from Okinawa to ensure final victory. I trust these orders are clear?"

Yahara looked from Cho to Ushijima, who stared back at him, his steady gaze confirming Cho's words.

"Perfectly," Yahara conceded at last.

Then Ushijima's gaze swung round to me and I felt a tightening in my throat. "No!" I cried, before I could stop myself, but he silenced my protests, "Kenichi, General Cho and I wish to die at the same time. Please don't force one of us witness the other's death and force Colonel Yahara to act twice."

I stared dumbly at Ushijima, unable to comprehend the enormity of what he was asking.

"Besides," he continued softly, "it is somehow fitting that you, a child of Okinawa, should be the one to deal my death blow."

"That isn't my wish, General!" I protested, unable to stop the tears. "I would gladly…"

"No, but it is mine!" he insisted loudly, and then he smiled his kindly smile, his eyes seeking mine, his voice gentle. "It is my wish, Kenichi."

"You would do the general a great honor, Kenichi," Cho said.

I turned to Yahara imploringly, hoping he might offer a way out, but Yahara had no clever alternative for me. He nodded once, his expression grave. He had failed me. I looked back to Ushijima, the great general reduced to this, and saw the fierce pride still alive in his eyes.

I heard myself speaking, the voice distant, as if coming from another part of the cave. I felt a single breath pass my lips, and with it a single-word answer. I heard myself agreeing to assist in the suicide of the officer in charge of Japanese forces on Okinawa. I heard myself agreeing to kill Lieutenant General Ushijima.

Yahara and I left the generals alone to prepare for their final act of the war. They sat cross-legged together, smoking and composing poetry, which they exchanged back and forth. Cho's final lines read:

We have used up our withered lives,
But our souls race to heaven.

Ushijima responded:

Green grass of Yukushima, withered before autumn,
Will return in the spring of Momikoku

Cho drank his favorite whisky, King of Kings, while Ushijima sipped sake contentedly. They discarded their army uniforms and wore simple white shirts, onto which Cho had written his departure poem:

With bravery I served my nation, with loyalty I dedicate
my life.

The generals wished to see the rising sun once more. It was a desire no Japanese could refuse. Yahara took me outside and by the sickly light of the false dawn, showed me how to wield the sword correctly to ensure a clean cut. He had me repeat the action over and over for the best part of an hour, until he was satisfied.

When the sun's first rays broke over the horizon, the generals made their way onto the cliff-tops. My eyes were on the sea, my ears alive for the sound of an approaching patrol boat, but the generals had no such concerns. They knelt side by side and shaded their eyes so they could watch the sunrise.

"I will see you at the Yasukuni Shrine, General," Cho said.

"It will be a happy reunion," Ushijima replied.

The sun cleared the horizon, huge and red, the same sun that always rose over Okinawa, impervious to the affairs of mortal men, bestowing the same brilliance on all beneath it, young and old, high and low, friend or enemy.

"Such a beautiful day," Cho whispered.

"A beautiful place," Ushijima said without turning. "Keni-chi, your island is a splendid place to pass one's final moments."

I couldn't find words to answer him. We watched the living emblem of our country rising over the eastern sea, an emblem that demanded two more deaths by its new light. The faintest buzz broke the stillness. It was a patrol boat, though not yet in sight.

"So little time," Ushijima said, reaching for his short sword.

"A curse on the foreign devils," Cho laughed grimly, taking up his own sword.

Yahara and I stood behind them, our long swords held high. There was no sign of the patrol boat. For a moment, the sound of the engine disappeared. I guessed it had stopped to investigate something in the next cove to ours. The generals waited until the sun finally cleared the horizon and they could see it in its entirety. "Hai!" Ushijima said, signaling the beginning of the end. "Long live the emperor," they said loudly as one, cutting together, groaning as the blades penetrated deep into the lower abdomen, then grunting in agony as they sliced across their own flesh. As soon as the cuts were made, I saw Yahara's sword flash. I didn't wait to see what happened but struck at Ushijima's neck as I'd been shown.

The force of my strike ripped the sword from my grasp and I held onto the hilt by my fingertips, but my strike had been good. The general's head was off. Cho's body fell to the left, his severed head just a short distance away, but Ushijima fell forward and his head rolled on and over the edge of the cliff. I turned to Yahara in horror but he smiled to reassure me. The cut had been quick and clean. The general hadn't suffered. It was all that mattered.

I saw the black shadow of the patrol boat, heard the roar of its engine and the staccato blast of the machine gun, but still I jumped in surprise as the rocks began to ring around us. We ran back inside the cave. There were new voices coming from the main shaft. The Americans had penetrated our headquarters. We were trapped. I looked to Yahara for a solution, but he had no more idea than I.

"Outside is safer than in here," I said, "Let's make for the beach. If we can evade the patrol boat, we might stand a chance."

"Split up!" he said, following me from the cave. He turned left and pointed for me to go right. "Good luck, Kenichi."

The patrol boat had gone farther out, assuming we had disappeared, but the sharp-eyed gunner spotted us and raked the cliff-side with bullets, enjoying a little extra target practice at two fleeing figures.

"Good luck to you, Colonel," I cried, launching myself down the cliff-side. My last sight of Yahara was of him slipping and tumbling down a steep slope. I wondered if he would make it to Tokyo. I prayed he would, so that the High Command could be shown the error of their ways and the tragedy of Okinawa would never be repeated.

I hit the beach and ran along the fine shingle to take cover in a pile of rocks at the southern edge. The patrol boat turned around and pursued me to the rocks, hunting me. I saw it coming around to investigate from my left. If they beached up and came to look for me, I would be easy prey. On my left was the open beach, on my right only water and a sheer cliff that I couldn't hope to climb. The patrol boat neared. I heard the voices of the Americans. My mind was made up. I slipped into the water on the far side of the rocks and swam along the length of the cliff. A minute later, I heard the boat round the rocks on the other side, still searching for me. I dived beneath the surface and swam under water as far as I could. Coming up for air, I floated on my back so my head wouldn't bob above the waves, sucking in air for another dive, but they saw me and gave chase. The cliff stretched for another hundred yards before there was another beach where I could get out. I put my head down and swam for my life.

The machine gun cackled cruelly at my attempt to escape. Bullets streamed past me into the depths. I waited for the final agony of a bullet, two bullets, three bullets, ripping into my flesh. I saw myself sinking into the blackness, a wisp of crimson the only trace of me, saw my body come to rest on the ocean floor, so close to the land of my birth, yet not on it. I would have preferred to lie in Itoman Bay where I'd swum as a child, but Mabuni wasn't far from Itoman. Nowhere was far on my island. I wondered how many more of my countrymen were in the water nearby, or buried under rocks, or lying unrecognizable in the mud, with no gravestone to mark their location, no ashes for their children to honor, no bones for their descendants to clean. I wondered if Yahara would be my closest companion in death, or was there anyone closer.

The pain didn't come. I interrupted my stroke to glance over my shoulder. The patrol boat had halted. The firing had stopped. I will never know why. Perhaps they took pity on me. Perhaps they decided I was a civilian after all, as my clothes suggested, and left me alone. Perhaps they didn't want to waste any more ammunition on such a worthless target. I heard the crackle of the radio, and the boat swung away and headed off in the other direction. I breathed steadily, holding down the panic, and made for the beach.

I made my way westward toward the little village of Kyan where my grandparents lived. If my family were anywhere, they would be there. I prayed I would find them alive.

The path led me through an unearthly landscape of pock-marked hills, black stubs of trees, shrapnel and shell casings mixed with mud and baked hard with the end of the rains. A pile of discarded Japanese rifles had been left beside a broken truck. A haphazard pile of helmets lay a little further ahead. It seemed some of our soldiers had decided to surrender after all.

At the top of a rise, I looked out and saw an ocean filled with enemy ships. A giant oil slick covered the ocean, giving it the blue-grey sheen of gunmetal. I noticed how well the dull battleships blended in with their surroundings. Black smoke hung in the fetid air, a reminder of the carnage of earlier battles. I stood watching, I don't know for how long, until I heard the drone of an engine behind me that quickly grew to a roar. It was a single Zero coming in from high and diving toward the American fleet.

A hail of bullets and shells erupted around the Zero. Unde-terred, it chose its target, a destroyer, and flew at it. A cloud of destruction enveloped the plane. Then, through a gap in the flak, I could make out the dome of the pilot's head. What was he feeling, I wondered. Was he grim-faced and determined, eyeing his target as a wolf eyes its prey? Or were his eyes closed in terror, his lips moving in silent prayer? Perhaps neither. Per-haps he was serene, simply another blossom falling from the cherry tree, already basking in glory at the Yasukuni Shrine for serving his emperor with such devotion.

His right wing disintegrated, thick smoke streamed from his engine, great chunks of metal flew from his bodywork. Glass shattered, the shards exploding in all directions. Did I see a streak of crimson in the maelstrom? I couldn't be sure. The nose pitched forward, the whine of his engine reaching an ear-splitting pitch. He began to spin. The elegant line of his approach degenerated into the lurching, stumbling advance of a drunk who would never make it home. I willed him on with my entire being, my fists clenched white-knuckle tight, my lips curled back in a silent scream, but my prayers were not enough. He hit the water fifty feet from the destroyer. The Zero flipped five times and came to rest just yards from its target before sinking swiftly into the black water.

I remained frozen on the cliff-top. A boat spotted me and the crew began taking pot shots. Bullets hit somewhere close by, but I was immune to them. I turned slowly and ambled away without a backward glance.

THE DEATH OF JUN

Professor Shimoji reappeared outside Miyagi's door, but one look at his face told Miyagi that this time, the professor had no new comfort or amenity to offer him. Shimoji's brow shone with sweat, and a deep furrow divided his forehead between thick grey eyebrows. His mouth was set firm, like a cut across his face, his lips tight, unwilling to utter the words that he needed to tell Miyagi.

Miyagi stared at him wide-eyed, unwilling to invite the man inside, knowing that whatever he had to say it would be agony to hear, and hoping against hope that it would be something simple—they needed to move out of their house, or share their space with another family, or reduce their water consumption—knowing already in his heart that the man had come to deliver news far worse than this and steeling himself for words that would that would tear his wife's, his children's, and his own heart apart.

The professor did not wait to be invited inside. Mrs. Miyagi and her children stopped what they were doing as he entered their living area and stood, his hands fumbling, not knowing what to do with them, his words starting and failing several times, his eloquence as a one-time teacher now long gone.

"I bring grave news from the front," he began. "Tragic news, I regret to say."

Five faces watched him. None said a word.

"The name of your son, Jun Miyagi, was listed as killed in action. I have no details at the moment of where or when, and it is not confirmed. However, I felt you should know. It is with deep regret that I bring you such news. Rest assured that I will tell you more the moment I hear. Now I will leave you in peace. Please forgive my intrusion."

At this, Professor Shimoji left the silent house and the noble family that had once been the pride of Okinawa. He was scarcely able to hold back his own tears for how far his island and its people had fallen.

THE CORAL TOMB

When we had been young, my brothers and sister and I had often played in the water tank near my grandfather's house. The tank was concealed in a niche between two rock faces and invisible from the road. It was the best hiding place I could think of, and I prayed my family had thought of it too.

The path to Kyan was strewn with the corpses of soldiers, some serene in death, others torn apart, their mouths still twisted in the shapes of their final agonies. Body parts were as common as shell casings and shrapnel, and lay side by side with the agents of their destruction. Where the bodies of the soldiers ended, those of the civilians began. Civilians is the wrong word, a cold word. These were my people, my neighbors, the young woman who worked at the bakery, the old man who moored his boat beside my father's, the farmer's boy who tended the pigs, chewing on a stick of sugarcane.

Some were clothed while others were naked or burnt black, their mouths open, but no word of complaint uttered. I hardened my heart. It was the only way I could continue. I walked on, no longer looking left nor right, determined only to find my family.

As the sun rose higher, I became aware of my raging thirst. I knew of a brook a little way ahead and turned off the path to reach it. I knelt beside it and cupped my hands into the bubbling water. When I raised them to my lips they were filled with maggots. I threw the water away in disgust and ran, stumbling with exhaustion, until, quarter of a mile upstream, I reached clear water and drank my fill.

Kyan was quiet, although I could hear the pop of rifle fire and the chatter of machine guns in the distance. I passed numerous caves and family tombs buried deep in the rock where I knew people would be hiding, but I didn't try to enter in search of my family. I knew where they would be and made my way directly to the water tank.

Standing before its door, I hesitated, preparing myself for the worst. I knew for certain that I wouldn't find my entire family alive, and my heart ached at the prospect of finding which, if any of them, had lived.

I opened the door and saw a small child squatting in the shadows. I guessed one of the local children had found the hiding place. Then the child raised its head, terrified that it had been discovered, and I saw the face of my sister.

"Yuka."

She stared at me, uncomprehending.

I went to her and pulled her slowly to her feet. She was covered in fleas, lice crawling in her hair and in the cuts that covered her face and body, her legs smeared with excrement, but it was her eyes that shocked me most. They were black and hollow, unlit by the spirit that had once occupied her body.

I pulled her close to me and held her, horrified by the skeletal thinness of her, the sharpness of her ribs in my hands. Whatever hardship I'd suffered had been nothing compared to what she'd undergone. I dreaded to think of what she had endured, dreaded to ask the question that I had to ask.

"Mother and father? Yasuhiko and Tatsuo?"

She shook her head.

I could ask her nothing more. Not yet. "We have to go," I said quickly, before grief overwhelmed me and made me useless.

"It's safe here," she said in a tiny voice.

"The Americans are coming this way," I said. "They'll be here in a few hours. We need to leave now."

"Where will we go?"

"Chinen is the safest place. We should make our way there."

"Chinen is far."

"Yes, so we need to make a start."

She followed me out of the water tank as meekly as a child. We picked our way through the debris of war, stopping only to scavenge food from the packs of dead soldiers, or root around in the fields for sweet potatoes and radishes. We passed caves and tombs, occasionally peering in to see who or what was inside. In some we were driven away by Japanese soldiers who didn't want civilians in their midst. In others, we found local people, huddled in silence. Sometimes they drove us away. Other times, no one said a word. When we found people who would speak, they spoke of American atrocities: torture, rape, the murder of children and babies. The Japanese soldiers nearby had urged them to take their own lives rather than fall into enemy hands. Some had given out hand grenades so the civilians could kill themselves quickly. This often created dreadful results. A hand grenade was enough to kill one person but not a whole group. We found children bleeding in agony beside the bodies of their dead parents, parents who had tried unsuccessfully to kill the whole family. There was nothing we could do for any of them—we walked away. Those who had no other means of a swift death jumped off the cliffs. They did so in such numbers that the cliffs along the southern coast of Cape Kyan became known as the Suicide Cliffs.

When shells began landing nearby, we took shelter in a cave ten miles northeast of Kyan. The cave mouth was crowded, but no one said a word as we squeezed in. It was occupied by children and old people. There were no soldiers to order us out. As we made our way toward the back of the cave, the stench of human excrement and decaying corpses was so overwhelming that I felt I might faint at any moment.

A moment later, we heard English booming over a loud-speaker outside. We couldn't understand what they were saying, but the voice terrified the little children. I held my sister tight as she shook uncontrollably. The end was in sight—the Americans would kill us one way or another. We waited a long time for the end to come, but the Americans were patient. Eventually a different voice came on the loudspeaker. It spoke Japanese in a heavy accent, and urged us to come out. We wouldn't be harmed, it told us, and repeated its message over and over, until one grandfather decided to take his chances with the enemy. He led his terrified wife and what looked like five grandchildren out into the daylight. I expected to see them cut down by gunfire in the mouth of the cave, but all was quiet. I guessed the Americans wished to torment them later. I was sickened at the thought of what would happen to them.

Soon other old people and children began to leave the cave too, until only Yuka and I remained. "Better to die in here than in the hands of the foreign devils," I said to Yuka.

"Yes!" she said, her voice small but certain.

"For the emperor!" I said.

"For the emperor," she repeated weakly.

The loudspeaker issued its final warning. Then came the crunch of boots in the cave mouth. I covered Yuka with my body.

"No," she pleaded, not wishing to be left alive alone, but I couldn't allow her to die while I lived.

The dull thud of a grenade landing nearby, too far to reach and throw back. Too far too smother with my body. I enveloped Yuka in my arms, pressing her face into my chest, my eyes screwed tight shut, waiting for the deafening end of my war. Waiting to rejoin my family and my ancestors. Waiting for peace.

A BED IN GENKOKU

I heard Yuka's voice from another room. She was saying my name. I was answering her, but she couldn't hear me. I heard her calling to me again, closer now. Through half-closed eyelids, I could make out a blurred shape hovering over me. I could hear the gentle chatter of unfamiliar voices, speaking in tongues. The memory of the cave and the grenade were with me, but didn't seem so terrifying now, merely an afterthought from the past, an unpleasant incident best forgotten. I was floating on air with my sister beside me. We were safe, free of the horrors of the war and the cruelty of our tormentors.

I opened my eyes a little wider and saw her face beside me. She was smiling. She had died too and she was by my side, coming to the afterlife with me. We would be reunited with our family together.

"You're not dead," she told me gently. Her voice sounded so real.

"Then where are we?" I asked, playing along.

"In a hospital."

"Which hospital?" I asked. I'd caught her out already—there were no hospitals left on our island.

"An American hospital."

I laughed, and somewhere far away I felt a dull pain in my back that seemed very real. I stopped laughing. "Seriously Yuka, tell me, where are we?"

"It's true," she soothed, "You're in an American hospital. They gave you morphine for the pain."

I lay for a moment, letting it all settle in my head and then tried to sit up. A searing pain cut through my body and I slumped back onto the bed. "What about you?" I asked, suddenly terrified that what she was saying might be true.

"I'm fine. There's no need to worry."

"But the grenade!" My tongue felt heavy and useless in my mouth, getting in the way of my words.

"The doctors removed shrapnel from my arm and hand," she told me, holding up a bandaged arm for me to see.

"You were injured?" I asked, suddenly aware that I wasn't the only one in the hospital.

"Just a flesh wound," she assured me, "Your injuries were far more serious." I waited for her to continue. She smiled sadly. "You saved my life," she said, and tears welled in her eyes. "Most of the shrapnel went into your legs, but a few pieces went into your back. You are very lucky to be alive. When the soldiers took you out of the cave, there was blood everywhere. I was sure you were dead."

"Yahara came back!" I said in astonishment.

"Yahara?"

"Colonel Yahara of the Japanese army," I explained, "my commanding officer. He must have gathered fresh troops from somewhere, organized a counter-offensive."

She shook her head slowly. "No, Kenichi. It was the Americans who saved you."

Then it hit me. The strange voices were speaking English—American English. I raised my head and looked around, ignoring the pain. There was an orderly standing beside the next bed, discussing a patient with an army doctor. The man beside me was a Japanese soldier although he was wearing civilian clothing. He was unconscious and close to death.

"They killed him!" I shouted.

"No," my sister reassured me, hoping to hush me, "they're doing what they can for us."

"So they can torture us later. We have to get away!"

"They operated on you twice, saved your life," she insisted gently.

I didn't know what to believe. She stroked my hair gently, and then took my hand in hers. "They removed the shrapnel from your back in two operations. Some shards had gone very deep. There is still a lot in your legs. They told me they'll remove it later, when you're stronger."

I stared at her, trying to take in what she was telling me. "You've been here for four days," she continued. "They've been letting me visit you each day. I've been watching you sleep." She leaned closer, speaking close to my ear, "I've been watching them, too. They are not like the Japanese soldiers told us they'd be. They've been feeding people, caring for the injured, housing refugees and orphans," she looked around to make sure no one could overhear us and then continued, "and there seems to be no limit to their supplies. Their store rooms are filled with food, clothes, medicines, even candy."

I closed my eyes. My head was swimming with this new information. The holy war had come to a filthy, rain-soaked, blood-soaked end, and here I was, lying in an American hospital, being cared for by Americans, fed by Americans. The Japanese had deceived us. The propaganda leaflets had deceived us. Parents had murdered their children and young women had thrown themselves off cliffs—all for no reason. We had truly lost the battle for Okinawa. I turned away from her in despair.

"Miyagi is alive," she whispered.

My sister was clever. She knew how to reach me. The words echoed around in my morphine-fuddled mind for a few moments. Still confused, I turned back to her.

"He's nearby, in Genkoku. I saw him in the street and introduced myself. He was so very happy to hear you're alive."

"How is he?" I asked.

"Unharmed, but very thin and pale. Kenichi, he's not the man you knew before the war. We spoke for a long time and he confided in me. Why, I don't know, but he seemed to want to talk forever, as if saying these things—terrible, painful things—would ease the pain in some way."

"What happened to him?" I asked, dreading the answer.

"Two of his daughters were aboard the Konanmaru when it was sailing to Kyushu."

"The Konanmaru was hit by a torpedo."

"Yes," she answered.

"Which daughters?"

"Tsuneko and Shigeko."

I closed my eyes in despair.

"And his son Jun was killed in the fighting."

I had known Jun well. I could not imagine him gone.

"And Mrs. Miyagi?" I asked.

"She is well enough, considering what they have been through."

"And Miyagi himself was unharmed?" I demanded, my mind still furry from the morphine.

"He is ill, Kenichi."

"Ill? How do you know he's ill? Did he tell you?"

"No, but I know the signs. The past year has been too much for his heart."

"Not Miyagi. He's as strong as an ox."

"This isn't a matter of strength," she said quietly, her hand on mine, "He's suffered too much tragedy. Most of his students are dead. You're one of the few survivors." She smiled, but her eyes glistened with tears. "Do you remember Jinan Shinzato?"

"Of course, he was my Sempai, but he wasn't here on the island. He went to Kyushu."

"He volunteered for the kamikaze. He hasn't returned."

I closed my eyes and steeled myself for the question I had to ask. "And what of our own family, Yuka?"

Her silence spoke the words for her, long before she could bring herself to say them aloud, in a choked whisper, "All dead."

"How?"

I needed facts, something to cling to, to examine, to contemplate, anything to block the awful realization of my worst fears.

"I can't say," she cried softly. "Not yet, please don't make me, Kenichi," her voice barely audible. She was struggling to hold herself together. If recounting the manner of their deaths was so terrible, then perhaps I should let it be, at least for now. I wasn't sure if I could bear to hear it myself.

"You're certain? You saw it with your own eyes?" It was all I could think to ask.

"No, not with my own eyes, but our neighbor, old Mrs. Mura, she told me. She saw what happened to mother and father. I don't know what happened to Yasuhiko and Tatsuo. Nobody does. I've made inquiries everywhere."

I reached for her hand and squeezed it. Perhaps there was hope for our brothers, after all. She rested her head on my chest and wept for a long time.

I wondered how my parents had died. My mind quickly filled with terrible images, which I chased away—there was no good in imagining such horrors until Yuka could tell me the truth. Instead, my mind turned to Shinzato and the image of the single Japanese Zero came back to me, flying into a miasma of gunfire, the sickening shriek of metal torn asunder and crashing into the sea. Had it had been Shinzato in the plane, I wondered.

I would never know for sure, but ever since that day I have always believed I was an eyewitness to his glorious, tragic, pointless death. Shinzato never returned from Kyushu. His first successful mission had also been his last in this bitterest of battles, and his name was listed, with so many others, as "Killed in the Battle of Okinawa."

Yuka visited me each afternoon and stayed until evening. When the medics learned of her nursing skills, they got her to treat Japanese patients who still refused to trust the American doctors. Yuka's English was good, even better than mine. She soon picked up some basic medical vocabulary, and I would watch her explaining some treatment or other to a wounded soldier or one of the pitiful children in the ward. Sometimes it took her over an hour to calm them enough so that an American doctor could examine them.

I understood their revulsion. The feeling of American hands on me made my skin crawl. The doctors inspected my legs and my back, muttering to themselves as they did, drawing on my flesh with ink pens, planning their cuts with diabolical calm. They removed the shrapnel from my legs in a series of operations that spanned three weeks. One particular doctor stopped by my bedside regularly to examine my wounds. He would speak with Yuka as if I wasn't there. I found I could understand his slow drawl well enough, but had no wish to speak to him. His concern for my welfare wasn't born of mercy or compassion but simply the guilty contrition of a conqueror who had destroyed an island and murdered its people. Yuka translated the doctor's words dutifully. She said my muscles had been badly torn and would need time to heal. There would be a long period of rehabilitation. I heard the doctor say there was a chance I'd never walk again, but Yuka didn't translate this.

Eventually she persuaded me to stand up and take a few faltering steps, but the pain was excruciating and I quickly returned to my bed. Each day she would beg me to try again, but after a while, even she couldn't get me to stand. Finally, the Americans moved me to an infirmary in Genkoku where the wounded were convalescing, and Yuka moved in to look after me.

She was offered a permanent nursing job in the hospital, and accepted, since there was no other work anywhere. Each evening she would return home with supplies: tins of spam, Lucky Strike cigarettes, cans of soda. Most of it she sold on the black market, but occasionally we would share some candy or open a tin of fruit immersed in a sickly-sweet syrup that we rinsed away before eating. The skin had been peeled, the pips and stones removed. Each piece was uniform and perfect. Our island had once produced all kinds of delicious tropical fruit in abundance. Now it was barren, and to taste that sweetness again, we were forced to open a tin that had come all the way from America.

THE FINAL AIR RAID

On the same day that I left the infirmary, a plane took off from Tinian in the Marianas and flew to Kyushu, the southernmost of Japan's main islands. In stark contrast to the massive air raids on Tokyo and Yokohama, this was a single bomber with a single bomb. It flew unopposed in the clear skies above Hiroshima and released its payload—code-named Little Boy— killing 80,000 people.

Three days later, a similar plane with a similar bomb flew over Nagasaki, and it too released its payload successfully. This bomb—code-named Fat Man—killed 40,000 people that day, and many more died in the aftermath.

Japan surrendered a week later. The war was finally over.

A Visitor from the Past

When the field hospital in Genkoku shut down, Yuka got a transfer to the new medical center in the Kadena airbase. I didn't approve, but I couldn't argue—she was bringing home US dollars, the island's new currency, together with food rations, clothes, and morphine.

We moved into a tiny room in a squat accommodation block in nearby Koza, which was growing quickly to accommodate the sprawling airbase. Every day Yuka would urge me to get on my feet and walk, to rebuild the strength in my legs. I promised I would, but I needed morphine to overcome the pain. She brought me vials, which I stored under my bed. I assured her that I was walking each day while she was at work, but my sister was never easily fooled even as a child, and she was no more gullible now. When she insisted on walking with me, I got angry and shouted at her. At this, her frustration spilled over and she screamed at me. She began taunting me, goading me to try and catch her and beat her. Finally she began to withhold my vials of morphine, but I went into a black rage for days until finally they reappeared by my bedside. I accepted them without a word and returned to my soft oblivion.

Dozing one afternoon, I found myself in a particularly vivid daydream. I was in the entrance hall in Miyagi's house and staring at one of the portraits hanging on the wall. It was an old black and white photograph of his ancestor, an uncle I believe, who had been the head of the Miyagi clan before Chojun had taken that position himself. I rubbed my eyes. I was getting too used to the morphine.

"How are you, Kenichi?"

Miyagi's uncle was speaking. His voice was real. Suddenly I was awake, lying in my cramped room in Koza, and looking into the face of Chojun Miyagi. It had been less than a year since I had seen him, but it might as well have been a lifetime ago. His hair was thin and grey, his cheeks sallow, hanging loose over his wide jaw. Livid spots covered his face and hands. His shoulders, once so massive, had shrunk leaving hollow pleats in his over-sized shirt, and his ragged pants hung loosely from his waist.

I struggled to rise from my bed. "I am well," I lied, "very well, thank you. How are you, Master? I was so delighted to hear you were safe."

"Well enough, under the circumstances," he answered with a wave of the hand, "but you aren't well. Can you walk at all?"

He already knew the answer; it was obvious my sister had asked him to come. I avoided the subject. "I'm so sorry to hear about your family, your losses."

"Thank you," he said, nodding slowly. I saw a flash of pain cross his eyes so intense that it shocked me to my core. My master, once so strong, was broken with grief, yet he fought it down and stared at me intently.

"How is Mrs. Miyagi?" I went on.

"Mrs. Miyagi is the strongest of all of us," he said with a smile, "but what about you? Your sister tells me you need to rebuild your strength."

"The muscles need time to heal," I answered.

"Your sister told me the muscles have already healed. Now they must be used."

"It's still too early," I said apologetically.

"Too painful?" he asked, his eyes examining the wall above me, though I knew his mind was intent on my answer.

I shrugged.

He smiled and sat down slowly beside me on the bed. I saw his eyes rest on the cigarette butts piled on a chipped plate beside my bed. I waited for him to admonish me—he was always lecturing his students on the hazards of smoking—but he made no comment. "Have I ever spoken to you of Bushido?" he asked instead.

I nodded slowly. I'd heard him talk of the samurai code countless times.

"Then you know *The Way of the Warrior*?" he asked deliberately.

"*The Way of the Warrior* is resolute acceptance of death," I answered, repeating what he'd told us so many times during his evening lectures.

He nodded slowly. "So tell me now, after all you've seen, what do you think of this code?" His eyes returned to the wall behind me, giving me time to collect my thoughts. The stark image of General Ushijima's final moments came to me, the brilliant white kimono, the moving exchange of death poems with General Cho, the head, rolling down the cliff as the patrol boat opened fire. I thought of the single Zero flying toward the American fleet, the hail of bullets, the carnage on the waves.

"I've seen Bushido at work many times over the last few months," I said, "And I'm forced to ask myself is it really our way, to seek death so eagerly? We are Okinawan, after all, not Japanese. What is our way?"

"We are a small island," he said, "a small nation caught in a battle of giants, but the code isn't wrong, merely misunderstood. The warrior doesn't seek death, he simply accepts its

CHOJUN

possibility—its inevitability even—with firm resolve. Once he has done this, he is free to engage in battle unburdened by fear for his life. In many ways it is an important way to preserve life."

The idea turned around in my head. I tried to grasp it, but my mind was a fog. "I never considered it that way before," I answered, unsure what to make of what Miyagi was telling me.

"Have you accepted death, Kenichi?" he asked.

I was stunned by such a direct question, and considered it for a long time.

"Twice," I answered eventually. "Once, in the sea, I was swimming, a patrol boat was firing at me, and once, in a cave, when I was hiding with Yuka and the Americans found us."

"Death didn't accept you," he said quietly.

I examined his eyes, wondering what he was driving at. He stood slowly and I noticed a new rigor in his posture. For a moment, the old strength was there again, coursing through his body and limbs. "I'm reopening my karate school," he said.

I stared at him blankly, my mind still furred by the morphine.

"Where will you train?" It was all I could think to say.

"Anywhere," he answered briskly, "until we can build a proper dojo. You're now one of my most senior students," he continued, flashing a sudden smile, "Who would have thought it, eh? The boy caught in the storm all those years ago is now the sempai. Now it's his turn to set an example."

I began to protest but he cut me off, "I will let you know the details in due course. It will be good for you. Moving in shiko dachi will rebuild the strength in your legs."

I winced at the thought—shiko dachi was the low, squatting stance that featured heavily in Miyagi's kata. I knew how painful it could be even without shrapnel wounds in the legs. What he was asking would be agony. I also knew I couldn't refuse.

THE LIGHTS OF KOZA

I didn't mention Miyagi's visit to Yuka, but the next morning, once she'd left for work, I reached under the bed for the morphine vials and took them down the corridor, past the washroom and toilet—farther than I had ever gone before—and stepped out into the yard. I threw them on the ground and stamped them into the dirt quickly before I could change my mind, and then I walked unsteadily into the bustling streets of Koza.

The Americans were everywhere, their loud voices, their cheerful faces, their pockets brimming with dollars and cigarettes, chocolate and bubble-gum, their radios blaring their fast, rhythmic music. A queue of refugees was waiting by a truck as two GIs gave out rations, tins of spam that they believed we liked because we eat pork on Okinawa. They even gave us rice, and our people were forced to accept it.

I walked on, an uncontrollable hatred of our new occupiers mounting inside me, despite how well they had treated Yuka and me. The house on the corner of our block had been made into an orphanage. I could hear the happy chatter of children behind the wall and stood by the gate to see what was happening. A tough-looking American sergeant was playing a game with the orphans, whose heads had all been shaved because of lice. It was hard to tell who was a boy and who was a girl. They were all enjoying themselves, and for a moment I was touched by the American's kindness. Then I heard him calling out military style commands, and realized his game was teaching them to drill like soldiers. The children were all laughing noisily and marching out of time. I yelled at them before I could stop myself.

Did they know they were playing games with the man who'd killed their parents?

The children stared at me open-mouthed, while the sergeant regarded me with pity in his eyes. He must have taken me for one of the many sufferers of what was known in those days as *combat fatigue.* I turned away and walked quickly back to my room, relishing the pain shooting through my legs, ready to burst with sadness for my island and my people. I stumbled into my room and roared in fury, collapsed to the ground, then rose again and threw up my mattress against the wall, searching hopelessly for a vial I might have missed, desperate for the oblivion it might provide. But I'd been thorough. All the vials were gone, their precious contents wasted in the dirt. I lay down on the mattress and steeled myself for the hardships ahead. My battle was not completely over after all.

Each day I ventured a little farther on the tawdry streets of Koza. The place had been a sleepy backwater for many years, but now, with its proximity to the giant American airbase at Kadena, it had suddenly become the island's busiest town. New bars and restaurants appeared every day, with brightly painted signs to attract a new clientele. I read an advertisement in a shop window: *Wanted, Beautiful Women of Okinawa, aged 18 – 25, to welcome occupying troops in an important mission for national unity. Full board and lodgings provided.*

I peered inside. It was mid-afternoon and the bar was almost empty. Only two young Americans sat at the counter talking to the barmaid. She was older than either of them by a long way, but quite beautiful, and it was clear the GIs thought so too. It took me a moment to place her, dressed as she was in an American style skirt and blouse. She'd been General Cho's mistress. Her eyed flicked to mine and she recognized me, but her attention returned immediately to the GIs. The GIs looked around to see who was there and on seeing me, turned back to the bar without comment. A young Okinawan man was of no concern to them. And now, with new masters to serve, he was of no concern to the former comfort woman either.

It was the same story everywhere. When the sun went down, the young GIs would appear in their droves and the young men of Okinawa would vanish from the streets, fading into the background unseen. Then the *panpan* girls would emerge, standing beneath streetlamps or leaning with one foot against a wall, their skirt hitched casually above the knee. They dressed like American teenagers in tight-fitting blouses and knee-length skirts, their hair cut shaggy and loose, so unlike the long, carefully combed style of before.

I saw my first black GIs on the main strip of Koza—five of them huddled together on a corner, smoking and laughing. I passed close by to get a good look, trying not to stare too obviously. They were all taller than I was, even though I was tall for an Okinawan, and their skins were truly black, blacker even than the Indonesians whom I'd seen in Naha before the war. Their voices were deep and loud, their accents different to the white Americans. They didn't notice me. I was just another wounded Nip wandering the streets in a daze. I became fascinated with the black GIs and looked out for them each day as I walked. They kept apart from the white soldiers, drinking in different bars, listening to different music, eating different food, and using different girls. Koza was becoming like other

American cities, divided into ghettos of white, black, and Asian by invisible lines that were rarely crossed.

My legs healed slowly. Each day I walked a little farther and pushed my pace a little faster. When I got home, I performed squats in the yard before going inside to bathe. One day I had walked almost to the end of the strip, the farthest I had ever walked. Crossing a road, a Jeep appeared out of nowhere, traveling fast. I hurried to the sidewalk to get out of its way, and a spasm in my knee made me stumble. I leaned over and clutched it in both hands, waiting for the pain to ease. When I looked up there was a pretty girl standing in front of me. She was dressed in the fashion of the day—a skirt sewn from American tent canvas, a tight flowery blouse, and open-toed sandals. Her hair was short and kept off her face with a colorful scarf tied in bow.

"Kenichi," she said with a smile. "I heard you were alive. I was so glad when Yuka told me."

"Fumiko." I hadn't seen her since she'd treated my wounds after the bombing of Naha harbor, and I found to my surprise that despite her new style of dress, I was very pleased to see her. "I'm so glad you're well."

She must have seen me eyeing her new clothes disapprovingly because she smiled apologetically. "A lot's changed since we last met," she said lightly. "Are you really alright? I saw you stumble just now."

"Shrapnel," I explained, "Every now and then, I discover a new piece."

"Do you want me to help you?"

"No!" I said quickly, embarrassed by my weakness. I stood a little straighter. "You've helped me enough already. I never got to thank you properly for that."

"There was no need," she said, stepping forward to take my arm, "I was a nurse. It was my duty." Her arm felt good in mine. "Anyway, where are you going in such a hurry, Kenichi?" she asked.

"To the end of the strip. It'll be a new record for me to walk so far," I said with a grin. "How about you?"

"Oh, I'm just running an errand, nothing important. I'll come with you."

I hesitated.

"Medical back-up," she offered with a smile.

I couldn't refuse. We walked arm in arm, and it felt good to be close to her. Her skinny arm was surprisingly strong. "What are you doing in Koza?" I asked, "Still nursing?"

"No, not any more. I work in a restaurant now."

"A pity, you were good at it."

"Thank you, but I've had my fill of nursing," she said quietly.

"That's understandable," I said, thinking back to the young nurse I'd seen with Colonel Mita's troops at Sugar Loaf Hill, remembering the horrific conditions she'd faced.

"Where's your restaurant? Is it near here?" I asked quickly, hoping to return to a lighter mood.

"Not really. It's a new place. You wouldn't know it."

"I know Koza quite well from my daily walks."

"Sometimes I don't think I know Koza at all," she sighed. "It's so different from before. I used to come here to visit my grandmother."

I didn't ask about her grandmother, not wishing to dampen her good humor. "Too many foreign devils," I said instead.

"They're everywhere. It's so hard sometimes."

"Do you speak any English?" I asked.

"I'm trying to learn. You have to nowadays."

"Yes, but it's such an ugly language," I said. I'd enjoyed learning English at school, but it was abhorrent to me now, the language of our slave-masters. "Their talk sounds like farmyard animals in a barn."

Fumiko giggled. It was the sweetest sound I'd heard for such a very long time. I tried to recall the last time I'd heard something so lovely, dredging my memory, but not one instance would come to mind. I needed to hear it again. "And the way they smell," I went on, "Don't they even know how to wash?"

"Kenichi, be careful, someone will hear you!"

She was shocked, but still there was laughter in her voice, delicious laughter. I needed it like I'd once needed my vials.

"They won't understand," I said in a broad Okinawan drawl. "Even if they speak Japanese, they can't understand our accent."

Fumiko shook her head and covered her mouth to stifle her mirth. "Have you tried their food?" she asked mischievously.

"The pink meat in a tin?" I said loudly.

"Yes that stuff—what's it called?"

"Spam."

"That's it!"

"Yes, Yuka gets it from the base. Have you tried it?"

"Once. I was nearly sick."

"How can a country with so much money choose to eat something so awful?"

"I've no idea." She laughed once more. The sound was addictive. I had to hear it again.

"And their music," I added quickly.

"Actually, I like their music," she said to my surprise.

I shrugged. It was true, the Americans' music wasn't so bad, but I didn't want to admit it.

"Have you heard their Rhythm and Blues?" she asked.

"What's that?"

"Black music."

"Black?" I asked, uncomprehending.

"The black soldiers—they listen to different music than the whites."

"How do you know?"

"Black soldiers come to our restaurant. Actually, very few whites ever come in now."

"You don't mind?" I asked.

"No, I have nothing against them," she answered. "Do you?"

"Not really," I said. "I hate them all equally. I just pray for the day when they're all gone from here."

"That day might be a long way off," she said quietly.

She was right, but I didn't want to think about it. We'd reached the end of the strip and the row of hastily erected shops and bars stopped abruptly. Beyond were fields that had once been swaying pampas grass, but which now contained piles of building materials and a parking area for trucks and bulldozers. "You did it," she said, her smile returning suddenly. "You walked all the way to the end."

"With your help, Fumiko."

"But it still counts as a new record, yes?"

"I'll have to think about it," I said, stroking my chin with mock seriousness.

"Please say it does, Kenichi. Please!" Her expression was so sweet I couldn't refuse her. "I'll have to confer with the Olympic committee."

"Oh Kenichi, say it does!"

"Okay, it does," I relented.

Her pretty face lit up, and I was drawn into her warmth. I had an overwhelming urge to take her in my arms and kiss her, but just then two black GIs appeared on the other side of the street and called out to us.

"Hey Coco!"

I didn't turn to answer, thinking they were calling to someone else.

"Hey Coco? Konichiwa, Coco!"

I turned to get a better look at them but they weren't looking at me, they were looking at Fumiko, and calling to her as if they knew her.

"Excuse me, just a moment," she sighed, letting go of my arm and mumbled a curse under her breath as she crossed the street. I watched her speak to them for several minutes. One of them put his hand on her arm repeatedly, but she pried it away patiently each time. I saw them gesture toward me and watched her smile and shake her head.

Then she was beside me again. "Don't worry about them," she said breezily. "They're customers at our restaurant. They left me a big tip and now they think they can try it on."

"But why were they calling you Coco?"

"I don't want them to know my real name."

"You should be careful of the foreign devils," I said seriously.

"I am careful, Kenichi, but thank you for your concern."

We walked on in silence for a block, until it dawned on me that Fumiko hadn't mentioned my sister once. "Have you seen Yuka recently?" I asked.

"Yes, we see each other now and then. Please say hello from me."

"I will," I promised.

"Look, we're back where we started," she said happily, "Did you enjoy your exercise?"

"Very much, and I need to get fit."

"Well, don't rush. Take your time. There's no hurry."

"Yes there is," I said. "Master Miyagi's karate class starts next week. I need to get ready for it."

"Karate?" she asked. "I didn't think anyone was doing that any more."

"Miyagi thinks it's important. It's part of our heritage."

"Maybe so, but just don't injure yourself needlessly."

"You worry too much about me, but thank you for your concern."

"It's nothing. You're my friend's brother, after all."

We stopped and turned to face one another. "It was so nice to see you again," she smiled.

"It was nice to see you too."

I examined her face. The wide-eyed innocence was still there, though she must have seen things in the war that no young girl should ever see. I took in the curve of her breasts beneath the tight-fitting blouse and her slender legs. She wasn't as beautiful as Wa Cheun had been, but there was something lovely about her, comforting and warm. I hadn't thought of any other woman apart from Wa Cheun since retuning from China, but that seemed a lifetime ago now.

"Perhaps we could meet again?" I ventured.

"I'd like that," she smiled.

We made a date, and despite the agony in my legs, I walked back to my room with a new spring in my stride.

I found Yuka sitting in the dark. Now that the effects of the morphine had gone from my body and my mind, I began to notice a change in her. The stronger I became, the more she withdrew. It was as if she'd devoted the last of her strength to my recovery, and now she had none left for herself.

"I saw Fumiko today," I told her, hoping to cheer her up.

She smiled faintly. "Oh, Fumiko, how is she?"

"She looks well, different though—she's dressing like an American now. She has a job in a restaurant, did you know?"

"Yes, I heard something like that."

I detected a note of disapproval in her voice. "Maybe there were no nurse's jobs," I offered.

"The money in the restaurant business is good. A lot better than nursing."

"What do you mean?"

"Nothing," she said wearily, "nothing at all."

It wasn't like Yuka to be judgmental and I wondered what was affecting her. I realized how little I knew of what she'd endured during the battle.

Some weeks earlier, she'd told me how our parents had died. How mother and father had perished within twenty-four hours of one another, both from machine gun fire as they had fled south after the collapse of Shuri. Mother had died quickly. Father had taken longer, almost a day. Mother had been hit in the neck and died in father's arms. Father had been hit less than an hour later in the abdomen and the thigh. He had lain by the roadside as a convoy of hospital trucks went past. Old Mrs. Mita, the neighbor who'd seen it happen, said she'd tried to get a truck to stop so a medic could attend to him, but he was just one among a sea of wounded and dying. None did. Father had lived throughout the night—she didn't know how, considering the seriousness of his wounds—and had died stoically the next afternoon, with no word of complaint on his lips. I wanted to find this woman and squeeze the whole truth from her, demand to know every detail of his passing, but Yuka told me Mrs. Mita had died from a mortar blast shortly after meeting Yuka.

No one knew what had become of our brothers. They had been conscripted into the Blood and Iron Brigade and sent to Kochi. Neither had been heard from again. Their wives and children had gone north to Motobu, but that was all the information we had. We never found them, despite searching for over a year.

Yuka had served as a student nurse in Haebaru, the main hospital cave complex near Shuri, but more than that she would never tell me. I lit a lamp and sat beside her, taking her hand in mine. "Tell me what happened to you, Yuka."

"There is nothing to tell," she said bleakly.

"It might be good for you to remember."

"I can't," she said in the tiniest voice.

"I hear you crying at night. You shout terrible things in your sleep. Let me share your sorrow."

"You've suffered too," she said.

"I'm strong now," I promised, squeezing her hand.

She was silent for what seemed like an age. Then tears began. She cried for so long that I thought she would never stop. I held her as she shook, her small body a bag of bones in my arms. Then she began speaking in a whisper.

YUKA'S STORY

Over two hundred young women joined the Maiden Lilies Corps. We were all so very proud. We couldn't have been prouder. We were going to help the young heroes who were fighting the foreign devils. For women to be allowed to serve the emperor this way—it was so modern, so exciting.

We were sent to the new military hospital in Haebaru. It was built deep inside a cave complex and was impregnable. Everything inside was shiny and new. It was filled with doctor-officers, nurses and student nurses like us from the Maiden Lilies Corps. There were just a handful of wounded men inside and our tasks were very simple. We brought them drinking water and emptied their bedpans. We didn't have proper bedpans but that didn't stop us. We improvised with old catering tins instead.

There was an officer, Lieutenant Saito, who visited us regularly. He was very handsome in his uniform, with a sword on his hip. He would tell us the news from the front and we would hang on his every word. He told us the Americans were in the north of the island and they'd had some easy victories, but the real battle hadn't begun yet. They were being lured south into a trap, where they would be crushed in a decisive battle that would change our fortunes in the war. We were all in love with the Lieutenant, but when he began flirting with one of the prettiest girls, we became jealous and no one listened to him any more.

Even when the bombings began, it wasn't so bad. When the first victims of fires and explosions came to the hospital it was shocking, but we had doctors, we had medicine. It all seemed somehow quite romantic. We knew our soldiers would soon make the Americans pay a hundred times over and the horrors would be ended once and for all.

The bombardment became constant. It was our job to fetch water and supplies from outside and the American pilots began using us for target practice. Several girls were wounded. A bomber scored a direct hit on the complex and there was a cave-in. Two of my school friends were trapped inside. It took seven hours to recover their bodies. It was so strange. Mariko looked completely unscathed—she must have died of suffocation—while Sakae was unrecognizable except for her hairband. It was the only way to identify her.

When the Americans attacked Kakazu Ridge, the hospital was swamped with wounded and dying. Trucks filled with new casualties arrived every hour. We soon ran out of space and supplies. The floor was swimming in blood and puss and filth. It was impossible to get clean. Men with terrible wounds were left lying on the muddy ground. There was no morphine for them. Their cries were pitiful. Some of them called out for their mothers. Some swore at us. Some raved while others begged us over and over to kill them. I couldn't bear it so I hummed to myself all day long and at night I stuffed cotton wool in my ears.

Patients with minor injuries began to die of dysentery and lockjaw. Their wounds became infested with maggots. Did you know maggots are actually good for wounds? It's true, they keep them clean, but they're agony for the patients. I can still hear them weeping in frustration whenever I close my eyes.

By the time Shuri came under attack, we couldn't accept any more wounded, and only high-ranking officers got to see a doctor. When the evacuation was ordered, there was no way to transport the patients. One of the doctor-officers gave out little packets of white powder which he told us to hand out. I didn't know what it was until someone told me it was cyanide. My patients begged me to take them with us, but all I could do was give them the powder and tell them to take it before they fell into enemy hands. Some of them thanked me so earnestly, as if I were a savior rather than a murderer. I wanted to stay with them, but I was too frightened—I wanted to live.

When we began the evacuation southward, we saw the impact of the war on the local people. They looked like ragged skeletons, wading in the mud and rain. Some were dragging themselves on their hands and knees, their eyes lifeless. They looked right through us like hungry ghosts. There was a group of them huddled near a truck, hoping to get food. I warned them not to stand there because the Americans targeted trucks but they wouldn't listen. Soon after, a shell landed nearby, killing a whole family and several others. One of the men burst into flames and ran into a river. He never came out.

I remember a woman with a baby on her back. She died instantly, but her baby was thrown into the air and landed in soft mud at my feet. It cried for its mother, "Anma, Anma!" I wanted to take it with me, but I couldn't. I walked away. Afterward I felt so guilty that I looked up to the sky, hoping for a shell to end my misery, but none obliged me. When I saw another baby, even smaller than the first, clinging to the teat of its dead mother, I couldn't leave it, I picked it up. It was a boy.

We were near a village where everything was made of stone. I took him into a deserted house and held him. He didn't even cry. It was only then that I heard the shriek of an approaching shell. I woke up much later to find myself buried under rubble.

I could hear voices somewhere above me and rescuers lifted me out. They had seen my hair sticking out from the rubble. I had barely a scratch on me. It was a miracle. I told them I'd had a baby with me, but they couldn't find him. I begged them to search deeper. They were shouting unknown words at me but I couldn't hear. My eardrums had burst from the explosion. They left soon afterward but I stayed to search through the rubble alone. I searched all day but never found the baby. Maybe one of the rescuers took him while I was still under the rubble? I don't know. I'll never know.

When I arrived at the hospital caves in Makabe, the doctor-officer examined me. There was nothing wrong with me, which was fortunate, since there was nothing they could do for anyone. He assured me my hearing would improve in time.

When the Americans arrived outside, Fumiko and I left through a small exit in the hills. We walked all day and hid in a cave with a lone Japanese soldier. He gave us a grenade so we could kill ourselves if the Americans found us. We thanked him for his kindness.

Next morning we went south, through an area of thorn bushes to the coral beach. People were walking out into the sea, as if searching for a way off the island, but there was none. We saw a family of eight throwing themselves from the cliffs.

An American boat patrolled the coast, urging us to surrender. They were using a loudspeaker, speaking in Japanese. Their accent was strange. They spoke like devils. We were hungry and desperately thirsty, but we didn't even consider surrender. We didn't believe them. Then we saw a Japanese soldier strip to his loincloth and swim out to the boat. The Americans pulled him inside. We were surprised when they didn't shoot him. He simply sat on the side of the boat in his underwear, his head bowed. The marines paid him no more attention. He was no longer a threat. They just continued with their message, urging us to surrender and promising food and water and medical care for those that did.

That night, flares lit up the sky like an eerie daylight. An artillery barrage to the south drove us back toward the stone village, or at least what was left of it. In the garden of what had been a fine house, we came across a couple having sex in the bushes. It seemed so surreal, we giggled like the schoolgirls we once were. Then a new flare lit up the sky and we saw it was a Japanese soldier having sex with a corpse. The girl's face was quite beautiful. I'll never forget her lifeless eyes, looking at us accusingly. Did she resent us for being alive? She had no right to—she at least was safe where she was, far beyond the degradation being visited on her, while we had more to endure.

Fumiko disappeared later that night. I don't know what she did, or where she went, but I think she gave herself up to the Americans, and I didn't see her again until recently, when we came to Koza.

GUSHIKAWA

"You have a letter, Kenichi," Yuka said, dropping the carefully written envelope in my lap. It was a note from Miyagi, informing me the address of his new home in Gushikawa, and the date of our first karate class.

On the allotted day, I hitched a ride in a truck driven by three Filipinos who had come to work on the construction projects that had sprung up all over Okinawa. I tried speaking English to them, but they understood less than I did. I guessed they might understand Japanese better, but had no wish to inflict the language of their hated former occupiers on them. I wondered why they had picked me up at all, and we sat in silence until the road took us into Gushikawa and they let me off on the main street.

It took me a long time to find Miyagi's home. It was in an old row of houses that nested between two squat concrete blocks thrown up by our new masters. I imagined the entire row would be demolished soon, and wondered where Miyagi would live then.

The dojo turned out to be a small yard of beaten earth beside the house. I noticed the fence had recently been patched up to make it a little more presentable and a little less visible from the alley outside. A group of eight or nine young men, little more than boys, were gathered in the yard. I didn't recognize a single face. One of them saw me looking in and hurried over with a grin, "You must be Ota San," he said.

"Yes," I answered, wondering how he knew me.

"Master Miyagi told us you would be coming," he said with a grin.

"Where is he?" I asked.

"He will come later. He told us you would be teaching first." I didn't know what to say. "We're very pleased you decided to come, Ota San," he continued. "We've been asking Master Miyagi to teach us karate for some time, but he has always refused. We're sick and tired of the Americans pushing us around in our own country, and no means of defending ourselves, no weapons. But that's the great thing about karate, isn't it? No need for weapons."

I stared at the young man. He was little older than I'd been when I had first trained with Miyagi. I looked around at the others. Some were even younger. There were also two older men, both painfully thin. I wondered if they had learned nothing from the war.

"Master Miyagi said you persuaded him to reopen his dojo," the young man said cheerily.

"Me?" I stared at him.

"That's what he said," the boy beamed. "We've prepared training implements according to his instructions," he went on, pointing proudly to the collection of karate equipment lined up along the fence. "We're going to build a makiwara too. Master Miyagi said you would tell us how."

Looking at their faces, I saw something that I hadn't seen for a long time—enthusiasm. A sense of hope. It had been so long since I'd seen it in my countrymen, I'd almost forgotten what it looked like.

"I will," I said, touched by their simple faith.

They were easy to teach. Miyagi's classes had always been carefully structured. I simply followed the curriculum studiously. I showed them how to use the equipment: the weights, the gripping jars, the stone hammer, the iron rings, and the kongoken. My own strength was pitiful compared to before the war, but the students didn't appear to notice. In fact, they were amazed by my ability. Soon they were all working hard on a conditioning circuit. Watching one of the smallest of them struggling to move the stone-hammer with two arms, I was filled with admiration for my brave young countrymen.

Finally, I showed them the basic stances of karate, just as I had been taught. Squatting low in the horse-riding stance, I felt my scarred muscles complain, refusing to stretch as they had once done so easily. "Lower," I ordered, squatting lower myself, ignoring the pain. We suffered together.

I was so immersed in my teaching that it took me a moment to notice Miyagi from the corner of my eye. I hadn't seen or heard him enter, but the gate to the yard was closed again. I wondered how long he had been watching. I called a halt to the class and we bowed to Miyagi, who returned our bow.

"*Onegaishimasu*," I said, a formal request to my master to teach us.

Miyagi accepted and stepped to the front. Standing before a class once more, he seemed different again. Still smaller and thinner than before, but there was a new rigor in his posture, a new firmness to the set of his jaw. He examined his new class slowly, looking at each new face in turn, a new light in his eyes.

He taught for an hour, then ordered the new students away, so only he and I remained.

"You are a good teacher, Kenichi," he said, and I felt a rush of pride at his compliment.

"I simply followed your methods," I replied.

"That is a good way to begin," he said with a happy smile.

"It's a great honor to teach these young men," I said, "but you have other students who are my seniors and far more qualified: Miyazato, Yagi…"

"Don't concern yourself with Miyazato and Yagi," he smiled. "They're already teaching elsewhere. You are here, now. Come. It's time for you to learn a new kata, one that will be good for your injuries."

That evening I learned a new kata called Seiunchin. Unsurprisingly it used the low horse-riding stance extensively. With its slow movements and deep breathing, each low stance had to be held for a long time before moving onto the next. I struggled to concentrate on the complex hand movements as my thighs burned in agony. When we changed to a more upright stance, I breathed a sigh of relief. My relief was short-lived. Seiunchin is a long kata—twice as long as any other kata I knew—and soon we were back in our low horse-riding stance. The pain, it seemed, would be interminable.

An hour passed before Miyagi was satisfied that I knew the basics. He left me to practice alone, returning half an hour later with a chair. He sat down to watch me. I had never seen Miyagi sit in the dojo before. He had always stood ramrod straight, or patrolled the edge of the training area, his eyes searching for the slightest error, the slightest lapse in concentration. Knowing what it must have cost him to sit before a student, I redoubled my efforts to perform correctly.

Finally, Miyagi invited me into his new home. It was tiny, little more than a hut, and I was saddened to see his family so reduced. I greeted his wife Makato, who wept silently when she saw me and went to fetch some refreshments, despite my protests. Miyagi's younger children had grown since I last saw them, their childish faces lost, changed forever by what they had endured. Mrs. Miyagi returned with refreshments and I knew she would be offended if I refused. We ate a few mouthfuls in a warm silence. Mrs. Miyagi didn't ask about my family. I imagine she didn't want to spoil the happy occasion. Her restraint made the silence all the more poignant.

Miyagi and I sat at a little table by the kitchen window and drank tea. He told me a little about my new kata, Seiunchin, explaining its background and purpose in a way he had never done before. I listened as he went into detail, conscious of the honor of being taken into his confidence, yet saddened by the words of tragedy that remained unsaid, words of parents and children, of brothers and sisters, words too painful to be spoken aloud. Karate was our salvation in more ways than one.

We didn't talk for long. Miyagi would have talked longer, but Mrs. Miyagi hovered in the doorway, and when Miyagi ignored her, she told him that I had to leave because I had to get back to Koza that night. Miyagi grew angry and spoke sharply to her, ordering her to stop interfering, but I could see he was exhausted and made my excuses shortly afterward. He walked with me to the main road and waited with me until I succeeded in hitching a ride back to Koza.

A Boat to Iejima

It was early on Sunday morning, and the only person on the street was an elderly street-sweeper. It was refreshing to walk in Koza without the American soldiers about. The street-sweeper was busy clearing all reminders of their presence and his cart was filled with crumpled cigarette packs, empty bottles, candy wrappers, and condoms from the night before.

I arrived outside the restaurant where Fumiko had a room on the upper floor, and waited. There was no sign of her. I watched the street-sweeper at work. He bent easily to collect the rubbish, and stood erect with a dignity uncharacteristic of such a lowly profession. I wondered what he might have done before the war. Perhaps he was a nobleman ruined by the conflict, or an officer of rank in disguise. I examined his face, but didn't recognize him. He'd never been in the command center in Shuri. Perhaps he'd commanded a brigade in the Motobu Peninsula in the north, where I was planning to go with Fumiko. If he'd been based there, I wouldn't have seen him. Maybe he was the last of his men left alive, playing out this lowly of existence to atone for his shame in avoiding an honorable death.

I called Fumiko's name softly from the sidewalk, not wanting to wake anyone by knocking. There was no response. I called again. Eventually her head appeared at the window, her hair disheveled, her eyes bleary. She signaled that she would be down in a moment. I continued to watch the old man working his way methodically along the street, determined to eradicate all trace of the invaders from his city. I felt a flush of guilt. My own pockets were filled with American supplies that Yuka had gotten for me from the air base, I didn't ask how: cigarettes, candy, chewing gum, and condoms that I hadn't asked for but that Yuka had given me anyway. I hoped I might make use of them later in the day.

Fumiko appeared in the doorway and looked at me expectantly.

"I thought we might go to Motobu," I said casually.

"What's in Motobu?" she asked in surprise.

"Nothing," I smiled, "just some quiet woodland and empty beaches. Maybe we can even get a boat to Iejima."

She considered it for a moment, then shrugged. "That sounds nice. Have you got a jeep?" She knew I didn't have a jeep, but I didn't want to spoil the mood by challenging her. "I thought we could hitch a ride."

"Okay," she smiled.

We caught a ride in a van as far as Nago, then walked for a mile before hitching a ride on an ox cart that took us to the north of the peninsula. The ox moved no faster than walking speed, but it gave us the chance to relax and chat in the back of the cart. We talked of growing up in Okinawa, the beaches where we had swum, the islands we had visited, the school trips we had gone on, laughing about the pranks we had played on our classmates, and they had played on us, taking care to steer clear of any mention of the war.

The cart dropped us off at Motobu town and we walked to the seafront. I hired a local boat in exchange for a pack of Lucky Strikes and sailed toward nearby Iejima. It was the first time I'd been in a boat since the night sailing and the storm, but this was the sea I had always known, returned to its natural green and blue, moving in slow swells and decorated with white tips where the wind was stronger, farther from shore. The day was pleasantly warm, the sky clear and blue. The boat was smaller than my father's had been, but reminded me of his, and of being at sea with him. I waited for the familiar stab of pain that accompanied any thought of my parents, but to my surprise, it was a good memory. My father was with me again. I felt a warmth I'd not felt for so long. I looked at Fumiko, wondering if she had noticed my changing emotions, but she was facing into the breeze, her eyes closed, thinking thoughts I would never know.

As we approached Iejima, an American patrol boat came toward us at full throttle and passed close by without slowing. Three sailors stared impassively into our boat. Their bow-wave rocked our little craft so violently that Fumiko screamed. I expected the Americans to turn back and interrogate us, but they didn't. Making Fumiko scream had been enough for them.

We moored on a deserted beach of white sand. The water was quiet during the midday lull in the wind. I stripped to my shorts and waded in up to my knees.

"Do you like it here?" I asked.

"I love it," Fumiko said, joining me.

"Then come in," I urged her, falling backward into the welcoming water. "Cool down. The water's fine."

"I can't remember the last time I swam," she said.

Myself, I could remember all too well. It had been escaping from the patrol boat at Mabuni caves, but I didn't want to think of that now. "Then it's been too long," was all I said.

"I don't have a swimming costume," she protested.

"You don't need one. There's no one here but us."

"There's you!" she said with a frown.

"No there's not," I said, disappearing under the surface and staying under for some time. When I emerged she was laughing. "Turn around," she ordered.

"I'll do better than that."

I took a deep breath and dived again, this time swimming far out into the cool embrace of the deep. By the time I emerged again, Fumiko was in the sea, her skirt and blouse left on the sand. She swam out to join me and we floated on our backs, as weightless as two sand flies resting on the ocean's surface.

When we returned to the shallows, I lay in the little breakers as they sloshed onto the beach, while Fumiko remained a few feet away in the deeper water. As the waves broke around me, I rocked from side to side. "Arhh, the waves!" I screamed, mimicking her earlier cries when the patrol boat had passed us.

"Oh, you are wicked, Kenichi!" she cried furiously, splashing me over and over.

"How can an Okinawan girl be afraid of waves?" I asked between gasps.

"Those were not proper waves. Those were foreign-devil waves!"

"Oh, I see," I nodded, coming closer to her despite the splashing. "You have a point. I didn't think of that."

"No you didn't!" she said, splashing me ever more furiously, until I seized her by the wrists and held her hands down by her sides. She struggled to release them but I was too strong. Finally, she went limp and looked away in exasperation.

"Okay, I apologize, it was very wrong of me to say such things."

"You're not sorry!" she said.

"Yes I am," I said, slowly releasing her wrists and drawing her to me.

"Are you?" she demanded, turning to me.

"Yes."

I kissed her and for a moment she responded. Then she pushed me away hard and I fell back into the water.

"I don't believe you," she yelled, laughing now, as I flailed in the waves, then splashing me again as I emerged from the water. The water went into my eyes, but even so I caught a glimpse of her nipples and the dark triangle of pubic hair showing through her wet underwear.

"I'm getting out now," she said.

"Okay," I said, turning away so she could get dressed. When I joined her, I noticed her blouse was wet around her breasts.

"I'm thirsty," she said, bending forward and wringing out her hair. It was short now, little more than shoulder length. It wouldn't take long to dry.

"I have water in my bag," I offered.

"You don't have any soda?" she asked, shaking her hair and brushing it off her face.

"No, but I have candy, if you like. And some rice-balls."

I laid out what I'd brought and we shared it happily, then lay back and dozed side by side in the sun for a while.

"What shall we do now?" she asked lazily.

"I can think of something," I said.

"What," she asked innocently.

I rolled over slowly, until I was on top of her. She seemed surprised, but didn't resist. We kissed for a while.

"What if the patrol boat comes by?" she asked.

"It won't."

"But what if it does?"

I looked around. There was a palm grove at the end of the beach. "Come," I said, standing and offering my hand. She took it and I helped her up. We went into the welcome shade of the trees. The wind had dropped, as it often did at midday. The heavy air smelled sweet, with a hint of spice. The waves licked the shoreline gently.

Fumiko sat on one of the sloping palms that stretched low across the sand. I stood between her thighs and kissed her. Her lips were warm, soft, and yielding. I felt the tip of her tongue probing my mouth and I pushed mine into hers. She accepted it. Her hands pulled hard against my back, drawing me to her. I slipped my hand between her legs and her thighs parted oblig-ingly. I broke off our kiss for a moment to remove her panties and slipped a finger inside her. Her eyes closed and she began to moan as my finger moved inside her, exploring her. I felt her wetness descend, and soon her cries were so loud that I feared she would attract attention and someone might think I was attacking her. I covered her mouth with my hand and she bit hard into my flesh. Her hands gripped my wrist, urging me to go harder, faster. Her arousal excited me like never before. I barely had time to put on a condom and enter her before climaxing.

I looked into her eyes, there was a moment of awkwardness, and then she slipped out from under me. She put her panties back on quickly and headed back for the beach. I followed her, buttoned my shorts as I did, wondering at her total abandon. When I'd looked into her eyes a moment earlier, her gaze had been so far away. When her focus returned to me, she'd looked at me in surprise, as if seeing a complete stranger. I wondered where she'd gone to in her mind.

"What do you want to do now?" she asked. "Do you want to go back?"

"No," I said in surprise, "do you?"

"Not really."

"Let's walk along the beach," I suggested.

"Fine."

We collected our things and I took her hand. The sand was hot, so we walked in the shallows, stopping now and then to collect a brightly colored shell. We saw a flying fish streak across the surface. Fumiko clapped her hands in delight, and for a short while, we might have been on Okinawa before the war. Then we came across a scattered pile of shell casings, half buried in the sand.

We made love once again in a tiny sheltered cove. Fumiko was so wild that I could barely hold her, her eyes screwed shut, her lips parted. She thrashed beneath me, urging me on with language I didn't know she possessed, and when we'd finished she opened her eyes and looked around in surprise, taking a moment to recall where she was. I wanted to lie beside her and doze in the warm breeze, but Fumiko was restless and wanted to walk despite the heat. We walked further around the island, and made love a third time, Fumiko as frantic as before.

After returning the boat to the harbor in Motobu, we hitched a ride back to Koza in a truck driven by a marine who dropped us off on the main strip, not far from Fumiko's room.

"I can walk back from here," she said, "but thank you for a lovely day, Kenichi. I enjoyed myself so much, really I did."

"It's okay, I'll walk with you," I said. "It's no trouble."

"There's no need."

A group of black GIs was talking and laughing loudly outside one of the bars. "I insist," I said, taking her by the hand.

"Do you think black soldiers are more dangerous than white soldiers, Kenichi?" Her tone was light, but I sensed a certain weight behind the question.

"I don't know," I shrugged. "Perhaps. I don't know much about them."

"Well I heard they didn't fight in the war," she said.

"There were some fighting units, but not in the marines, as far as I know."

I wondered at her interest in the black soldiers. She was watching me, waiting for me to say more. "Mostly, they were given other jobs to do," I continued.

"What sort of jobs?"

"Menial jobs like cooking or digging latrines and graves."

"You think they weren't brave enough to fight?"

I thought back to what I'd seen during the battle. "No, it's not that. They had dangerous jobs too, like delivering ammunition to the frontline troops and carrying the wounded off the battlefield. I'd say they were brave enough."

"But they didn't shoot guns?"

"None that I saw. Why do you ask?"

"Then the black soldiers didn't kill anyone."

"Maybe not, but only because their superiors didn't trust them with guns."

"You think they wanted to kill people?" she asked, and I noticed an edge to her voice.

"I don't know. I have no idea what they think."

"Really?"

"No."

"You can't imagine?"

"No, and why would you imagine that I could?" I asked, bewildered by her questioning. I had nothing in common with the black soldiers.

Fumiko didn't answer and we continued arm in arm in silence. I noticed new garbage on the streets that hadn't been there in the morning. The old street-sweeper would have more work to do tomorrow. The silence between us continued until we reached her room above the restaurant, where the dark glass window made it difficult to see what was happening inside. We stopped by the entrance and Fumiko extracted her arm gently.

"I had a good time today, Kenichi," she said cheerfully.

"Me too," I nodded, "It was fun."

"Yes, it was a good idea. Iejima was lovely."

"I thought so too," I said, suddenly sorry that the date had somehow ended on a sour note.

"Thank you so much," she said with a smile, but she didn't kiss me. She turned and disappeared quickly through the entrance before I could ask her for another date. I watched her shapely legs dancing lightly on the steps and wondered what had just happened between us.

As I began to walk toward my room, two black GIs ambled past, each with a local girl on his arm. The girls were deeply tanned and I noticed, to my surprise, that they had braided their hair close to their scalps to resemble black women. I found it doubly strange, since dark skin was traditionally considered inferior, and Okinawan women, who were naturally darker-skinned than Japanese, had usually done everything possible to keep out of the sun.

A cooling evening breeze was blowing now across the central plain of the island, uninterrupted by the hills to the south. I was almost home when the implication of Fumiko's questions hit me—that as an Okinawan, I should empathize with the black Americans because we'd been treated similarly by the Japanese during the war. I found the idea preposterous. The situation was entirely different, and walking back to my room,

I thought of all the many reasons why it was so different. Yet by the time I'd reached my door, I'd come to the angry realization that there was more to Fumiko's point than I cared to admit.

A GAME OF GO

Miyagi's new students had been busy. Since he would still accept no money for his tuition, his house had been repainted and refurbished since my first visit. Mrs. Miyagi must have registered my surprise as I looked around the new interior. "The local people have been very kind," she explained. "Nothing is too much trouble when it comes to the great Sensei Miyagi. Such luxury! It's almost as if we were back in the old times."

"Almost," Miyagi smiled, "especially now that I have also managed to obtain a game of *Go*." I saw a board had been laid out on a kitchen table by the window.

"Shall we play?" he asked.

I accepted happily. It was a great privilege to play with Miyagi. I took a seat and reached for my pieces, but Miyagi's hand snaked out with astonishing speed and caught my wrist. He turned my hand upside down. The yellow staining of nicotine was faint but visible on my fingertips. It was a bad habit I'd picked up during the war. He didn't say anything, but his disapproval was all the incentive I needed. I quit that day and never smoked again.

We played our first game in silence. I lost quickly, no match for Miyagi. During the second game, Miyagi began to probe gently into what I had done during the Battle of Okinawa. I started at the beginning, from standing on the battlements of Shuri Castle and watching the American landing. I told him of Colonel Mita on Sugar Loaf Hill and my fight with the dark American. I told him of the conflict between Yahara and Cho, and of my role in the death of General Ushijima. I told him how I had escaped from Mabuni and found Yuka, and how we had been trapped in the cave and captured.

Then Miyagi told me his story, how he had led the families from the cave in Henoki, and how the interpreter had given him a candy bar. He reported it all in a matter of fact way, but I sensed he was keeping his emotions in check. I wondered what it had cost him to surrender so meekly to the enemy.

"You acted correctly," I said bleakly, "and I got it wrong. I could have gotten my sister killed."

"Don't be too hard on yourself, Kenichi. I was unsure about what I did. It was only worth the risk to spare the innocents in the cave."

"You did them all a great service."

"Did I?" he laughed hollowly, "Now we must all live with the indignity of defeat. It is a bitter pill to swallow."

"Sometimes I think it would have been easier to have died in battle with the emperor's name on my lips," I said quietly, thinking of Colonel Mita on Sugar Loaf Hill. His soul was happy now, his duty done, performed to perfection without the slightest blemish on his character. His spirit could take its place with pride at the Yasukuni Shrine along with the warriors of the past.

"It is our way to endure hardship, not turn from it," Miyagi said, knowing my thoughts, as always. "And now there is much work to be done."

I waited, the game of *Go* forgotten. He picked up a *Go* piece from the board and turned it over in his fingers. I felt he wished me to ask what that work was, but I dared not. I was afraid of the answer. In the end, he continued, "In China there are countless fighting arts: Shaolin Fist in the north, White Crane in the south, tai chi, pakua, and hsing-I from Wudang. In Japan there are also countless martial ways: kendo, iaido, jiu-jitsu, aikido, judo. In our tiny island, there is one art to rival all of these. There is karate. Karate is our cultural heritage, unique to Okinawa, and I have come to believe it must be passed on, not only to our children, but to the whole world."

He continued to turn the *Go* piece in his fingers.

"Even to the Americans?" I asked.

He looked up from the board and stared hard at me. For a moment I feared I'd angered him, but if he was angry, he held it in check. "One day, when I'm gone."

"A long time in the future, then," I said lightly.

"Not so long," he answered softly.

"Master?" I waited, holding onto the bitter silence, unwilling to hear the words I knew were coming.

"My health isn't what it was," he began.

"The war has taken its toll on everyone," I cut in quickly.

"I know my own body, Kenichi," he said with a thin smile, "My ki is weak. It can't be restored through medicine or strengthened through exercise. I am learning to accept this, and you must too. Only one thing gives me strength to continue and that is the thought of passing my art onto the world."

I wanted to speak, but the words refused to surface.

"Time is short," he continued. "The focus of our training must change if I'm to pass on my knowledge before I go."

"It will take a lifetime to pass on what you know."

"My knowledge is contained in the kata. The entire knowledge of karate is contained in the kata. There are twelve in our system. I will teach all of them to you. It doesn't matter if you don't understand them now. One day you will. Just retain them as they are. In time, their secrets will be revealed to you."

An Orange Soldier

Miyagi taught me his kata, and I worked diligently to learn each one. When I asked to learn the meaning of a movement, he would demonstrate his brutal techniques with a power that belied his failing health, smashing my ribs, tearing at the tendons of my elbow or shoulder, knocking me unconscious with a swipe to the neck, or slamming me into the hard earth, until I dared ask no more questions.

At other times, I continued to teach Miyagi's new students. They built two sturdy makiwara in the yard according to my instructions, and the thuds of their strikes grew louder each week as their hands grew accustomed to the blows.

It must have been the off-beat rhythm of the two makiwara being struck that attracted an unwanted visitor to the yard. His intrusion began with a knocking at the gate, which I ignored, but the knocking returned the next day and didn't stop. No Okinawan would knock so persistently—they would know that to train with Miyagi would require an introduction, or at least a respectful approach at the right time and in the right manner. It could only have been a foreigner.

Sure enough, I heard an American voice outside, asking in faltering Japanese that we open the gate. I replied in Japanese that we didn't understand.

"Are you training in karate?" he asked in his laughable Japanese. Again, I said we didn't understand, and eventually he went away again. I thought nothing more of it until, several hours later, it was time to go home. I stepped out of the yard and found a tall, gangling American waiting in the alley. His red hair had been bleached orange by the sun and the freckles on his broad face had joined into one across his nose.

"Konichiwa," he said with a smile and a stupid bow.

I held my hands wide, a pained expression on my face, "No speak Ingerish, soh soh-rry!"

He made another attempt at Japanese, saying he had heard of karate and wished to learn. I waved my hands and shook my head, saying I didn't understand in a dialect so broad that only a local would be able to follow me. He tried again. I had to admire his persistence, but I wouldn't be moved. I waited for him to finish—it wasn't a good idea to be rude to our new masters—then apologized once more.

"Thankrou very much," I repeated dumbly, over and over, hoping he would give up and leave. He shook his head with a smile. He guessed I was stone-walling him. "Maybe later?" he said cheerily.

Two days later, when I arrived to unlock the gate to Miyagi's yard, he was there again. My students were also waiting in the alley and it seemed he had been trying to talk to them. They were making fun of him in an Okinawan dialect he could never hope to understand. He smiled benevolently, knowing he was the object of ridicule. Something about that smile touched me, and when he followed me into the yard, I didn't stop him. The other students looked at me in outrage, but I ordered them to begin their training. The orange soldier watched them go to work, his eyes alive, darting from one to the next, trying to drink in all the things they were doing at once. I was reminded of my own fascination with karate that had begun so long ago, a passion that had been nurtured by Miyagi and continued to this day, and to my surprise, I no longer saw a foreign soldier, an American, an enemy. I saw only a young man enchanted by karate.

I told to him to wait and went inside to speak to Miyagi before I could change my mind. Miyagi was writing at his kitchen table by the window, his head bowed close to the paper. He looked up, his forehead still creased in concentration, his eyes struggling to refocus in the dim light.

"There's a young man who wishes to join the class," I told him.

"Who is he?" Miyagi asked with a frown.

I realized I didn't know the American's name. "I forgot to ask," I said.

Miyagi's frown deepened.

"He just appeared outside," I continued. "I think he heard the makiwara and decided to look in."

"Where is he from?" Miyagi asked.

"Kadena, I imagine," I answered.

Miyagi blinked slowly before speaking. "If a young man comes to us with no recommendation for his character, then we're forced to use our judgment. In this case, it's you who will be his teacher, so I'll leave it up to you."

Miyagi hadn't understood the significance of Kadena.

"Not Kadena village," I explained, "Kadena airbase. The young man is American."

Miyagi's face darkened ominously. "I am surprised at you Kenichi, that you would trouble yourself and me with such a request."

"I apologize, Master," I said quickly. "I will send him away immediately."

Miyagi returned to his writing without another word. As I left the room, I heard a slow output of breath leave his body.

The American was waiting where I had left him, still watching the others in their training. His expression brightened when he saw me.

"Miyagi Sensei so sorry, not possible karate! Not possible. So sorry!" I said quickly.

"Thank you for asking," he said in his stilted Japanese, bowing courteously, and to my surprise, he left without further argument.

After the class, I went back inside to see if Miyagi was angry. If he was, he didn't show it. However, he didn't invite me to stay and play *Go*, and Mrs. Miyagi kept a studied distance from the kitchen. Miyagi leaned back in his chair and smiled, though his eyes didn't, "Don't trouble yourself about the Americans, Kenichi," he said.

"I'm not troubled," I reassured him "It's just that, well, he was the first, but he won't be the last."

"You wish to teach him?" Miyagi said, his voice rising incredulously.

"Not especially," I answered quickly, "but the Americans are here to stay."

Miyagi glared at me, his eyes aflame, "The Americans don't have the right spirit for karate."

"This one seemed quite determined," I said.

"How do you know if he was determined?"

"He came three times, asking to train," I said.

"Three times?" Miyagi said icily.

"I thought…" I began, but he cut me off.

"The Americans might be determined, but only for a short time. They grow bored quickly. Karate isn't for them."

"Karate is for the whole world," I said, shocked at my sudden boldness in repeating Miyagi's own words back to him. He glowered furiously. I'd gone too far. I looked away but didn't apologize. Sooner or later, it was an issue we would need to confront.

Miyagi was silent. Despite his anger, he knew that what I was saying was true. "One day, maybe," he said quietly, "but not in my lifetime."

"As you say," I nodded firmly. Miyagi regarded me silently. I couldn't see his features in the deepening shadows, but I sensed their brooding menace. I bowed and left without another word, feeling his glare boring holes in my back as I slipped through the door and out into the yard.

I hitched a ride back to Koza, but I didn't go to my room. Instead, I walked on the main strip, watching the Americans. Their faces had changed since the end of the battle. These were not faces of the combat troops who had destroyed the 32nd Japanese Army. Those faces, hard-boiled by the horrors of war, had left the island, posted to new areas of conflict or returned to the United States to receive medals and be with their loved ones.

These were fresh faces, the endless supply of eager, ignorant youth, the lifeblood of every army. These eyes didn't share the same memories of what had occurred on the island. They regarded us simply as a defeated foe that needed to be kept in line. We were an endless procession of funny little *Nips* that cleaned their rooms, washed their clothes, served their food. Our cute little children milled around outside the wire fences of their bases and watched wide-eyed as they sped past in their cars.

I found myself across the street from the restaurant where Fumiko worked. I didn't go in. Instead, I stood in the shadows, watching the soldiers going in and out. The outer door was propped open. I watched a local girl and a serviceman emerge from the restaurant and go upstairs together. I waited, wishing I still smoked, pacing up and down until I saw Fumiko come down the stairs, closely followed by a tall black soldier.

They stood out on the street talking for a short while, and then he put his hand on her hips and squeezed her buttocks. She laughed and pushed him away in mock surprise, as if some maiden aunt might see her from an upstairs window and berate her. The soldier seemed to take this as a challenge and pulled her closer. She screeched and beat his chest with her tiny fists. He leaned down, demanding a kiss. She refused. He wouldn't release her until she did. Eventually, she complied.

"Hello Fumiko," I said, standing beside her now.

"Kenichi!" she said, her eyes wide, "I didn't know you were coming."

"I can see that," I said.

"This brute thinks he can take liberties," she said quickly, "just because he comes to our restaurant."

"If he pays enough money, I guess he can." I stared at her, waiting for her to answer, but the soldier spoke instead.

"What's up with this guy, Coco? Is he your brother or something?"

Fumiko ignored him. "You should have told me you were coming, Kenichi."

"Should I? What difference would it have made?"

"Hey leave it out, man," the soldier said, stepping forward and placing his hand on my chest.

I could have broken his arm, snapped it at the elbow like a dead tree branch, I could have struck him so hard that he'd be unconscious before hitting the ground, but there was no anger in me—only bitterness at my own stupidity. I ignored him and looked instead at Fumiko. If my words had hurt her, the pain had already passed. Her eyes looked through me, seeing a thousand yards past me. She was untouchable now, beyond all feeling, beyond all pain, and for a moment I envied her. She was truly free.

I turned and left without another word. I heard her say my name, her tone matter-of-fact, as if she'd forgotten to tell me something before leaving. I didn't answer or look back. I heard the soldier say something, which she ignored. I couldn't hear what.

"Kenichi," I heard her call a final time in a voice even more devoid of emotion. If she'd screamed and cried, or run after me, if she'd pleaded, or if she'd shouted at me furiously, I might have stopped, I might have turned and gone back to her. I might have forgiven her. I wanted to. But whatever she felt for me, some yearning for some remembered happiness, some lost innocence, it wasn't what I needed now. I continued without a word or a backward glance and cursed myself for my own stupidity.

TURNING PALMS

In the weeks that followed, I busied myself with karate training and tried to forget about Fumiko. Miyagi obliged me by teaching with a renewed sense of purpose. Despite the speed with which he was teaching the new kata, he wouldn't accept a single error in my performance. There was no time for a game of *Go* by the kitchen window. Instead, I spent every spare hour of the evening repeating the kata over and over, and many more hours at home, until I knew each new movement in my bones.

Miyagi corrected me mercilessly, and I left the yard each night feeling like a beginner all over again. He was never satisfied with my performance. Even the occasional words of encouragement that I'd enjoyed as a boy were no longer heard. Instead, I sensed his struggling to keep the frustration from his voice when he spoke.

I wondered if the incident with the American visitor had anything to do with his new coolness. It wasn't like Miyagi to bear a grudge. He was the most gracious man I knew, but the war had wounded him deeply and I had reopened that wound. I felt guilty and redoubled my efforts to learn his kata to his satisfaction. Several times I left his yard so late that I was unable to hitch a ride back to Koza and dozed by the roadside until the dawn traffic appeared on the highway.

When I was finally able to perform a kata to his satisfaction, we moved immediately onto the next. I was deeply troubled by such a swift progression. I hadn't even begun to feel comfortable performing one before moving onto the next, let alone feel I might one day master that kata, but I dared not complain, knowing the reason for Miyagi's haste.

Each new kata had a new name that held a new significance. Most were Chinese in origin, with names based on Chinese numerology—*thirty-six, eighteen, thirteen*—with a meaning I could only guess at. When I pressed Miyagi, he was evasive, and when I suggested my own interpretations, he rarely commented one way or the other. I had the feeling he was leaving me with a giant puzzle to unravel when he was gone.

The months passed quickly, taking us through autumn and winter and into the brooding skies of the typhoon season. As my knowledge of the kata grew, Miyagi seemed to diminish, spending more time each day teaching from his chair, rising only occasionally to demonstrate a new sequence or correct a movement. We spent all of spring learning a particularly long kata called *Suparinpei*, the last of the kata handed down by Miyagi's master, Higaonna. The monsoons had made the ground soft and muddy underfoot and my feet slipped constantly. I cursed to myself as Miyagi watched me slip and slide in the mud, his mouth turned down in disapproval. The wet ground churned up quickly under my feet, making changes in direction impossible to execute with any elegance or power. I struggled to simply remain on my feet. When I performed the high crescent kick in the final sequence, I kicked mud up into my eyes, blinding myself momentarily. I continued, blinking furiously, determined not to give Miyagi more reason for complaint, performing a jumping front kick and finishing with the traditional return to a ready-stance and bow.

I wiped the mud from my eyes and glanced at Miyagi. My kicks had sprayed dirt over him. He stood slowly, ignoring the dirt, and corrected a small aspect of my hand position in one sequence before leaving me to practice alone.

By summer, the rain clouds had receded and the ground had returned to its hard-baked form. I could step and kick without fear and grip the ground with my toes. The good weather seemed to lift Miyagi's spirits and he watched me perform Suparinpei, over and over, without comment or correction. The next day he had me perform all the kata one after the other, and when I'd finished, he rose from his chair and stepped toward me.

"*Hai,*" he said briskly.

This simple "yes" was all he ever said when I had performed a kata to his satisfaction. It signaled acceptability rather than praise. Nevertheless, from one who expected nothing short of perfection, it was high praise indeed. He had said "Hai" to all of my kata. I felt the thrill of reaching the summit of a high mountain after a long and fearsome climb.

"There is one more kata I must show you," he said with a smile.

My heart sank at the thought of another kata to battle with, but another part rejoiced at seeing Miyagi smile for the first time in so many months.

"This one is quite simple. It is called *Tensho,* which means *turning palms.*"

Miyagi rose from his chair and pressed one palm on top of the other before him in preparation. Even as he stepped forward and his arm snaked out, describing an inside curve and then an outside curve, I sensed there was something unique about this kata. His stance was firm and rooted, but his hands flowed in powerful circles and straight lines, drawing their power from his body like the limbs of a supple tree.

"Follow," he ordered. I stood beside him and aped his movements. Within five minutes, I had learned Tensho. Miyagi returned to his chair and watched me perform it several times, correcting only occasionally and calling out instructions from his seat. When I had corrected these small details, he told me to stop, a half-smile on his face.

"Good, you're learning quickly Kenichi, picking things up easily now."

I didn't know what to say.

"What do you think of Tensho?" he asked. The half-smile was still there, but the seriousness of his question wasn't lost on me. Miyagi had never asked my opinion before. I hesitated, unsure what to say, my mind groping for some insight that might satisfy him. "It seems different to all the rest," I ventured cautiously.

"Different in what way?" he demanded.

I shook my head, searching for the right words, "Like Sanchin, but softer, more flowing."

"Go on," he ordered, his eyes exploring mine, and I wondered if he could read the thoughts that I couldn't yet articulate. I sighed, exasperated at my inadequacy.

"What was in your heart when you performed it?" he asked suddenly. "Don't think. Just say!"

"Joy," I blurted out.

"Why?"

His eyes were boring into mine.

"I felt all my training coming together in the smallest movement," I said, then stopped, searching in vain for words to express what I'd felt deep within.

"Go on," he urged.

For many years I had believed there could be nothing more demanding than living up to Miyagi's exacting physical standards, but now his questioning filled me with a new sense of hopelessness. I was grappling with the deeper meaning of karate, attempting to fathom something that Miyagi said was as deep as an abyss. I felt myself teetering on its edge, reaching for something solid in a void and filled with a sudden despair as I realized that Miyagi wouldn't be able to fill it for me.

"Speak up, Kenichi," he smiled reassuringly, and suddenly my old master was back, if only for a moment, and I was a young boy, protected from the storm by the typhoon-man, delivered back to the safety of my home in his powerful arms.

"The techniques work on many levels," I said the words tumbling from my lips of their own accord. "In their basic form they are escapes from wrist grabs," I demonstrated as I spoke, showing the motions I was referring to, "but the same movements can be hooks, open-handed strikes and breaks using the palms and wrists."

"Hai," he nodded.

He was satisfied, but I didn't stop. There was more, much more. "On yet another level, it combines hardness and softness quite perfectly." Hardness and softness were the twin cornerstones of Miyagi's style, the ever-changing interplay of opposing forces that the martial artist must master. "If Sanchin kata is the root of power, this is its final exposition, taking power from the earth's core, using yielding and redirection of the opponent's force, then striking with the force of an iron whip."

I examined his face. He seemed thoughtful, but I could read nothing more from his expression. "Where is it from?" I asked finally. "I don't remember ever seeing it before. I have never heard you mention it."

"You like it?"

"Very much."

"It is my own creation," he said, watching my reaction with studied nonchalance.

I knew how Miyagi frowned on creating new kata, or even adapting existing ones. True, he had created two kata of his own before the war, but these had been designed with a specific goal in mind, to train a simple, some might say brutal, martial spirit in his students. Now, after a lifetime of karate, he had left a lasting legacy of his genius in Tensho. There was no need to hide my feelings. I was thrilled.

"It is the perfect union of your methods," I said.

"Why do you say that?" he asked.

"Before there was only Sanchin, which could be considered an internal kata. Now there are two," I mused.

"Beware of thinking too strictly about internal and external," he warned. "It is a distinction I use for beginners, to help them concentrate on one thing rather than two. In reality, all the kata combine internal and external training."

"Yes," I said, knowing it was true.

"What is internal?" he asked.

Again, my mind knew what it thought, but my clumsy tongue had no idea how to express it.

"Just say," Miyagi said, nodding encouragingly.

"With an internal kata, my concern is my own body. My rooting to the earth. My balance. The power of the ki flowing through my body and limbs."

"Your attention is directed internally?"

"Yes."

"And external?"

"With external kata, I picture my enemy before me. I imagine his attacks and my counters. I project my attention outward onto my opponent."

"Good. Very good. You've been thinking. But tell me, can a kata be both internal and external?"

I had never considered this before. "It depends how one decides to practice it," I began, hedging my bets.

"But can it be both at once?" he persisted.

I was at a loss. The idea of projecting my concentration both inward and outward at the same time seemed flawed, since only half would go in each direction, where total concentration was required.

"I would ask you to tell me the answer, but I know you won't," I replied.

"I will tell you," he corrected, "but I warn you, knowing it is irrelevant. Understanding it is what matters." He took a deep breath, preparing himself to divulge his answer smoothly without faltering, so I might grasp it more easily. "Internal and external, like hardness and softness, are Yin and Yang—opposites contained within the whole—as I have told you many times."

I nodded, hanging on his words, eager not to lose any part of his explanation. "At some point, it is important to leave all ideas of Yin and Yang behind—all issues of form and non-form. Only by transcending such concerns can you be at one with the universal Tao. That is the supreme expression of our art."

I tried to imagine the perfect kata, so perfect that issues of form were no longer of concern, where awareness of self and enemy were universal, seen from inside, outside, and all around at once. My mind struggled to even entertain the concept.

"I will try," I said weakly.

"Then you will succeed," he assured me.

"You think so?"

"I know it," he said seriously. "You are a seeker, Kenichi, like me, and they say that to seek is to find."

"I hope so," I said, happy that Miyagi should compare me even in some small way to himself.

"So you like Tensho?" he asked again, and I sensed my approval had real meaning for him. This time there was no need to think before answering.

"It is a masterpiece."

Miyagi held my gaze for a moment, then blinked and turned away quickly, "Good, come inside, Kenichi. Makato has been asking about you. She wants to see you, and it's been some time since we played *Go*. Do you think you can beat me yet?"

"I have a new strategy I want to try out," I told him, even though I hadn't.

"It won't work," he said without looking back.

"How do you know?"

"I know," he said, holding the door open for me to enter and waiting patiently until I had stepped inside.

When I got home, it was two hours after midnight, so I was surprised to find Yuka still awake. Her red eyes warned me of grim news even before she spoke, and I steeled myself for whatever it was.

"Fumiko has been raped."

I could think of no response. Yuka continued, reporting the facts as she knew them, as if informing a doctor of the status of a new patient. Fumiko had also been badly beaten and was in the hospital at Kadena airbase, where Yuka was working. Yuka had persuaded one of the American doctors to take a look at her, and after what he saw, he had called the military police. The case would be investigated. Charges would be pressed.

I told her I knew who it was—the tall black soldier whom I'd seen her with before. I turned to leave, struggling to keep the rage inside me, at least until I found him. "No!" Yuka cried, clawing at my arm to make me stay. "It was three white marines. They're saying it was a deliberate act to antagonize the black soldiers who hang out where Fumiko works."

"You're sure?"

"Yes."

"Then I need their names."

"I don't know them," she said, her voice cracking, "and even if I did, I wouldn't tell you. If you do something stupid, they'll kill you, you know they will."

"I won't do anything stupid," I promised her, icy calm now.

"Please don't Kenichi, I beg you," she sobbed, "I can't lose you. Not now."

"You won't," I promised. I took her in my arms and held her tightly, stroking her hair, reassuring her that I was calm, that she was right, that I would leave it all in the hands of the authorities—and all the while my mind racing, planning how to get their names, hunt them down, and destroy them.

THE WITNESS

There had been no problem in identifying Fumiko's attackers. She had given her own description, which in itself wouldn't have counted for much, but an American soldier had come forward as a witness and backed her story. His word had been taken seriously and three marines had been arrested.

I discovered the identity of this witness by chance. Yuka came home from the hospital in a rare state of excitement and drew up a chair close to mine. Her eyes shone with a purpose I'd not seen for a long time.

"Something so strange happened today," she said, "you will never guess. I was giving routine inoculations in the clinic. Charles was there—I mean Doctor Day," she corrected herself quickly. "He was the doctor who examined Fumiko. Anyway, he mentioned that one of the patients in the queue was the witness in Fumiko's case. I asked him which one and he pointed him out."

"What was his name?" I asked.

Yuka rolled her eyes. "It's very difficult to pronounce, but it sounds like *James O'Leary*."

I nodded for her to continue. "Anyway, when it was this man's turn for the injection, I smiled at him. He asked if the needle would hurt. I think he was trying to make conversation, practice his Japanese, so I told him to look away and he would feel nothing more than a scratch. He asked my name and we spoke for a while. He said he was from Ohio. He said he was interested in Okinawan culture and especially karate. I told him my brother was a karate-man who trains with a famous master in Gushikawa, and guess what he said?"

"Miyagi," I said quietly.

"Yes, but how do you know?" she demanded in surprise.

"This O'Leary, he's tall, with orange hair?"

"Yes."

"He came to Miyagi's garden dojo several times, hoping to train."

"You didn't accept him?" she asked.

"No."

I examined her face, searching for clues to her thoughts. Yuka knew the complexities involved, but I sensed she disapproved of our refusal.

"It was Miyagi's decision," I said lamely.

She smiled sadly. "This O'Leary seems like a good man," was all she said.

The next day I told Miyagi of Fumiko's rape and of the witness who had come forward. He nodded without comment, and I didn't press the point.

Two days later, he invited me to sit with him in his kitchen, at the table by the window. "I've been considering the future of karate," he said seriously, pausing to tap his fingertips on the table pensively. I waited for him to continue, wondering what he had to say that I hadn't heard countless times already. He adjusted the angle and position of his fingertips as he tapped, experimenting with the most effective way to strike with his fingers even then. "Karate is unique in all the world," he continued at last. "It is Okinawa's national treasure, the pinnacle of our cultural heritage." I nodded gravely. I'd heard him say this many times before, but he was speaking as if revealing some important news to me. "One day, karate will be practiced all over the world."

"I believe it will," I said dutifully.

"Not just in Japan, but in Europe, Asia, everywhere."

"That will be a great day," I said.

"If it is to be, we can't keep our training to ourselves, Kenichi."

I watched his face carefully to ensure I understood his meaning correctly. "You wish to recruit new students?" I ventured.

Miyagi's face took on a pained expression. He had never once sought students in all his years of teaching. He had never advertised his dojo and had always fought to keep his ability hidden from all but his closest students. "If foreigners earnestly wish to learn karate, we should not refuse them."

"All foreigners?" I asked deliberately.

"All? Yes, of course all!" He glared at me accusingly, as if I'd been the one who had prevented the American from training with us.

"Hai!" I said, accepting the blame happily, knowing what it must have cost him to change his mind. He turned away. I found myself struggling to keep sudden tears from my eyes.

"Good, I am glad we are clear on that now," he said absently, "and now that you're here, perhaps you would like to play *Go*? Do you have a new strategy yet?"

"Yes I do," I lied.

"Better than your old one?"

"A lot better."

"Good, because your last strategy wasn't very successful," he said, taking the checkerboard from the nearby shelf and placing it carefully on the table.

"This one is different," I assured him.

"We'll see."

I saw the doubt in his eyes, and as I laid out my pieces, I knew another quick defeat was in store.

THE MESSAGE

I asked Yuka to deliver a message to James O'Leary, letting him know that our karate classes were now open to foreigners, but when she came home that evening, her eyes were red from crying. I knew something terrible had happened before she began. "O'Leary has left Okinawa," she told me, her voice heavy with resignation.

"What do you mean?" My mind was reeling with the implications, "Where has he gone?"

"Home, to America."

"What about the trial?" I said, my voice rising, knowing the answer all too well.

"With no witness, there can be no trial," she said quietly, "The charges against the marines have been dropped."

"How the hell could O'Leary leave?" I yelled.

"No one's saying anything," she insisted.

"But you know!" I said, seeing it in her eyes.

"Charles made inquiries," she said, her voice soothing, but it only made me more angry, "The official story is that he was posted back to the United States for his own safety. Unofficially, O'Leary was beaten up and stabbed. He's lucky to be alive."

My head was spinning. O'Leary had almost died and Fumiko's rape would go unpunished, and I was to blame for all of it. If I had stayed with her, tried to persuade her to give up her work as a prostitute, she might have listened to me. If I had taught karate to O'Leary he might have been able to defend himself.

"It's not your fault!" Yuka said urgently, "Don't do anything foolish. Promise me, Kenichi!"

"I won't," I said, rising from my seat, "not any more."

"Where are you going?" she cried, following me to the door.

"Don't worry, I'm just going outside. I need to think."

She gripped me by the wrist, her tiny hand surprisingly tight. "Be safe."

I put my hand on hers to reassure her.

Outside, I walked quickly in the cooling evening air. The rage inside me had to be controlled, concealed where it couldn't affect my demeanor. My actions had to be governed by a clear head. I walked until an icy calm descended into the core of my being and my mind was clear. There could be no mistakes. No evidence. No trace back to me. I was going to kill three marines—I just needed to figure out how.

First, I needed to discover their identities. Yuka would never tell me for fear of what I would do. I would have to find out another way. There was only one other person to ask and that was Fumiko, but she was still in the hospital in Kadena, and the air base was off limits to Okinawans.

I waited almost a week until Yuka had a day off and took her security pass. Dressed in the drab overalls of a base-worker, I held up her pass and looked the security guard straight in the eye. He waved me through without a word. One Nip looked the same as any other—male, female, boy, girl, it was hard to tell the difference. It took me half an hour to find the hospital and another twenty minutes of searching to find Fumiko, but on the way I had picked up a mop and bucket from an open cupboard and no one thought to challenge me.

She was alone in an empty ward. Her face still bore the faded yellow signs of bruising. She seemed small in the roomy bed, shrunken like an old woman. She took a moment to recognize me. Her eyes had lost their indifference. She had the look of a wounded animal, awaiting the hunter's final bullet. I sat on the edge of her bed, careful not to touch her.

"I'm sorry to hear about what happened to you," I said.

"Why are you here, Kenichi?"

"I need their names."

"Why?"

"So justice can be done."

"Justice can never be done."

"Tell me their names, Fumiko," I said, looking her in the eye.

"What's the point? We lost the war. There is only justice for the winners."

"We can make our own justice," I said firmly. "Just tell me their names and it'll be done."

"It has nothing to do with you," she said.

"Yes it does. Tell me."

"So you can have revenge for your wounded pride?"

"Call it what you like. Just give me their names."

She stared into my eyes and I felt her hatred for me, almost as strong as for the three marines. "I can't say them," she said at last, turning away in disgust.

"Say them!" I urged her, seizing her arm.

"I can't pronounce them!" she said, turning back suddenly, her face ugly with hatred. "I don't know how."

But you know them, you know their names?"

"Why are you so insistent?"

"Just tell me," I ordered.

When she spoke again, her voice was small and faraway. "They were written on patches that were sewn onto their uniforms. It was all I could think of when they were attacking me—they didn't even bother to hide their names."

"Can you write them down?" I asked.

Her eyes examined mine, searching for my motive. I didn't try to hide it. I wanted revenge. "Can you write them down, Fumiko?"

"I'll never forget them."

I handed her a piece of paper and she wrote each name in block letters, then drew a neat box around each, just as they'd looked on their army badges:

EVANS

NEWMAN

PIERCE

She hesitated before handing it to me. "What are you going to do?"

"Don't concern yourself with that."

"I don't want you to suffer any consequences for my sake."

"I won't," I promised, taking the paper from her, "Where are these men now?"

"Somewhere here, on the base," she answered, her voice quavering for the first time.

"Do you know which unit?"

She shook her head.

"I need to know what they look like. Can you describe them?"

"White. They were all white."

"I know—but more than that?"

"No!"

I didn't press her. "It's alright. I'll find out some other way."

"I know where they drink."

"Where?"

"The Red Rooster."

"I know it."

She bent her head, her face hidden beneath her unkempt hair. I wondered if she was crying. I thought of putting my hand on her shoulder, but didn't know how she would react. I kept my hand by my side.

"You shouldn't stay here," I told her, "not now that they've been released."

"I'm leaving tonight."

"Where will you go?"

"I have an aunt in Kerama."

I stood slowly. "Take care, Fumiko," I said awkwardly. She didn't look up. I didn't know what else to say. I waited a moment, in case she wanted to say something more, but she was silent. I left the room quickly, shamed by my callousness, my lack of patience, my inability to forgive her for what she'd become.

I walked through the hospital until I found what I was looking for, an office filled with piles of paperwork. Two American doctors were chatting happily with two nurses. None of them noticed the new base-worker who entered and collected a handful of mail from the post tray. I made my way over to the main barracks and walked through the corridors until I found an Okinawan man working in a cramped office. "Please can you help me," I said cheerily, "I have only started working here today and I'm hopelessly lost. The foreign devils have built an airbase that's bigger than a city!"

"You'll get used to it eventually," he chuckled, "The layout is very simply all straight lines and square blocks."

"The Yankees are not like our people!" I smiled.

"Our people prefer a little more variety," he agreed.

"There's been a mix up with the post. I'm looking for these three names," I said handing him Fumiko's list. He opened a file and leafed through the pages until he found one of the names, Evans.

"There are four people named Evans on the base," he said with a frown.

"I think they are all in the same unit," I offered hopefully.

He smiled and found the other two names quickly, confirming that all three soldiers were in the same barracks.

"How can you read their funny names so quickly?" I asked.

"Necessity," he smiled, "It's the only way to eat."

"The sad truth," I nodded. "Thanks for your help."

Outside the barrack room, I checked Fumiko's note a final time, committing the names to memory before tearing it into pieces and stuffing it into a wastebasket. I took up my mop and bucket and went inside. Most of the men were wearing vests, their uniforms hanging up or folded by their bedsides. I set about cleaning the floor, moving systematically from bunk to bunk, until I saw PIERCE on an army jacket hanging over the end rail of a bunk halfway down the room. The marine lying on it was short and dark haired, his skin as brown as mine, his face hard and pinched. On the bunk beside his, I saw the uniform folded on the chair had the name-badge NEWMAN. Newman was big, broad, with tight brown curls and a heavy brow. On the bunk beside his, I couldn't find any evidence of the man's name.

"Excuse me, you are Evans-san?" I asked the marine on the bunk.

"Who wants to know?" he asked, looking up. He was tall and lean-bodied, with glasses and blond hair, a long narrow face.

"I have a post-letter for you from USA," I said, grinning happily.

A post-letter?" he snorted.

"Ah, yessir."

He held out his hand.

"You are Evans-san?" I asked, keeping the letter back.

"Yes, I am," he said slowly, as if speaking to an imbecile, "so give me the goddamn letter!"

I handed him the letter and he scanned the address, then got up off the bunk and thrust it hard into my chest.

"This isn't my letter, you stupid fucking Nip!" he said.

"No?" I said astonished, checking the front of the letter with a frown.

"It says Edwards, not Evans!" he shouted.

I ran my finger under the name slowly.

"Why the fuck are you reading it when you can't fucking read?" he yelled.

The other marines began to laugh. I stared blankly at the letter, letting it feed the growing fury inside me, then left the room, their laughter still ringing in my ears.

THE RED ROOSTER

That evening Yuka and I ate together. Somehow, I didn't ask how, she'd managed to obtain bean curd and had made miso just as mother had once done. It was good too, as good as mother's, and I told her. She smiled, and for the first time in many months, I thought she looked truly happy. It had to do with more than miso, that much I knew.

"You have something to tell me, Yuka?" I probed.

"I do," she blushed, and for a moment she was my little sister again, standing by the hibiscus at the back of our house, watching the rough and tumble of her older brothers, too cautious to join in. "He's a doctor."

"An American?"

"A good man," she said quietly. "His name is Doctor Charles Day." She pronounced the name so clearly, I guessed she'd practiced saying it aloud many times.

"You've mentioned him before."

"Yes, and I'd like you to meet him."

I didn't answer. It seemed too fast, too soon. One minute the Americans had been bombing us, killing us in our hundreds and thousands, the next they were our friends, our providers, our lovers.

"It won't be easy for the two of you," I answered instead.

"It wouldn't have been easy for you to bring an American into your dojo."

Yuka was right. I couldn't argue with her. I had seen something in O'Leary that had transcended all matters of race, creed, and color. I had seen a man with the same passion as mine, the same heart as mine. "It wouldn't," I sighed.

"Then you'll meet him?" she asked eagerly. "You'll meet Charles?"

"If you insist."

"Thank you, Kenichi!" she said with relief. She looked into my eyes to try and gauge my mood. She was so happy that I couldn't be glum about it.

"I will soldier on," I sighed.

"With the warrior-spirit of Japan!" She chuckled mischievously, repeating a much-used wartime phrase, and we laughed together for the first time since I could not remember when. The last time we'd laughed together, we'd been little more than children.

I waited outside the Red Rooster in Koza. This part of the strip was lit by a solitary streetlamp and a row of neon signs that gave the street an unhealthy glow. It was still too bright for what I had in mind. I needed somewhere dark and secluded. I scouted out the area and found an alley around the corner from the bar that would be perfect.

I wanted to smoke, but I'd quit, and forced my hands to stay by my sides. I waited over an hour, keeping my breathing slow and deep to remain calm. When the first of the three marines emerged, I stayed in the shadows outside the arc of the solitary street lamp. I wanted them all together, one target, complete. It was Evans. Newman joined him a moment later and they lit cigarettes. Two *panpan* girls had come out with them. They waited, laughing and joking, until the door opened and Pierce emerged. He looked around, bleary eyed. His gaze rested on me for a moment and I thought he'd seen me in the shadows, but he looked away and joined his buddies.

While they were deciding where to go, I stepped from the shadows, my plan taking form as I approached. I walked past their group, muttering to the girls in our language as I went, "These are the three who raped that girl."

"Hey, what did that guy just say," Newman demanded.

"Which girl?" one of the panpan girls called after me, ignoring Newman.

"Fumiko Higa."

"We don't know any Fumiko Higa," she called back.

"He means Coco!" the other girl said.

"Yes, Coco," I said, turning.

"Hey, who's this fucking Nip?" Evans shouted, pointing his stiff fingers in my direction.

"You girls should both come with me now. You're not safe," I turned away again and continued down the street.

One of the girls broke away from the group and I could hear her heels clicking swiftly on the tarmac. "Are you sure it was them?" she asked, panting as she caught up with me. I looked back, ignoring her question, to see the other girl walking away in the other direction.

"Hey, where the fuck are you two going?"

It was Evans. He was coming after us. I took the girl's hand and wheeled her into the alley that ran down the side of the Red Rooster. It was dark, almost black, with only the dim glow of the club's low lighting coming from two small windows. "Run," I ordered. She didn't need to be told twice and set off at speed for the faint slit of light at the alley's end.

I looked around urgently, assessing the territory. There was a long arc of shadow to my right, behind a big garbage container.

It was too obvious. Instead, I moved in front of the container and crouched into a small triangle of shadow just before it.

Evans rounded the corner and saw the girl disappearing down the alley. He didn't see me. He called after her, ordering her to come back. He didn't even consider me a threat. It was a mistake.

I rose from the shadows and slammed a ridge-hand strike into his neck. He crumpled to his knees with a sigh. His head lolled forward. I seized it, my left hand under his chin, the fingers of my right hand around the back of his head. I thought of Fumiko's empty stare in the hospital and felt a charge of murderous fury load my hands.

"*Whatthefuck!*"

It was Newman, shouting, and he was almost upon me. He let fly with a punch. I released Evans' head and raised my forearm to block, my other hand already out, fingers tensed, seeking Newman's eyes in the darkness. We wrestled for a few moments. I felt my finger in his eye socket, and then he roared, clawing my hand away. He was strong. I felt him turning me expertly. He was a skilful fighter. He bent low to tackle me to the floor, but I threw my legs back to resist and hammered my fist into the side of his head. He released his grip and as he did, I aimed a knee at his face, catching him hard. He stood, wobbled, but didn't go down. I smashed a punch into the side of his head and then stepped through, placing my leg behind his and driving him to the ground with my elbow. Keeping hold of his hand, I stamped his head into the concrete. Newman didn't move after that.

I felt myself lifted suddenly into the air, my arms pressed so tight to my sides that I couldn't breathe. Evans had recovered and now he had me in a powerful bear hug from behind. Worse still, Pierce had realized what was happening. I saw his silhouette approaching at a run. I heaved with all my might to move my arms, but they were pinned by my sides. My feet were off the ground, I could draw no power from the earth. I flicked my heel back, up between Evans' legs, and heard him grunt in pain, but he squeezed me even harder. I threw my head back into his face and heard his nose crack. At the same time, I kicked forward, catching Pierce hard in the stomach. The force caused Evans to overbalance and his grip loosened as we fell. I twisted into him, keeping his body pinned to the floor with my hands. Pierce came at me from behind. My foot lashed out with a back-kick and I caught him in the groin. I heard him gasp, felt him crumple to the ground.

Evans gripped my lapels, attempting to pull me down. I snaked my hands over and under his grip and jerked free. I was still standing between Pierce and Evans. It wasn't a good position. I stepped away, looking at neither enemy, but getting a sense of both. Evans was scrambling to his feet, but Pierce was the greater threat. He was seething with rage from the two kicks and struck out at my head with his fists.

I sidestepped him, parrying his punch and driving my own fist into his face. I trapped his outstretched arm against my chest and turning, struck him on the back of his neck with the inside of my forearm. With the same movement, I propelled him into Evans. Now both my adversaries were before me. Pierce was dazed and stumbled into Evans' outstretched arms. Evans manhandled him out of the way and came at me. He was the tallest of the three and broad.

"The little fuck knows judo." He approached me more cautiously now.

I waited for him with my hands outstretched, offering him to grapple with me. He lunged forward to seize me with both hands. I slipped beneath his right arm, passing close to his body and ramming the inner ridge of my palm up into his groin. He doubled up and I kicked him hard across the face. He hit the floor unconscious. Now there was only one left.

Pierce stood ready to tackle me, his right hand forward. It took me a moment to realize why he was in this position—he had a knife. He slashed at me and in the darkness, the blade was an elusive glint, seen and then gone. I felt a hard blow across my hand, then another across my jaw—an inch lower and it would have been my neck. I didn't stop to think of the consequences. If I did, I knew I would falter, and hesitation was my enemy. He circled, I moved in, hoping to seize his wrist, but he was moving too fast. I sensed a change in direction and he thrust the knife upward toward my stomach. I crossed my arms before me and blocked two hard stabs, then seized his wrist with both hands.

He punched me in the face with his left hand, but I wouldn't release his knife-arm. He tried to pull back. I followed him, directing a fast kick between his legs. He grunted in pain, but was too pumped to feel its effects. I twisted and took the knife-arm high in both hands, aiming to bring it down hard over my shoulder and break it at the elbow. Pierce reacted quickly, circling away to escape the limb-break. I twisted the other way, using his movement against him and took his knife-arm over my other shoulder in a single arm throw. I felt the knife press against my stomach. It might cut me, but it wouldn't kill me. I raised my hips and Pierce flew over my shoulder, landing hard on the concrete. Still holding his arm at the wrist with one hand, I punched his head into the hard ground of the alley-way, and then wrenched his arm across my thigh. The elbow joint snapped with a loud pop. He bellowed in pain. I drove my forearm across the hand that held the knife, breaking his wrist, and the blade hung useless in his fingers. I took it and held it to his throat. He was still conscious. I could feel the tension in him, hear his harsh breathing as he prepared to die. He didn't plead or say a word. I guessed he'd faced death before. His silence made it easier. I pressed the blade into his skin, one quick draw and it would be done. I breathed in and prepared.

With that breath, I became aware of two hands resting on my shoulders. I wasn't startled. They weren't the hands of an enemy. They were familiar. Their heavy warmth infused my body, sending a gentle wave pulsing through my limbs and into my fingers. I eased the pressure on the knife. The hands worked their way down from my shoulders, feeling the condition of the muscle across my back, fingers pressing, testing, probing, the hands as hard as oak. They were the hands that had guided me since I was a boy. They held me by my sides, just below the shoulder, and lifted me to my feet. I released the marine and stood over him, breathing deeply to steady myself.

I could smell the scent of my teacher's body, the fresh sweat on his tunic, a familiar whiff of his hair tonic. I could hear his soft, rich voice muttering to himself, making notes on my condition, *Hmmm, yes... yes... strong...* The sequence for his testing was always the same and I knew what was coming next. His iron palm tapped my solar plexus twice, then slapped hard. Its weight was extraordinary. I gasped at its sickening power and struggled not to gag.

Pierce looked up at me in surprise. I threw the knife into the shadows and walked to the end of the alley. Then I ran.

HAWAII

The islands reminded me of home. I watched each one appear and disappear from the rail of the ancient tramp steamer. Like the Ryukyus, they resembled a length of knotted rope strung out across a limitless ocean, each jungle-clad peak a monument to the fury that had erupted long ago when the earth was still young. I tried to imagine the creation of these islands, the chain reaction exploding across the ocean like giant steps, hurling fire and water miles into the sky. It was difficult. The islands seemed so tranquil now, resting on the azure sea. Only the smoke from the ship's funnel reminded me of their fiery past.

The main island of Oahu came into view late in the afternoon, its jagged outline rising higher on the horizon as we neared Honolulu. The bustling port brought memories of Naha before the war, but Honolulu was larger and the ships more modern. Further west on the same coastline was the deepwater port of Pearl Harbor where, in one sense, the first shots of the Battle of Okinawa had been fired.

Miyagi had arranged everything. The tramp steamer was owned by one of his business associates. It plodded between Japan and America, stopping off in Okinawa and Hawaii on route. There was a sizeable Okinawan community in Honolulu who knew Miyagi and revered him. Before the war, he'd been invited to teach karate in Hawaii by a local newspaper and had stayed for several months touring the islands. I carried his letter of introduction in the single kitbag containing all my worldly possessions.

After the fight with the marines in Koza, I'd gone straight to his house and told him everything. He'd listened dispassionately as I relayed every detail, and when I'd finished, he had only one question: "What prevented you from killing the marine?"

"You did," I answered truthfully.

He didn't ask how. Instead, he reached out and put his hand on the back of a chair for support, his eyes never leaving mine. "You have fought and won the greatest battle of karate," he said in a low voice. "How does victory feel?"

"Hollow."

Miyagi gave a grim laugh. He'd eaten the same bitter fruit himself. He knew how much sweeter revenge would have tasted, how much simpler it would have been, how instantaneous. Forgiveness, in contrast, was a long drawn-out battle against self-doubt, a feeling of emptiness, and a sense of loss.

"Sit," he ordered, patting the back of the chair. "I have some contacts. I will make arrangements."

Within a week, I had a place on a ship bound for Hawaii. I said farewell to Yuka, promising I'd write as soon as I landed. I would miss her terribly, but I wasn't worried for her now. She was happy. She was in love with her American doctor and I knew she'd be safe.

When I went to take my leave of Miyagi, he greeted me with a certain formality. At first, I thought he was angry with me. He lectured me sternly in a way that reminded me of my early training with him, telling me of the importance of karate, repeating his mantra that it was Okinawa's unique cultural treasure. At the end of his speech, he said he had a task for me in Hawaii. I imagined it was to deliver something, a package or a message perhaps. In some ways, it was.

"You must open a dojo," he told me firmly.

I examined his eyes and saw he was completely serious. I wanted to protest that I wasn't qualified, but Miyagi had requested it, and it would have been pointless to argue.

"If you believe me qualified, then I will do my utmost."

"I do," Miyagi said, "and you must."

A contract had been signed between us. No pen or paper had been necessary. It had been written in something far more permanent, the blood and sweat of the dojo that flows from teacher to student, mingling on the hardwood floor.

With the business of karate taken care of, Miyagi poured two tots of *awamori* and we played *Go* and spoke long into the night. At dawn, a car appeared, to take me to Nakagusuku and the ship sailing for Hawaii. I took my leave of my sensei in just a few brief, inadequate words.

I never saw him again.

I was greeted in Honolulu by one of Miyagi's many admirers and taken to a small guesthouse. My room and board had been paid for in advance. I never found out by whom. A job at the shipyard had been arranged and a small dojo of Hawaiian hardwood had been earmarked for me. The Okinawans on Oahu had long memories and recalled Miyagi's pre-war visit well. They came to the dojo eager to learn. A group of eight young men helped me polish the flooring, build a *makiwara* in the yard, and create the traditional training implements of the dojo.

On the evening of my first lesson, standing before them as their sensei, I felt a fraud for teaching Miyagi's art so poorly, but despite my self-doubts, my classes quickly became popular. Local Japanese immigrants and young Hawaiians were also keen to join, and soon American servicemen were training with us too—white, black, and Hispanic. Miyagi's dream was coming true. His karate was spreading across the world. More than that, it was uniting the world under one roof. If ever there was a place where creed, color, and race had no bearing, it was in the dojo—where money bought no greater respect or easier passage, and rich and poor sweated alike, separated only by their ability in karate. I was pleased with myself and proud of my achievements, and just when I thought we could be no more harmonious or cosmopolitan, a new student appeared at the door to bring me a new world of conflict.

On first seeing her, I'd imagined she was waiting for her boyfriend, and from the frown on her face I'd guessed he was in trouble—such a beautiful woman would not appreciate being kept waiting. The class had already begun its warm-up, performed exactly as Miyagi prescribed, so I ignored her, expecting one of my students to ask to be excused at any moment to go and speak with her. None did, and by the time we'd progressed to our strength circuit, I'd all but forgotten she was there. When I finished my exercises with the stone hammer, I moved to grip the water jars and noticed her, still in the doorway. I set the jars down and went to her.

"Are you waiting for someone, miss?"

"I'm looking for Sensei Ota," she answered.

"You've found him."

She looked me up and down in surprise, and I wondered whom she'd been expecting to see. Her eyes locked onto mine and I was taken aback by the intensity of her gaze—Japanese girls were brought up to be demure, but the girls in Hawaii adopted a more Western manner. Even so, the boldness of her stare made me expect the worst, and I braced myself for some accusation or other. "Can I help you?" I asked warily.

"I heard you teach karate here."

I looked over my shoulder at my students, who were working hard, as I'd trained them to do. "I can't deny it," I replied, still wondering what she wanted.

She blinked and her frown returned. She licked her full lips hesitantly and looked around the dojo. As she did, I stole a better look at her face. Her wide-spaced eyes were a deep black that caught the light like two precious stones and sparkled as they moved. Her cheekbones were high and cut at an extraordinary angle, and her skin was a smooth golden brown. Her thick black hair was swept back off her face and hung long down her back. Her looks were at once familiar yet exotic, different to any face I'd seen before. Later I learned her mother was Hawaiian and her father Japanese—an immigrant who'd settled in Hawaii to work on the plantations before the war. "I saw Master Miyagi perform karate once when he visited the islands," she said at last.

"That was a long time ago," I said, enchanted by her unexpected revelation.

"I was a young girl at the time," she smiled at the memory.

"Master Miyagi was my teacher. *Is* my teacher," I corrected myself.

"That's what I heard. I wanted to see for myself."

"We've been training for almost a year now," I told her, surprised that I'd misjudged this young woman so badly, and finding myself enjoying our conversation now.

"Master Miyagi's demonstration was wonderful," she said. "I remember it like yesterday. My father took me—he was interested in karate. I watched from his shoulders."

"You were lucky," I grinned. "Master Miyagi rarely demonstrates in public. I've only seen him do it once in all the years I've trained with him, and I've known him since I was a boy."

"He was promoting karate in Hawaii," she explained. "There were very few people who knew his style, so he performed his kata for all to see. He announced the name of each one before beginning. I can't remember them now, it was so long ago. But I remember his performances. Those I'll never forget."

I nodded knowingly. "Master Miyagi's kata are nothing if not memorable."

"You know them?" she asked.

"He taught me all of them," I nodded proudly.

"I would like to learn them," she said.

"I'm afraid I don't teach them outside the class," I said, sorry to disappoint her.

"Then perhaps I might join the class?"

I stared at her, wondering if she was serious. Her face told me that she was. I hadn't considered a woman might wish to join us. It was unheard of in Okinawa, but then I remembered another young woman I'd met—a lifetime ago—a woman who'd also been a martial artist and more, a warrior. A woman who'd fought and died for what she'd believed in. I looked at this young woman doubtfully, wondering how she could possibly cope with the rigors of karate training. She was of medium height, athletic-looking, with broad shoulders and a narrow waist. The sleeves of her plain blue blouse were rolled up revealing forearms that hinted at a sinewy strength. Her calves, visible beneath the cut-off khaki pants, tapered to a strong ankle and broad, flat feet. She had a great figure, the sort a man imagines running his hands over rather than slamming with his iron palms. I wondered if she had any idea what the karate class entailed.

"Karate can be very physical," I said.

She stared into my eyes again, and I realized her frown had not been annoyance, but simply preparation for the rejection she'd known was coming.

"I saw Master Miyagi testing a student," she said. "The young man was not allowed to move." She tensed her arms in a good imitation of Sanchin, "It looked very painful."

"It is. And every student receives the same treatment."

"I understand," she said.

"I'm glad," I smiled. I felt sorry for ending her dream of learning karate.

"I still wish to train," she said, and I noticed an undertone of defiance in her voice.

I shook my head. "It would be difficult for you to train with the men, I'm sure you understand."

"Difficult for whom?" she asked.

It was a good question. She knew she would be training with men, and was prepared for it. It was the men who might find it difficult to adjust to the idea.

"For you," I said, unwilling to concede to her argument. My expression hardened and all warmth left my voice. "I train them to hit hard."

"Then you will train me to hit hard, too."

There it was again, the defiance, but spoken in such a gentle tone that it was difficult to take offense. Perhaps it was not so much defiance as a challenge. I was reminded of the last time I'd met such determination to train. It had been outside Miyagi's makeshift dojo in Gushikawa. I'd rejected O'Leary then. I didn't want to make the same mistake again.

"Like I said, our karate is very physical, and we make no allowances."

It was my final warning, but she mistook it for a refusal and pursed her lips. "I wasn't asking for any," she said, turning to go.

I watched her take two steps before calling after her, "Then you know what to expect."

She took another step before turning back with a question on her lips, examining my face to be sure of my meaning. "I do?"

I found myself captivated by those eyes, and looked away before I was lost in them. "I believe I've been most clear," I said sternly.

Her mouth opened, her lips moved, but it took an extra moment for the words to come: "Oh yes, Sensei. Very clear."

"Good."

Thank you, Sensei Ota," She beamed, and I noticed a swift blush of redness on her cheeks at her sudden exuberance. It was the moment I fell in love with her, although it would be much later before I admitted it to myself, and later still before I admitted it to her.

"Don't thank me," I said, still avoiding her eyes. "You'd better tell me your name."

"Lani," she said breathlessly.

"Surname?"

"Yamashiro," she answered.

"Age?"

She blinked, surprised by my questions.

"I need some details, for my records," I explained seriously.

"Eighteen," she answered. "I'm eighteen, Sensei."

"Good," I nodded.

"Do you want my date of birth?" she offered.

"You can give me the rest later," I said. "Come back tomorrow evening and we'll fill in the details."

Now I was at a loss. I knew how Miyagi would frown on any form of liaison between us, and so I treated Lani as hard as I treated any of the men—harder, in all honesty—in the hope that she would leave and free me from my unhappy dilemma. Night after night, week after week, I struck the body that I wanted to touch and hold, and left angry welts on the smooth flesh that I dreamed of caressing gently with my fingertips. Unfortunately, and to my own detriment, I was a good teacher and Lani was a good student. She learned as well as any of the men, better than most, and her fierce pride meant she showed no pain despite the severity of my testing.

The men in the class had accepted her without any great drama or protest. I hadn't made any mention of the fact that a female had joined us, and they simply followed my lead in treating her like any other new student. For her part, Lani had taken to the class quite naturally, though she struggled with the strength work. At first, she was so far behind the men that it was laughable. Here slim fingers couldn't grip the earthenware jars for more than a few seconds, and her narrow wrists turned the stone hammer just a few inches from the top of the handle rather than the bottom, where it is supposed to be gripped. But there was a fierce determination in her eyes when she did these exercises, and she made a little progress each week. When I watched her performing the kata she'd come to learn, there was a beauty in her movements that filled me with a joy that I struggled to conceal. "Hai," I would say, as Miyagi had to me, to signify acceptability, nothing more.

Soon after she joined, more young women began coming to the class. Most left quickly, but several stayed and Lani became their unofficial mentor. To my dismay, they progressed quickly too—there was no hope of Lani leaving anytime soon, and if she had, the class would have been considerably poorer for it.

I continued my hopeless battle for almost a year, never speaking to her unless it was to bark an order or criticize a technique. For her part, Lani remained polite and respectful, and if she resented my harshness, she hid it well.

My defeat took place at the New Year celebrations of 1948. Our class had gathered at Waikiki beach to join the evening festivities. The combination of music, atmosphere, and strong American-style cocktails disarmed me. A steady stream of young men had been asking Lani to dance. She had accepted some, though not all, but after each one she'd retreated to her group of girlfriends from the karate club. I joined in the fun of the occasion, chatting amicably with the young men from my dojo and dancing with the girls, including Lani, since it would have been noticeable if I hadn't.

The hour was already late when I spotted her sitting a little apart from the crowd on an upturned boat, her face serious despite the occasion. I went and asked her to dance with me again. She accepted dutifully, no doubt wondering if it was some new test of mine to endure, but as we danced, I complimented her on her dress and she smiled. We danced a little closer. Later, we walked on the beach as fireworks lit up the sky and dabbled our bare feet in the silver foam of the shallows. My talk was unromantic—it was all karate, I knew of little else that might hold her interest. I told her how I'd first met Miyagi during a storm, how he'd smashed a makiwara before my eyes, how we'd visited an old dancing man and even sailed to China in search of an old master. Lani probed each of my stories, demanding details, seeking explanations, laughing at my mishaps, and when the sun began to rise, we found ourselves sitting side by side on a secluded bench.

A short silence had descended. "Miyagi would like to see your karate," I told her gently.

She looked at me suddenly, her old suspicion returning—was I mocking her?

"I mean it," I smiled, hoping to reassure her. "You've learned it well."

She looked away. I thought she was annoyed, though I couldn't imagine why, until I saw the glistening line of a tear on her cheek.

I reached for her hand and held it. "Your karate is beautiful," I told her.

Her frown returned. It was then that I realized what weight my words carried for my students. I was no longer a young man practicing karate for his own purposes. I was a sensei, someone whom my students looked up to in the same way as I'd looked up to Miyagi. "Like you," I added quietly.

She turned to me and I could only see the outline of her cheek and the occasional flash of her dark eyes, illuminated by the fireworks. My arm circled her waist and my lips brushed hers, nothing more, then she turned away and I kissed her neck. I felt her hand on mine, squeezing it gently, the pad of her thumb caressing my skin, but I felt she was on a knife-edge of indecision. To begin a relationship with me might be to lose her sensei, and I knew how much her karate meant to her. I tore myself away from kissing her delicious skin and rose, stretching with exaggerated slowness.

"Let's get back to the party. People will begin to wonder where we are."

She rose and we returned to the celebrations hand-in-hand. In the early hours of the morning, I walked her home, and when she returned to the dojo some days later, it was as if nothing had happened. Nevertheless, we began dating, and by the next New Year's celebrations, we were engaged. A year later, we were married and in the summer of 1951, Lani gave birth to the first of our three children.

We were happy, living close to the dojo, visited by students who came by to help around the house in exchange for a little extra karate tuition. They helped in our tiny yard or minded the children while Lani and I enjoyed an evening in town. I went to college in the evenings when I wasn't teaching karate and studied English. On graduating, I got a job with the port authority controlling the entry, exit, and customs red tape of shipping. Watching the local fishing boats coming in and out of the harbor reminded me of home. It was a good life, a happy life, one that I couldn't have imagined even a few years earlier.

I wrote to Yuka, telling her my news, reassuring her that all was well in my new life. She replied saying that she was moving to America with Doctor Charles Day, who had gotten a new position at a hospital in San Francisco. I took my young family to meet them and we attended their wedding in San Francisco Bay. They spent their honeymoon with us in Hawaii. Yuka told me she'd received a letter from Fumiko, who hadn't found her aunt in Kerama so had gone to Tokyo, where she was studying, Yuka didn't say what. They had written a few times before losing touch.

I also wrote to Miyagi and received long, carefully written letters in reply. He had left his temporary home in Gushikawa and moved back to Naha, where he continued to teach karate in his garden. He demanded to know details of my students, insisting I list each one by name and inform him of their knowledge, ability, and progress. Soon he was writing instructions for students he had never met, often with remarkable insight. That was always Miyagi's way. I urged him to come and visit us in Oahu and he promised he would—he had very fond memories of the island and its people. But the years passed, and Miyagi didn't visit.

Seven years went by quickly, until the day when the old postman stopped me in the street and handed me a letter. It was postmarked Okinawa and the return address was Miyagi's, but my name and address was written in a hand I didn't recognize. It wasn't Miyagi's. I guessed it was from Mrs. Miyagi and steeled myself for the words I knew would be inside.

The letter was long, and I read most of it through my own tears. Mostly, Mrs. Miyagi asked about my new life in Hawaii, demanding to know all about my beautiful wife and baby, urging me to send photos, asking about my sister Yuka, urging me to tell her of Yuka's new life in America. But before all this, at the beginning of the letter, she'd written the news I'd been dreading, and with the letter she'd enclosed a small printed note detailing the arrangements for the funeral of her husband, Chojun Miyagi.

When I finished the letter I clutched it to my chest, crushing the paper hard against my body, so hard that I might make it disappear and the news with it, but the paper remained, and the news remained. I could not escape it. My sensei was dead.

THE GHOST MASTERS

Stepping from the aircraft at Naha airport and standing at the top of the steel stairway high above the runway, I saw a city I didn't know. Only the blueness of the sea and outline of the distant islands was familiar. The old wooden buildings of the capital had become concrete blocks. The dirt roads had given way to tarmac. Even the smell of my island was gone. The warm pines, the sea hibiscus and salt air was drowned out by the heavy fumes of aviation fuel that made my head spin.

I passed through the lofty terminal building in a daze, struggling to recall what the airport had looked like before. Outside, a line of taxis was waiting but I strode past, not wanting to be driven. Instead, I hired a jeep at considerable expense and set off through the busy streets. The rickshaws and horse-drawn carts had been replaced by mopeds, cars, and trucks. The haphazard shops with hand-painted signs were now uniform squares with shop-finished neon above their doors, and the sturdy little typhoon-proof houses had become squat stucco condos. I drove on, searching for the city limits, but they never appeared. The old road between Naha and Shuri didn't exist. The countryside didn't exist. Shops, offices, and flats had taken its place between the two, creating one town.

I had a day to spare before Miyagi's funeral, so I headed north toward the central plain, eventually leaving the sprawl of Naha behind. Memories of driving in the staff car with Yahara flooded back, but the beauty of the Amekudai countryside had all but vanished. The soft fields of waving sugarcane and pampas grass had been buried beneath a patchwork of concrete runways. The rolling hills, once dotted with the turtleback tombs of our ancestors, were home to uniform grey squares that could have belonged to any country of the world. I drove on to the Motobu Peninsula where I'd once spent the day with Fumiko. Whole hills and valleys had disappeared from the landscape, flattened by the unrelenting fist of the bulldozer. I continued into Kunigami where we had fetched timber in the little boats. The forests had been cut back from the roads and the roads widened. The small timber mills had become gated factories. A new convenience store had opened on the outskirts of Hentona and I saw a group of American hikers with their backpacks, drinking soda outside.

Turning south, I hugged the eastern coastline past Nakagusuku as far as Yonabaru before pulling over just outside Mabuni village. I wandered down toward the cave where we had made our final stand. I couldn't find the land-side entrance, or the hatch that had once led down to the caves below. There was no sign that a cave had ever existed in that lonely hillside. I thought about going down to the beach and climbing around, up the cliffs, to try to find the entrance where generals Ushijima and Cho had committed seppuku, but something made me stop. I didn't want to see that place now. I wanted to keep my memories of it the way it was, unchanged by all that had happened since.

I was just a short drive from my home town of Itoman, but I wasn't ready to go there yet. I would attend Miyagi's funeral first, tomorrow, and pay my respects to his memory. Then I would go to the site of my home and pay my respects to my parents and my lost brothers.

I climbed into the jeep and chose a little known track through the hills to take me to my hotel in Naha. On the way, I came across a tomb belonging to a family I'd known as a boy. The tomb was a patchwork of old and new stone from where it had been repaired. An immaculate shrine stood beside, complete with flowers and offerings, which had clearly been built after the war. A little way above, guarding the tomb from a rocky peak, a bullet-scarred lion-dog was looking out to sea, the only trace of the battle that had once raged so fiercely on our island.

Miyagi's funeral was a grand affair, befitting a nobleman of his standing. Hundreds of people had come to pay their respects and leave offerings at his gravestone. I stood back, not wishing to get in the way of the grieving family. Later, when we retired to the Miyagi family home in Naha, I walked around the garden where he'd trained in his final days. There were three makiwara sunk into the earth, the heavy earthenware gripping jars, the iron wrist rings, and the huge oval kongoken weight that he had brought back from Hawaii.

I picked up the stone-hammer that was used to strengthen the wrist. The wooden handle was dark with the sweat of countless students who had performed endless painful rotations of the chiishi, and that sweat included Miyagi's. Someone touched my arm and I turned to find Mrs. Miyagi beside me. She seemed even smaller than I remembered her, her hair a lighter shade of grey, but her eyes were still bright and full of life.

"I am so happy you could come, Kenichi," she said.

I wanted to pay my respects," I said quietly, not knowing what to say to her. I wondered about offering my condolences, and how to phrase them, but Mrs. Miyagi took my hand and squeezed it tight, as if to reassure me there was no need for such formality between us.

"You came a long way," she said, "farther than anyone else."

"It wasn't so far, not for Master Miyagi."

"He knows you're here," she assured me in a most matter of fact way, "He is very happy that you joined us." I searched her face and saw that she was convinced it was true. "He loved all his students as if they were his own children," she continued, "and you, Kenichi, you were always one of his favorites."

"He had many fine students," I said.

"Yes, but you took him to China," she smiled. "He spoke of that trip many times. It was one of his most treasured memories."

"But he didn't find what he was looking for."

"What was he looking for?" she asked with a frown.

"Some deeper meaning to karate."

"Pah! Miyagi was always looking for something in karate," she smiled sadly. "It was as if nothing else existed. All day he would practice, practice, practice, and at night, he would dream about it until morning."

Despite her words, I knew how much she loved and admired her husband. I couldn't imagine the hole he would leave in her life. She must have read my thoughts as expertly as her departed husband had once done because she squeezed my hand to reassure me. "Don't worry about me, Kenichi. Our house is full of ghosts. Chojun is still with me, still giving me instructions about my health, still inventing silly new exercises, still playing *Go* with his friends and talking about karate, karate, karate, all night long. You don't know what it was like to live with someone like Miyagi every day!"

She was clutching my arm tightly now, as if losing her grip would cause her to her fall into a chasm of despair. Her eyes had filled with tears, but I could see the joy behind them as she spoke of him. Miyagi was with her always. "I can talk to you," she laughed, "because you understand. You shared his passion. You still do."

"Then tell me more," I ordered gently.

"More?"

She sniffed, shaking her head slowly as she allowed the thoughts to come. "You know, other women used to worry about their husbands having affairs, but my husband loved karate so much that at times, I felt I was the mistress. He was always out somewhere, teaching, training. Even in the house, he never stopped. Do you know what he would do? Exercises for his eyes! He would move them up and down and side to side to make sure he could never be caught unaware." She did a demonstration of Miyagi's eye exercises, moving her pupils this way and that, and I wondered what the other guests at the funeral would make of her curious antics. It didn't seem to concern her in the slightest. "Do you know what else he would do? He would get me to whisper in another room and try to hear what I was saying. He never got it right until I spoke too loud and then he would become annoyed. In the end, I wouldn't say anything and then, when he guessed, I would tell him he was correct!"

We both laughed at the memory and the laughter soothed our hearts. She continued her tirade, her voice getting louder. "At night, he would place a bamboo stick by the bed and tell me to wake him with it in the morning, in case he mistook me for an attacker and hurt me."

"Did you use it?" I asked, fascinated by the idea.

"Of course not," she laughed. "In the morning, he would get out of bed and punch the mosquito net one hundred times. He said it developed a different sort of power to the punching-post in the garden."

"I'll have to try it," I said mischievously.

"Oh don't be ridiculous, Kenichi!" she said sternly.

"Tell me more," I begged.

"Miyagi talked in his sleep. Even when he was young, he would murmur certain things, strange Chinese-sounding words that I didn't understand. But after the war, around the time you left for Hawaii, he began to hold whole conversations. When I asked whom he was talking to, he wouldn't tell me, until one day, several weeks after it began, he came to me and we walked in the garden, just as we are walking now. It was good exercise for Miyagi to walk a little each day. Then we sat. He held my hand and we spoke for some time, longer than we had for many years. It reminded me of the time when we were young newly-weds discovering one another. He told me he was visited in his dreams by the ghosts of the Chinese masters who had created the kata. They spoke to him of their art, their intentions in creating the kata and the universal principles contained within them. It means nothing to me, of course, but I thought you would be interested to know."

"I am," I assured her, hoping for some new insight, "He was always seeking answers to karate. I'm so glad he found them."

"Perhaps," she said, "but when the seeking was over, his karate was over, and so was his life."

I was happy for my master. He had found his way across the abyss. He had seen blurred, half-formed ideas and suspicions brought into sharp focus. He had grasped the ethereal nature of karate in his fist. "His karate will live on," I offered.

"Yes, I believe it will," she said her eyes alight behind the tears. "There are already several schools here and on the mainland, and I understand there is also one on Hawaii."

"A small one."

"It will grow," she assured me. "Now, come and have some food."

All at once, I was transported back to day when Mrs. Miyagi had invited a young novice into the house and given him sweets while he waited for his teacher to arrive. "I will, thank you. Your sweets always tasted so good."

"You were a good boy," she smiled. "Look at you now, a big man, and broad, too. Hawaii must agree with you."

"Hawaii is good," I smiled. We walked back among the crowd of mourners. Mrs. Miyagi turned to me suddenly, "Will you come again before you leave, Kenichi? I want to know all about Hawaii."

"I will," I promised.

"You must. I heard you married a lovely Hawaiian girl and have two beautiful children."

"Lani—she's half Japanese," I said.

"You brought photos?"

"I brought photos."

We stepped from the heat of the garden to the cool of the house and she looked up at me suddenly, as if remembering something vitally important. "Of the children, too?"

"Of the children too," I laughed. "I wouldn't have dared to come without them."

I left the jeep where it was parked and walked to Itoman. Traffic rushed past on the new tarmac, motorbikes and scooters where rickshaws and carts had once ploughed their trade. No one stopped to talk. People didn't seem to know each other anymore. They were strangers passing in a blur.

Itoman appeared sooner than I remembered, so soon that I wondered if a new town had sprung up out of nowhere, until I saw a sign saying *Welcome to Itoman*. I found another town I didn't know. I searched for a familiar street in vain. My house had been demolished long ago, I knew, but I'd expected to find something intact, my street perhaps, or some notable feature nearby. There was no sign we had ever lived there—my parents, my brothers, my sister, and me. I gave up my painful search and made for the harbor. This at least I recognized, despite the extensions to the marina and the sight of the sleek motorboats in the water.

At the seashore, I turned south and strolled along the beaches where I'd once run as a boy. Sand got into my shoes so I kicked them off and rolled up my trousers. This, at last, was a familiar place. Shells still protruded from the golden grains, sand flies still hovered above the black seaweed that marked the waterline, and crabs still scurried in shallow rock pools. I walked on, lost in my reverie, and found myself on the cliffs at Cape Kyan. A stiffening breeze whisked up a foam on the wave tops, and powerful breakers crashed against the rocks. Here was a landscape still unchanged by the hands of humans, a sea that moved as it always had, a sky that was as fathomless as it had always been.

I removed my shirt and felt the warm caress of the wind on my skin. The familiar smell of sea and pine filled my nostrils. The sun was setting before me, massive in the western sky. The nearby palms rustled in the breeze, and on the higher ground, the twisted typhoon trees swayed in the grip of the stronger wind.

I stepped forward, gripping the earth with my feet, drawing its power up through my body and limbs and into my fists. I inhaled, withdrawing my hand slowly, drawing the strength of the island into me. I'd no breath of my own, no body of my own, no fists of my own. The wind was my breath, the trees my body, the tide my limbs. The forces that moved the universe moved through me, coursing through my veins like the starlight that was beginning to appear in the sky. It was a power available for all to harness—all who submitted their bodies to ceaseless practice and opened their mind to the possibility of this union.

There are many gateways to this power. Miyagi's way was through karate. He led me to the entrance and gave me the key. It was a gift I'll treasure to my dying day, one that I've sworn to pass onto others, who in turn, will pass it on again. This is already happening, and Miyagi's karate has spread far beyond the shores of Okinawa and Japan, even beyond Hawaii.

I imagined sitting with my sensei, in his kitchen perhaps, or on his terrace, playing a game of *Go* and telling him how his art was being practiced in all four corners of the world. I imagined how happy it would make him to hear this news. Then I smiled at my own foolishness. Chojun Miyagi had a sixth sense. He'd always known what I was thinking, and why should now be any different? He already knew.

HISTORICAL NOTES

It's no coincidence that when Hollywood was looking to create the archetypal karate master, it chose the name Mr. Miyagi. The real Miyagi, Chojun Miyagi (1888–1953), founded one of the world's premier styles, Goju Ryu karate. While other masters may have created larger schools or led more colorful fighting lives, Miyagi was the epitome of the Okinawan karate master, powerful and humble, stern and kind, simple and wise.

His life has been dramatized in *Chojun*. However, both his character and the events that took place in his life have been written faithfully to what is known of him. Most of the information on Miyagi comes from memoirs written by his former students. Miyagi's own extensive notes were destroyed in the war and only a few brief articles remain, but these are enough to give some indication of his character and his approach to karate. Their tone and style correspond with the portrait painted of Miyagi by his students: a meticulous man, studious, open-minded, obsessive about karate, demanding of his students, warm-hearted, and remarkably modest, especially considering his elevated status both as the head of a noble family and a karate master of wide renown.

Miyagi's humility was perhaps his greatest virtue. He never advertised his school, he performed in public only rarely, and he never engaged in duels or challenge matches, yet despite this, his ability was never in doubt. His willingness to admit to seeking a deeper understanding of his art is a remarkable strength in itself. In one article, he writes:

I have been practicing karate for a long time, but I have not yet mastered the core or the truth of karate. I feel as if I walk alone on a distant path in the darkness. The further I go, the more distant the path will become, but that is why the truth is precious. If we go forward to find the truth of karate with all our strength of mind and body, we will be rewarded little by little, day by day.

While many starting out in the martial arts may believe a master knows everything, the true master cultivates a restless lifelong search, grasping at unattainable perfection and looking beyond the physical to the spiritual dimension of the art.

When it comes to the Battle of Okinawa, the subject is rarely given much attention in karate histories. This is understandable since once the fighting had begun all formal karate training ceased, and afterward, neither Japanese, Okinawans, nor Westerners, united by karate, wished to reopen old wounds. Nevertheless, the effect of the war on Miyagi's life was immense. He lost three children and many of his former students, including his protégé Jinan Shinzato. His home was destroyed, and his island was devastated. It seems safe to assume that his health suffered greatly as a result of these tragedies. He developed a heart condition after the war and died of heart failure in 1953.

Considering the scale of the Battle of Okinawa, it is relatively unknown in history. Overshadowed by Iwo Jima before it (the first raising of the American flag on Japanese sovereign territory) and Hiroshima and Nagasaki after it, it is something of a forgotten battle. Okinawa was the largest combined air, sea, and land battle in history, far larger than Iwo Jima, and costlier in civilian casualties than Hiroshima and Nagasaki combined. In his book on the subject, George Fiefer calls it

The Stalingrad of the Pacific, and in Okinawa, it is remembered as The Typhoon of Steel.

The American invasion fleet was the largest ever assembled in the Pacific and second only to the Normandy landings. The scale of the fighting on the tiny island was titanic, and the loss of life staggering. The Japanese lost over 100,000 troops, the Allies (principally the United States) suffered more than 50,000 casualties with over 12,000 killed, while the Okinawan civilians, caught between battling giants, were the gravest casualty of all with over 120,000 dead.

Okinawan men and women were assembled into units such as the Blood and Iron Corps and the renowned Himeyuri Nurses Corps (which translates as *Maiden Lilies* or *Princess Lilies*)—a unit made up of 297 highschool girls and teachers forced to serve on the front lines. Of these, 211 lost their lives during the 3-month long Battle of Okinawa.

The battle itself is accurately described in *Chojun*, as are the officers in charge of the Japanese defenses: Lieutenant General Ushijima, Major General Cho, and the master strategist, Colonel Yahara. When the battle was lost, Ushijima and Cho committed ritual suicide at Mabuni cliffs. Yahara tried to escape and bring word of the defeat back to Japan, but was captured as a prisoner of war. Years later he went on to write a personal account of the fighting: *The Battle of Okinawa*, which is available in English translation.

Japan surrendered shortly after the Battle of Okinawa. The island of Okinawa was already over-run with American troops and became a convenient place to concentrate US forces in the Pacific without encroaching too heavily on Japan's main islands. Thus the American presence was felt far more keenly in Okinawa than anywhere else in Japan. Okinawa remained under American control until 1972, when it was finally returned to Japan, though some argue little has changed.

In the post-war years, the Okinawans survived on American aid and commerce from the giant air bases on the island, most notably Kadena. Okinawa became a staging post for American forces on the way in and out of Korea and Vietnam. The usual industries sprung up to service the servicemen on leave, with a thriving red-light district near the airbase in Koza, now called Okinawa City.

American actions and behavior on the island was as mixed as the characters that were there. There are tales of compassion shown to civilians and orphans, and tales of heavy-handedness, brutality, and worse. The reputation of each nation is at the mercy of its individuals. During the American occupation, there were several high-profile rape cases involving American servicemen, and understandably tensions ran high. The case in *Chojun* is fictitious, as are the characters involved.

When it comes to Miyagi's students, Jinan Shinzato is widely acknowledged as an outstanding practitioner and, if he had survived the war, would have been a potential successor to Miyagi. In *Chojun*, Ota is mistaken in his belief that Shinzato joined the Air Force and later the kamikaze. Shinzato remained on Okinawa, where he fought and died in the battle, killed by a bomb blast while standing in the entrance of a cave.

Miyagi had other senior students of note who went on to found their own schools of Goju Ryu karate on Okinawa, most notably Eiichi Miyazato (Jundokan), Meitoku Yagi (Meibukan), Seiko Higa (Shodokan), and Seikichi Toguchi (Shoreikan). Miyagi also taught Gogen Yamaguchi who founded the world-renowned Goju Kai in Tokyo. One of Miyagi's later students, Aniichi Miyagi (no relation) became the teacher and mentor to the internationally renowned Morio Higaonna of IOGKF.

There is much debate—sometimes heated—as to who was Miyagi's true successor. Miyagi left no clear instructions on the matter. This is understandable considering he taught many talented practitioners over the years, several of whom had already begun teaching their own clubs while Miyagi was still alive. It would have been both difficult and unnecessary for him to choose between them.

Today, despite their political differences, all Goju Ryu schools remain united by the kata that were collected, and in some cases, created by their remarkable founder.

Further Reading

By far the most detailed and extensive biography of Chojun Miyagi and Goju Ryu karate can be found in Morio Higaonna's excellent *History of Karate: Goju Ryu*. Now a master in his own right, Morio Higaonna (no relation to Kanryo Higaonna) has spent a lifetime researching the origins of his style and its founder, including several trips to China in the footsteps of Miyagi.

There are also several articles available online, the most poignant of which is *Memories of My Sensei Chojun Miyagi* by Genkai Nakaima. This writing gives a valuable insight into Miyagi's character and inspired much of the detail in *Chojun*.

There are several books dedicated to the Battle of Okinawa. Colonel Hiromichi Yahara's *The Battle of Okinawa* makes a fascinating alternative perspective to the many American books on the subject—the most memorable of which is Private E. B. Sledge's *With the Old Breed: At Peleliu and Okinawa*—a vivid memoir that inspired Spielberg's epic drama *The Pacific*.

Some of the best civilian perspectives come from women's writing, including *A Princess Lily of the Ryukyus* by Jo Nobuko Martin; *The Girl with the White Flag* by Tomiko Higa; *Mama, Mama, Don't Die!* by Fumiko Tanahara Bourne; and *Women of Okinawa* by Ruth Ann Keyso.

Acknowledgements

The writing of *Chojun* was both a thrill and a challenge for me. I wanted to express the passion I feel for my art—a passion I share with so many around the world—and recreate the atmosphere of training in Okinawa when today's karate was being created. I also wanted to do justice to a remarkable man who gave his art to the world, and to me.

If I have succeeded in some small way, it was with the help of many people, first and foremost among them Chojun Miyagi himself, without whom nothing could have followed. Sensei Miyagi would be at pains to acknowledge his own sensei—'*those who went before*'—most notably Kanyro Higaonna, who in turn would acknowledge his teachers in an unending line reaching all the way back to the Shaolin Temple.

Moving in the other direction, the lineage from Miyagi to me is a long and circuitous one. However, I would like to acknowledge certain sensei along the way, most notably Shihan Gavin Mulholland, my present day teacher, mentor, brother-in-law, and friend. I should also mention Shihan Dan Lewis who continues to inspire me, and sincerely thank Shihan Chris Rowen who first showed me the beauty of Miyagi's art, and Shihan Jose Claronino of Kyokushinkai, who first introduced me to karate.

When it comes to the writing of this book, I would like to thank the readers who gave their valuable time so freely: my father Michael, my sister Sasha, my sister-in-law Genevieve, and my wife Charmaigne, who is both my biggest fan and sternest critic, and without whom no writing would see the light of day.

Finally, I would like to thank David Ripianzi of YMAA for making the whole business of publishing such a pleasure, and my editor Leslie Takao for her thoughtful input and improvements.

ABOUT THE AUTHOR

Goran Powell is a freelance writer who holds a 4th Dan in Goju Ryu Karate. He teaches at DKK London, one of the UK's strongest karate clubs, and is assistant coach to the Mixed Martial Arts team DKK Fighters who compete successfully in Ultimate Challenge and UFC.

In 2002, Goran undertook the grueling 30-Man Kumite test and wrote of the experience in his first book *Waking Dragons*. It became an instant bestseller on Amazon's martial arts listing. In 2008 he edited the widely acclaimed karate book Four Shades of Black written by his Sensei, Gavin Mulholland.

His first novel *A Sudden Dawn* was published in 2010 and won three awards for Historical Fiction from USA Book News, eLit and Living Now. In 2011 he converted the book to a movie screenplay.

Goran Powell is married with three children and resides in North London, England.